THE COMPLETE EL SEPULTURERO

PHIL BUCK

ALSO BY PHIL BUCK

Santa Santera

AS WEDLAKE-BUCK

Whisper From The Alamo
Runaway Blues
Life On Maui

BOOK #1
EL SEPULTURERO

BESTIA

The rainforest wildernesses of Yucatán were like another world, a world where the ground and the sky spoke a different language. Uncountable time had shaped the landscape into a place where only hardy things lived amongst the trees. Every direction was dominated by rain forests littered with ruins that spoke to the ancient past, and cenotes that gave way to underworld caverns and lost lakes luminous with elemental color. Everything was smothered in the wettest of tropical heat.

This world was where Francisco walked now, and ever since they had driven to this new home there seemed to be nothing but the wild places, while all around him the dead whispered even as the howler monkeys called and the multicolored birds sang.

Sometimes it felt like wild places was all there had ever been.

As he walked, the sun beat down on Francisco's bleached white skin, but he didn't feel it. There was no sweat on his heavy brown, and no tiredness to his steps. There was just a huge figure in dusty black clothes and a concert tee-shirt with the name 'Desekratus' in stylised letters across his chest – a ghostly giant with dark hair recently cropped to his scalp who trudged forward, piercing eyes scanning the rough ground for the trail.

This particular one was easy to track. Blood stained the heavy prints that old boots had left on the empty road, and no effort had been made to conceal tracks that spoke of a stagger rather than an escape. Every now and then there were places where somebody had stumbled and collapsed, and they were getting closer and closer together. Without water, and cooking alive in the heat, Francisco knew it wouldn't be long now.

The tracks led him up towards an archway of old gnarled trees that led to a slope half-buried by scrub. Past it was a hidden little space, like a tiny valley, cooled by the shade of a large overhang from which jagged stone hung like predator's teeth. This was where the trail ended.

The body that was there was no shock to Francisco. Just like the other two he had seen it was strung up by the arms between two of the rock teeth, out of the sun, and gutted. The blood had gone, and the heart and lungs and liver had been dumped raw into azure painted bowls. Nothing was different – the ritual was identical.

<Are you here?> called Francisco. His growl of a voice did its best to travel. <If you are, let us make this quick.>

The sounds of rustling, of motion, answered as something stirred out of sight amongst the wet garden of trees. Francisco reached to the back of his leather belt where he kept a pouch of small thin stone tablets. Just pieces of slate to most. To him there was a far greater significance. He selected one and tossed it out in front of him, letting its painted symbol face upwards – a cobalt blue sigil depicting what looked like a hand with its fingers locked straight and pointing sideways and its thumb at right angles. At the centre of the hand were two circles that resembled a crude wheel.

Ch'am.

Francisco listened as the sounds of movement got louder, and the beast emerged.

He had no name for the juggernaut that faced him. There were no names for these things, no convenient categories to somehow make things easier to deal with. Nothing was easy anymore. All Francisco could do was take in what he saw and prepare himself as the beast advanced on him, an entity made of the pure unfiltered killing urge.

It was a hulk of a man, or at least had been once. A mass of pocked flesh easily 8 feet tall and ridden with blubber that hung off a shambling body hunched and contorted by its own weight. The skin was wet, too. Not bone dry like everything else out here, but slick and glistening with a grey pallor that made it look half dead, threaded with patches of decay. It was what it wore, though, that conferred the mark of true monstrousness. Around its waist was a thick leather felt from which hung hands, ones and even heads that had been hacked from the still screaming living and turned to trophies. Worse, covering the beast's own head, was a huge cow skull, bleached white and rendered demonic with its new purpose. The head of the beast.

Perhaps another might have faltered in the face of this horror, but Francisco was different. He was The Pale Ghost, The Ranger Of The Wilderness, and he would not succumb to cheap tricks. All he had to do was hold his nerve, and trust in the tablet and its sigil.

Ch'am.

The beast bellowed through its horned skull head and charged forward. There was no intelligence to its attack, just a primal instinct. It brandished a huge axe nearly its own size, built from bone and rock, and Francisco prepared himself. His window of opportunity was going to razor thin and he felt the anticipation in his body build. Five steps became four as the distance closed rapidly. Then three.

Two.

One.

The beast came within just the right distance to smash his reaper's axe down, and with one last footfall its foot fell beside the tablet.

The air around its obese form suddenly became like glue. Between the rock and vine, time seemed to solidify and catch the beast fast. It screeched in confusion, unable to command its thick limbs to move properly. The prodigious bestial strength it prided itself on was stolen away and instead something unseen held it with an invisible web. Strength drained, and it lost its grip in the axe.

Francisco had already seized upon the brief moment his trap had afforded him. A creature with this kind of size of strength would be held for only a few seconds, so there was only one course of action. A practiced one that demanded no subtlety, simply the brutal will to execute. He leapt forward as the beast screeched its last gestures of defiance, ignoring the still potent force of its roar as he grasped hold of the axe as it fell. The weight was enormous but as it fell out of the trap Francisco felt its momentum and made himself simply a vehicle for it, guiding rather than holding. It took on its new arc almost by itself as he span it back around towards its owner.

Sharpened stone cracked and penetrated the bone of the cow skull, splitting the malformed head underneath in half. The brain inside, broken and shrivelled as it was, took a second or two to realise it had died. Then the beast simply pitched forward into the dust, and Francisco looked down at the carcass. A death was always a tragic thing, however monstrous the dead.

First he would dig a grave. Then he would get back what was his.

*

Francisco shovelled one last clump of dirt onto the beast's grave and whispered a short silent prayer. Somewhere in the back of his mind he half expected the beast to erupt back out of the ground, conjored back to life by some enigmatic ancient force of the land. After all, he had seen far stranger things since he arrived here. But it didn't. There was just the animals of the rainforests and the wind that blew hot across everything.

Thankfully, nothing was going to return from the dead today.

He placed the cowskull he had hauled off the beast's head onto its burial mound. The face underneath it had been nightmarish, but removing it had seemed like the right thing to do. For Francisco, nobody should be buried nameless and without an identity. At least this way, however vicious a killer the beast had been, the spirits should know its name and know it had once walked upon the earth. All things deserved that.

Satisfied, Francisco returned to the carved corpse that still hung there suspended in the light. He would get around to that. First though he had to recover what was his.

A little way forward was a slit in the limestone, carved by processes both natural and artificial. It was large enough to allow Francisco to clamber through it with a little effort, and he assumed it was the beast's own gateway to what could only be its lair. There were always lairs, he had learned. The gap led to a slope covered in loose rock broken down by heavy footfalls, and the slope led down to a cavern. Slivers of light from cracks in the rock illuminated little parts of it that gave the place almost the feeling or a church or a shrine, hidden away in darkness. Francisco could hear rats scurrying about everywhere, and the gloom revealed hints of bone and gnawed flesh that still glistened with raw wetness.

He stepped into the cavern with a new caution born of experience, listening to water drip from everywhere. Traps were common out here, but it seemed the beast was not a creature of guile or intelligence. It simply carved its brutal way through life to feed. Francisco could see that it wasn't selective in its choice of meals, as the flayed corpses of human victims lay next to butchered animals. All had been rendered down to simple meat, while blood stained very surface and the stink of the rotting dead burned into Francisco's nostrils. It was a smell he had tried to become used to over the years.

At the centre of the cavern was a broad rock perhaps a metre high, ankle deep in water and angular in shape perhaps a metre high. This was where the beast kept its treasures, and a beam of light revealed some of them. The hoard was composed of weapons, from simple guns to ornate daggers, from complex scientifically designed bows to makeshift explosives. Some had been handled, others simply left where they had been tossed. Francisco scanned them, recognising that each one of these discarded devices represented a life, however corrupt, that had been destroyed at the point of an axe. He could only guess how many of those people had tried to fight back only to be torn apart and then consumed, left to fester in this cavern without a grave of their own. Now though, there was little to bury – just remnants of humanity, a broken skull, a half-eaten ribcage. Nothing whole remained, and whatever was left over was a hearty meal for the rats.

Then eyes that were adapting to the darkness picked out the object of the search. Half buried under a cache of old looking revolvers, its distinct leather wrapped handled protruded out.

Francisco smiled. This was what he had come here for, and reached out for it.

He grabbed the hilt and hauled his prize from the beast's cache. His eyes greeted it like an old friend and the weight felt familiar and powerful in his hands. It was a sword, but not one known to any modern technology. Easily over a metre and half long, it was a long thin wooden rectangle, bound with colored cords in criss-crossed patterns of blue and orange. Embedded in the edges of the wood all the way around were perfectly cut blades, rectangular also and made of razor-sharp black obsidian that swallowed up the light in their glass surfaces.

Francisco had seen those ebon blades slice through leather and flesh alike, and whatever they cut they never seemed to lose their edge. That was their power, and Francisco's prize. His sword. An old relic of a lost world that defied time with its pure killing ability.

Now he knew its name.

Macuahuitl.

He felt the strength of it flow back into his body as he took a length of thin chain out of pocket and connected to both ends of the weapon. Then he slung it over his shoulder and across his back. It had taken six men to take it from him weeks ago. He was determined that wasn't going to happen again. Their trail had led them hear and he was certain some of them had been slaughtered by the beast. Francisco took a grim satisfaction in that, but no pleasure. One or two of them had got away, smart enough to use the wilderness to their advantage and hide from the things that lived out here.

People sometimes saw Francisco as one of those very things. A giant with the bleached white flesh, possessed of strength and sight created out of the substance of the desert rock itself. But he knew that wasn't true. He was a just a man, and there were far worse things that existed outside the crumbling cities and hasty constructed outputs where faith in science and God merged into one. This was a place of monsters now.

And in this place, Francisco only friend in battle was *Macuahuitl.*

The sword.

His sword.

He rummaged through the weapons stash, looking for anything of value or purpose. It was easier to see now as his eyes had acclimatised, and he could see most of the guns were spent or broken. After a moment he discovered a battered sawn-off shotgun with three barrels. Shotgun shells were easy to come by and there were two still loaded when he broke the weapon open, so he took it and tucked into his thick belt. There was something else as well, something a little more unusual that caught his eye.

Burrowing through the detritus he pulled it out what looked like a metal claw sculpted like an eagle's talon. He kept pulling, and found that the claw was connected to a long thick leather cord reinforced with fine metal chain.

Maybe it had been some sort of bullwhip once, or maybe it was something else again. But it was certainly something that had use. That, and it intrigued Francisco, so he looped it carefully and slipped the coils onto his shoulder. That would have to do until he had the light and the time to properly examine it. He had seen a church a mile or so back – there were always communities at churches however small, which meant food and drink and rest, so that would be his next destination.

As Francisco took one final look at the weapons, something alerted him. A new sound way back in the recesses of the cavern like a constant scratching. But not scratching against stone. It sounded more like the slow deliberate carving of wood, splinter by splinter.

He squinted into the gloom, and saw a door that shouldn't have been there.

The scratching continued, its eerie echo bouncing off the cavern walls. The sound had a rhythm of sorts, it had a changing tempo and it had peaks and troughs, its volume rising to sudden urgency and then falling back into a quiet near imperceptibility. Francisco listened to it intently. He tried to pick out something he could recognise, some kind of phrasing that might tell him what might happen if he levered open the heavy doorway. All he could make out was that it wasn't random, but rather had a purpose. What that purpose was eluded him.

Even so, Francisco had to know.

The planks of the door looked old and ridden with endless cracks in their smoothed finish. As Francisco put his ear to them to listen to the scratching, he felt a little warmth coming through as well. The cavern was cooler than above ground and he had expected the substance to feel dead. He had expected it to be made of wood as well. But it was neither of those things.

Francisco ran his hand over the surface. His skin on his fingertips detected the same warmth, and he realised the texture was dry and cracked like ancient leather that had left to dry out. As he looked more closely, he founds rips and patches where it seemed that damaged areas had been hastily replaced, though clearly not in a long time. It reeked of neglect.

<Anybody back there?> demanded Francisco, and abruptly the scratching stopped. For a moment that stretched out forever there was utter silence in the cavern, and then something began to hammer hard from behind the door. There was power and need behind the hammering, but Francisco had seen enough doors to know that one could never know intention was behind them. And it bothered him there was no voice.

The hammering continued, getting louder and louder like some insane drum beat, and Francisco made his decision. He brandished his new shotgun as his other had felt its way to what felt like a heavy chain and an old rusted padlock. The uncountable years had weakened it, so Francisco has able to break it apart with a few hits of the gunbutt.

<Gonna open this door,> he growled. <If I don't like what I see, I won't be asking any questions.>

The hammering subsided. Francisco noticed that the sounds seemed to respond to his voice so he assumed their hidden creator was listening and understood something. He hoped that for their own sake they at least understood that he would have no hesitation in shooting them.

Straining, he hauled open the door as long-disused hinges screeched their resistance.

A person suddenly collapsed forward. From behind them from what seemed like a tunnel a vast on-rush of stale air that smelt of age and decay rushed out into the cavern. It stung Francisco's eyes and made him gag a little, even make him stagger a half-step back. Recovering, he looked down and realised that the form of a young woman lay sprawled at his feet. Dressed in only the barest of filthy rags, he saw that she was emaciated and barely moving. Fingers were ripped and bloody, and yellowed eyes rolled in cadaverous eye sockets, barely able to focus.

Then Francisco realised why there was no voice behind the scratching and the hammering.

The woman's mouth had been sewn shut.

Francisco put his weapon aside and crouched down next to the woman. Though the cavern remained ridden with gloom he could tell that she was just barely defying the urge to die. The breaths in her bony chest were shallow and slow, and she wheezed from lungs filled with whatever it was that saturated the contaminated air around him - air that still stank of the dead. Yet, somehow, she *was* alive.

Water, thought Francisco. She had to have water. He recognised a victim when he saw one, and he couldn't permit this wasted creature to die nameless in a hole in the ground that was filled with the cannibalised remains of the torn dead. He reached to his belt again and took out a flick-knife, popping it open and slicing through the dirty thread that sealed the woman's lips together. They parted, and a whisper escaped out from her freed open mouth

At least, thought Francisco, she could breathe. Now he needed something else.

He looked about the cavern and something caught his eye. Walking over he looked behind the stone that bore the cache of weapons and found some old canteens and tin cups, undoubtedly discarded from violated corpses that no longer required them. Some were broken, others were stained with dried blood and the residues of death. He picked the cleanest one he could see and took it back over to the wall near the open doorway. The rock walls were dry but they were down under the ground a little. Perhaps there would be something he could use.

There was a recess, rendered dank and all but hidden from light, and as Francisco went over and peered down he could see something growing on the stone. Not much, some sort of moss that covered a patch barely an inch square. Another tiny piece of life that clung on to its existence out in the Wilderness. But it was enough. He scraped some off into the cup with his knife and returned to the woman, sitting cross legged on the ground beside her.

As he took two small vials from his belt Francisco pictured into his mind exactly what he needed to do. A process he had performed many times before, a simple thing yet one which had saved many lives. including his own, on more than one occasion

The first vial held a kind of gel, viscous and translucent orange, and he allowed three thick droplets to fall into the cup. Then he poured some of the contents of the second vial, with its bluish powers flecked with glimmering grains of crystal, careful to make sure only the right amount fell. And then one final drop of the gel, just at the right moment.

The contents of the cup instantly began to smoke and fizz violently. What seemed like a tiny little cloud seemed to form briefly inside, forming a bubbling seething froth that expanded like boiling milk. It seemed more violent a reaction that before, and for a second Francisco thought he might have got the mixture wrong someone. Perhaps the proportions were incorrect, or something had contaminated the compound. Or maybe he had simply forgotten something vital. But he needn't have worried. The knowledge was instilled within him now, a part of him. There was one final pop as huge oily bubble expanded and burst, and it was done. Francisco leaned forward and cradled the young woman's head as lifted the cup to her dry and painfully cracked lips - the cup that was now full with cool, fresh, pure water.

As metal and skin touched, bloodshot eyes suddenly snapped open and gnarled twisted hands thrust out.

The young woman had no strength in her wasted muscles and her grip faded almost instantly. Everything about her was dry, almost desiccated, and when the water touched her lips it was hungrily soaked up by paper thin skin. She was so weak her tongue and lips couldn't move, and the rattling breath in failing lungs told Francisco that however much water he had it probably wasn't going to be enough. He had seen enough people facing death to know the signs.

Francisco tipped the tin cup a little, trying to coax the woman's useless throat to swallow. She struggled, rabid with hunger and thirst and staring crazily at him with those reddened eyes. Whatever had happened to this woman behind the wooden door had taken away her humanity, and whatever remained of her mind was working on simple instinct. And that instinct was to resist, to fight.

Even if she did drink the water would only help little. Francisco knew she would need alot more to have any hope of reaching any semblance of health. More water, food, clothes. She would need a bed to rest in and the care of a physician, if one could be found who wasn't obsessed with hacking off limbs. In these times, the true doctors were hard to come by. But if he could contact one and keep the woman alive long enough for them to arrive, she might have some sort of way back to the land of the living.

Francisco looked again at her fingers. Broken and split where she had gouged and ripped with her last moments of strength at the unyielding door, and caked in wet and dry blood all at once.

<How long were you in there,> Francisco mused to himself.

He laid the woman's head onto her makeshift pillow. Supplies were low and there was not much let of the moss to use as a base, so he needed to find something to help. Anything. The cruel irony of the cavern struck him – the place was filled with meat, yet only suitable for the cannibal's stomach. Francisco ran through the possibilities and recalled a clump of cacti he had seen a little way back on the trail that led to the entrance to the cavern. That would give him at least some water, and if they were the right species he could pulp some of the flesh to use as a medicinal balm. It was an old trick, one used for so long nobody could recall who first came up with it. But it was all Francisco could think of.

As he stood, he felt the temperature in the cavern drop suddenly. A sibilant whisper drifted out of the darkness back beyond the doorway. The sound carried a chilling sensation into the back of his mind. It made the hairs on his chalk-colored arms raise up and a flash of nerves roll across his stomach. Francisco peered into the tunnel he had opened, trying to make out what might be in there. There was nothing he could see. Even though his eyes had adjusted to the low light of the cavern, this tunnel was pitch black. It stubbornly denied his sight, refusing to allow him to see anything.

Francisco took a step closer. There was something there, he was certain of it. The whispering sound began to intensify and coalesce around him, floating out into the air as it formed into a chorus. He took another step, almost to the threshold of the door and its tunnel, and that was when he knew for sure.

Down there, deep in the darkness, he knew that something was watching him.

The tunnel growled. Its sides seemed to pulse a little and the solid rock suddenly took on a softer sense, something that could almost have been wet slick flesh. Francisco watched the stone move, trying to convince himself this was an illusion - that some property of the cavern or this tunnel was conjuring ghosts of the mind to confuse him. It wouldn't be the first time. The impossible chemistry of so many places did strange things to the brain. He had met more than one man who had sworn he had seen God under the influence of some hallucinogenic underground cave.

Francisco felt the paranoia of being watched boring into him, screaming at him to run and hide. But he refused to bow to it. The mysteries of places like this drew him in, the perfume of hidden things irresistible to his mind. The whispers, the unfaltering dark that festered, and now this – this feeling of touching something alive.

In that second, Francisco realised the door wasn't wood or leather, but coated in skin.

The tunnel growled again, and Francisco's hand reached for the wrapped chainlike cord over his shoulder. He slowly drew it off and let it fall out of its coils as he kept his eyes focussed on the doorway. As he looked, his perception of it began to change. The doorway seemed to be less carved and more as though it had opened of its own accord, splitting apart like some gaping mouth. And the tunnel beyond it, the walls and the floor and the roof rippling with their grotesque life, appeared to be nothing less than a throat. The throat of something born out of the underground rock itself. Living within it, unseen behind the door made of skin.

Until Francisco had opened it.

Another growl rolled out of the tunnel, and the young woman stirred. Francisco could see she was afraid, and he couldn't deny he shared that same feeling. Something was stirring down in the depths, somewhere that he couldn't see. Each growl was louder than the last as the whispers chattered to each other with their own chorus. As Francisco watched the tunnel began to spasm, slowly at first and then faster, as though it were preparing to disgorge something from its depths. The stink of acid and dead bodies burst out in waves, forcing Francisco to cover his mouth and nose to stop gagging. Then with shocking suddenness, the whispers began to cry and scream. They began to weep like lost souls cast into Hell, then howl with rage. The noise was thunderous, echoing endlessly back on itself to make the cavern itself cry out with a deafening anger.

The young woman began to moan as well, caught up in the vortex of unnatural sensations of sight and sound and vision. It seemed to caress her body with invisible hands, and Francisco realised it wanted her back. It sought to reclaim its prize, its victim. Maybe even its bride.

And in that second of realisation, the chain cord in his hand began to speak to him. Not in words, but in sensation. A kind of static electricity that sparked across its length and discharging itself into Francisco's hands. It was not random but somehow had a pattern, and as Francisco lifted it up to look he saw that the carved claw at the end of the cord had changed.

Once a simple piece of carving, inert and solid, it had transformed to become the huge living claw of a raptor that clutched at the air again and again, desperate for the hunt. Francisco instinctively knew that this weapon, this whipclaw, was ready. He gripped it as the tunnel growled its loudest and something from inside it came for him.

Gigantic, with its surface slick with dirt and pus, a vast serpentine limb burst out of the tunnel. Ridden with pock marks and sores it was stitched together from muscle and sinew, red raw and bloody where metal and bone had been used to sew its skin. At its tip was a bulbous growth, encased in leather sewn together from flesh and teeth and hair, and woven through with a crown of jagged metal. For a second Francisco was captivated by it, unable to tell if this was some monstrous creation of the land or simply the dark magic of his own mind.

But real or unreal, it slammed into the ground and hurled him off his feet.

He rolled away as best he could, slipping on the bloody remains. The stitched rancid limb, which seemed for all the world like a tongue, blindly groped the walls, trying to latch onto to what it had sensed. Its bulbous end, dripping translucent slime with every motion, slid across the surface of the cavern. As it did the whispers spoke to it, guiding it, becoming its eyes where it had none of its own.

Francisco moved back behind the rock where the weapons lay, and the limb followed his motion. He guessed it couldn't see, at least not the way Francisco understood, but it could clearly sense. Almost to confirm it he heard the whispers change. They buzzed excitedly, a thousand ghostly voices once again forming into a single entity that summoned the limb. Hearing their call it homed in on

Francisco's location, feeling the way he had moved through the air. As it searched, the sounds changed as well, ebbing and surging with their instructions.

Everywhere the stink of the thing had become overwhelming. Acrid and rotten, it hurt to breath the air that this monstrosity seemed to revel in.

As he crouched, Francisco tried to form a plan.

Reaching up to the pile of weapons he grabbed one, and saw that even that tiny movement drew the limb's attention. He threw the gun across the cavern, letting it clatter onto the rock. The limb whiplashed towards, its terminus tasting the air. But it didn't attack. It seemed unsure, held back by the caution of the whispering, unwilling to commit itself until it had a solid target to latch onto. Perhaps, thought Francisco, this creature was not as strong as it was trying to pretend to be. Perhaps it needed to save its strength. Or perhaps it had no strength of its own, but was simply a ghost in his mind only given substance and power by the fear that radiated from all sides.

As he thought that, the whipclaw spoke again in his hands. Silently, subtly, its surface began to flow with tiny tingling sparks of static electricity, shooting up and down Francisco's arms as the claw itself grasped and spasmed. It was once again as if the substance of the cord was trying to tell him something in a language so utterly unknown there was no way he could understand its meaning.

But at least he could guess.

In his head, Francisco counted to three and leapt out, screaming his defiance as he cracked the whop forward as hard as he could. It was all he could think of as the limb reared up, sensing its killing blow as the whispering voices excited it.

It loomed for a second like some alien hooded cobra, and then lunged.

The whip cast through the air, and as Francisco watched the claw seemed to guide itself. It arced around and reached its talons wide, wider than should ever have been possible. Then it was on the rotting limb itself, piercing its head and gripping deep in the flesh. The limb lashed furiously but the claw had become a vice, a mantrap that crushed down, squeezing until its prey started to bleed and ooze. The stitching fell away and the bulbous head opened like a ripped sack, sickly pulp slopping out onto the ground where it hissed and smoked against the dust.

Francisco saw the claw rip and gouge by itself. It tunnelled into the substance of the head, boring through layer after layer, skin and flesh and bone alike, until there was nothing left to destroy but an infected mass of dead tissue. All around the whispering eager voices suddenly cried out in agony all at once. Then they were silent.

The limb, dead and inert, flopped onto the ground. It was nothing but a wreck now, a torn wounded skin without function and awareness. Unmoving, it simply oozed filth. Beside it, the claw had done its work and lay inter on the ground again. Just a carving attached, unmoving, to a length of chainlike cord.

Francisco stood there for a moment. The cavern was silent now, though his own heartbeat thumped in his ears. The fight was fading like a dream, the limb dissolving and even the smell disintegrating to nothing without its host to sustain it. He couldn't help but wonder how many people had been locked behind the door of skin, sentenced to be consumed by whatever it was that dwelt there whether at the jaws of a monster or at the hand of terrified plague and starvation. Soon there would be no evidence of either and Francisco would never know why the beast with the cowskull head had made his charnel house here.

Some questions were simply not meant to be answered.

Francisco had no desire to stay in the cavern any longer. He collected the whipclaw and coiled it over his shoulder, then swung his sword back over his back and gently lifted the young woman. She was quiet again now, and weighed almost nothing as he carried her up out of the cave and out into the light once again.

The sun made him blink through the treetops, even though his own pale flesh defied its burn. He could already see the patch of fat fleshy flowers he wanted to harvest for the young woman. They would certainly help. They would give her strength with their pulp and their water. They had small red buds that would help with healing, their sweet incense would encourage her muscles to recover, and her mind to regain itself from whatever madness it had had to endure.

Francisco realised he had left his jacket in the cavern, but it didn't matter. Once he had stabilised the girl he would set the whole place on fire. He would torch it out of existence. There was nothing there to bury, no being that he could put in the grave to allow it to pass over.

As he collected the flowers and pulped them, he found his hands touching the whipclaw at his shoulder. Perhaps, he thought, it was destined to take him to other places, lost places, and perhaps terrible things would be waiting. To be fought, overcome, buried. Our here in the endless rainforests.

Perhaps. But then again, wasn't that the life of the Gravedigger?

MEDUSA

Francisco woke up from a dream he couldn't remember. For a moment he lay there, savouring a comfortable mattress and the cool air from the overhead fan. He missed these simple things, these simple comforts that his life out in the Wilderness and the wildernesses so often denied him. As he sat up, he realised he couldn't remember the last time he had slept so well.

It was strange sensation. He still slept but rarely for long, so to lose a whole night was unusual. It felt good though. It always did when he was in the little beach town of Playa Del Mantarraya. His new home, somewhere between an old disused resort in the North and the reefs of Quintana Roo further South. Whenever he came back here Francisco had a routine, a simple one that he never ignored. So he drank his coffee and then took a run along the white-sand beach.

For a long time people had been alarmed by him. The sight of this giant with his chalk white skin thundering through the surf was enough to scare even hardy souls who had braved the Wilderness just as Francisco did. But over time he became a part of the town, even expected, and missed when he wasn't there.

Every time he ran he saw an old woman with a face made of leather smiled at him with impossibly bright teeth. Francisco always smiled back. That was the extent of their interaction. They never spoke, and he didn't even know her name. In his head he simply called her Old Lady Rosalee.

Francisco always ran for miles. He didn't sweat and the heat didn't affect him, so he was only beholden to his own strength. Sometimes even that surprised him, and he often wondered just how far he could push himself. Perhaps it was better not to know. Perhaps it was better just to enjoy the warmest sun and the bluest waters, and relish the short freedom from his seemingly endless journey.

The beach from Playa del Mantarraya didn't really end, it just merged into the next one as he left the town behind and the ruined towers of Cancún loomed up in the far distance. He never went there. It wasn't the city it once had been since the wall, and the violence that had followed. There was no sense courting the kind of trouble that lived in the ruined hotels and streets now.

Something caught its attention and he slowed to a walk. A few metres ahead there was something there in the surf. It seemed gelantinous, half translucent. Unmoving and easy to spot against the white sands, it lay there as the froth of the waves washed over it.

Francisco looked around. He was alone as far as he could see. There were no buildings here. The beach was unoccupied and the beach backed onto sea-washed limestone slopes and a sea of bright green palm where nobody lived. If somebody had dropped this discovery here, they themselves had long since departed. This made it unusual, and unusual things always interested Francisco.

The 'something' looked dead, a ruined mass of jellyfish substance, and as Francisco looked down at it a human face looked back.

Dead eyes gazed up out of the inside of the jelly, and a mouth lolled open in what could only have been a last expression of sheer disbelief. The skin was discolored and warped, splitting apart from itself as acid and decay ate it away, and half the support of the skull was missing.

Then Francisco realised some of the jelly itself was the remnants of the destroyed brain, dragged out of its bone casing.

He crouched next to the mass. He had seen a hundred beached jellyfish before. They were common - washed up colored blobs littering the sand after a storm or a surge tide alongside dead fish and horseshoe crabs. This was different somehow, and he couldn't quite put figure out how. Its color maybe, its size?

Or simply the fact is contained a human face.

The mystery was not Francisco's forte. His nature was the confrontation, the combat, and the burial. The mass required trained eyes, so he needed an expert. He took an old beeper out of his shorts and pressed it.

Back in town, sitting on a comfortable chair at her kitchen breakfast bar, Dr Sonja sipped a first morning coffee as her own beeper went off. She rolled her eyes. This was not what she wanted for today.

<Ana, I have to go out. Make sure you are ready for school.>

An unenthusiastic moan came from upstairs. That was a good sign, so Dr Sonja grabbed her keys and headed outside into the sun.

It took 20 minutes for Dr Sonja to pull up near Francisco in her battered beach buggy with the faded red paint. <I hope this is good. I have to open surgery in an hour and Cynthia is off on a sick day.>

< I found something on the beach. Its weird.>

<Is this another one of your strange animals that turns out to be a beached dolphin or something?>

<No, this is different. Promise.>

Dr Sonja had obviously already seen the gelatinous mass, and her gaze was directed straight at it as she got out of the buggy and walked over to Francisco

<Well you don't often see that,> she observed drily. <Definitely weird.>

Francisco nodded and as they stared at the discovery another wave flowed over it. At first Francisco thought it was a trick of the water, an illusion. Dr Sonja's reaction told him that it wasn't.

The eyes of the dead face had begun to move, and the jellyfish slowly crawled forward towards them.

<Holy shit> said Dr Sonja.

The jellyfish continued to move, slowly as though it were wounded and weak, but still animated. Its direction seemed to follow the eyes of the head, still empty and grey but rotating in their sockets as though desperately trying to find something.

She couldn't help but be repulsed, and at the same time this monstrous blob fascinated her too. Not in the way it interested Francisco, but from the perspective of science. She looked at it through the filter of more years than she cared to count of training and working as a doctor. She picked out details, looked for familiarity to try and establish some sort of cause and effect mechanism.

She crouched down, tying her long black hair into a pony tail. She always did that when she was concentrating

The jellyfish and its amputated face continued to slide across the hot sand leaving a wet trail behind them. Dr Sonja could see the brain matter within the gelatinous body as well, and the missing hemisphere of the skull form where it emerged. It seemed impossible that such an amalgamated being could have any kind of life. Yet here it was, if not sentient then aware, moving, seeking.

The mouth moved a little as well. Dr Sonja looked closer, thinking that the motion of the mass itself was causing it. Perhaps it was, but she couldn't be certain. Perhaps the mouth was moving on its own. But what reason could there be?

For one moment, Dr Sonja wondered if it was actually trying to speak to her.

She shuffled forward a little, and then suddenly jerked back. Something stabbed into the down mass with a sudden explosive force, penetrating right through the head and burying itself deep into the sand.

Francisco loomed over her. He hadn't really cared about the whys and whats. He had simply reacted, taking the old shovel that Dr Sonja habitually kept in her buggy and slamming it through what he could only see as an abomination.

The two of them stared at the mass. Perhaps two metres across, and now pinned to the beach by a shovel, it looked even more out of place than before.

<Is that your solution to everything?> barked Dr Sonja. <Just kill it?>

<It belonged dead> answered Francisco.

The doctor couldn't disagree. Whatever this thing had been, it had not been born out of any natural existence she could comprehend. And even as she though that she realised that it continued to defy the natural order.

The metal of the shovel blade was beginning to smoke. It started to bubble and seethe and hiss, and once again the mass of jellyfish started to flow forward.

Not even a minute passed before the shovel blade dissolved enough to fall backwards into the beach. The mass was resealing itself already, and within it the face began to reconstruct too, even though the broken fragments of skull did not. Instead they hung suspended within the gel as the eyes, the nose, the mouth and the skin bearing them reassembled themselves. Not perfectly, more like a crude replica patched together in haste to leave gaps and holes.

It could not possibly be alive. And yet it moved. Steadily and inexorably, it continued its journey.

<I…don't understand> said Francisco, finally.

Dr Sonja didn't either. She was the surgical precision to the big man's brute force. Each had their place, and in his world Francisco needed to be strong and powerful. But here, faced with something that refused to abide by natural laws or all rational definitions, that physicality was meaningless. Trying to kill it with a shovel had not worked, and Francisco had nothing else.

This was a time for the mind, not the body. Despite that, Dr Sonja simply couldn't form any kind of theory. Even in her small corner of the changing world she had seen many things. Not as many as Francisco as he ranged across the Yucatán. But enough to know that the rules were different now. And in each of those encounters Dr Sonja had at least been able to form some kind of a theory.

This, however, defied even the basic truths of life and death.

Dr Sonja stood, moving her hands to see if the dead eyes of the face were tracking her. They didn't respond. Instead they followed their own impulses, apparently unperturbed even by being attacked. Did they even see anymore, Dr Sonja wondered. And if they did, what did they perceive?

Was there some veil those eyes could penetrate, one that was denied to the living.

<We need to contain it>? she said finally. <I have something in the buggy that should work.>

Francisco wasn't surprised. The buggy always seemed to contain all types of useful things, and he wondered if Dr Sonja was able to foresee exactly what she would need. With that sort of insight she could back a fortune out in the Wilderness, where new beliefs so often superseded science and religion.

He walked over to the buggy, and as he started to lift the box he found there his attention was drawn to something new. At first it was just faint sound, a low almost imperceptible buzz. As he looked back from the beach, he saw a rippling black cloud rise out of a crack in the green of the trees.

It was a swarm.

Los Insectos Del Diablo, they were called.

Once they might have been beetles or flies. Now they were vicious biting winged creatures, big as locusts and vicious as wasps. Swarms were common, and everybody knew to avoid them. Even the venom of the red rattlesnake paled in comparison to the bite of the Devils' Insects.

They were killers, purely and simply. Thousands of them, attracted by the pheromonal scent of Francisco and Dr Sonja.

She hadn't seen them, and Francisco quickly looked around for shelter. There was nothing. Just the buggy, which had no roof and would offer no protection. It was too slow to outrun the swarm as well. He had seen faster vehicles overwhelmed and their occupants turned into masses of suppurating bites before dying convulsing and in agony.

<SWARM,> shouted Francisco.

Everyone knew the word. Dr Sonja snapped her head back, her eyes widening as she saw the cloud in insects approaching. Francisco ran towards her, picking her up like a rag doll and heading for the water. If they could get far enough out to sea maybe the insects would lose interest. Maybe they salt would distract them, or maybe something in the buggy might get their attention. Dr Sonja always kept food in there somewhere.

It was a plan born out of desperation, Dr Sonja knew that. But she trusted Francisco to protect her, so she clung on as he powered into the water. Behind them the sound of the swarm, its malignant buzz, got louder and louder, and Dr Sonja imagined all those pairs of mandibles dripping with their sickly yellow venom.

She hated the insects more than almost anything else.

The two of them glanced back as Francisco tried to get them away from the shore. Even with his massive body and the sheer strength it possessed, the sea was implacable. It slowed him down, forcing him into submission. Dr Sonja slipped free and splashed down next to him and they both waded out further. The surf gave way to warm Caribbean water, and the sandy ocean floor sloped steeply until she was out of her depth so she started to swim.

The swarm was coalescing into its killing form. It was reshaping itself, each member becoming a cell with a new ephemeral creature that almost possessed a murderous intelligence all of its own. Dr Sonja had seen it before and it was always terrifying.

<Hold your breath,> instructed Francisco.

Dr Sonja complied, and the two of them dove down beneath the surface.

Under the water everything was so different.

Sound, light, all were transformed by a place that existed as another world entirely, apart from humanity's conquest of the lands. It was so beautiful here, it felt like nothing could possibly hurt Dr Sonja. But that was when she was diving with her air-tanks and her radio.

This was something else, something more primal and frightening.

Francisco would be able to remain submerged for minutes. But for Dr Sonja, it was barely thirty seconds before she started to feel the strain on her unmoving lungs and the burning in her chest. Her mind started to scream at her to breathe.

This was what it must have felt like to drown.

She held on for as long as she could, counting off each second as her vision starting to blur with bloody static. However strong she was, however at home in the sea, it would always be a losing battle, and it was barely a minute and a half before she broke the surface, gasping to suck in precious breaths.

Beside her, comfortable and relaxed, Francisco watched her struggle and finally surface. He braced himself, ready to grab her and full her back down at the first hint of trouble. Instead, her hand gently reached down to him, tapping him on the arm.

Francisco rose up out the sea like some pale titan summoned from the ocean depths. Even Dr Sonja could still be surprised by his appearance, his sheer size, and his albino skin reminded her why so many people called him the Pale Ghost.

Next to him, she was tiny. A beautiful black haired doll. The two of them were utterly different in almost every day, but Francisco knew that Dr Sonja held the real strength. She had been the one who had been there when Francisco had come back. She had treated him and cared for him, and watched as new strength had gradually built up inside him.

They could almost be family.

As the two of them started back towards the beach they heard that the noise of the insects had ceased and the air seemed clear. Francisco knew that it wasn't unusual for swarms to dissipate quickly if they couldn't track their prey, and that was what Francisco had banked on. He was thankful it had worked. The swarms were easily capable of coping with water, and he had had no back up plan.

Francisco watched some silver fish dart by as he followed Dr Sonja back to the shore, enjoying the water as he waded back into the surf and onto the sand.

When he got there, he and Dr Sonja both realised why the air was so quiet now. The entire swarm was dead.

Thousands of tiny carcasses littered the beach. Not one single member of the swarm had survived. All had been cut down, transformed by death as they lay on their carapace backs, smoking as they seemed to burn from the inside.

<I really don't understand now> said Francisco.

Dr Sonja tried to make sense of it as well. Swarms were usually unstoppable forces of nature like a tornado. One simply took whatever shelter they could and waited for Devil's Insects to pass. This kind of extinction was unheard of.

All she could divine was an idea from the way the bodies were giving off little clouds of foul-smelling gas. It was the same thing that seemed to have happened to Francisco's shovel. She had guessed it was some kind of acid then, some necrotic substance that ate away the metal. Now she wasn't so sure.

Now she wondered if there wasn't something far more directed at work.

<I'd better get this thing in the box> said Dr Sonja determinedly. She as determined to conduct some tests, and try and glean some sort of scientific insight. Mysteries were nice, unsolved ones not so much.

Francisco nodded, but when he picked up the discarded container he looked down at the thick blob of jelly.

The face was gone. There was no hint of brain or bone, no assembled flesh or dead staring eyes. All there was, was a dead jellyfish lying on the beach, like all the others Francisco had found except for the mass of dead things that lay around it.

Dr Sonja had seen it too, and the two of them mirrored each other as they locked eyes, looked, down and then back up again.

<Shall we just say this was a jellyfish>? asked Dr Sonja, <and try and pretend this didn't ever happen.>

Francisco smiled a little and nodded. Nobody would care about dead bugs, and the seabirds would soon consume them

all. It would be like they had never existed. He knew Dr
Sonja needed answers, but he had also learned that the way
this world was now those answers were harder to come by.
Much harder. Sometimes, things simply happened.

Today there would no explanation.

<Are you hungry?> Dr Sonja asked. <We should get
some breakfast.>

Francisco nodded and they clambered into the dune
buggy, excavating tyre tracks into the sand as Dr Sonja
floored the accelerator and headed back to the town.

Behind them, forgotten, the jellyfish began to crawl back
towards the sea.

CENOTE

Francisco loved markets, wherever he found them. In old towns, in lost backstreets, and way out past so-called civilisation and into the Wilderness, they were little oases that filled the belly, clothed the body and all things in between.

This one was out into the north of the peninsula, outside a town called Chicxulub. Or at least what used to be a town. Things had changed, and now most of the human traffic flowed past it and to the market, one that had used to be a villa buried out in the scrub and painted bright white. For a while there had been neon signs, but they were switched off because people rarely ventured out there at night. Not anymore.

Francisco visited the Chicxulub market often. He liked the food, and always made sure he got his fill of the cochinita pibil that was a speciality of one of the street food stalls. He could smell the churros cooking as well. Dr Sonja said they were bad for him and told him to eat the sopa de lima instead, but she knew he wouldn't. The best she could hope for was that Francisco restricted himself to just a few sweets, rather than emptying out the whole stall.

As he ate, Francisco noticed a clothing stall. He missed his old jacket and had been wanting a replacement. The vendor was selling ponchos, and Francisco has always wanted to own one, ever since he was a child. One in particular caught his eye, a dark burned orange color and sewn with geometric patterns of lines and triangles in blues and golds.

The vendor caught the interest straight away and assessed the size of his giant new customer.

<Sangre.> said the vendor. Francisco was puzzled until the man, old and skinny with parchment skin, pointed at his tee-shirt. <Good band. Heavy.>

Francisco nodded his approval. Sangre were one of his favorite bands, and there were rumours they would be playing somewhere close to his home sometime soon. Like many rumours it would probably never happen. Especially after what happened to the last band that played the area. Even a year later they hadn't found all the pieces of the drummer

<How much for the poncho?>

<300 my friend. For a Sangre fan I drop to 250.>

<Still too much for me.>

The vendor leaned in, conspiratorial and close. <Maybe I can do something about that.>

Francisco finished eating his churro. <Something like what?>

<Please, come into my office. I have a proposition for you.>

The little room Francisco found himself in was hotter even than outside. The air stank with perfumes and incense, and a hundred different skulls were painted on the walls, each one with its own unique colorful sense but all of them carrying the same feeling of the grotesque. These were not the skulls sold to tourists that had become so popular. These were something different. Empty eye sockets gazed down from ragged hand painted work, making the room feel as though it was being watched by sentinels from a darker, unseen place.

<Please, sit> said the seller.

Francisco took one of the two wooden chairs either side of a rough table with one leg shorter than the other three. A single tiny square hole was the only thing that let the light in, illuminating the dancing streams of dust that were everywhere. Other than the plain furniture, the room was empty. Stripped almost, so that nothing could get in the way of the scent that dominated everything else.

Francisco felt it in his nostrils, and he did his best not to breath too much of it in. It made him feel nauseous, even a little light-headed.

<Are you trying to sell me something else?>

The vendor smiled, thin lips receding over dark gums and yellow teeth that spoke of a person who didn't eat or drink enough. It was no surprise – there was so little money out here in the wilderness that even the best vendors could only scrape by. Without tourists, there were only travellers.

<I see your skin, so I think you are the Pale Ghost. You do favors for people. I need a favor.>

Francisco shifted in his seat. Too many of these sorts of encounters ended up with guns. <What sort of favor do you want?>

<I speak to people, people who come by here. They say that you are the one who can deal with things.> The seller mimed a slashing motion with his wizened hand. <Permanently. I need this service. I throw in the poncho for free. I heard the story of the beast with the head of a skull. It breathed fire and summoned demons from the rocks, and you cut off its head and burned the serpent that lived under the ground until it begged for mercy.>

<That is not…>

The seller waved him to silence. <I know these are made up stories to scare travellers. But there is always truth in every story.> He reached into his jacket and pulled out a tiny clay model no more than six inches tall. It was roughly made, perhaps by a child, yet it clearly showed something with teeth and claws and a tail that tapered to a spike. <We want you to kill *our* demon.>

<*The story of El Carnivoro was told to me by my father and his father before him. It is an old story. It is said that the first person who saw him was a young girl who lived in a small town built here by American settlers. They knew nothing of the land, and they tried to make their life in places that people should not live in. On their first day when the settlers raised their flag a terrible sound came across the mountains. On the second day the settlers awoke to find that their finest cattle had been slaughtered, leaving only the sick and the young. The settlers took up their guns because they believed that Mexicans tried to take revenge upon them for the loss of their land to America. But there were no men there.*

The settlers search for weeks, looking for caves where their enemy could hide. They found nothing. There were no more events, no more sounds and no more slain cattle. The settlers thought perhaps that had simply scared their enemy away and proceeded to build their new lives as they had planned. Then one day, a young woman, the child of a physician, went out to collect some cactus flowers. She walked many miles from their town with five strong men to protect her. They took horses and provision, and they believed themselves safe against the snakes and the coyotes. But it was not the native animals that watched.

When the party did not return after six days the woman's father became concerned. He petitioned the sheriff of the town to ride out to look for her and demanded that he join them should his daughter have become unwell. And so eight men rode along the same trail. After half a day they found a dead horse, gutted and half eaten like the livestock before it. The flies told them that death had come very quickly, and soon they discovered more horses and the bodies of men. They were ripped and torn, limbs scattered about the rocky land where their blood stained the earth and red flowers grew. Their guns were used, their supplies gone. But there was no sign of the physician's daughter.

The physician became afflicted with panic, and he rode his horse hard to try and find his daughter. The sheriff pursued him alone, not wanted to lose any more of his men, while the others returned to protect their growing town. But there was no town anymore. Every man and woman and child had been slaughtered, just the same as the riders and the animals. Not a single life was spared, and a dark vapour hung across the place as though the spirit of death itself had laid claim to their homes and their lands. It claimed the sheriff's men too.

The sheriff knew nothing of this as he pursued the physician. But eventually they found his daughter. She was clinging to the last spark of life, hiding in a tiny crevice deprived of all food and water. She begged her father and the sheriff to leave their settlement behind and return home. She said the land itself had spoken, and the mountains had sent forth a monstrous demon that walked like a man. It had blazing eyes and a tail like a serpent, and its jaws could crush the strongest man with a single bite.

The very sight of it had driven her to consume her own flesh.>

As Francisco stepped back out into the open air, the story the vendor had told him rolled over and over in his head. He had heard a hundred of these legends, each one of them forming the basis of a new folklore over time that had spread from town to town. As things had changed and the collapse had begun more and more people looked back to these stories to given them hope. But myths always spoke of the unnatural, and now everybody seemed to have a tale of monsters and demons.

Francisco couldn't argue that things lived here in the Wilderness now that he couldn't explain or understand. Of course, the strange gases in the caves made people see all kind of terrifying things, but Francisco knew that it was more than that. Some things were real. He himself was evidence enough.

The vendor had given Francisco a hastily sketched map before he had scuttled off to try and reclaim the sales he might have lost, targeting a small group who had driven in in an old battered school bus that had no school children in it. The map wasn't much but at least it gave Francisco a direction. He could drive for a while but then the Chicxulub terrain would force him onto foot.

He just hoped he could avoid the Hotspots.

Like so many things in the Wilderness they were hard to find and unpredictable, and too often it was only when a car engine died or a dog went suddenly rabid that anyone would even realise they were in such a Hotspot. They seemed to defy all knowledge and reason. Dr Sonja had tried to analyse them, yet even she could only identify that they occurred within the hidden boundaries of the vast crater. Francisco had not paid much attention. That had been the same day the new Erebor album had come out. He wasn't missing that for anything. With the Internet gone he had had to travel a long way to get a copy of an old CD, so all he could remember about Dr Sonja's talk between bursts of thrash as that the crater was big, and the asteroid that had caused it had wiped out the dinosaurs. Francisco had thought that was a shame. Like a lot of men he had loved dinosaurs as a boy.

The clay model that the vendor had also given him reminded him a little of a dinosaur. But nothing like the ones in the books.

Francisco went back to his car, the dark red sedan with the jet-black roof and hood, and the coffin bound to the roof via steel moorings, that he had driven since the day his skin had turned to chalk. He got in and perched the map on the dash, just under where a tentacled pendant that someone had given him hung from the rear-view mirror. It had become a sort of good luck charm, even though Francisco didn't know what it was meant to be.

Like he always did, he pinched it between his thumb and forefinger for luck, and then drove away in a huge cloud of dust.

From his stall the vendor watched him go.

Half a day later Francisco sat on top of an old ruin and looked out over a landscape of trees that stretched over every horizon. This was one of his favorite lookouts, a forgotten crumbling Mayan tower that few people visited anymore and fewer still cared about. Bandits and animals and the legends of the damned kept people away from sites like this until eventually even the knowledge of their existence was all but lost.

Francisco preferred it that way.

He hadn't known it back when tourists flocked to all of the sites, especially the ones in Campeche but he could imagine that he would have hated it. All these old temples and pyramids had probably felt like they teamed with life - armed with cellphones, all swarming with their sodas and junk food, every one keen to get their perfect picture opportunity while their children ran amok and didn't care.

This tower, Francisco's tower, didn't have a name anymore could remember. It was overgrown with nature now, the grey stone of the place half covered in running plants and vines inhabited by armies of insects. Their sounds formed a hot sunlight buzzing chorus, and it was endless as the landscape shimmered with heat haze. The isolation allowed Francisco to pretend he was the only person in the world, and he could sit there for hours watching the landscape.

And once, occasionally, he would be able to see something more.

That was why he had climbed the collapsing rocky steps today and picked his way through the growth. This place, this outlook, was where he had first seen a glimpse of that other place. The place of bright colors and strange shapes that sang a song of the past and the future, or perhaps both merged together. And it told Francisco things. Whispered secrets nobody else could hear.

It had scared him at first, even though he had been told that first day that this was part of him now. Something in him, that he would carry. Just like the sigils he was able to draw on the small slate stones he kept in his belt pouch, it was part of some greater knowledge of which only tiny fragments had been imparted. It only ever happened on this spot too. Francisco had tried to listen in other places, other ruins, but only this one gave him anything to listen to.

So Francisco always came back to this tower, a little way North and a long way past the half empty tourists' cities. He sat, letting his legs hang over a huge broken stone as the clay monster figurine the vendor had given him sat in his lap alongside a scrawled and illegible map. He never knew quite what to focus on, or quite why some days worked and other didn't, but he hoped that today if he concentrated hard enough on these two new objects that something might happen.

As he tried to let his mind drift, a harsh voice barked out in brash American English. "What the hell are you doing here?"

For a moment Francisco thought that Dr Sonja or maybe even her sister had followed him, just to make certain he didn't do anything stupid. It wouldn't have been the first time, and the woman who ran up the broken stone steps towards him had the same strength and bearing about her.

The sun was behind her and it took a moment for Francisco to realise that it wasn't someone he knew. As she resolved from a silhouette, he saw that the woman wasn't local, and not even Hispanic. It was impossible tell how old she was, and all that Francisco could really identify was that she had hair with blonde streaks in it, and that she was very angry.

"This is a private dig," shouted the woman, in strident English. "So you need to…"

She stopped, as everyone did, the second she saw Francisco's sword. He hadn't thought about it too much as he was so used to it, so had had just put it next to him on the ground while he concentrated. He always forgot the impact it tended to have on people. After all, it was a weapon with one single purpose.

Francisco braced himself.

"Oh my God…" began the woman.

Here it came…….

"Where did you get that artefact? That is incredible. I've never seen one in such good condition before. Where did you get it?"

Francisco was confused. There was no running away or eyes bulging in disbelieving fear. All the woman's eyes held was a burning excitement, and she seemed to have instantly forgotten why she was supposed to be angry.

"It was…given to me," said Francisco, unconvincingly. He rarely spoke English and was a little hesitant. Not that he ever said a great deal anyway, in any language.

The woman strode right up to him, her face brimming with the energy and enthusiasm of an explorer who had discovered their own personal Holy Grail.

"May I?" she asked. Francisco nodded, and the woman knelt down by *Macuahuitl*. "My name is Rae, by the way. Oh my God this is amazing. Really incredible. The cross-bindings are perfect. And the blades look brand new."

Rae began to talk to herself, but something else had distracted Francisco, and when he looked out over the trees again he realised that something had changed.

The air had begun to almost invisibly peel, to fold back on itself like a fading flower, and Francisco watched as his vision began to reveal something new.

The sky phantoms danced.

Out of the bright blue perfect sky, their shimmering outlines swam through the air like fish in water. Unseen yet so undeniably there, Francisco was always bewitched when they chose to appear. He didn't know where they came from or what they were, just that they conjored themselves out of the nothingness of the hot air to play.

They were all shapes and no shape all at once, fluid and unformed as they slipped from one configuration to the next without care or consequence. Even Francisco, who had seen them so many times before, found it impossible to follow their intricate movements. All they revealed of themselves was a haze, a glimmer. One that anybody else would simply discard or not even perceive at all. Occasionally there would be the briefest flash of color, polished metallic gold or deep rich emerald, but only occasionally.

Fascinated as he was, Francisco knew that he had to watch closely. Somewhere in the movements and the light was something else, something so subtle and concealed that the simplest of distractions would cause to vanish entirely.

Because the sky phantoms also brought a gift.

"Excuse me," said Rae.

Francisco physically jerked, and the show was instantly over. The glimmers and the ghosts disappeared and the air sealed itself back up so that nobody could see what secrets it hid away.

<Fuck it> he growled.

"Sorry, are you OK?"

Francisco wasn't OK, and Rae in turn could tell he was tense. Unnerved even. Seeing that in a giant man with chalk white flesh was disquieting to say the least. "Yes, fine," said Francisco. "I thought I saw something."

Rae shrugged it off. "Well I'm sure I can help you with that, if maybe you can answer some questions for me about this amazing artefact. My camp is nearby. I can't offer you luxury but we have some water and some food. One of my guys can do amazing things with tinned meat."

Slowly, Francisco nodded. He was intrigued at how Rae had gone from so hostile to so friendly in seconds and he guessed that she must be an archaeologist. They always had that passion for the past that overtook everything else.

As Francisco picked up his sword, with Rae's gaze glued to it, neither of them saw a telltale shimmer in the air behind them as a phantom watched.

Rae led the way down the steps of the old ruin, her steps sure and quick to evade the flaws and cracks in the stone. Francisco guessed she had been here for a while. Exactly how long he couldn't tell. It had been months, perhaps even a year, since he himself had visited the tower, and when he came his attention was always outwards to the land.

The camp was not much more than a half mile hike from the base of the monument, and it had been carefully assembled around a thick clump of trees. There were tents and benches and equipment all dominated by the whirring of small generator, with so little space given over to any kind of living that the whole place spoke of a dedication to their task. An obsession almost.

Francisco didn't like technology too much. It made him uncomfortable, and he didn't really understand why people were so willing to give their existence over to it. None of it worked here anyway.

Chicxulub was not a place of progress. It was a place of old lands.

As Rae took Francisco over to her own workstation, two benches ridden with equipment and her beloved laptop, a second person joined them. A man this time, dressed in fashionable wilderness clothes and a big wide hat, who eyed Francisco suspiciously.

When he spoke it was with a French accent. "Who is this?"

"Ah, this is…" began Rae, and then realised she didn't even know Francisco's name.

"Francisco," growled Francisco, and Rae carried on without missing a beat.

"…Francisco. Francisco, this is Vincent Maurier. Vincent, just look at that." She pointed to the sword that Francisco had slung over his back. "Isn't that incredible."

Vincent was older than Rae, his features gave that away. His skin was thin and age had brought out aquiline features dominated by a hooked nose. He didn't extend his hand to shake, and neither did Francisco. Instead the older man started to pace around, looking at Francisco as though he were nothing more than an exhibit in a museum.

"Oui, c'est incroyable," he said, quietly.

Francisco didn't speak French, so the words did nothing to alleviate the sense of tension he felt radiating off Vincent. Rae was clearly ignorant of it, but Francisco knew it all too well.

He wasn't at all shocked when Vincent pulled out a gun.

"Vincent, what the FUCK…" shouted Rae.

"Silence. You know who this is. Le Fantome Pale. Pale Ghost. He is a monster. A devil. I was told you were coming, Ghost. You are not supposed to come here. Why did you not stay away. I will kill you."

Francisco wasn't listening. He could already tell that this old Frenchman wasn't used to violence and had never held a gun before in his life. Despite that there was something strong behind his actions, a kind of power that came from somewhere other than muscle and bone.

"Vincent," pleaded Rae. "Please put that gun down." She couldn't understand what was happening. Her twenty year friendship with Vincent had taught her a set of behaviours, of expectations, proven again and again, and as a scientist she absolutely believed in that. Now it was as though the man in front of her was speaking with somebody else's voice.

Francisco saw that too and had little patience for it. He simple swatted the older man away when he steeped to close. Not hard, but enough to throw Vincent almost ten feet and crashing down into one of the other benches. The noise alerted others, and two, three then four young faces – students – all appeared at the openings of their various tents. None of them made a move to intervene. They were simply too scared as they all was a huge man with a sword on his back, and their beloved professor lying on the ground with blood oozing from his nose and mouth.

Vincent reached for the weapon he had dropped but Francisco had already kicked it away into the trees. Then he grabbed the old man by his jacket and lifted him bodily off his feet.

Rae was screeching at Francisco to stop, to leave, to just go. She simply couldn't reconcile Vincent with the gun so she could only blame the newcomer, the freakish pale giant that her mentor and friend had seemingly recognised. She blamed herself for being so openly blind. For inviting someone she knew nothing of into their camp – their home. In a vain attempt to help she hurled herself forward at Francisco in the hope she might be able to affect him in some way. It was like running into a wall.

Francisco looked into Vincent's eyes, and he saw what the ghosts of the air had been trying to tell him. He saw another life behind the one he held in the air, another spirit. And then he saw that whatever it was laughing.

"You think you are strong but you are not." Vincent took something out of his pocket and held it up. It was a stone object of some kind, flecked with white crystals that fluoresced a little and carved into the shape of a coiled serpent.

Francisco didn't recognise it but he knew exactly what it meant. A signal.

Something new was being summoned. Something bad.

Monsters weren't supposed to come out during the day. They were supposed to hide their faces until darkness and then creep out of their caves, hiding their reality in the pages of tabloid newspapers and drunken stories in bars.

Francisco knew differently. Even as he dropped Vincent onto the ground and stamped the fragile substance of the object into fragments, he knew it was too late. Whatever silent signal the old man sent had been received, and that was what the sky phantoms had tried to tell him in their ethereal language. He just hadn't seen it in time.

It wouldn't be long now.

"What did you do," demanded Rae, horrified at the words Vincent had said. He looked back at her with eyes that no longer cared.

"He has to die," spat the old man. "You see, yes?"

"No," said Rae. "No I don't see. What are you doing?"

One of the students screamed. It was a young man with bleached blond hair combed across his face and he pointed out of the camp back towards the monument. Whatever he had seen or thought he seen was hiding itself, and Francisco tried to track it. It defied his attempts as he reached to a pouch on the back of his belt.

The pouch where he kept his thin slate tablets.

Vincent just smiled a dead man's smile, lying there in the dirt. Whatever had happened to him had broken him, and whoever he had once been was gone now.

The sound of trees crashing and splitting made more people cry out as they scrambled for some sort of safety. Once, long ago, Francisco would have done the same but now he knew that there was no real cover, no way to conceal oneself from the impossible predators of the Wilderness.

When the attack started it was swift and brutally sudden. The blond student was snatched off the ground, and the sounds of him being brutalised became the only sounds. It took mere seconds for the body to be cast down again, flesh peeled from bones and tissue burned to stinking residue.

Rae wanted to puke when she saw the ravaged corpse.

"Everybody run for the truck," she shouted, looking at Francisco for some sort of support. If he had some he didn't give it. Instead, as everyone scattered and panicked, he carved a symbol onto a slate piece, the knife in his hand moving with a practiced ease as it traced the simple whirls and curves of a sigil.

K'ak.

There were maybe nine people in the camp and they all howled and begged and ran from the tent. Possessions were abandoned and friendships forgotten as everyone stampeded for the supposed safety of a vehicle. It was simple fear, and Francisco that it was what the monsters out here depended on. There was no point in saying anything because the people wouldn't listen. They couldn't.

Francisco wished he could save them. He knew that it didn't matter if they were in the truck or not. Around him another person died, then another, all ripped and scorched in the briefest of seconds before being reducing to smoking ruins. They fell almost like meteorites out of the sky, breaking as they hit the earth.

Vincent lay there, forgotten, as Rae instinctively looked to Francisco as a shield. Perhaps the sword or his size seemed the safer option, but anything had to be better than the alternative as she looked at the bodies of people who had trusted her with their safety. She felt the shame of self-preservation as another person was plucked out of existence, and the disgust at Vincent who simply watched it happen, all his emotions stripped from him to leave only a husk behind.

Then something else took her attention.

"Oh my fucking God," she whispered. "What is that?"

Slowly, the trees themselves seemed to have let go of their shadows in the harsh sunlight. At the edge of anything she could perceive, Rae saw smoke-like almost invisible shapes drift out into the air, twisting and coalescing with a life of their own.

There were no features, no identity to hang onto it. Instead it was like a sensation of dread, as though the sap from the trees had been corrupted, made cancerous, and then silently spawned an invisible fear that crept relentlessly forward. But it was that silence that was the most terrible thing. It seemed as though whatever unseeable apparition had apparently been born to the world existed outside of sound.

Francisco hurled his carved slate forward.

K'ak.

The second it hit the ground it began to spark, spitting out fountains of firework orange and white that caught onto the trees and set them alight. Rae gazed, dumbstruck, as she watched the flames hop impossibly from tree to tree, jumping across unbridgeable gaps to form what could almost be called a web, its burning filaments transforming dry brush into wildfire as they wove their way onward.

Thousands of incendiary splinters flew out of the fire to burn air as easily as wood. The flames became like liquid as they rolled in the air, transforming themselves into their own monster, a firestorm that sought only to consume what it had been conjured to destroy.

Rae gazed, trying to reconcile these impossible phenomena, as Francisco turned to her and simply said "Run."

Francisco and Rae sprinted through the trees, he following the slightest of paths and she simply following in his footsteps as best she could. He was fast for his size, and not simply because of his stride. There was something more to this man, and even as they ran she was determined to find out what it was. Somehow, even with the horror she had witnessed and the fading hope her students had found some kind of safety branded into her mind, she simply had to understand.

It was her nature.

Francisco didn't care about any of that. The flames behind themselves were already burning themselves out after not even a moment, and once gone the barrier they had formed would no longer protect them. Then whatever it was that Vincent had called upon could pursue them again.

He drew his sword and hacked through growth that blocked their path, barely losing his stride as he did so. Behind them he already could hear the trees begin to crack again.

"Where are we going?" gasped Rae. She prided herself on keeping fit, but she knew she couldn't keep up this pace for very long. The heat was already sapping her strength, and her head was starting to thump as her body started to dehydrate. It happened so quickly out here there was almost no warning.

Francisco didn't answer straight away. The way the rock and earth was lying beneath his feet was telling him something. With each step he detected little telltale hints of geography that the instincts he possessed revealed to him. Their language only came in little fragments but he knew enough to be able to piece it together, and if he was right, those hidden signs spoke to him of a destination.

Then he shouted "This way."

He changed course, powering through a thicket that burst apart into dust and spores. Rae choked on it and nearly stumbled. Ahead, Francisco had already cut open a makeshift gateway and behind her she could feel the shape, the monstrosity, gaining ground.

Rae had to admit she was terrified. Her long-planned expedition, two years of her life, had been transformed into a massacre in a moment of Hell on Earth, and somehow she had taken a step out of the comfortable world of lectures and classrooms with which she was so familiar and into a different, frightening and alien place. One where people died so hideously and so instantly, and where her only apparent chance of survival was a man with a sword.

So she ran after Francisco.

Not ten feet past the gateway he had created the ground was suddenly gone, and Rae fell.

*

All around, the air was thick and blue. Mirages of the old and the new fractured and reformed endlessly. Figures of men and women were transfigured to animals, buildings were rendered back into their basic stone shapes, and above everything a vast serpent dominated the skies that swirled with every color. There was no sound, no thought. There was just a vast primal landscape, painted in hyperreal glows, where the jaguar and the eagle hunted and ghosts danced between the trees.

Francisco tried to remember who he was as the panorama seeped into his brain, beckoning for him to become a part of it. His vision warped as his eyes tried to focus, yet the harder he tried the less he could grab hold of. It was a dream, a mirage that danced at the very edge of his awareness.

And in an instant it was gone.

Francisco opened his eyes and realised he was drowning. There was nothing around him other than impenetrable water that took away any sense of direction. No up or down, no gravity or the slightest sense of light to show the way. There was just the breath in his lungs separating him from slow sinking inevitability. It made his chest burn as he strained to orient himself, but panic was taking over.

Even with all the things he had seen, this was true terror for Francisco.

Desperately he tried to swim, to find some way of seeing anything that might guide him. Already the hands of unconsciousness were creeping in, little black smudges at the edges of his consciousness. Awareness was starting to dim and in a few seconds he would start to choke on the water.

Just a few short seconds.

Finally his muscles gave way and bubbles flooded out of him, surrounding his body in his own last breath frozen into perfect spheres that taunted him. If only he could take them back in. If only....

Francisco looked at what he hoped was upwards, and impossibly there was light. Not the sun, but a glow in the water itself. The air bubbles started to light up like lanterns as all around him lit up with luminous blue. Somehow, it calmed him. The pain in his chest was gone, and the fear that gripped his gut began to faded away

Was this it, wondered Francisco. Was his last sight on this earth, his final experience - a beautiful lightshow conjured out of nothing to ease his transition?

As he let himself relax, a shape appeared out of the colors. A figure smothered in feathers that flowed like hair in the water, silent and serene, swam effortlessly towards him and reached out with a golden hand.

Francisco opened his eyes and realised that he was alive. There was rock under him digging into his back, and his clothes were dripping wet in a heavy uncomfortable way that could only be real. He blinked the water out of his eyes and let them focus a bit before he tried to take in any more detail.

"Thank God," said a familiar voice. "I was pretty sure you were dead."

Rae was sitting next to him, just as soaked.

Francisco slowly propped himself up on his elbows. His head swam a little and echoed his heart with a steady thump. But it seemed that his desperate idea had worked. They were both alive, and whatever it was that had chased them could never come down into the cenote. Like so many things he didn't know how he knew that. He simply did. The pure waters of the cavern would cast out anything dark and impure.

Perhaps they had spat him out too, and he was only breathing because he himself was something the underground lake wouldn't tolerate.

"Look, I'm glad you're not dead and everything," continued Rae. "But we've been down here for hours now and I'm cold and wet and I still don't know who you are or what is going on. Oh, no wait a second. I do know something. And that is that since I met you my entire life has gone FUCKING INSANE."

Francisco's head hurt as he sat up. Hours, she said. He'd been unconscious for hours. All he recalled was jumping, and then feeling too heavy. Other than that, nothing. Just the vaguest hints of what could only have been a hallucination. Dr Sonja had told him about that sort of thing before with swimmers and divers. Something to think about another time.

"Thank you," said Francisco.

"For what? I didn't do anything. Jesus, you think I could do anything with you, you're like 10 feet tall. So, have you got any more magic stones that can get us out of here?"

She pointed up to the cenote entrance, perhaps thirty feet overhead. It wasn't a large opening but the cave beneath opened wide, just as Francisco had hoped. That meant there was probably a linking tunnel somewhere, eroded out of the rock just like the cenote itself. At least he hoped there was.

He checked his belt and its pouches. A few things had been lost to the water but nothing he couldn't easily replace. *Macuahuitl* the sword was just next to him as well, undamaged and sprinted as ever, and as he idly wondered how it had got off his back Rae got his attention, pointing at the far edge of the cavern. There, in an area cloaked with thick shadow, a huge shape lay quiet and still.

Rae's eyes widened as she saw what it was. "Oh you are kidding!"

The shape was an animal but not like any other. Large, reptilian it was lying on its side, a thick scaly abdomen moving up and down with pained laboured breath, and there was a ragged gash on one side, dark with dried blood. As Francisco and Rae carefully approached to see through the shadows the animals body became visible –grasping arms, huge thick legs and a long fat tail that curled open and closed.

When the head of the creature revealed itself there were teeth within titanic jaws, horns that arced back of its muzzle and head, and small yellow eyes that peered weakly at its observers.

"Is that…" whispered Rae, unable to quite believe what she was seeing.

Francisco had left his little clay sculpture from the market in his car, but he knew straight away that this beast, wounded though it was, was what he had been looking for. That crudely formed object was now a living thing, defying extinction and evolution and simply laying there.

Reaching down, he grabbed his sword.

"Wait, what?" demanded Rae, snapping out of her trance of disbelief.

"Gonna kill it," said Francisco.

"No you are NOT. Do you even understand what this is? Holy shit I guessed you weren't you weren't too bright but this is unbelievable."

Rae stood defiantly between the creature and Francisco. Very quickly he realised that there was little point in arguing. Yet again he saw the spirit of Dr Sonja in front of him, and knew that whatever primitive plan of execution he had formulated was going to have to change. The sense of how he felt was so familiar to Francisco. Maybe, he thought, this Rae woman was some sort of distant relative of Dr Sonja. That would explain a lot.

"What do you want to do."

"Well, we examine it. It's obviously injured so we should see what's wrong and then see if we can do something."

The animal was easily fifteen feet long but a lot of that was tail. Even so it was clearly muscular and powerful, in particular sinewed scaled limbs ending in ebony claws that looked like they could disembowel with only a casual flick of motion. Whatever they did was going to take time, and

Francisco decided it was best to place himself somewhere that if the creature started to react he could at least attempt to subdue it. Quite how he would do that, he wasn't certain

Rae fell back into the power of science once again and all else was forgotten as she began to examine, every movement cautious and carefully planned with nothing random. It didn't take her long to find something.

Buried in the flank of the animal was a huge metal hook.

"Can you get this out?" asked Rae.

Francisco found it puzzling how this woman's dedication to her science seemed to override everything. It was almost as though she became possessed by some secular force made of facts and analysis, and all thoughts of what and why of the death and the terror were suppressed. Even Dr Sonja didn't do that, and she was the smartest person Francisco knew.

For a moment he wondered if Rae was a robot from the future. Unlikely, he concluded. They didn't exist, and if they did she surely would have short-circuited by now with all this water.

He looked at the hook embedded in the animal's side. Too big to be wielded by a man, and old by the look of it. It was made of iron and rust covered most of the roughly worked surface. It looked like some kind of claw that had been snapped off a giant metal version of the creature itself. The wound around it had sealed a little, though not enough to start healing. That told Francisco this was a recent injury.

Gently, he touched the hook and the pale flesh of the animal's abdomen. It juddered a little, wincing with pain, and the growl came again. It was obviously weak and there was no real way to judge what removing the vicious hook would do to it. The metal had penetrated deeply so there could be all kinds of damage. Even moving it a little might cause a catastrophic bleed, and this wondrous discovery would just die in front of the two of them, forever unknown.

"What do you think? Can we get that out of him. Or her?"

"Up to you."

"Oh yeah, sorry. I forgot you just wanted to kill one of the greatest scientific finds literally ever. Let me have a look."

Rae pushed him aside and began to study the wound. Francisco watched for a moment, and it became clear that she knew exactly what she was doing. He guessed she wasn't simply an archaeologist. Instead he began to search for a way out along the sides of the bulb-shaped cavern. There were all sorts of limestone formations to marvel at, time having formed intricate pillars and spires and webs. He had seen them before of course. Sometimes he and Perdita visited cenotes just for fun, and he made a mental note to bring her to this one. Its structures were especially beautiful, lit by that elemental blue light coming from the water.

Finally Francisco saw something that might be useful. It took a little bit of a climb to get to it, and he reached to his belt to take out a small vial of liquid that he shook to life to create a bright yellow sodium glow.

He held up his makeshift light to the opening he had found and peered inside.

Through the crack in the rock, Francisco saw things that shouldn't have been there. Nothing definite, just hints of shapes at first as his eyes did their best to penetrate the darkness. But even the shapes made no real sense. He could see carved geometry next to organic curves, and the hints of something that could have been something crystalline embedded within the dust white of bones. Huge bones as well. Whatever space lay beyond the cenote wall had to be vast, and Francisco imagined it containing within it a place of arches constructed from stone and ribs and walls laced with elements moth natural and man-made.

All he could really see were hints. The light from the vial revealed only tantalising glimpses into something that could not be reached despite its brightness. The crack that Francisco had found was not big enough to accommodate even a small person, and even the power of water had taken untold millennia to carve its way through the solid rock.

He glimpsed little torn pieces of what looked like big fibrous eggshells, and a little film formed in his head of the baby animal crawling out into the world for the first time, others of its kind gone deeper or gone for good.

It made Francisco smile to think that this huge animal had once been mall enough to crawl out of the crack in the wall – a barrier to a hidden underworld. Another hidden place in the Wilderness.

Francisco slid back down to the rocky ground and looked over to where Rae had been examining the animal that could only really be called a dinosaur.

Like so many young boys, Francisco had loved such things. He had always been on the side of the monster in the old black and white movies they never showed anymore, and as a boy he collected the different dinosaur models that he kept on a shelf by his television. Idly, he wondered what had happened to them.

It didn't really matter as he was looking at the real thing now. A giant reptile that everyone said shouldn't exist anymore. How long had it been here? It seemed small, perhaps a juvenile, so maybe there were others scattered in the underworlds of the cenotes. Enough to have built the legend the man at the market had told him perhaps? Had they been here for all that time?

There were too many questions that made Francisco's head hurt. On top of that he was getting hungry, it was easily later afternoon and he still didn't have a way of getting out of this pit. Mentally he cursed. The whipclaw would have been useful but he'd left it back in the car. In future he'd make sure he carried it on his belt.

By the water, largely ignoring him and everything else, Rae had started to examine a part of the dinosaur's neck, where the greenish color of the skin seemed inflamed and reddened. Running her hands across the scaled flesh she found a part that felt almost like an opening and pressed it.

Francisco started at a sudden scream that echoed around the cavern, and he ran to Rae's side as she collapsed back, clutching at her face. Something had spurted out from the creature, covering her face. She cried for help and scratched at her skin while Francisco tried to calm her, slowly prying her hands from her face.

Rae looked up at Francisco with eyes that were suddenly becoming as yellow and reptilian as the dinosaur itself

As Francisco looked at Rae's changed eyes the dinosaur began to thrash, its body convulsing from head to toe, and as it did Rae bent double in sudden stabbing agony. She tried to speak but couldn't get any words out, just gasps and cries of pain.

Francisco tried to help her but she pushed him away, instead fixing him with her altered unnatural gaze.

"Get it OUT," she hissed, before another wave washed over her and forced her back into spasm.

Francisco desperately tried to connect everything up, not knowing what to do. He was used to being able to take action immediately, unambiguously. His job was to track and to fight. This was something different, a problem that couldn't be solved with a sword.

He looked back and forth between the two of them woman and creature, and suddenly something in his head clicked. As he watched, the creature was reaching for the hook embedded in its side, clawing at its own body. It was futile because its forelimbs were just too short. But then he saw Rae clutch her own side, and the place her hands went was slick with what looked like blood weeping through her clothes.

In that second, Francisco realised he wasn't dealing with two things but one.

He reached to his belt and pulled out another stone, one that was elongated almost into a jagged rectangle. As he moved to the dinosaur's side he used the base of the hook to scratch a crude symbol, a head with a hooked nose and jutting chin. It wasn't perfect, and after the firebomb he had used for their escape whatever effect it produced would be weak. But perhaps it would be enough.

Francisco grabbed the hook and counted off his timing. It would have to be perfect, otherwise there would be a lot more blood. With a single movement he pulled the hook right out of the creature's body. It screeched out in pain and licked out one of its taloned legs but he dodged it and drove the hastily scratched slate straight into the wound.

Hoy.

Rae suddenly arched her back with one final agonised scream that bounced around the cavern, and then she lay still and quiet. The dinosaur did the same, its violent thrashing subsiding and its breathing regular and relaxed.

Francisco dropped the bloodied hook and crouched next to Rae. It took a moment, but then her eyes opened a little, still yellow like the reptile. But there was no time for any sort of explanation or understanding. Before either Francisco or Rae could decide what to say a gunshot sounded, and a bullet chipped stone just a few centimetres away from them.

"You did not think you would get away from me did you," shouted Vincent. He stood silhouetted at the lip of the cenote's entrance. "You will die Ghost. You think you are clever but I will kill you and the woman you have corrupted."

Francisco couldn't tell if the older man had missed accidentally or by design and wasn't about to take any risks. But there was no cover and he had no weapons to hand. Anything he could possibly do would simply take too long.

"Vincent," croaked Rae, her throat dry. "Why are you doing this?"

Vincent didn't hear. Even if he could he didn't want to. The power he had been promised had failed so utterly that a churning rage had taken over in its place. Around him, something began to coalesce in the air. It was something demonic, the same terrible force that had stolen away Rae's students' lives but somehow more focused, more intense. More real.

It made the air ooze and twist like thick tar, and slowly flowed around Vincent's body, picking at it. It smoked a little, and as it touched Vincent his body smoked too, becoming translucent in brief seconds showing bones, sinews, even the blood that boiled in his veins.

The older man relished it. It made him feel strong. Standing there at the rim of the cenote, all he had to do was wait. The water down there, the purity of it shouldn't have stopped the power he could command. He didn't know what it was about this place, but there was something down there was a barrier for the malignant whirlwind that snapped and bit, anxious for its next meal.

Something to do with that grotesque pale abomination Francisco.

It didn't matter. Vincent would not be stopped.

It had taken him along time to find his power, and the lives of students meant nothing. Just food for this monstrous spectral thing. But power or not, he would have what he craved. There wasn't going to be any way to stop him from reaching his goal, that obsessive thought branded into his mind. If he couldn't go down into the centre Rae and the living ghost that had corrupted her could die down there. So he fired again. The gun jumped in his hand and the slide cut him but he ignored the pain and the noise. He just wanted what he was due. The power around him, his personal demon spirit, wanted it too. They were connected. The same.

The second bullet ricocheted off into the water, and Francisco searched for somewhere to hide. There was nothing, not a single crevice or hole that would accommodate even one of them, let alone too.

Then he heard Rae say one single whispered word.

"Stop."

Beside them there was sudden movement as the dinosaur reared up and was on its huge therapod feet. Its wound had mostly sealed and although it had been weakened it still had the strength that had been granted it by evolution. Its huge mouth opened wide and it bellowed a terrifying roar that dropped Francisco to his knees, his hands clapped over his ears, while Rae lay next to him seemingly immune. Then it reached down and grasped the hook in one hand.

As they watched, the creature leapt onto the side of the cavern and began to scale it impossibly quickly. It darted from point to point almost like some gigantic man-lizard, able to defy gravity and scale surfaces that would intimidate even the most skilful spider.

Vincent saw it coming and emptied the clip in his gun, shot after shot thundering out. Whether he missed or whether the creature ignored them didn't matter, because with one final leap it was on him.

All around, the terrible spirits that churned in the air tried to consume this new creature but they could not. There was no humanity to latch on to, nothing to feed upon. Instead it howled impotently as the creature smashed Vincent's body to the ground with the hook, crushing bone and organs alike, and his last sight was of those terrible jaws yawning wide for his flesh and filled with vicious pointed teeth.

And as he died, inch by inch, the malevolence in the air died too. Its rage faded as Vincent's body shut down into lifeless butchered meat, until it was nothing but a whisper in the air, and then nothing at all.

Below, Francisco and Rae watched, almost in disbelief, as the creature tore Vincent's body apart and began to feed.

Slowly Rae got to her feet. She was unsteady and weak, but as Francisco supported her he saw that the wound that had opened up in her side was gone, leaving just a darkened stain. She in turn looked up at the creature as it gorged, and couldn't help but feel a sense not of sorrow but of deep relief. Whatever Vincent had become, he was not the man she had come to this place with. Perhaps one day she would find out what had happened to him.

Francisco picked up his sword and slung it over his back. Rae guessed that he had seen a great many stranger things than this, and that she herself had taken a first step into a new world that this man had made his home in a long time ago.

"I'm going to name him Ceratocarnus Rex. King Of The Horned Meat Eaters. Maybe Hook for short," Rae said, finally.

Francisco smiled a little. "Good name. Like a thrash band."

"Glad you approve. So, how bad do I look."

"You will need some sunglasses."

"That bad huh. You know it's odd. I was scared for a moment but it actually feels fine. Splitting headache though. Got anything for that in your magic belt."

Francisco shook his head. He guessed the pain was a natural part of some process, some supernatural empathy that had chemically connected human being and reptilian beast together. And if it was part of the way things should be, he had long ago learned that it should not be interfered with.

All he really had to do was think of what to tell the vendor back at the market.

"What are you going to do?"

Rae frowned for a moment. "First thing is to find my students. Hopefully some of them are still alive. Then I need to find out just what happened here. And it seems like I have some help now." Hook bellowed his approval as he gulped down the last of the human meat. "You know I can kind of see into his head. It's hard to explain but it feels amazing. The adrenaline is really pumping. Really very weird….. oh, you know he doesn't want to hurt people, right? Before you get any ideas…."

Francisco shook his head. "Good. I don't wanna have to come back."

"Yeah, I'd rather not see you for a while if that's OK with you."

The two of them looked at each other with a kind of mutual understanding, and Francisco glanced back up at Hook as he seemed to sniff the air protectively, fired with a new purpose and a new awareness.

"So, we got a way out of here now?" he asked.

Overhead, Hook let out a magnificent roar of victory that echoed around the cavern, and Rae broke into a broad smile.

"You know, I think I can arrange something…"

NAVIDAD PIÑAS Y CERVEZA

Away from the *posadas* and the *pastorelas*, a man ran as though the Angel of Death was upon him. His chest screamed from the exertion, and all the flab around his middle rubbed itself sore and bloody as his did his best to escape. He headed out of the streets and into the dusty outskirts of town, deaf to the celebrations of Christmas that went on all around him. It seemed everyone was happily lost in the party, singing and eating and doing their utmost to forget about what lived out in the Wilderness.

This particular man couldn't forget. Not anymore. He had seen them, and they had seen him back. Eyes out of the darkness but not the eyes of human being, or even the demons of the Bible. No, this was something else entirely. Something that wore a shape that didn't quite fit properly, with limbs and features that should never exist. It saw him, and the man was terrified down to the bare essence of his soul.

The man's name was Miguel, but he didn't think that really mattered anymore. All he cared about was running, trying to get away. He hoped as he fled that his knowledge of his own town, its twists and turns and hidden streets, would help him. Maybe give him a hiding place that no being either natural or otherwise could find him. It was the hope of a very desperate man, but it was all Miguel had to hold onto now.

Around him the sounds of Christmas were fading fast, swallowed up by the roar of blood in Miguel's ears. He felt sick, and knew he wouldn't be able to keep this pace up for much longer. Just long enough to reach some safety he hoped. Just long enough to get away.

He hurtled passed the last lit liquor store on the street beyond which lay nothing but moonlight darkness, ignoring the revellers who waved drunkenly. Another twenty or so steps, and Miguel's body finally succumbed and he stooped, sucking in whatever breath his unhealthy lungs could cope with.

It wasn't ten seconds before he threw up and sank to his knees.

Terrible ugly thoughts swept through his head. He imagined the ground opening up wide like the jaws of a shark, tearing the flesh form his ones and pulling him down to a netherworld of the damned. The hallucinations of fatigue conjored up bloodthirsty devil bats and snake women who wanted to suck him dry in the worst most agonising ways. That image alone forced him back to his feet, and once again Miguel began to move forwards. A wretched stagger this time, all hope of running lost to flabby muscles that had long since succumbed to age and inactivity. Miguel took a few shaky steps, trying not to vomit again, and he looked back at a neon beer sign he had passed that shouted sweet cold refreshment.

Perhaps, he thought, drunken oblivion was the better option after all.

That was the exact instant a giant fist knocked him down.

Miguel lay on the ground, unsure for a second if he was still alive. His head swam and it felt as though his brain was floating loose in his head, banging against his skull as it did. He puked again, down his already sweat-stained tee-shirt, and looked up at his assailant.

A beast of a man looked down at him.

From where Miguel lay half unconscious, this man looked eight feet tall and built out of rock. Massively broad and with cropped jet-black hair, it seemed that his body contained the strength of ten men or more. Then Miguel wondered if this was a man at all. Even in the half-light cast by the liquor store behind him the giant man's skin seemed oddly pale, almost white, and from a black shirt the image of a drooling monstrous demon head stared down too. Written beneath it were three words.

Danza del Infierno.

Miguel squinted, confused. He'd seen that exact band with that exact image on the stage only last week. Hardcore thrash with a bleached-blonde female singer whose voice spoke of fantasies and fear all at once. He tried to imagine her face as he vomited again, and the man reached down for him with hands the size of his head.

<Please don't kill me>, whimpered Miguel. He couldn't think of anything else to say. <I love Danze del Infierno too. I won't steal anything again. I promise. Swear to God.>

Black eyes peered into Miguel's wide open, slack jawed face.

<Not here to kill you,> growled Francisco Garza.

Miguel instantly wet himself in relief. He didn't care. As long as this giant was holding him almost bodily off the dirty ground, he felt sure no supernatural creature was going to try and rip his soul out through whatever orifice it chose.

Francisco could only pity the man.

He had hoped there would be more to someone who had chosen to play with unknown things. Clearly though this was just another drunk and feeble-minded idiot who had found something out in the Wilderness, something he didn't understand, and tried to unlock its secrets with cheap booze and a dead chicken. What exactly he had found wasn't important. Most likely a small fragment of something that should have stayed buried deep in the dust. But even fragments had power, and when that power had leaked out and faces had appeared in the glass of broken mirrors, Francisco had needed to act.

He dragged Miguel back to the side of the liquor store and dumped by a bin filled with old cardboard and bottles.

Something else was waiting there too.

Miguel huddled himself into a ball and tried to pretend none of this was happening. The shape that waited just out of the light was the thing that had been pursuing him, and now he knew it was here and the chase was done his mind started to fracture a little bit.

<I'm sorry,> he whispered. <I'm sorry I'm sorry I'm sorry....>

Francisco ignored him. Without the fragment of whatever object it had been, Miguel was of no interest. He didn't have it on him and had probably dropped it when he started running. That could be retrieved later.

What fascinated Francisco was the ethereal form in front of him.

It had substance of a sort, while at the same time it shimmered like an apparition of the heat. The hard lights of the store just passed through it somehow. And however hard Francisco stared at it, he couldn't make out any more detail that if it had been half-glanced from the corner of his eye. It seemed to relentlessly deny any attempt to focus on it. All Francisco could really tell was that it was spindly, like a skeleton covered in flesh that faded in and out of focus, with long arms and long legs and long fingers like needles.

And then there was its head.

No eyes, no mouth, or at least not all the time. Just a misshapen lump that even without sight was looking down at Francisco and further still to Miguel's slumped body. Bulbous and irregular, spines poked from everywhere on the apparition's head and then moved around constantly, the substance that supported them completely insubstantial.

Francisco though it looked a like a pineapple. So perhaps, he thought, this was *El Demonio De Piña*. The Pineapple Demon. Surely that had to be one of those somewhere. Francisco had hated pineapples since he was a boy, so perhaps this meeting was always going to happen. El Sepulturero and Piña, old enemies finally face to face.

Then Piña decided to speak. Not with a voice, but instead through the air, making the empty space sing in a tone that was heard and felt at the same.

<*You are…unafraid?*>

<This is not my first meeting with your kind,> answered Francisco. He had no idea what this entity wanted, although he could guess. Instead, suddenly, all that mattered was the opportunity to simply talk. The irony of meeting this creature, this Demon, at the festival of Christ was not lost on him.

<*I taste The Other upon your flesh. You are of the Grave. Why do you waste your strength upon this animal? Grant me the existence of the wretch. I shall consume it.*>

Francisco looked up at Piña at it towered over him, trying to focus on some kind of familiarity in the morphing mass of its head. There was nothing to be found but even so there was a horrible fascination to that blankness, as with so many of the things that dwelt in the Wilderness.

Maybe, thought Francisco, he should write a book. Or at least try and get Dr Sonja to do it for him. Writing wasn't his strong suit.

<Why do you speak like that?> asked Francisco, finally.

Piña didn't reply straight away. Instead the night air filled up with the sweet rotting scent of ageing fruit, and a hot breeze drew in the pungency of stale beer and discarded sweets. Two people staggered out of the liquor store and ambled off, unware of anything.

Then, finally, it said <You confuse me with your question.>

Francisco shrugged. <Always 'Give Me The Mortal' and 'You Are Of The Land Of The Dead'. Why is that?.>

Long talons reached up to scratch a chin that did not exist. <Your question confuses me.>

<Well, maybe you guys need to just calm down. Maybe you should have a beer. I can get you a beer from this store right here.>

<Beer.>

<Yes, beer. You know, alcohol. A cold one. Can you drink beer?>

Slowly, something resembling a mouth formed like a slit in the substance of Piña's head. Little tiny teeth like those of a piranha spouted, and the demon held out one hand.

<Give me beer. I shall judge this.>

<OK good. Hold there while I get one. And don't destroy the wretch.>

Piña just continued to hold out his hand, so Francisco headed into the store where a clerk was half drunk himself, drowned in bright light as he watched flies commit suicide on the electrocutor. He didn't move as a beer was taken from the fridge and a note thrown onto the counter. For all the clerk knew or cared nobody had ever come in at all. All he wanted to do was go home and get laid for Christmas.

Outside the demon hadn't moved at all, and Miguel still lay there in an expanding pool of his own piss. Francisco handed over the drink, wishing he'd bought one for himself. Piña considered the cold bottle for a moment, and then put the whole thing - glass and all - into its newly grown mouth.

There was silence. Francisco decided it wasn't important to tell the demon that generally you only drank what was inside the bottle. Maybe Piña preferred the glass to the beer. Who really knew what such beings liked or did not like.

Finally, The Pineapple Demon spoke one final time.

<This offering is good.>

Its form rippled like smoke, and then it was gone.

Francisco leaned back a little against the wall of the liquor store and breathed a sigh of relief. He had no idea how or why that had worked, and had learned that it was often not even worth asking those questions. When things did work he assumed there was something somewhere, some hidden mechanism of supernatural existence, that had been satisfied. Best to let cleverer people work it all out.

At Francisco's feet, Miguel looked up. <Is it over?>

<Get out of here. No more digging or the demon will come back.>

Miguel didn't need telling twice, and this time when he started running again he was heading for the largest loudest mass of people he could find, even though he smelled like a toilet. That didn't matter, because his stories about fighting off a demon would be legendary over the holiday season.

Francisco watched him go. Maybe a lesson had been learned tonight but he doubted it. People always did stupid things, but at least he hadn't had to bury anyone or anything tonight. And he could be certain that Miguel wouldn't be going back out into places he shouldn't anymore, looking for things that came from places everyday people had no business looking into. That, after all, was the job he had taken on.

He went back into the store and bought a sixpack. This time the clerk stared at him, at his hulking frame, his monster faced tee-shirt and his chalk white skin. Francisco just said "Christmas" and left, leaving the befuddled young man to his own conclusions and his fried bugs.

The walk back to his car, Francisco's old faithful with the coffin strapped to the roof, took no time at all, and he resisted the temptation to crack open his first beer. No sense getting pulled for drinking and driving, and all the more to enjoy over the spectacular meal that waited for him.

As he opened the driver's side door, a group of young people, American sightseers, waved and smiled.

"Dude, Happy Christmas," shouted one of them.

Francisco smiled back. *"Feliz Navidad."*

Sometimes Francisco really hated driving. The seemingly endless hours along the same rough bumpy roads surrounded by trees frustrated him, with nothing in every direction but brush and trees to look at. Other people loved this sort of thing. He knew plenty of people who had driven and ridden the length and breadth of the peninsula looking for, so they said, adventure. How many bikes had been bought, he wondered, for just that purpose?

The backwater glamour of those long road trips eluded Francisco, and as the miles racked up and the landscape didn't change he couldn't help but wish the time away.

It was a chore anyway, but a necessary one. He needed his supplies from The Crone, so the hundreds of miles were necessary for the cardboard box in the back seat to be filled with the things he couldn't get anywhere else. The Crone's prices were generally low, which was good as money was not plentiful. Francisco wasn't the only person she supplied, but he was certainly the one who her used the most. She never asked any questions either, which he appreciated. He had no desire to tell stories of the things he had seen.

The Crone had other things on offer as well, so Francisco usually fuelled up and got the car serviced. The women he didn't go near. Not since Perdita.

He thought of her as the outside went by.

Dr Sonja's sister the police officer, with the single vivid blonde streak in her black hair. Her career had made her hard in many ways, but slowly Francisco was starting to learn more about what was hidden under the layers of armour. Not much, because they so rarely had time together and more often than not they just enjoyed each other's bodies.

She liked guns, the more unusual the better, so Francisco made a point of looking out for them. She had been very happy with the three-barrelled shotgun he had found, so much so she had decided to wear the burlesque garter belt that he wouldn't ever have guessed she owned that evening.

Francisco smiled at the warmth of the memory, even the part when she had told him she would shoot him if she mentioned the garter belt to her sister, and put his foot down slightly as he slipped a new CD into the car's ageing player. Suddenly the driving was even more frustrating than before now he was thinking of Perdita, so hopefully some good music would take the edge off.

A band called Matando's raw guitar ripped out of the speakers. Good hard thrash, no frills, and a drummer who sounded like he was channelling the impossibly intricate beats of Hell.

As he let the music fill up the car and become a soundtrack for the drive, Francisco spotted a sign that caught his attention. It was one that he didn't remember seeing before, and it instantly intrigued him.

'Museo de Cosas Imposibles'.

The sign led to a small side road that wound into the trees and off the maps, so Francisco decided to park the car and take the route on foot. He made sure he was fully equipped, the pouches on his belt properly filled and everything in its proper place, right down to the whipclaw that he would never leave behind again. *Macuihuitl* the sword felt strong across his back, and the poncho he habitually wore now for no other reason than he liked it hung comfortably. All these things had become a part of him now, a part of his new identity, as much as his faded old black boots and his bleached white skin that rejected the burning heat of the Wilderness.

And so the man they called the Pale Ghost, El Sepulturero, walked forth.

There was path of sorts in amongst the trees. Little more than a sandy line worn away by footsteps, and every hundred metres or so another sign appeared. They were all the same – a smiling skull face and an arrow that pointed every onwards. With each one Francisco's curiosity grew. He knew it got him into situations he would rather have avoided far too often than was good for him, but that did nothing to deter it.

In a way, that was why he was who he was now.

Finally, the path opened out in a small dusty clearing dominated by an old steel gate. Either side of it was fencing that had long since fallen into disuse, ridden as it was with holes and breaks. The bolt on the gate was gone as well, and it let the solid frame and its wire mesh panels hang open, uncaring as to who was admitted.

Another sign with another smiling skull sat on top of the gate, the paint peeling off an old wooden board that appeared to splinter more with each passing moment. Underneath the grinning dead mouth was the single word **Entrar**, written in livid red letters that had streaked the wood either by accident or design like blood. Francisco wasn't sure how this was supposed to entice anyone inside, but he knew he had to see what was beyond.

The gate creaked as he opened it, and it half hung-off the hinges that had rusted almost to the point of being useless. If there had been booby traps or other hidden surprises they had also succumbed to age, and nothing greeted Francisco but the sounds of the insects and the birds. He checked though. He always checked these things, just like Perdita had taught him to do.

One could never be too careful, she had said. And she should know. She had seen more than one person, even professionals she had worked with for years, miss something and reap the consequences of lost limbs and blindness.

As he moved on the trees started to thin out, and up ahead he could see something reflecting the sun back at him. Something plastic perhaps, or glass.

The second he saw it he began to hear the sound of laughter.

Francisco walked towards the object, his eyes adjusting to the glare the same way his body had adjusted to the heat. Around him the laughter continued, softly at first and then growing louder with each step he took forward. It was an odd sound to hear anyway, and as it began to revolve in his ears it became eerie, wrong. Not the sound of joy but a corrupted noise, far more like the giggles of the insane.

As he looked around Francisco could see nothing in the trees except a bird he didn't recognise that watched him for a few seconds and then flew off. Perhaps the laughter had scared it off too. It was certainly unnerving, and even Francisco felt a little kick of adrenalin leak into his system on the back of a heart that beat just a tiny bit faster.

<Anyone there?> called Francisco.

He hadn't expected anyone to respond, and the laughter just continued so he walked towards the source of the reflected light that had caught his eye.

There was an archway made of wood and painted with symbols by what could only have been the same hand who had painted the signs and the head over the metal gate. The same roughness from the same hands. But what was beyond it made Francisco forget all of that.

He found himself in what looked a like a courtyard. A simple white wall bordered the space, with a metal gate buried in each one, and at the opposite end to the arch was a new structure, easily fifteen feet high and sealed shut with wooden slats, that backed onto a house that hadn't been fully built. Francisco could see bricks and metal lying around, even though the courtyard itself was sparse and clear.

Except for all the jars.

Lined up on what looked like old shelving units from a warehouse, standing free in the open air and aligned like a neat grid that a person could comfortably walk around, were glass containers of a hundred different sizes. There were so many of them that Francisco couldn't even begin to count, and each one had been perfectly placed in relation to all the others. This was no random collection. It had been organised, categorised, presented. It had been designed to be seen.

It was one of these, a jar the size of a garden pail, that had reflected the afternoon sun into Francisco's eyes, and as he peered at it he saw something familiar.

There, hanging in yellow water, was a fat glob of what looked like a jellyfish, and inside was the face of a dead man, eyes rolling and mouth opening in some silent speech.

Francisco recoiled, his mind taking him back to the beach and the glistening gelatinous thing that had crawled across the sand. Was this the same one? Or another of its kind, another dead thing caught and preserved here as a different kind of portent?

What did it speak of? The last time there had been a swarm of insects, and if they returned here there was no shelter, just a desperate run back to the car.

But nothing came.

Instead Francisco knocked against another of the shelves and immediately turned to grab it so it wouldn't collapse. When he did he started to see the contents of other jars. There were eyes and hands, but not human eyes or hands. There were preserved parts of grotesque foetuses, and strange little goblins that hung suspended for all time, pickled and shrivelled. As he looked further, he saw that there were larger containers on the ground which held heads that bore the features of demonic intervention. There were faces with singles eyes and pointed jagged ears and horns of malformed bone that twisted out in different directions. Animal heads as well, nothing he could recognise but one was similar to a horse.

Maybe.

Nothing presented in the jars represented any normal line of evolution. Instead, it was a harvester's gallery, the remains of other life gathered from dead and dying beings that didn't appear in any books.

Francisco took it all in and wondered if he had stumbled across something like a graveyard. Perhaps one that preserved the last vestiges of the things that formed that unending dark system of life that dominate the Wilderness. With the sheer variety on display, he had to admit that even with the things he had seen and killed and buried, it seemed that he had barely seen the half of it.

Maybe, Francisco thought, he should take something. He knew Dr Sonja would be fascinated by any one of these specimens, from the curled ammonite creature that was made of flesh rather than shell to the thing he couldn't even begin to identify with its cactus-like spines and petals that fanned out like teeth.

It almost felt wrong disrupting the perfect organisation of the collection, but surely thought Francisco one tiny little thing wouldn't be missed. It was just a matter of finding just the right specimen.

Then he caught sight again of the dead face hanging there, its wide eyes moving to track him, and heard the laughter again. It was much louder now, feeding in and out of itself in an echoing symphony of what was clearly more than one single voice.

Movement caught Francisco's attention, on the other side of the display in front of him, and he realised that wasn't alone any more in the courtyard.

Francisco moved quickly, silently, his hand going instinctively to *Macuihuitl*'s hilt as he slipped around the corner. His body tensed a little as it always did when he smelled confrontation, that perfume of the unknown that was slightly different every time.

What he saw was not anything he expected.

There were two women standing there, dressed in colorful long dresses and laden with golden and jewellery. They giggled unceasingly from mouths twisted into crazed frozen grins and their heads lolled constantly from side to side like broken marionettes. Those same heads bore faces painted eerie white, adorned with patterns just as the skull at the gate had been, and out of them looked eyes that were seemed dead - pale somehow in a way that made them seem blind and empty. Except that they weren't blind, and their zombie gazes fixed directly on him in a way that made him feel unnerved in a completely new way.

<We love Dr Horta> said one of the women, her voice almost singing the words before she started giggling again.

The second woman, blonde and definitely not Hispanic, nodded. "We love Dr Horta," she repeated, in an accent that Francisco couldn't identify.

Francisco didn't quite know what to do. There was no feeling of hostility from either of the women, indeed they seemed more like puppets than people. He waved a hand in front of one of their faces and she didn't respond. The fogged eyes didn't blink and the locked terrible smile didn't waver for an instant. All she did was loll and giggle.

<Who is this Horta guy?> asked Francisco.

"We love Dr Horta," said the blonde woman, mindlessly.

There was clearly nothing to be gained from trying to talk to these women. Something had clouded their minds to the point where it seemed they couldn't even think for themselves. Francisco had heard of shamen out past Mexico City up in the mountains who practiced some dark magic. It was said they could command the senses and summon a person's hopes and fears to suck away their souls. In his old life he would have dismissed it as laughable but now, after he had seen the spirits for himself, Francisco took those kinds of stories very seriously indeed.

Whatever it was that had happened to these two women he had no idea how to identify it, let alone try and release them. Different sigils sprang to his mind, yet nothing came to him that he could carve, and if he did he could so easily do more harm than good with some sort of understanding.

A deep heavy thump distracted Francisco, and he looked to the end of the courtyard. There, the slats on the front of the unfinished house had ground into life and slowly began to open.

The two women did nothing but giggle as Francisco's brow creased, trying to put the parts together yet finding nothing to connect them. All he could do was watch as the heavy wooden slats slid upwards like a blind, and stare at what they revealed.

There, chained by the neck in some sort of hollow pod and dressed in dirty ragged clothes was another woman, but this one was utterly different from the two who had greeted him. Her skin was smooth & copper, and along her arms were beautifully intricate curves that flowed together into arcane patterns. Francisco could see nails on her hands and feet that had grown into sharp talons, and what looked like ragged points to her ears behind a huge cascade of jet-black hair that had matted into the beginnings of dreadlocks.

Then Francisco saw the horns. Small, a foot long at most, but somehow perfect as they curved out of her forehead, not the heavy structures of a ram of a bull but beautifully tapered like those of a gazelle. Seeing those, most would have reacted to her as something demonic, conjored out of the collective fear of Hell and its legions. Not Francisco. To him she was quite beautiful.

Despite all of that she had the same clouded whitened eyes as the other two, and Francisco realised the same affliction had claimed her. Whatever mind lay within her had been suppressed. This time though the effect was frighteningly violently different. But instead of giggling, this horned woman roared and spat and hissed as though she was a rabid dog. She strained to free herself from her collar even though every attempted brutally choked her back.

<You came here to steal my collection, didn't you> said a voice.

It boomed out of hidden speakers buried in the walls where they couldn't be seen, yet even the echoes didn't disguise its pitch. It was high and petulant, almost like a child, and Francisco guessed this was the still-unseen Dr Horta who liked his women docile and chained up. That alone was reason enough for Francisco to dislike him and want to hurt him.

<Don't try and deny it,> continued the voice with its odd malignant squeak. <My slaves have been watching you. They know what you come here for. You are not the first. See what happened to the last ones.>

Something mechanical clicked, and the base of the pod underneath the raging demon girl opened. Two corpses flopped to the ground, wet with decay and stinking of death as their rotten contents spilled out. The sweet scent was something Francisco would never get used to and it burned a little in his eyes as the two painted women just continued to giggle.

<I'm going to teach you the same lesson. KILL the interloper.>

In the pod, the collar around her neck suddenly released, and the horned woman screamed as she hurled herself through the air at Francisco.

Francisco had no time to react to the sheer ferocity of the attack. The horned woman was instantly on him, nails digging into his flesh and drawing blood as the two of them locked together in a beast's embrace. Francisco tried to push her head away without hurting her, but she was impossibly strong. Her jaws snapped closed again and again as she tried to bite at his neck, while the painted women looked on, blank and grinning and emptily unaware.

<You see> cackled the voice of Dr Horta. <This is what happens to people who steal from me.>

"We love Dr Horta," said the blonde woman.

Francisco span around and tumbled to the ground, away from the racks of specimens and as close to the archway as he could get. *Macuihuitl* dug into his back but he ignored it. He felt like he was fighting fury incarnate, a whirling rabid slashing devil that had been set upon him like an attack dog with one singular purpose.

The nails sliced him again, opening a wound on his chest, and though the pain was dull like it always was, Francisco still felt it. He tried to prise the horned woman off him but she wrapped her legs around his body, the strength in thighs crushing hard against his ribs. She tried to sink her teeth into his neck again but he covered himself and rolled over, trying to pin her. Knees and elbows smashed into him from every angle and cut after cut opened up on him. She squeezed his body harder, aiming simply to break him, and he tried to lock up her arms. But the strength of this feral woman made it so hard to get any advantage, so he dropped forward and tried to bar an arm over her throat.

She choked, reacting like an animal and focussing on the new threat. She clawed and bit at Francisco's as he reached to a pouch, instinct guiding him to the right place for the right thing. It had taken too many seconds to figure out what to do, and already she was prying his arm away. Her heels kicked into his kidneys hard, bringing a new level of nausea and pain, and she raked at him with feet that felt like the talons of a hawk.

Francisco realised he was losing this fight. And if this didn't work, he had nothing.

The horned woman ripped Francisco's arm from her throat and threw him onto his back, her hand at his throats, snapping and biting. There was nothing in those whitened dulled eyes other than pure killing instinct, and the two of them rolled into the dust again. Francisco struggled desperately. His hand took something the pouch, something rough and crystalline, as he felt himself held fast against the ground. Bones were at breaking point now, muscles stretched, blood seeping.

Now all he had was a little blue gemstone that glowed with an eerie light, and he desperately tried to force it towards the horned woman's forehead.

The woman grabbed Francisco's arm, staring at the glowing thing in his hand. Then, somehow, there was something new in her eyes, or perhaps old. Some tiny spark of will that reasserted itself, driving her to grab the gem.

Instantly she screamed a terrible scream. She arched her back so hard Francisco was thrown off, and writhed and contorted and thrashed as the crystal burned away the control. Body rigid and agonised, her eyes widened as far as they could and she gasped a long deep rattling gasp.

And then it was over.

The violence ended, the rage gone, and she lay there, unconscious. Francisco breathed deeply as he climbed to his feet. He bled all over, and while most of the wounds were superficial he could tell that a few had penetrated deeper than he would like. Too often he forgot that while he was strong, he wasn't indestructible. This was more proof, if he really needed any.

The courtyard was cloaked in an odd silence. The voice had ceased its prattle, and Francisco guessed whoever this Dr Horta was, he had decided to run away. There was no point trying to look for him. This was his domain, and whatever hidden places it held were only for him to know.

No doubt he would return here when he felt safety again. It was obvious from what he had said that his collection was far too precious for him to desert

Francisco felt like burning the whole place down before he could come back. Then again, there was so much here to examine. He was torn. Dr Sonja would get so much knowledge from the specimens, and that would mean Francisco would be better prepared in future. Then he saw the two painted women, and suddenly the decision didn't mean anything anymore.

They both lay there, face up with their eyes closed and their faces released from those mindless grins. They were asleep now. Maybe they had been all along, and it was just that the waking nightmare they had been trapped in was over now. It was impossible to know for certain, or how long they had been caught here. There were no wounds or blood, no marks or signs, nothing to show what had happened to them. Just the make-up and the dresses. It was as if they had simply been let go from invisible puppet strings and needed time to recover.

And so Francisco did what he always did. He helped them. One at a time he carried their bodies tenderly out to his car and placed them in the back seat, trying to make them comfortable as he could far away from the courtyard of jars and oddities. He spoke a quiet prayer to each of them in turn, hoping their sleep would end soon and they would be able to return to whatever ordinary lives they had left behind.

There was a vow to his words as well. The name Dr Horta and his strange child voice were not going to be forgotten by Francisco.

A shadow fell across the car, and he looked up into the sunlight.

<Thankyou,> said the horned woman. *<Dios dios dios,* thankyou soooooo much.>

Francisco nodded and stood. He looked into her eyes and saw deep brown rather than obscured pale sclera. She seemed completely peaceful now, the psychosis gone as she stood there, clothes in rags. With her left hand she offered back the blue gemstone, dark and inert once again.

<How long have you been here?> asked Francisco, taking the stone.

She smiled a little, a sad smile that so many people wore after they had been to the Wilderness. <I don't remember. I just …It….No, I'm a positive person so I'm going to not think about it.>

A determined look set on her face, and it was a relief for Francisco to see. So many people broke after bad things happened to them, which was most of the time it seemed. Bad was almost the way of things, and he was just happy he had helped to release her from what could only have been purgatory. <What's your name?> he asked.

<Moya,> said Moya. She smiled a lovely smile with bright white teeth, and then looked down at herself. <I think I need some new clothes. I don't usually run around in dirty rags. *Mierde* you're bleeding. A lot. Did I do that? *Dios* I'm so sorry.> Her smile suddenly transformed to sadness.

Francisco shrugged. He had had a lot worse, and there was no reason to punish Moya for what he been done to her.

<I have some clothes in my car. Old stuff.> He led Moya over to the trunk and she picked out a long plaid shirt that turned into a blue checkered dress on her, and gave a little twirl. Francisco didn't quite know how to respond to that.

<It's OK to ask me about the horns if you like. Everyone asks about the horns. Just don't do the horny joke. I hate that.>

Francisco smiled a little. <I like them.>

<Oh. Uh, you know, I really didn't expect you to say that.>

<Last week I met a woman who can talk to dinosaurs now, so…> Francisco tailed off, his point made.

Moya's eyes widened. <Dinosaurs? *Dios* that is amazing.> She smiled again, and Francisco found it irresistibly charming in its innocence. The urge to help welled up in him and became overwhelming. Just like always.

<*Chica*,> he said. <I have some friends. Maybe we can help you out. It's a long drive though. Unless you have somewhere to go.>

Moya shook her head. < That is so so sooooo kind of you. I promise to be no trouble.> She paused as Francisco walked around to the driver's side. <Just one question. Um….. why do you have a coffin on your car?>

COMPETENCIA

Dr Sonja held up her stopwatch. Next to her, Ana-Maria watched on in excitement. She loved the beach, and today was even more special because of Moya.

Ana-Maria thought she was beautiful. Like a copper goddess with horns that made her seem a little bit like a devil, but a smile and a face that contradicted that completely. Ever since Francisco had rescued Moya she had been the subject of everyone's conversation, and the admiration of men and women alike. There had been so many presents, flowers, even items of exotic-looking underwear that couldn't be found anywhere but the black market, that Ana-Maria had lost count.

Dr Sonja was just as fascinated, but in a different way.

And that was why Francisco and Moya were lined up, facing down the beach, ready to sprint.

<And…GO.>

Francisco was big, and because of that people often forgot that he could be fast as well. He accelerated off across the sand, powering forward, just as Ana-Maria knew that he would.

But what they didn't expect was Moya to keep up. And not only that, she overtook him, graceful and fast like a gazelle, barely even out of breath as the two of them crossed the makeshift finish line that Ana-Maria had drawn.

Dr Sonja clicked off her watch. <Not bad,> she said to herself. <A new personal best. He must be trying to impress her.>

<Was he fast mama?> asked Ana-Maria, a little impatient.

<He was very fast. But Moya was just a little bit faster.>

Ana-Maria didn't like the sound of that. For her, Francisco was always the strongest and the fastest, no question. Perhaps Moya was some kind of devil after all. Surely only someone with magic devil powers could be that fast.

Francisco and Moya jogged over across the sand, already comfortable in each other's company. They seemed at ease with other and had become good friends in the few short days. Yet still they knew little about her. Moya Olmos, the woman from a place called Ciudad Volcan that none of them had ever heard of. The Horned Woman.

<Uncle Francisco> squealed Ana-Maria, and she launched herself up into a hug. Francisco smiled widely and held her up. <Mama says that Moya was quicker but you let her win didn't you. You were just being nice . Weren't you.>

<So was I faster?> asked Moya.

<You were. Nearly a second faster.>

Moya punched the air in delight. <SI.> Then she looked suddenly a little crestfallen. <Sorry, did I embarrass you. Dios I hope not. That would be awful…>

Francisco shook his head. <Didn't embarrass me. We all wanna find out what you can do.>

Dr Sonja handed them both cool bottles of water from an icebox which they gratefully guzzled.

<So what's next?> Moya asked.

<Weights,> said Dr Sonja, and she saw a glint in Francisco's eye.

Francisco heaved the weight up, pushing his muscles farther than he had in a long long time. The sun never affected him and he never sweated, but even so Dr Sonja could tell he was straining. Moya had topped out at just over 220 kilos, and Francisco was simply pushing his own limits now, just to see if he could. Dr Sonja had loaded the bar at nearly 360, heavier than any of her previous tests.

He braced the weight over his head, and then dropped it hard to the sand. Moya lay back on the beach next to him, stretching her arms that felt is if they had popped and split. She had never tested her strength before, but she knew this pale man was one of the strongest, maybe even on a par with her brother back home. How she had ever come close to overpowering him back in the clearing, under the power of Dr Horta, she would never know. Perhaps some hint of the beast had been brought out, so she wasn't enslaved so much as regressed. Made into an animal.

It still made her a little sick to think about it, but she always pushed those kinds of thoughts away. Here, at Playa Del Mantarraya, she could just relax and enjoy the sun and the sea. These people, Francisco, Dr Sonja, even little Ana-Maria, had all been so kind. They had made her welcome and encouraged her to stay before she began her long pilgrimage home, countries away.

It was nice to wake up in a comfortable bed and feel like herself again.

<I think that's it,> said Francisco. Ana-Maria handed him his water and he winked at her.

<You're still the Champion, Uncle Francisco.>

Dr Sonja wrote some notes down on her beloved writing pad.

<You seem to be getting naturally stronger. It's like the longer time has passed, the more you're adapting.>

<Does that mean he'll get stronger and stronger until he's the strongest in the whole world?>

Dr Sonja smiled and gave her daughter a little hug. <Maybe, *chica*>. She looked over at Moya. <And you're no slouch either Miss Olmos.>

<I think I tore something>. Moya groaned. <I've never lifted weights before.>

<Well, you're pretty good at it. Bar about three I've tested, you are the only one I've met who comes close to Francisco, and believe me I've been doing this a while.>

<So there are lots of people like us here?>

<In town? Not so much. Out in the Wilderness though, Francisco has met a few tough guys. Everyone is different. And there's nobody like you around here.>

Moya shielded her eyes as she looked up at Francisco. <So just how did you get so strong.>

Francisco shrugged. <Lucky, I guess. Some parts aren't so good.>

<How can any of that not be good.>

Ana-Maria piped up excitedly, unable to contain herself and desperately wanting to be part of the conversation. <Uncle Francisco doesn't like his skin being all white and chalky. He says he wants to look Mexican again.>

<Uh, sweetheart we said we weren't going to embarrass Uncle Francisco. OK, you two guys get something to eat. This afternoon, Swimming. Everyone likes swimming, right?>

<Holy SHIT.>

Francisco covered Ana-Maria's eyes and turned his own away, while Dr Sonja just stared at Moya, dumbfounded.

<What?> said Moya. <You said swimming, right.>

Dr Sonja nodded, slowly. <That is correct. Usually we keep our clothes on for this activity. I notice that you are naked.>

Moya seemed puzzled. <You swim with clothes on?>

<So I assume that you don't?>

<We have the thermal pools and they are always better on the skin. Wearing clothes in the water is just silly.>

<Ok, well, just for this time, can you put something on.>

Moya shrugged and headed back to where she had stripped off. Francisco did his best not to watch her go.

<Uncle Francisco,> said Ana-Maria. <I hope you're not peaking.>

Dr Sonja gave him her sternest look, the one she shared with her sister that could cut the strongest men down in an instant. <This isn't funny.>

<Kind of a little,> said Francisco, stifling his own smile.

<Why am I not shocked. You're a guy, why would you be bothered by naked amazon women on the beach.> Dr Sonja shook her head. <Disappointing Francisco, very disappointing.> She crossed off something on her writing pad. <5 second penalty on the swimming.>

<WHAT? How is this fair?>

Moya emerged from her hiding place, wearing just her beach shorts and a cheap white vest that she had bought at one of the local vendors. <This is very weird. You really want me to swim with my clothes on?>

<We all do,> said Dr Sonja, not taking her eyes from Francisco. <Don't we.>

<Yes,> he said.

Moya grinned widely. She smiled a lot, as though happiness was the most natural state for her. It was infectious too, and even Dr Sonja felt her own attempts to project professionalism melting a little.

<Come on snail man,> said Moya. <Race you to the water.>

Francisco and Moya hit the ocean at their top speeds, and vanished in a huge spray of surf. Dr Sonja clicked on her stopwatch, and watched how the two of them seemed so different in the waters of the Gulf, yet both so at home.

She knew how Francisco swam. He was like a dolphin, vanishing under the water for a minute, two minutes, at a time and moving as though his skin was immune to the friction. It was almost inhuman how he could do that, and yet somehow Moya was keeping pace. She swam with a fast and relaxed body, each strong stroke powering into the next like an athlete, her head down as her horns cut through the cool surface.

They both reached the end of the little peninsula of rock with its cluster of green palms that reached out from the outskirts of town, and turned, heading back to the beach.

Francisco stood first, but only just. As Moya emerged next to him, Dr Sonja covered Ana-Maria's eyes again and decided that she would have to persuade Moya to buy a decent swimsuit at some point.

<Wow, how do you do that?> asked Moya.

Francisco shrugged like he always did. <Don't know. Like the rest, I just do it.>

<As far as we can tell,> explained Dr Sonja, striding up to the two giants as she scribbled on her pad. <Francisco has had knowledge psychically embedded into him. That's how he knows how to use all the artefacts on his belt.>

Moya nodded her appreciation. <Well, I'm glad you can do all these things. Otherwise I'd still be Zombie-Girl.>

<To be honest, Moya, I think some of that came from you.> said Dr Sonja. <I have a feeling you weren't as far gone as you might think you were

<Really???>

<I got that,> added Francisco. <Like you were fighting it. Meeting me half way.>

<So, positive thoughts?>

<Yes, positive thoughts,> said Dr Sonja. <And by the way, you swim like a professional. You did amazingly well to keep up with Francisco.>

<My father taught me, and my brother too. Where we live there is a big lake heated by the volcano and we all like to swim there.>

<Naked, obviously.>

<Yes, naked.> Moya nodded and grinned widely. <So, what next?>

Francisco fixed her gaze. It was his favorite time of day. <Next, we eat.>

As the sun started to sink, Francisco had a fire going, and the four of them sat on the sand, soaking up the remainder of the day as little fish cooked slowly on old metal pans. Dr Sonja had taken the cooler from her jeep and handed out the cold beers, while Ana-Maria happily drank her water. She didn't like juice or soda, and her mother was glad for that, even though she knew that it was far more a result of Francisco's influence than her own. No doubt when she was old enough, she and her uncle would be sharing those beers.

Still, health was a valuable commodity now, and keeping it safe was important. Especially now, as so many people abandoned it as life became harder and the dark things crept ever closer from the Wilderness.

Sometimes, addictions were easier to live with than the monsters.

<So,> said Moya, <How did I do?>

<Impressive,> said Dr Sonja. <All your physical abilities are way above baseline normal. Based just on today I'd put you in the top two percent of the Yucatán population. And that means everyone. And everything, human and otherwise. Just what do they feed you in the volcano city of yours.>

<Ciudad Volcan? Lots of us are like this. Some of us are horned and some are not, and always the people with horns are stronger and faster.>

<This really is fascinating. A bio-ethnically divergent isolated population.>

Moya looked over to Francisco who gave her one of his shrugs as he built a sandcastle with Ana-Maria. <Never really know what she's saying.>

<He likes to pretend he just hits things. So do you have any tensions.>

<No,> said Moya. <Mostly everyone gets along fine. Sometimes we have problems but that is mostly when someone goes with an outsider. That can be a bad when family gets involved. Some are old fashioned.>

<So are you the Princess of a magic city?> asked Ana-Maria, wide-eyed and fascinated. <Why did you leave?>

<I wish I was a Princess. Sorry *chica*. And I wanted to travel and see the things. Everyone in our city talks of the strange powers of the Wilderness and I wanted to come and see for myself. It turns out its good and bad.>

<Mostly bad,> said Francisco.

As he spoke, a heavy rumble of noise rolled through the air, and overhead the gloom of grey clouds was starting to form, coming together almost impossibly quickly out of nothing but wisps of white in the blue sky. Francisco had already picked up the change in the air, and Moya felt it too.

<Storm is coming.>

TORMENTA

Storms were so much more frequent since the Black Day. It seemed as though not a single month passed without the winds and the rain pummelling everything while beautiful forks and sheets of lightning lit up the thunderhead skies. There were so many they didn't even have names anymore.

Ana-Maria loved watching them. She loved watching the winds drive the rain almost horizontally, and especially loved closing her eyes after an especially violent arc of electricity so she could see the imprints left behind. So whenever the storms came she positioned herself right by the window upstairs in her room and became enraptured by the elements.

Her mother didn't share the passion, particularly at dinner time.

<Ana,> said Dr Sonja. <Are you going to stare out of the window all evening? We have guests coming.>

Reluctantly, Ana-Maria dragged her gaze away from the window. <But mama I want to see the storms. Francisco said they are spirits who live in stormclouds and if you close your eyes after the lightning comes you can see them.>

<Is that what Francisco said?> asked Dr Sonja, folding her arms. She wasn't entirely sure whether it was true or not, and there was certainly no harm in it, but she would rather her daughter focussed on math and science homework than stare into space searching for whatever might be out there.

Ana-Maria was clearly not in the mood to do any homework at all. She simply nodded enthusiastically as the tempest raged outside the window and rain hammered on glass. <Do you think Francisco can talk to the lightning spirits?>

Dr Sonja smiled a little. Her daughter was not even ten years old and yet her awareness of the way the world was now was growing by the day. She had asked Francisco to shield Ana-Maria from the knowledge of reality so he told her stories instead, stories of magic and princesses. But Ana-Maria was smart, and she was making connections. And while she had never seen anything the way that her mother had, it would only be so long before she experienced something for herself.

<Maybe we can ask him when he comes over. OK?>
<OK mama>.

Ana-Maria nodded and took a last look out of the window, a little forlorn and not keen to drag herself away from nature's show. Her gaze happened to fall onto the path down onto the beach, and she saw something moving. A shape of a person but somehow not a person. It was much bigger, bulky and hunched over, and as it shambled through the rain Ana-Maria saw something else.

In a gnarled hand were what looked like daggers.

*

The kitchen bustled with activity as it always did on Sunday nights. Dr Sonja made it a point that everyone got together to eat proper food once a week, and escape at least for a while the endless diet of fat and sugar that Francisco and Perdita tended to subsist on in their travels.

By the time Ana-Maria came down to help with laying the table and setting the places both of them had arrived, and the little girl smiled widely.

<Hi Uncle Francisco,> she called, and ran up to give him a hug.

<Hi little *Princesa*, how are you?>

<I'm good. Mama said you would tell me more stories tonight.>

Perdita raised an eyebrow as she glanced over at her sister who stood expectantly at the doorway to the kitchen. <Is that what Mama said?>

Dr Sonja rolled her eyes a little. It seemed she had little choice now, and it was certainly better that Francisco told her stories than anybody else. Especially Perdita. Perdita's stories always ended in someone being arrested or shot in the head. Frequently both.

As Francisco took off his coat and Ana-Maria buzzed around him expectantly, Perdita joined her sister.

<You seem less stressed than usual.>

Dr Sonja nodded. <I have a new secret weapon.> She gestured into the kitchen where Moya, her copper skin, her marks and her horns formed a bizarre contradiction to her casual jeans and teeshirt, was expertly continued preparing five dishes at the same time. Looking up, she gave the sisters a smile and a wave. <Is there nothing this woman isn't good at?>

Perdita nodded her appreciation. Moya still made her a little nervous, but she had to admit that over the past weeks the horned woman had gone out of her way to be as helpful as possible and to allay any fears. Often by singing. Everyone liked her and she simply fit in. She certainly wasn't the strangest looking person in town, but Perdita was built from suspicion and she found it almost impossible switch off. She also didn't like the glances she had seen Moya make at Francisco from time to time. He had dismissed it as simple gratitude.

Then again, Francisco often wasn't the most perceptive guy, so Perdita was happy that he was sitting down with Ana-Maria and nowhere near the kitchen.

<Oh oh, Uncle Francisco guess what,> said Ana-Maria, almost babbling with excitement. <Guess what guess what guess what?>

<Tell me.>

<I have a story. Guess what? I saw a monster.>

Dr Sonja froze at those words, and Francisco suddenly realised that everyone had gone very quiet. Ana-Maria remained oblivious as Perdita shot the big man a look. He realised that he suddenly had to be very careful indeed.

<Oookay,> he said, a little hesitantly. He didn't want to say the wrong thing and risk the wrath of the Castellanos sisters. One was bad enough, two would be quite simply terrifying. <So, what do you think you saw?>

<It was a monster, I know it was a monster Uncle Francisco. It was out in the rain and it walked across by the beach and it had knives.>

All the adults in the room liked this less and less, and even Moya had started paying attention as the contents of saucepans bubbled and steamed.

<Knives?> asked Francisco.

<In his hands. Like the man in the films where they come out of his hands but they were his whole hands and it was like a big monster claw>. Ana-Maria was utterly oblivious to the impact her words were having as she made a claw shape with her own hand.

<Well,> cut in Dr Sonja. <I've never heard of a knife monster. Have you, Francisco?>

<Err no. No, I have not.> He looked to Perdita for help. <Right?>

Slowly Perdita nodded. <No knife monsters.>

Relieved, Francisco did his best to guide the conversation elsewhere. <See. All the monsters were chased away a hundred years ago by....>

<By the storm spirits?> asked Ana-Maria, deadly serious with her question.

<That's right. By the storm spirits. Sometimes you can see a picture of them when they've been good, but they can never hurt anybody.>

<So I saw a picture of a monster?> Ana-Maria was confused, but Francisco reassured her.

<That's right. When there's a storm sometimes you can see them like a photo but they can't hurt you. They are just like clouds now.>

Perdita mouthed <Good save> as Dr Sonja called her daughter over.

<Can you help Moya in the kitchen Ana.>

Apparently satisfied with Francisco's explanation, Ana-Maria skipped out into the kitchen. She and Moya had become firm friends, and Dr Sonja was more than happy for Moya to teach her cooking songs rather than listen to horror stories. Everyone started to relax a little, nightmares and difficult questions averted.

That was when they all heard the first gunshot.

The sounds of gunfire were nothing new. In some places, especially in Cancún and some of the lost and broken towns deep in the peninsula, it was the pulse of existence. The gangs feuded, the vigilante groups hunted, the drug squads murdered and all of them shot each other all the time. Perdita dealt with it daily, and Francisco spent entirely too much of his life being shot at.

But Playa Del Mantarraya was not one of those violent places, and so in this quiet beachside town a gunshot was still a sudden and frightening sound.

In the kitchen Ana-Maria wrapped her arms around Moya's waist, and she in turn gave the young girl a reassuring squeeze, even though she didn't feel like there was any reassurance she could offer. Moya hated guns.

Perdita had simply slipped into her police officer persona, one that she barely dropped at the most relaxed of moments and which now was wholly dominant as she looked out of the curtained window and scanned what she could see. The storm reduced visibility to virtually nothing, and as further shots rang out the winds hid the direction of their origin.

<Gangs?> whispered Francisco. Perdita nodded.

<Sometimes Los Cuervos come down this far. That's Cíclopes' crew. They usually keep to themselves so something must have triggered them off. Don't know what. There's no turf issue down here.> She caught Francisco's look. <Don't tell me....>

<Not saying anything. Just a coincidence that Ana sees something....>

More gunfire cut into their conversation. This time it was automatic fire, not the individual pops of single shots. Whatever was happening had taken a step up in Perdita's book, so she took her gun where Dr Sonja made her leave it on the cabinet by the door. It was her favorite one, with the compensator added to increase the length of the barrel. She said it helped her aim, but Francisco teased her that she just liked it because it looked cool.

<Seriously?> called Dr Sonja. <You're going out there? Literally there could not be worse conditions.> Perdita didn't answer. She never did. She would not be questioned on matters of the job she took very seriously indeed. Dr Sonja knew that too, so she switched her attention to Francisco. <Make sure you look after each other.>

Francisco wasn't keen. He tended to try and avoid gang situations as long as they avoided him. If he was honest, he could see the appeal, the sense of family that they provided. And if they wanted to steal cars and sell drugs, so what? The things Francisco had encountered did a lot worse than that.

<Ready?> asked Perdita. Francisco couldn't have said no if he'd wanted to.

So he nodded, and the two of them slipped out into the storm.

The wind and the rain blasted Francisco and Perdita instantly, and it took real effort to even stay still and standing. Scant seconds soaked them both to the skin almost instantly, but they did their best to try and ignore the storm. Instead they focussed on the gunshots as they continued unabated. Perdita guessed easily six different weapons were firing, and in amongst the gunfire Francisco ears could hear voices as well. Voices crying out in fear, in panic.

This is bad, thought Francisco. He wasn't thinking of the guns though. In his head, the image of what Ana had described was coming to life, and it reminded of something he had seen before, out in the Wilderness.

And that thought became the second of decision. The one that always happened, that differentiated those who could fight from those who would run. That primal instinct over which no person had any control, and yet which defined the bravery or insanity of the hero and the shame of those who thought themselves cowards when they were not. Often the most sensible people were the ones who ran.

For Francisco there was never any real choice.

He and Perdita started to power their way through the storm, barely able to muster a run as they tried to orientate towards the gunfire. There were no cinematic flashes of light to help, just the relentless sounds that crossed each other to form almost an orchestra of their own, whipped around and distorted by the wind of the storm.

Turn after turn, corner after corner of the town presented them with nothing, just the expected dead ends and streets made empty as everyone took shelter. They passed the store and the old church, and then they approached what had been the old school building before they had moved to bigger, nicer premises.

The spaces of the grid-patterned streets opened up into a huge concrete area, once an old playground with the hints of painted lines still left on the courts, and only partially fenced off with wire that had been torn down and ripped apart.

Now, it was an arena of conflict.

Perdita counted eight cars and easily twenty men, all armed and emptying clip after clip in blind fear. They shouted and screamed at each other, their ornately tattooed faces contorted into the kind of disbelieving terror that so many people shared when they encountered the inhabitants of the Wilderness. She had to admire their bravery at standing their ground.

Next to her, Francisco looked only to their enemy.

<Holy shit,> hissed Perdita.

Rearing up out the dark and the wet was Ana-Maria's monster made flesh.

It was a terrible thing, a mass of armoured flesh and jagged blades bound together into a swollen grotesque form. There were filthy bandages and strips of ripped leather that linked together broken remnants of metal from behind which rancid flesh bulged cancerously. Its face was hidden behind carved grubby bone that seemed too small for the vast body that bore it, and one of its hands was a mass of rusted razor blades, just the way Ana-Maria had described. Perhaps it was a small mercy she hadn't seen the other one, a fat stump of a hand encased in raw scar tissue and bearing two huge hooks that looked like some horrific lobster's claw.

Francisco guessed that this new abomination was easily ten feet tall, and every part of it was gripped by an irresistibly violent and greedy psychosis. It effortlessly shrugged off every bullet that hit it and was eerily silent as it ripped gang member after gang member apart with preternatural brutality.

For all the good their weapons were doing them, the Los Cuervos fighters might as well have been firing at a tank.

The huge claw grasped one man around the throat and tore his head off the shoulders, then the claws ripped through another and split his body into shreds that hung then as his innards spilled out onto the concrete. And there was so much blood now that it stained the rain and the pools it formed on the ground red.

Perdita raised her gun and fired, hitting the abomination in the head twice, dead centre. There was almost no effect except for a slight rock as the attack was dismissed and more men died. As Francisco watched, she strode out into the courtyard and emptied the entire magazine from her weapon into the abomination's body. If she had hoped that her trained aim might have helped, she was mistaken. All that happened was that the abomination focussed its two empty black eyeholes on her and started to moved forward.

All around the gang members shouted for her to run as she replaced the clip and chambered to open fire again. One driver tried to force his car between them as a makeshift barrier. Instead claws smashed the metal chassis inwards and tore away the hood and the doors. The driver followed, screaming as sharpened metal slid through his body and his lungs, and he was cast aside as the abomination focussed entirely on its new target.

It advanced, step by heavy step, ignorant of everything else as Perdita opened fire again, planting every single shot in the clip directly into the bone mask hoping that she might be able to crack it and get to whatever was underneath. Even before the slide locked back on her gun, empty, she realised it was a waste of time as she braced herself to run.

Out of the rain Francisco hurled himself forward and slammed into the abomination as hard as he could.

It staggered and fell back into the wrecked car, while Francisco himself tumbled to the hard ground. He felt like he had rammed himself into the jagged rock of a cliff, and realised he had already been hurt as the sting of bloodied open wounds registered on his arm and shoulder. Tough as he was, this armoured bladed thing existed on an entirely new level.

But he had knocked it back, and he had to press the advantage. He clambered to his feet and jumped up onto the abomination as it lay there like a beetle on its back, dazed and unfamiliar with the sensations it was feeling. Nothing had struck it like that before, and it was still trying to comprehend in its tiny primal head as Francisco started to rain down hammering blows, all of them smashing at the bony carapace that surrounded its little shrivelled head.

Because if painful experience had taught Francisco anything, it was to go for the head.

He hit again and again, as hard as he could, desperate to create some sort of tiny crack in the armour that he could try and exploit. He saw the marks of the bullets where they had dented the substance of the mask, but that was all. Not a single hole.

Francisco tried to ignore that as he pummelled. Somewhere behind him, a voice shouted through the wind to stop firing and the Los Cuervos fighters ceased instantly, watching in some kind of awe as this giant hulking man with chalk white skin beat down what they could only describe as a monster. They had watched as he had knocked it down, and almost felt each of the hammering blows as they smashed down, each one so obviously capable of breaking a normal skull.

But not this skull.

Slowly, the abomination started to recover itself, and a heavy foot reared up and kicked out. Francisco took the strike directly in his chest and went flying, crashing against the fence and collapsing. He felt like throwing up, and knew something had broken, but he forced himself to stand up anyway. A few of the gang members had started cheering for him and called out for him to attack again as the abomination started to clamber out of the car wreck.

Francisco just watched, trying to force strength back into his battered body. The rain just kept falling and it dropped off him as he rose to his feet. All he could do was try again, try to find the weak spot. But this time he knew the abomination wouldn't be so easily knocked down. This time it would be prepared - somehow the piercing pincer and the razor claws on its hands seemed sharper, more malignant than before.

<FRANCISCO,> shouted a voice.

It was Perdita, and he looked over to her she threw something to him.

Francisco reached up and grabbed his sword, feeling its strength merge with his own as his hands circled around the leather-wrapped hilt.

The hilt of *Macuihuitl.*

As the gang members watched him stand, stronger, empowered, they saw something else to. A madness they all shared perhaps, a mirage brought on by the adrenalin and fear that gripped all of their bodies and minds. But to a man, they swore that they saw some kind of outline flicker around Francisco's body. Etched in hints of arcane light, just for a second, there was the impression of a vast warrior dressed like some titanic beast, raising an ancient weapon for combat.

Francisco felt his muscle burn and the blood in his veins surge. The pain fell away leaving nothing but the fight, the arena, and he could taste the metallic hint of blood in the air. His senses magnified themselves a hundred times over and he became aware of every single individual raindrop as it fell in timeless space, glittering like crystal. He gripped the sword, and nothing mattered but the abomination.

It had to die.

It moved towards him in lumbering slow motion, every tiny detail of its substance picked out and every movement drained of urgency. The seconds ticked away, fragment by fragment, and Francisco picked the exact instant, that perfect point of timing and precision.

The abomination lunged forward…

..and Francisco moved. The vicious attack simply missed him to strike only empty space, and he buried the blades of his sword into the gut of the monster. They cut through everything, armour and flesh alike, and dug deep into the abomination's guts. It stopped dead in is tracks, and Francisco ripped the sword back and outward, disembowelling with a single clean motion.

The movement continued almost naturally, arcing around into the air and accelerating back as Francisco swung the sword back down as hard as he could, with every drop of strength that was his own and otherwise.

Macuihuitl hacked straight through the abomination's neck, and its head fell forward onto the ground. The body, too stupid to realise it was dead, quivered for a moment, standing there, before it too crashed downwards.

There was utter silence except for the rain and the wind. Francisco dropped to one knee, exhausted and propping himself up with the sword as Perdita ran over to him.

They looked up, and every member of the gang stared at them.

Nobody moved. Nobody spoke.

Francisco sucked in air while Perdita put her hand onto her gun, tucked back in her jeans, and too it out to reload with the clip she had collected from the car.

Everyone seemed frozen into a tableau, a standoff that stretched one moment out into what felt like endless time, as the rain swept at the abominations decapitated corpse and the skull-head that sat there on the ground, unseeing.

Finally, a car door opened. A man climbed out, not old or young but in between, his face smothered in the same tattoos as the others that spoke of their unspoken allegiance, and his eyes covered by a dull grey metal visor, dented and blackened and strapped to his shaven head by thick leather.

A single gesture seemed to relax the tension, and Perdita breathed a sigh of relief as she saw guns holstered and shouldered. Her own hand relaxed off her weapon and she tried to support Francisco. No more shooting today.

The new man walked over to the body of the abomination and looked at it through the black glass of his visor. His face betrayed nothing as he turned himself to face Francisco, who with Perdita's help climbed back to his feet. He was hurt and bloodied and everything hurt, but he would heal. Now all he had to do was listen.

<I think you done this before,> stated the man with the visor.

Francisco nodded slowly, wincing with the burning pain in his ribs.

<This your place?> came the next question, as the visored face looked around.

<Most of the time,> Francisco replied.

Neither Francisco nor Perdita had known what to expect, but it certainly hadn't been the hand of friendship this man now extended. <Cíclope. These are my boys.>

Perdita couldn't quite believe what she was seeing. She had been taught every day of her life that gangs only brought trouble, and now she was here, next to the body of some unholy horror that ripped men apart like paper, it was one simple gesture that astounded her the most.

Francisco took Cíclope's hand and shook it. <Francisco.>

Cíclope nodded. <Made a friend here today, Francisco. Good to have friends these days.>

<It is.>

Cíclope turned his gaze to the wasteland of torn bodies that surrounded them. <Any chance you can help us out with my boys.>

Despite his injuries, Francisco dug eight graves out of town near some old palms. Two of Cíclope's men helped with the other three, but mostly they simply watched the giant scoop out the earth almost effortlessly. They didn't speak to him, in large part because having seen what they had seen tonight they wondered if this man was really human at all.

Francisco didn't mind. He was used to it. Sometimes, on nights like this when after monsters had come, he wondered too.

The bodies of the slain had been collected carefully, respectfully. Each one had been cleaned and bound in the colors of Los Cuervos, and Cíclope had overseen everything as the process unfolded like a well-oiled machine. Most of the time he didn't even need to speak, such was the sense of connection that he shared with his gang.

Cíclope's face continued to show nothing from behind the visor, no emotion at all. Perdita guessed that was his way. He was a soldier, leading soldiers, and he was the strength that guided them. But she knew like any soldier he felt the loss, especially of so many men. He would have known their names, their families. They would have drunk together and fought together.

They could not be replaced, only remembered.

She and Francisco stood back from the gravesite as Cíclope spoke for Los Cuervos over the remains of their honoured dead. The storm still raged all around them and his words were lost to the elements, but prayers for the dead were the same all over. Francisco had spoken a great many in his time, because whether good or bad or lost somewhere in the mire of grey that was normality now everyone deserved a prayer as they lay in the ground.

A few of the gang members lit some torches and stuck them into the graves next to makeshift crosses they had carefully built. It had taken time, and it felt like hours to Perdita since the violence had ended. She said nothing. She knew the rituals of death meant something to Francisco as he watched the torch flames flicker and flap under the force of the wind. But not one of them went out.

Cíclope turned to give one final nod to Francisco, and he nodded back. Then the ceremony was over, and one by one the men of Los Cuervos followed their captain away into the darkness.

Perdita wanted to get home. She was soaking wet down to her panties, and she wanted to be back in the warm to reassure everyone that everything was OK. But Francisco still had one final task, so she followed as he wearily trudged back towards the courtyard and prepared himself to dig one last grave.

As he turned the last corner to the old school begin his work, he stopped dead.

The corpse of the abomination, and its skull-masked head, were gone.

CANCÚN

Cancún was a ruin, the wreckage of paradise laid out on the peninsula of white sand and warm blue waters that surrounded it. The tourists were gone, the hotels were empty, and the life that remained as dark and violent and twisted out of shape. Nobody had ever come back to try and fix it, and so it became diseased, cancerous.

Everything fed on itself here, parasite upon parasite, prey upon prey. The rules no longer applied, and life was broken and weak. Like any lawless place the real power was in strength and violence. Every person who lived here was tainted, and at the centre of it all was the blackened burned-out edifice that had once been the most luxurious hotel of all. Now it was the dead monument to everything this place had become.

It watched impassively as endless acts in the urban theatre of guns and knives played out beneath them in the language of survival.

Francisco and Perdita stood at the hotel's entrance, where the doors didn't fit their frames anymore and the glass was long since shattered and lost. They were a strange couple – the giant man and the slim athletic woman. They didn't seem to fit together and yet they did. There was a sense of balance there, of raw strength combined with quiet authority, where each one needed the other.

Perdita was certainly happy to have Francisco with her, even though he had insisted on wearing the poncho he had bought from some Wilderness marketplace she had never heard of and never wished to. She hated the poncho, but at least she had been able to persuade him to ride in her car. His vehicle, with the coffin bound to the roof, just made her uneasy. So she gave him some leeway – she was simply glad to have him with her. Most of the detectives, even the ones who had survived wars, just didn't want to come to places like this.

Perdita had asked one of them one, a scarred white haired detective named Arturo who nobody thought was frightened of anything, why they didn't come here.

He had told her <Wars have rules. That place doesn't.>

He didn't need to say any more than that. The city had been left to curdle in its anarchy, and only the very worst situations would bring any response.

<This is it?> asked Francisco.

<This is it,> confirmed Perdita. <Somewhere inside this shithole building is a very frightened young boy and our job is to get him out of there. I don't much care who we have to shoot or how many bones we have to break to do that.>

Perdita realised that Francisco wasn't paying attention and so she rounded on him irritably. He was looking upwards to something him high overhead, and when she followed his gaze she realised what it was that had caught his attention

Up above, spread across the old broken signage of the hotel and nailed in place, was a butchered body.

The corpse, the way it had been carved and displayed, was familiar to Francisco. He had seen something like this before, another body arranged in all of its brutalised glory. Out among the rocks and the cactus, hung within an alcove of dry rock like a dead meat puppet. He had assumed it had been the work of the same beast he had killed. At that time it had seemed so obvious that both were part of the same bloody equation, intimately connected in the causal relationship of murdered and murderer.

Now, it seemed that wasn't the case at all.

How many more, wondered Francisco? How many more bodies were out there, lost and nameless victims transformed into nothing but the results of terrible dissection. How many?

<You seen this before?> asked Perdita.

Francisco didn't take his eyes off the body. <Once. Not so long ago.>

<You didn't mention it. >

<Thought I'd fixed it.>

Perdita knew exactly what Francisco meant by 'fixed it'. She had only glimpsed the world he walked in, and she often wondered how he coped with it. She had seen too many officers, the newest and the most experienced, crack under what the Penisula had become. What, she wondered, would it take for Francisco to crack?

Francisco stood there, a chalk giant in black clothes and the colored patterns of his poncho, the sword *Macuahuitl* strapped to his back and the worn heavy leather belt laden with the pouches he carried that contained all the little things he needed to do his work – the vial and potions and fragments of slate, all neatly packed and stored. She also noticed he had hung his whipclaw from his belt as well, coiled up on his left hip with its single eagle-claw hanging loose.

Francisco seemed to have really taken to the whipclaw. Not for the first time, Perdita wondered why he didn't carry guns. He seemed not to like them, and any ones he found she happily added to her collection.

But even with what she had seen him do, with the strength he had, she worried for his safety. Not as much as her sister Dr Sonja. She worried about every scratch and bruise. But still, always in the back of Perdita's mind was the thought that one day, maybe soon, something would be more that Francisco could handle.

She drew her own handgun and cocked it. <Ready?>

Francisco nodded. They stepped into the foyer of the hotel through the broken windows, and the first salvo of bullets began instantly.

The guns that fired were old and inaccurate, and the bullets they fired sprayed everywhere like water from a burst hydrant. Even as Perdita dove for whatever cover she could find, Francisco had drawn and thrown something from his belt. As he followed her through the hail of bad aim, smoke filled up the foyer.

Tezcapotli.

It was not normal smoke. Instead, thick clouds of gas swamped the whole place too quickly than could ever be natural. And as she settled behind her shelter, Perdita realised that somehow, she was able to pick out the silhouettes of their attackers in a way that should not have been possible.

She had long since stopped asking Francisco about these things. Instead she had learned to accept them, even embrace them when she could. Particularly now, as she saw the smoke began to choke the gunners. There were five of them in all, all trying to conceal themselves behind a large reception desk that had been gutted and turned into something like a child's fortress build from scrap.

Francisco was already up and moving, heading for one side of the desk as two of them gunners staggered outwards, desperately trying to clear their streaming eyes and burning lungs so they could carry on their assault. They tried to aim, and when that didn't work that tried to fight. Wild swings came, and guns were turned to makeshift clubs in the hope they might connect with something.

If they had it wouldn't have made any difference.

Francisco lifted one man off his feet and hurled him against the stone wall where he crumpled, bones broken and lungs punctured. The second man tried his luck as well, trying to push the barrel of his automatic forward towards the looming shape so he didn't have to aim. Francisco hit him so hard his attacker upended and his chin split wide open on the floor. The gun just clattered across the floor, discarded and irrelevant.

Perdita had taken the other side of the desk and already put one of the remaining men down. She had expertly crept up and coiled her arms around his throat, constricting like a python until his eyes rolled up into his head and he went limp. Then she lay him down on the ground, unbroken. She favored that approach. Where Francisco was like some sort of bulldozer, unstoppable and heavy in his tactics, Perdita always preferred to leave people as unharmed as she could.

Unless she had to shoot them of course.

She was thinking that exact thought when she felt the cold barrel of a gun press against her back.

Another man had come out from a side entrance, drawn by the cries and the air thick with violence. The smoke caught hold him almost instantly but in his few brief seconds of clarity he had marked Perdita, coughing up green and red as he advanced forward. It took him ten plodding steps before he felt his gun up against flesh, and as he went to pull the trigger something caught his attention.

He snapped his head around just in time to see a body cannoning towards him, unconscious and turned into a human projectile by Francisco.

The two of them crashed to the floor, beaten.

Perdita cursed her carelessness. Of course there would be more of them. Maybe the smoke had blinded her more than she thought. So when she felt the pressure of the barrel leave her back and turned to see her would-be killer lying at her feet, she made a mental note to thank Francisco properly later.

There were two more men who were still trying to get their bearings, and this time she wasted no time. She shot the first one in the leg and the second in the shoulder and let them collapse and wail at their injuries.

As quickly as it had appeared, the smoke dispersed to nothingness and left the foyer open and clear again. Francisco stood there, implacable as rock. The attackers who were still vaguely conscious kept on choking and spluttering, as if the acrid chemicals of the smoke had somehow lodged themselves inside their bodies and continued to torture them. Then gradually, one by one, they passed out.

Perdita observed the scene as dispassionately as she could.

<What was that?>

<Smoke bomb.>

<Fine. Don't tell me. It's a lot better than tear gas. Maybe you should start selling it to us.>

It was a joke with an edge to it. She knew Francisco was never going to give up his secrets to anybody, not even to her or her sister. It had taken enough persuasion to get him to help out the police. And nobody was going to try and force him – not even men like Old Gonzales back at the station who broke arms and legs for a living in these days of flexible due process.

<Which way?> asked Francisco.

There were two main corridors off the foyer, and it didn't seem to matter which one they took. Perdita decided immediately, and nodded her head right

Francisco stepped forward into the corridor, and froze as something clicked under his foot.

Mierda!

Perdita crouched down to look at the floor under Francisco's booted foot. She couldn't see much, but it was obvious there was a plate there, concealed under broken tiles that nobody would see if they weren't looking.

<Trap, I think.>

<Traps? I didn't know there would be traps. Why did you not tell me about the traps?>

<Shush. Let me figure this out.>

Slowly, carefully, with the practiced eye of someone who had done this a great many times before, Perdita tracked the wires back out of the footplate and into the walls. No great effort had been made to conceal them, so she could see the colors snake together and tangle up onto the ceiling and away down the corridor. What they connected too, she couldn't sure, not without scouting ahead.

<The good news is that it isn't explosives.>

<I can get my foot back now?>

<The bad news is that I don't know what it is. There's something up ahead, just can't see it.>

<How bad?>

<Depends on whose standards we're taking about. For you, maybe it's, say a 2. Which is more an 8 for the rest of us.>

<So maybe I should just see what happens?>

Perdita didn't like the sound of that. Francisco was not one to plan things, and she had never been certain if it was some sort of inability to look to the future, or that he simply couldn't be bothered. Perdita was not like that. She needed structures and processes and options. Her training dictated that. She needed to able to use models to predict the likely outcomes, and she absolutely did not like just seeing what happened. She was a detective precisely because she could see things other people couldn't. And she didn't have a huge sword or mystical bombs to solve problems when it all went bad.

<I think I should scout ahead.>

Francisco didn't answer. He had made his decision, simply because knew he had a better chance of surviving whatever might present itself. He took the sword off his back and braced himself. It was all Perdita could do to scramble to cover before he lifted his foot, and the trap was sprung.

For a moment nothing happened. As he stood there, *Macuahuitl* ready to taste blood and violence, Francisco wondered if this was just a dud. A trick within a trap, just to mess with people's heads. It wouldn't be the first time.

Then he and Perdita heard a sound, something like metal grinding onto metal, and then looked up as, a hundred feet away down the corridor, a grating fell open out of the ceiling. Maybe an old accessway for maintenance, or an air-conditioning vent. It didn't matter, though, as it was what dropped out next that focussed their attention entirely.

A snarling ball of fur the size of a large dog, spiky and vicious, spines pushing out every part of its body like a porcupine. What wasn't covered in those spines was just mouth, yawning wide with every growl, every snarl, and filled with jagged teeth designed to do nothing but rip flesh.

<What is *that*?> asked Perdita.

Francisco didn't know, and he didn't care to know. He had long since stopped being surprised by the things the Wilderness could throw at him. To him this was simply another thing, another creature of the wilderness to kill and then to bury. He watched it as it drove itself into a frenzy, looking for the openings and the weaknesses he might be able to exploit. It had no eyes he could see but he knew it could see them through rage-borne vision.

With a howling roar, the spiney animal hurled itself down the corridor, half running and half rolling as it did. It looked so unnatural as it moved, and yet it moved so quickly it almost caught Francisco off guard. He swung *Macuahuitl* hard and it caught the animal as it leapt forward onto the wall. The flat of the sword batted it away, and it crashed back down onto the floor.

As it did Perdita wasted no time in shooting it. She emptied an entire clip directly into the animal's body, and expected that it should be dead.

Instead it righted itself, a frenzy of sharpness and spitting venomous fury. The bullets hadn't even penetrated the skin, and the animal shook the shells out of its coat of spines, letting them scatter around.

<That was a whole clip>, said Perdita, disbelievingly. <Why does nothing die when you shoot it anymore>.

Francisco raised his sword again. He knew it had the power to cut things bullets and technology could not even scratch, but this time he felt something almost like an uncertainty. It was like a little whispering voice, doing its best to weaken him. But Francisco ignored it. He had to ignore it.

Enraged, the animal crouched low and then hurled itself into the air towards Francisco, and he swung.

This time *Macuahuitl* and its obsidian razors raked along the underside of the creature, picking their way through the spines and finding purchase on pale skin. It screeched out as blood spurted from the wound, deep enough to hurt but not to mortally damage. It landed awkwardly, slipping on its own fluids, its claws scrabbling as Francisco turned to face it, determined not to let it get the advantage again. But this time he saw something new in the creature's face, in its eyes.

It looked frightened, afraid. It huddled to the wall, and the seconds ticked by in a strange standoff of man versus animal. Slowly, Francisco started to realise that the creature wasn't going to attack again and he let himself relax as he slid his sword onto his back.

Perdita wasn't so sure. She held onto her weapon, however useless it was, even though she trusted Francisco's

instincts as he moved closer to the cowered beaten creature
and crouched down.

<You alright boy?>

He offered his hand, and the creature - that looked for all
the world now like a terrified puppy – sniffed at it cautiously.
All its rage and spitting fury was gone, and instead there was
curiosity. It was still a wild animal, Perdita could feel that,
but now it was calm, soothed.

Francisco tried to get behind the creature's eyes and get a
sense of what it might be feeling. He hadn't wanted to hurt
it but there had been no real choice. He had done his best to
pull his blow, and he was thankful that its guts weren't
splayed out all over the carpet. It didn't deserve to be killed,
however hard that might prove. Francisco reached down and
pulled something from the creature's neck, a fat red
wriggling thing that looked like a huge tick. He crushed it,
popping it like overripe fruit, and in that instant something
about the creature changed. Despite its injury its pain was
suddenly gone, and the thing that made it crazed was ended.

It locked eyes with Francisco for a second, almost out of
gratitude, and then it was gone, bolting along the corridor
and to the foyer, where the gateway back to its Wilderness
home waited for it.

Francisco watched it go, wondering if it had friends, a
mate. Children. Perdita watched too, still not quite
relinquishing her grip on her gun.

<How do you do that?>

Francisco wasn't quite sure. Another gift perhaps, an
intuition.

It was then that the smoke came.

<Holy shit what NOW?> barked Perdita.

The smoke billowed around them, sweet smelling and
acrid at the same time. It was suddenly everywhere, and
Francisco realised that it was different to the smoke he had

used to deceive their attackers from the foyer. This seemed to come not from a bomb or a vent but out of the air itself. It was almost liquid as it flowed, swallowing up everything within its yellowish folds.

Inside it, Francisco and Perdita almost felt as though they were floating. Without the walls of floors to anchor them, it seemed that gravity had simply surrendered and let them go. What felt like the sensation of being drunk began to wash over them as well, and their bodies were light heavy all at once, lurching from side to side and they disobeyed even the basic commands.

Francisco grabbed for Perdita's hand and she clasped it. They were blinded, disorientated, but if they could still keep that physical contact with each other, then maybe they could find the ground again.

Flashes of psychedelic light began to burst around them, fracturing and cascading into torrents of multi-colored power. Sparks became waterfalls of primary color and the yellow smoke itself became a vast ocean that sought to consume them.

<Cisco, what......>

Francisco didn't answer. He clenched his eyes tightly shut, forcing the lightshow out of his brain even as Perdita succumbed to its hypnosis. He felt her hand loosen, not deliberately but as though she had simply forgotten what it was and what it was for.

<Beautiful,> whispered Perdita, the empty smile on her face invisible. <So beautiful....>

Francisco could feel he was beginning to lose her to the power of the smoke. What that power was he couldn't know, but he did know it was the same kind of power, the same magic that touched his own soul and with that second of realisation he knew exactly what to do.

Perdita wanted to be consumed by the lights, and she reached out for them.

Then she cried out and the two of them were suddenly laying on the ground. There was no lightshow, no smoke, nothing. Francisco put his penknife back into his pocket, and Perdita rubbed her hand as it bled. She stood, angry but knowing she should be grateful, and looked around to get her bearings, to try and figure out which way to go next.

But somehow, impossibly, the hotel and its corridors looked different now.

Francisco had never liked hotels, and this one was no different. Maybe it was worse, with its sense of bad things dripping from every crack in the walls and oozing from every hole in the floor. He preferred the open spaces. This maze of corridors made him feel boxed in, claustrophobic, and every little sound made him wary of some new threat that would leap out of nowhere.

Beside him, Perdita was calmer as she led with her handgun. She was on her last clip now, and she hoped she wasn't going to have to unload into some new apparently unkillable creature. On the other hand she was more used to these sorts of places than Francisco. It felt like a crime scene, and there was a little buzz of anticipation in her stomach as she scanned the area, looking for something. Anything. Some hint as to how to proceed or where to go. There was always some sort of track to follow – it was just a question of finding it.

There couldn't be too many places to look. This was, after all the original epicentre. This was where it had all started that one otherwise normal day - where the birth of a little baby apocalypse had crept out and spread across the peninsula, shutting everything down and opening the gates to who knew where.

The same thing that had made Francisco into the man he was now.

Sometimes she wondered if he was still really human. She had adjusted to his skin, his strength, his weird mojo magic, but underneath that there was still a niggling feeling that something inside him, deep down, had become something else. Something different.

In truth Francisco felt it too, but at this moment he was far more concerned about the next thing that was probably preparing itself for some sort of new ambush. Shadowy corners looked like caves and all sorts of things could be hiding away in them. Everything in this hotel made him a little too tense, a little too cautious, where usually he was loose and relaxed.

<Nervous?> asked Perdita.

<Just don't like this place. Feels…..>

A sound stopped him, a noise that echoed in from the distance. Metal on concrete, a single sharp crack and then scraping. Perdita quickly picked up on its direction and nodded towards a door up ahead, half off its hinges and partly hidden by a tangle of wiring that hung out of the ceiling.

<That way.>

They approached it, slowly and steadily, and Francisco gripped the hilt of *Macuahuitl* tighter than Perdita had ever seen, so tight she thought the sword might fracture. It worried her. They had seen much worse than this, and yet as they took their positions on either side of the doorway she couldn't shake the feeling that Francisco was….scared.

It didn't fill her with confidence as she braced herself.

<Ready?>

The door came away from its hinges liked cooked meat from bone, and Francisco hurled inside as Perdita covered the room, scanning and moving in that professional practiced way that was in her bones now, the woman and the training inseparable.

What they had found was an old maintenance room, one that had once helped to hide the machinery of the hotel, the pipes and conduits and endless miles of cabling. It was a wreck, just like everywhere else, and the air was stifling hot, so hot that Perdita found it a little hard to breath.

Francisco never worried about the heat. It was not something concrete for him, and he never felt it anymore. Yet the sense of unease that was plaguing him hadn't diminished, and he didn't like it at all. It hung in this room, almost palpable, thick and dirty and just beyond reach.

<Over there>, said Perdita.

There was a huge chunk of masonry blocking off half the room, and Francisco was relieved that there was something he could physically do. It took him a couple of attempts to get his grip and then he lifted. The chunk was heavy but it moved, and as he dragged it out of the way Perdita's gun came up to cover the space he revealed.

Lying amongst some rubble was a body, only just dead, one hand a bloody stump and the head half caved in.

<More dead stuff >, observed Francisco.

Perdita looked a little closer. The body obviously hadn't made the noise, but when she looked at where the hand had been she saw that the wound was new, stained with the paste of a dead man's blood. An idea suddenly formed din her head – this corpse might not have made the noise, but whatever took its hand might have.

She looked around, up, down, and then saw what she was looking for. A hole, big enough for a person to get through, and not part of the natural destruction of the hotel. This wasn't random but something different, deliberate, Smashed into existence for a purpose.

Francisco saw it too.

<Don't think I'm gonna get through there.>

He was right. Perdita's assessment told her it was only just big enough for her, so she slipped the safety on her gun on and slid it into the back of her jeans.

<I'll check it out. You stay here. >

Francisco nodded slowly, and watched as she vanished into the hole.

Seconds became a minute, then two, and the sounds of Perdita scrambling in the tunnel started to fade. Francisco didn't like this at all. None of it – the hotel, the nervous queasiness it made him feel. It was almost as though it was watching him. As a kid he had seen a film about an evil hotel that made people go mad, and somehow coming here was praying a little on that frightened child and his nightmares about madmen and their axes.

Shaking his head he tried to dismiss the army of little paranoias that were creeping in. Instead, he found his mind leaping backwards, digging up memories he hadn't thought about in a long long time. He remembered the day that masked man with the knife had come to his school and taken away one of the kids. He remembered being locked in the cupboard with his teacher as she desperately tried to pretend she wasn't panicking. He remembered the smell of her sweat as he made himself not cry, just like his papa had taught him.

Men don't cry, papa had said.

Francisco started to feel how scared he had been, locked within that little room. He didn't understand how or why. He made his home out in the Wilderness, in the darkness of the caves and the ruins, and faced things that would break the hardiest of souls. Monstrous terrible things.

So why was this place affecting him so?

<Perdi?> he called.

There was no answer. His rational self told him she was simply out of earshot, but that same voice of reason seemed muted suddenly, less distinct. Instead the frightened child was trying to claw its way out. The child who had watched them find the body of the abducted boy with his body sliced open and his guts removed. The child who faced his father the solider, who told him this was how the world was and he had better toughen up and get used to it.

Worst of all, Francisco remembered being so scared his father, his papa, might hit him.

<Perdi>?

No answer again, and this time Francisco's stomach turned itself into a knot, that horrible sharp stab of panic, of real and genuine fear. He tried to force it out but it wouldn't leave, squatting there like a growing intangible cancer. Then he heard that sound again, that scraping. But not muted anymore - loud and immediate, and right behind him.

Francisco turned, but it was that one second too late, his reactions slowed by the panic that was gripping him.

A terrible shadow grasped him by the throat and began to choke him.

*

Perdita scrambled along a tunnel that seemed to go on forever, hunched over and wishing she hadn't thought this was a good idea. More than once she had thought about turning back, but her curiosity got the better of her like it always did. She was never quite certain if it was natural or part of the training, that urge to turn over every rock and look in every crevice. Whichever it was it was an integral part of her, and she chose to embrace it, pushing onwards.

The tunnel teemed to have been dug out of the ground but she couldn't tell how, only that it was angled downwards into the limestone rock. She ran he hands along the walls and the stone felt almost melted, liked cooled waves of lava.

Whatever had done this hadn't cared what they were moving through – the concrete walls or the ground itself. Clearly neither had been any sort of obstacle.

Once, a while ago, Perdita would have assumed there was a rational explanation for all of this. A drill maybe, or some sort of military thermal lance device. Now though, it could be anything. Literally anything. There were no rules anymore. There was just life, and the things in the Wilderness.

Up ahead Perdita saw some light, a sickly green yellow glow that didn't look healthy, and she pushed herself along the tunnel a little faster. There was another opening, this time into some sort of natural rock chamber, and as she got closer she could see something in it, something that shouldn't have been there.

Another few steps, and her gun was out, safety off, as she started to see what she was looking at. She saw flesh and bone and other things, held together by a frame of thorny branches and arranged into what could only have been a shrine. Candles of fatty blood-red wax burned with the acrid smell of some unrecognisable incense, and dismembered hands hung from sharp stakes of splintered wood buried into the rotting mass. It was a hideous thing to behold, and as Perdita forced herself to realise that this was what remained of the little boy they had been looking for. Stolen away and brought here for some monstrous purpose. All she could do was hope that he hadn't suffered.

Perdita had seen shrines and their rituals before. There were so many cults now she had lost track, and they had a person at the station whose job it was to keep track of them. Her name was Enriqua, and she would probably wet herself when she read Perdita's report about this.

There was an unnatural quiet to the luminescent chamber, the kind that always meant something bad would happen. And the universe didn't disappoint

Out of nowhere a figure appeared at the entrance, distorted and grotesque as it hissed savage threats in unrecognisable mad gibberish.

Perdita calmly raised her gun and fired.

As the gunshot echoed, something smashed Francisco through thin walls, lifting him off his feet and hurling him like he was nothing. All his strength was gone, and *Macuahuitl* lay useless on the dirty carpeted floor.

Fear was a blanket all over him now, penetrating through every pore, and he wanted nothing more than to run away and to escape. His attacker was already on him though, a shadow, grasping at him as it once again dragged him into the air and cast him down. This time Francisco smashed into hard stone and felt something break that shouldn't have.

He reached for his sword but a booted foot drove itself into his head, the head grinding down onto it as it tried to pierce through Francisco's hard skin and grind whatever it found to pulp.

In agony that he shouldn't have felt, Francisco looked up.

The face that looked back down at him was first a woman, and then the mask of the school knife man. It flowed between the two and then a third form, something misshapen, demonic. He could see only its outline as it sucked in all the light and even then only for a second as it become the woman again, a cruel faced woman with eyes like oil.

There was no expression at all. No hatred, no range, no sneer of victory. Just a dead mask that stared dispassionately down, a void of feeling that was shared by the shadow's voice.

<Are you afraid?>

The boot released Francisco's hand and kicked him so hard he landed twenty feet away. Things inside were punctured and bleeding, and he groped at his belt for something, anything to use. Then he realised that he couldn't remember what to do – the fear had stolen away not only his muscle but his knowledge, and he watched, broken, as the shadow walked towards him, shifted between its three faces.

Images collided and burst in Francisco's head, every fear or every day roiling around in a whirlwind. He felt his body failing and his consciousness started to fade, both overwhelmed by the shadow.

After everything, was it now time to die?

Then there were two sudden words, clear as day, out of nowhere.

<Hey, witch>.

The shadow turned, and the last thing Francisco saw on its face was something like surprise as it turned to face the owner of the voice.

Moya smiled, and hit the Night Witch as hard as she could.

*

Perdita almost threw herself out the tunnel as she heard Moya's voice. She ignored the fact she was covered in the sticky blood of whoever it was she had shot. She hadn't waited to find out. A bullet in the head had dealt with it, so she could go back anytime and find out more of the shrine, its collection of hands and its unchallenging guardian that lay on the rock.

She knew she had to get back to Francisco and even as she emerged out into the storeroom to see him gone, she knew something was badly wrong. The wall has half gone now, smashed apart, and there was a crackle of static in the air that surely couldn't speak of anything good.

Her gun out, she ran into the corridor. More wreckage, and that hit of electricity was stronger, so strong it made her come out in goosebumps. Was this, she wondered, what Francisco had felt? Was there something here that had made him seem to edgy, so nervous.

For a second she lost her perfect composure and didn't know quite what to do.

<Perdi,> shouted Moya.

Perdita looked over and saw things that immediately told her what had happened. Moya, tall and strong with her strange horns and her relaxed smile. Buried in the wall opposite her, a figure dressed in black clothes that looked to have had its head smashed inside out.

But the worst of it was Francisco, lying there, unmoving, beaten. Perdita couldn't comprehend how this was possible as she ran over to him and knelt down, trying to pretend she was being professional and distant.

<You were back-up,> Perdita barked. <That was the plan.>

<But I wanted to help with evil witchy witch here.>

Moya wandered over to the wall and prodded the body and its lolling head with toe of her cowboy boot, wondering if it might spring back to life. She was almost disappointed when it didn't.

Almost.

Then she noticed that Perdita wasn't talking anymore like she normally did, and suddenly things were more serious.

<Is he OK? Perdita? Is he OK?>

Perdita didn't reply to Moya. She just started repeating the same four words over and over again as she checked his body with a desperation that could only have come from love.

<I can't find a pulse. I can't find pulse. I CAN'T FIND A PULSE.>

DIA DE MUERTOS
FANTASMA

Ana-Maria loved this time of year. She loved the candles and the music, the sights and smells. She loved all the people who came to Playa Del Mantarraya to celebrate their loved ones. She loved her mother making up her face and the fireworks that cracked and burst overhead as the sun went down. And most of all, she loved that strange otherworldly atmosphere where the whole town was bathed in the oranges and reds of an endless web of lights - it felt like the worlds of the living and those of the passed came just within touching distance.

She felt sad for people who couldn't share in it. Her mother had told Ana-Maria that in other countries cemeteries were dour and grey, forgotten places that nobody wanted to go to. Nobody wanted to remember the dead because they were frightened of them, and everyone tried to pretend that it would never happen to them. Ana-Maria just didn't understand that. Perhaps it was her mother's work, seeing people die as they were carried out of the Wilderness sick or injured beyond repair. Perhaps it was Uncle Francisco and his stories of burial. Or perhaps it was simply that she had been born into a country which saw celebration where others did not. Whichever it was, Ana-Maria was immune to the despair and saw only the joy in Dia de Muertos.

She loved Christmas too, but nothing could beat the end of October. Her favorite thing was when she and her mother visited grandmamas grave, the one with the carved angle and the fresh flowers that Dr Sonja changed every week. They would sit there with all the other people with their white painted faces, laughing and smiling and telling each other stories of other lives. They would eat and drink and forget about the world around them, the real world where walls had been built and all those fancy digital technologies didn't work anymore. Yucatán was a place apart in many ways, but this time of year, this celebration, was universal.

Ana-Maria didn't mind that Francisco and Perdita hadn't been able to come this year. They were off on one of their adventures in the wreckage of Cancún, which sounded far too dangerous. They were always here in spirit, and besides, this was just as a much a time for a living mother and daughter as it was for remembering the dead. She squeezed her mother's hand. Dr Sonja grinned and hugged her daughter. She had been talking to an older couple, perhaps in their 60s, who had come here to visit a relative and become enamoured of the place. They were English, and Dr Sonja was pleased to be able to practice her language skills a little. She hadn't been able to in too long.

Ana-Maria wasn't interested in talking to English people. Something else had caught her attention. Over by the gateway to the graveyard there was a woman. Young and beautiful, her makeup intricate and perfect, her dress colorful and simple and her face topped by a blood red rose in raven hair. There was something else as well, as she smiled at Ana-Maria.

<Mama> said Ana-Maria. <Look over there.>

Dr Sonja excused herself from her talk and followed the direction of her daughter's excited pointing. There was nothing there.

<What did you see?>

Ana-Maria creased her head in puzzlement. The woman at the gate must have slipped away. People did that all the time. Or maybe she had vanished. Uncle Francisco had told her tales of vanishing people before, and he said there were spirits out in the Wilderness. A little buzz of nervous excitement ignited in Ana-Maria's stomach that day, and she had wanted to know more. She often daydreamed at school of having adventures like Francisco, and while she would never be allowed out beyond the town limits, maybe this could be her own little adventure.

<I saw someone. Can I go and look, mama. Please?>

Dr Sonja nodded and smiled. <Of course. Just don't go too far. Promise?>

<I promise.>

Dr Sonja leant forward and kissed her daughter on the top of her head. Anything else would ruin the make-up, and that would only spoil Ana-Maria's absolute love on the celebration. As far as Dr Sonja was concerned that could not be allowed, and she watched her daughter wander off towards the gate.

What a lovely young girl," said the English woman, and Dr Sonja nodded her thanks.

"She is wise after her years I think. Is that right?"

"Beyond her years I believe is the correct phrase," said the Englishman.

"Oh don't be such a fussbudget," said the English woman in a way that made Dr Sonja laugh. "Ignore him. I think wise after her years is much better."

Ana-Maria heard her mother laugh. It was a lovely sound, one that sometimes she didn't hear enough, but it didn't distract her from the task at hand. There was a mystery to be investigated here, and Ana-Maria was determined to have her own story to tell the next time she saw Uncle Francisco.

She walked out of the gate and looked around. There were still lots of people going about their business, but no sign of the young woman. Ana-Maria frowned. She bet that Francisco didn't have these kinds of frustrations.

She turned, and the young woman was standing right behind her.

Ana-Maria looked up at the young woman, and the young woman looked back with empty white eyes that were eerie and alluring at the same time, a part of her intricate beautiful skull design and somehow different. Ana-Maria was dazzled a little by the beauty of the woman with her rose and her pretty dress and her cascade of hair, but she tried to focus on details things the way Auntie Perdita had taught her. The paint for example, it seemed to be all over her body, and was more like Uncle Francisco's pale white skin than makeup. There was something ethereal about this woman as well. It wasn't just those eyes, but something more, something that made her almost seem not quite real. It was important to ask questions, said Auntie Perdita.

<What's your name?> asked Ana-Maria.

The young woman smiled. <My name is Ela> she said, her voice sounding like echoing whispers.

<I'm Ana-Maria.>

<I know.>

This puzzled Ana-Maria. <How do you know.>

Ela didn't reply straight away. Instead she just opened her hand, and revealed a piece of old-looking paper with beautiful scripted writing on it.

<For you.> said Ela.

Ana-Maria found herself drawn in by the script. It seemed almost mystical to her, shimmering in the half-light, and she read the words out loud as she took the note for herself.

Ela Muerta

Fallen star

Grant a wish

And watch from afar

The very instant Ana-Maria read that final word the paper dissolved into dust and then nothing at all in her hand. Ana-Maria didn't understand, and she looked up to ask her next question. But Ela Muerta had vanished as well, as though she had never been real at all.

GARAJE

Francisco lay on his back, the ground digging into his back as he sucked in breath. Around him everything was a dust storm of chaos and overhead the sky roiled red as though it were bleeding fire and blood. Clouds bursts apart and reformed, flowing like lava, and every particle lifted off the ground felt like it was trying to punch its way through his skin. A billion tiny little pieces of grit and dust and sand, all raging in the air.

The storm, because it could only have been a storm, was out of nowhere. There was no rain or lighting, and the air was silent even as wind raged like a hurricane everywhere.

As Francisco lay, he realised he couldn't remember how he had got here. He assumed he had been driving but couldn't recall, and definitely had no memory of crashing. He tried to figure out if he was hurt. His car had obviously spun out of control and flipped onto its side, skidding along the ground. He could still just about see it through the whirlwind of dirt – unbroken, the coffin still securely lashed to its roof but still perched on its side and rocking under the assault of the elements.

Francisco couldn't remember how he had got out either. He guessed the impact must have thrown him clear out the car, and hitting the road maybe knocked him unconscious but he had no memory of it. There was no sign of a broken windshield or wrecked door to tell any kind of story.

All he knew is that what was happening was not at it should be.

Happy his bones were intact and limbs were accounted for, Francisco slowly climbed to his feet. The wind, if that was what it was, silently whipped at him. It was neither cold nor not, neither wet nor dry, just a constant lashing pressure strong enough to feel that he could be cast off his feet and back onto the ground at any time. Overhead, high up in the sky, there was still just boiling crimson instead of the bright Yucatán sky.

None of this was right. None of this should be happening.

Francisco took a few steps towards his car, and the winds seemed to intensify, suddenly feeling that their only purpose was to prevent him from reaching any sort of safety or shelter. The air matched him move for move, and for every step gained he was pushed back a half. And with every loss, debris continued to rain down upon him, the detritus of everything from the earth to the trees to the bodies of the mosquitoes. Everything had been turned against Francisco by the tempest.

Shielding his eyes he anchored himself, and then he realised with a sudden paranoid stab that there was someone else there.

Watching him…

At first Francisco thought he was imagining things. First there was a shape, and then it became indistinct, fading in and out of the storm and the red air all around it like a haze. It flickered in and out existence, appearing in one place, and then another, and each time getting closer and closer.

But however close it got, Francisco still couldn't see what it was. It was as though whatever the phantom was, it deliberately lying to his eyes, making fun of him, turning the chaos of this place to its own advantage. All he could really know for sure that it was scarlet red.

Fantasma Rojo.

The phrase popped into Francisco's mind, and he wasn't certain if he had made it up or somebody else had put it there. Maybe it was the mirage's name, or something else's name for it. Whichever was the case, the shimmering unreal thing made Francisco nervous. His mind was clouded and it was hard to recall anything with any clarity. He remembered a hotel somewhere, and the feeling of the life being sucked out of his body.

And then, he had been here. Lying on a road, near the wreckage of his car, stripped of his familiarity and his weapons. There was no *Macuahuitl*, no whipclaw, no belt with his pieces of stone and his shaman's alchemy. There wasn't even his poncho. It was just him, in a world he didn't really recognise that seemed like the very air had been stained by blood. A world he very much wanted to leave, but didn't know how. A haunted world.

The scarlet wraith quivered, its hazy outline like the failing image on a broken television. It was by the car now, more settled and more focussed, and it looked as though it was investigating the wreck. It seemed to have hands that were made of smoke, reaching out and penetrating the metal of the vehicle. What it was looking for, Francisco had no idea.

Should he try and communicate with it?

Francisco didn't know. He wished Dr Sonja were with him - she always knew the right things to say. He preferred the physical world made from things that could be touched and known. The world of ghosts and demons, that realm that edged into the very edges of reality out of folklore? He hated that.

As the ghost continued to study its new treasure, Francisco looked around the road. At first it had seemed empty, just a long road through another wilderness. Then he saw something that hadn't been there before, or at least he thought it hadn't been. It looked like an old garage, rusted with disuse with a peeling sign that hung half broken from a pole.

That had to be something, thought Francisco, so he started to run towards it.

Behind him, he felt the Red Wraith follow.

The garage felt lifeless. Dead. Everything about it was decayed and old, yet nature had not reclaimed anything. There were no plants or bugs, just a forgotten structure that reflected the red power of the boiling skies and suffered against the dust whipped up by the unending storms. The pumps were long broken, the glass of the meters cracked and the hoses discarded on the ground, split and ruined.

Francisco took it all in for a moment. It felt like he had somehow wandered into the end of the world, and he started to try and work out what had happened. The clues were there but they made no sense. Just broken things, forgotten places. It was like a fragment of somewhere else cut out of where it should be and dumped in another place, a place that it didn't fit.

There was no familiarity. Everything was just alien, and Francisco began to wonder if something truly bad had happened to him. With this long road, this ruin of a garage, and the Red Wraith that haunted him, still unsolid and impossible to really see.

Was he dead too?

Was that what had happened to him? Had that shadow in his blurry memory taken so much of his life that he couldn't get it back, and now he was here? It wasn't how he had imagined the afterlife. There was no music and no color, and there was no joy from those who had gone before him.

Had it all been a lie?

Francisco felt unnerved, so he headed for the garage store. The windows were smashed and the shelves inside stripped bare, everything inside exposed to the unnatural elemental powers that seemed to never end. Overhead the clouds just endlessly reformed into scarlet shapes, and all around the eerily silent winds lashed and whipped and whirled. It could all so easily be Hell.

As he stepped through the doorway with the broken frame and the metal panels that hung half off their hinges, Francisco saw the Scarlet Wraith again. It kept its distance, and was watching him once more. Not with eyes. It didn't seem to have any. Instead, it was watching him from inside somehow, connecting with his spirit rather than his eyes.

<What do you want?> Francisco tried to say, but no words came out. Whatever power that made the storm silent stole away his voice too, even though he could feel the words coming out of his mouth. He felt like all his strength was gone, and so he could do nothing but step through the doorway.

In that instant, he was somewhere else and a friendly voice said:

<Morning. What can I get you?>

Inside the garage, everything was alive. Sun flooded in through freshly cleaned windows, and people shopped for snacks or drinks, and paid for their petrol. The kind looking old man stood behind the cash till, a patient smile on his face.

<You OK, son?>

Francisco wasn't OK at all. He looked back out of the door and saw cars in the garage and on the road, driving past. But they weren't modern cars. They seemed older, but not in a familiar way. Instead they looked as though they had been put together from different times and places, just like the people all around him. A woman who walked past him for example. She smiled, looking like a vision out of the 1950s movies, and yet on her wrist was a modern watch and in her hand was a cellphone.

<Seems like you could do with some help there.>

Francisco felt like he was about to collapse, so he grabbed hold of the cash desk to steady himself as the woman paid for her petrol and left, the little tinkle of a bell announcing her departure.

<I….don't understand> said Francisco, finally.

The old man's faced creased as he smiled widely, everything about him open and friendly in a way that instantly put Francisco at ease. After a few seconds, the anxious nausea in Francisco's gut started to fade. The old man had put a soda on the wooden surface of the desk.

<Go ahead, it's on me.>

Hesitantly at first, Francisco opened the old-fashioned ring pull, half expecting some hideous demonic creature to explode out and try to eat his face. He was grateful that didn't happen, and took a couple of gulps. It was sweet like honey, not like any soda he had ever tasted before, but when he tried to see what it was called the name on the can it hid from him, just like the Red Wraith had. All around, everything seemed to be slightly less than real, not quite solid around the edges. Like a move made by ghosts.

<That's good.>

The old man grinned. <The best we have. So what's a Krakatoa?> Seeing Francisco's confusion, he pointed. <On your tee-shirt.>

<It's a band. Metal. You know. Guitars?>

The old man just nodded.

<You know, I think there's another door for you, just out back here.>

The old man led Francisco back out of the store, gesturing for a younger man who hadn't been there before to take over. There was more space than Francisco would have believed was possible from the outside, and there was a corridor made of dark wood that led down to a single door.

<There you go. I was wondering who that was for.>

Francisco couldn't help but tense up his body, as though he was preparing to fight. Everything in him was screaming that he should smash his way out of this place, and yet the calm serenity of the old man kept everything in check. In truth, there was only one thing that Francisco could do.

<Am I....>

The old man shushed him.

<I don't think questions like that mean a whole lot, do you?>

Francisco had no idea how he was supposed to respond. The old man gestured towards the door with his kind smile, and as he did Francisco saw something on the skin of his arm. A tattoo, one that was immediately and frighteningly familiar, even as it seemed to shift and blur like a kind of smoke.

It was an image of the Red Wraith.

Francisco looked at the old man, face creasing in rage. This was a trick surely. This was some messenger who had been sent to calm him, cajole him with soda, and then cast him down into some hideous pit to scream and burn. But still Francisco couldn't find the strength in his body to strike out.

<What are you?> growled Francisco.

<It isn't what you think it is, son,> said the old man. <It'll be fine if you let it be.>

The door at the end of the corridor snapped opened wide of its own accord, and as Francisco stared at it, it seemed more like a giant mouth, its edges organic and elastic, yawning wide with hints of teeth made of fractured broken pieces of wooden frame. Something invisible grasped a hold of Francisco, the same power of the silent storm outside but reversed now, drawing him inexorably in. He couldn't fight it even if he had wanted to, and so there was no choice, no option.

As the old man watched, gentle and unthreatening, as the door took Francisco, lifting him off the tiled floor. Invisible unseen hands enveloped him, not painfully, not forcefully, but almost like a soft cocoon, carefully drawing him into a shield of safety as he was taken through the mouth that grew wide to accommodate him

The door slammed shut, and Francisco was gone.

*

Francisco fell or flew or floated, he couldn't tell which. Gravity meant nothing, and everywhere there was void that sparked and crackled with the hints of images. He couldn't remember how long it had been since had been sucked through the door. Perhaps moments. Perhaps centuries. It didn't seem to matter anymore. Space and time were gone now.

Images formed around him, memories and dreams merging together into a sticky mass that was hard to pull apart. He saw a black shape and the carpet of a hotel. He saw the explosion of shotgun. He saw the Scarlet Wraith and its unsolid form, flitting in and out of the face of the old man at the Garage. He saws faces that he knew – a beautiful woman with a gun, and another woman, taller, stronger, with copper skin and horns that curved from her head. There were other things too, things that weren't human. A hulking thing with a skull for a head. A dinosaur with a hook in its hand.

He knew them, but he couldn't remember their names as they were lost back into the whirlpool of chaos.

Around him, the unending vistas of the Yucatán Borderlands formed out of nothingness. Francisco could see every tree and every cenote across the landscape he knew so well and had walked through for so long. Yet now he could see it from a new perspective and he realised how it was an alien world, full of things that nobody truly understood.

Francisco reached out for it, to try and grab hold of some tangible part of his home, and it all transformed again like a dream.

All around him was a magnificent rainforest, the brightest greens under a blazing yellow sun. Dominating everything was a huge pyramid, grey stone steps tapering up to the heavens, and across it swarmed thousands of people. People long dead, living in a world lost to history. The Mayan world.

The sight touched deep inside Francisco's mind and heart, and he felt tears come to his eyes. And as they came a shape formed, a blur of light at first that gradually become more and more real, until in front of him was the most beautiful thing he had ever seen. A young woman, her body adorned with bird feathers, her head covered by an ornamental crest of rainbow colors and the polished beak of a huge eagle that hid her eyes in shadow. Vast ethereal wings stretched out from her back, and she seemed like an angel sent from the sky.

The vision reached out her hands, seeming like the only thing that was real in this endless transforming void.

<Francisco,> she said, her voice a whisper that echoed all around.

As the world of the rainforest and the pyramid started to fracture, Francisco reached out for the vision, and their hands touched.

*

Dr Sonja slammed down her hands, glaring at the frightened looking receptionist who had only started at the hospital two days before. It wasn't the hospital it had once been, but enough had been rebuilt and rejigged to create a place where people could at last have a chance of being made well, or of being repaired.

<Where is he?> demanded Dr Sonja.

The receptionist, Carla, had no idea what to say. Dr Sonja's reputation preceded her everywhere she went. She had been out in the Wilderness, and rumour had it she had been there they day everything had changed. She had seen things. Things that made Carla want to drink heavily and have meaningless sex with Luiz the porter to forget.

Carla tried to be confident, but her hands shook over the paper reports she had been writing up. Computers rarely worked too well anymore, so in the hospital the pen was king and queen.

<I'm sorry Dr Castellanos, I'm not sure….>

<Francisco Garza. The coma patient in Room 27. Where is he. I didn't give anyone authorisation to move him.>

Carla bustled at her papers, even though they had nothing to do with Dr Sonja's case, the one she obsessed over. Everyone knew about it – the huge guy with the mysterious chalky skin, unconscious for nearly three weeks now and apparently immune to any kind of medical treatment any of the doctors could dream up.

Not that Dr Sonja would let anyone else near him of course.

<I'm sorry,> said Carla. She just couldn't think of anything else to say.

<You're sorry, everyone's sorry. Nobody knows anything.>

Dr Sonja stormed off, and a very relieved Carla just watched her go. It was definitely time to track down Luiz.

A thousand different possibilities raced through Dr Sonja's mind as she walked. She had never seen Francisco down before, at least not like this. He wasn't immortal and he could be hurt, but no normal person could match up to him physically. So it had to be something else. Her sister had told her what had happened at the hotel and it still didn't make sense – something about witches and body that had just turned to nothing after Maya had shot it in the face. That wasn't even a place to start for the right questions, let alone the answers.

Dr Sonja stopped as she found Perdita waiting by the main entrance, her face a practiced mask of hidden worry as she smoked her first cigarette in years.

<So what's going on?>

*

Perdita was like stone as she checked gun after gun, cleaning, adjusting, making certain that every single one of them was in perfect working order. Her favorites were all there – the ones that Francisco had found for her on his travels. There was the '45 made out of gold he had liberated from a ranting madman who summoned screaming ghosts that drove people mad and made their eyes bleed. There was the three barrelled shotgun from a cave far far away where he had rescued a dying woman. And there was the revolver, the gun Francisco had dug up the day it had all changed, the one with the intricate descriptions carved into the nickel plating, the one that never ever seemed to miss.

Moya emerged from the back room of Dr Sonja's house, where plans were being made, and ducked like she always did now. She had got annoyed with getting her horns caught on the frame, but even without them she was just slightly too tall to get through the door.

<Have you got enough guns?> Moya asked, raising her eyebrows as she looking at Perdita's arsenal.

Perdita didn't look up from her work. <Have you?>

<Ay ay, I have the these.> Moya flexed her biceps. <Great for punching witches. What else do we need?>

Perdita didn't answer. Her mind was lost to a mass of emotions that she desperately tried to force into the mental box she had created long ago. But now the box seemed cracked, and everything was leaking out, flooding her, and she hated it. Moya understood that. Her own nature was to smile, to be happy, but she understood darkness. She had felt it touch her soul. And she recognised the fear that only love could bring.

<Ana is staying with Derek. So, you sure you want to come with us >?

Dr Sonja had followed Moya out of the back room, dwarfed by the horned woman but filling up the house in Playa Del Mantarraya with an authority that pushed everything else aside.

<Big yeah. Something's got Francisco. If there's asses that need to be kicked, I wanna do some of the kicking> said Moya.

<You've been watching those movies again haven't you.>

<One. Maybe three. Five tops. They are so fun though.>

Perdita zipped up her arsenal bag, cutting through the conversation as she looked to Dr Sonja and Moya, drained of everything except the desire to act.

<Glad you're having a good time. So let's find him.>

*

The rainforest at night sang with life. The howler monkeys were asleep, and so the insects and the bats and the frogs had taken over, filling the air with their bodies and their calls. On the ground jaguars that dwelt deep in the heart of Calakmul prowled for their prey, while snakes slithered and lizards darted. Everything had its place in the natural order, from the smallest prey to the most ferocious predator, and all of them lived their lives in the wet heat, in amongst the green lush trees and the wetlands and the ruins of civilisations old and new.

Once this place had been threatened by the outside world, but now it protected itself. People never really came here anymore, not even the bravest and most foolhardy hunters or poachers after too many of them had started to vanish. Instead nature had re-established its dominance, and then other things had followed. Things that also walked and crept and crawled in the night, glimpsed only by shining eyes and heard only through growls that chilled hearts.

Because on that day long ago, the day that the Wilderness and all its denizens had been unleashed, Calakmul had been transformed as well. Now, the darkness of the rainforest had evolved its own existence.

Through the trees, guided by a dim yellow light that didn't really reveal anything, two figures moved. One was slim, dressed in raggedy clothes and a hood that hid his face, while the other was larger, more muscular. She wore a half-mask as well, close-fitting and embroidered with gold and silver. The mask of a fighter. A luchadora

<You sure about this?> asked the man in rags.

<She said it was here. When has she ever been wrong?>

<This place stinks.>

<A few more minutes, I promise you.>

<I'm not enjoying this.>

<Its not meant to be enjoyable. It's a mission.>

<Yeah, mission. Why do these missions always happen in places that stink?>

The woman in the mask snorted a kind of disdainful laugh, and then stopped as the lantern she was carrying picked out something in the undergrowth. A few metres ahead, in a small clearing where some chubby hairy rats scurried about, there was a shape. It lay there, unmoving.

<So that's him, right?> said the man in rags.

The girl in the mask nodded, handing the lantern over as she knelt down by the shape, hefting and it and carefully turning it over with a strength trained into her muscles over a lifetime raised in a fighting family.

There, lying on the ground, unconscious, was Francisco.

NAVIDAD
EL DUENDE

Ana-Maria lay in bed, unable to sleep. It was the same every year. The excitement of Christmas simply stopped her being able to drift away into peaceful dreams. There was excitement from sharing and seeing everyone together opening their gifts after Mass. There was excitement from the feast that her mother and Moya had put together, which had left everyone full and satisfied. And there was excitement from the Parades and smashing the piñata, which Ana-Maria had taken particular pride in this year. She had secretly watched Uncle Francisco practice with his sword once, and tried her best to emulate the strokes. It had worked, and everyone had clapped when the candy had spilled out after one mighty hit.

All of this swirled around in Ana-Maria's mind, replaying her favorite moments over and over. Uncle Derek had managed to join them as well. Usually he was giving his own Mass at his own church, but this year he had made an extra special effort to get to see Ana-Maria. He was a huge happy bear of a man with a beard like a forest, and it had been so much fun so listen to him tell jokes and entertain his sisters. Even Auntie Perdita.

Auntie Perdita had not been happy since they had come back from the hotel. Ana-Maria didn't know the full details of what had happened. She had had assumed it had been another exciting adventure that Uncle Francisco would tell her about while they shared bacalao together. Bacalao was Ana-Maria's favorite, and she liked it better than the sweetness of candy. Her mother had told her this was a good thing, as too much candy caused things to go wrong with organs in later life. That was something Ana-Maria very much wanted to avoid.

Maybe Christmas Day would cheer Auntie Perdita up. Usually they all just talked and played games and enjoyed the quite after the busy rush of December, but this year would be different. They would visit Uncle Francisco in hospital. Francisco always cheered Auntie Perdita up, and Ana-Maria had long ago figured out that they were a couple, even though nobody talked about it. And Ana-Maria was looking forward to new stories. Her mother had said that Francisco wasn't very well, but Ana-Maria was certain it wasn't too bad. After all, Uncle Francisco was indestructible.

She checked the clock again. 2:10. Everyone else was fast asleep, and she could hear Uncle Derek snoring downstairs. Even Moya was happily curled up, and she rarely slept. Sometimes Ana-Maria wondered if her horns were uncomfortable, but they never seemed to bother her. She wouldn't look right without her horns anyway.

Ana-Maria reached over and picked up the book that Uncle Derek had given her as a present. It was a wonderful thing with all sorts of illustrations and stories about strange things from places she had never heard of. It had been something Ana-Maria had wanted for so long, and she had no idea what lengths Uncle Derek had gone to get it. She was glad he had though.

Abandoning any hope of sleep, Ana-Maria opened the book and turned to the first story – the title said, in magnificent letters, <CUENTO DEL DUENDE>.

<In a church on a Hill where two crows sat on a silver cross, there lived a Goblin. He was as small as a person's hand and had green skin, with a big belly and a crest of black

hair and a tail. He had no name and nobody knew where he came from. He had lived under the floorboards for a hundred years or more and every now and then people would see him. They might see him while they were praying. They might see him other times. But nobody could catch him or take a photograph of him. The minute they tried, The Goblin would be gone, using his power to vanish into thin air. This was all because The Goblin liked to play tricks on people. He liked to see the looks on their faces.

<*In his little cave under the floor the Goblin would draw the faces of the people who had seen him in old crayons on the walls. The people made all sorts of faces. Over the years the Goblin had drawn hundreds of people, and he decided it was time to make a book. Then he would play his best trick of all. He would take away all the little books in the church, and put his book in their place. Then he would laugh and laugh, and watch as all the people tried to find their own faces in his book.*

<*To make his book the Goblin would need more than just crayons. He would need paper and ink, and he would need leather to make a cover. All these things would be hidden away in the world outside the Church, and so The Goblin decided to make a plan. First he would find his paper. There was a library in the town at the bottom of the hill. They threw paper in their bins all the time, so he would creep in and steal some. Perhaps if he was lucky they would have ink as well. So The Goblin crept out into one of his tunnels and began his journey.*

<*It wasn't long before the Goblin, whistling to himself, turned a corner, and a big black hair rat blocked his way. The rat stared at the Goblin, and the Goblin stared back. This rat was not friendly, he decided. It glared with its beady black eyes, and sniffed the air. Its whiskers quivered, and The Goblin decided that the rat was his enemy. So he*

summoned up some of his power, and made the face of a hideous rat-eating monster in the air. The monster had horns and a mouth full of ferocious teeth, and it chomped and drooled. The rat froze, petrified, and then scampered away, squeaking to itself. The Goblin chuckled to himself. All the rats would be afraid of him now, or they would answer to the rat-eating monster.

<The Goblin continued on his way, and found a big hole in the wall of his tunnel. It was new, and the Goblin didn't like it. He peered inside, and saw the hairy fat legs of a tarantula squatting in there. The Goblin decided to leave the tarantula alone. He was friends with the Tarantula King, and so it had been decreed that all tarantulas had to be his friends too, whether they liked it or not. This particular tarantula seemed like he didn't like it, but he still had to follow the rules of the Tarantula King.

<The Goblin happily went on his way. After all, he had a far more important mission to complete, and books didn't make themselves.>

The sound of a breath or a whisper stole Ana-Maria away from her story, and she looked up. At first there was nothing there, out in the gloom beyond the light of her lamp. Then sat up a little and looked more closely, peering into the darkness.

She wondered if somebody was creeping around. Uncle Derek often needed to go to the toilet during the night, especially after he had eaten and drunk as much as he had, but it wasn't him. It wasn't Moya either, or her mother checking on her to make sure she was asleep.

In fact it wasn't anything solid at all. It was something far less substantial, and the vague outlines of it drifted across the room. They seemed to have no purpose or meaning, and they didn't seem to be forming any kind of shape. Instead they just drifted in the warm night air, like cigar smoke or steam from a boiling kettle.

<Hello?> whispered Ana-Maria, unsure if she was afraid or simply curious. Could this be an actual ghost? Her first ghost? Uncle Francisco spoke about spirits, and he said they could become solid like real people and do all kinds of bad things. This was different. It seemed to have no interest in doing anything except floating, nothing but the faintest of wisps.

The whisper seemed to reply, and Ana-Maria felt a sudden familiar sensation in her stomach and in her head. A sense of recognition, one that hurled her mind back a few months, to when she and her mother had gone to the graveyard for the Dia de Muertos celebrations. Ana-Maria pictured the beautiful young woman with the painted face and the blank empty white eyes as she had done so many times since. The strange beauty had captured Ana-Maria's imagination, and for second she though she saw a ghostly face there in the smoke. The face of Ana Muerta.

<Is it you?> asked Ana-Maria, keeping her voice as low as she could. She thought of the little piece paper that the woman had given her, the one that had dissolved to nothing in front of her eyes. What had it said again?

The wisps seemed to reach out for Ana-Maria's book, almost invisible phantom fingers that wafted forwards into the lamplight, and as they touched the pages they were gone.

<Come back.>

Nothing happened. There was no more whispering, no more ghostly smoke. Irritated, Ana-Maria lay back on her bed and turned over to start reading her book again. Then she stopped dead, and her eyes widened, not quite believing what she was looking at.

There, squatting on the table, munching on a piece of candy, was the Goblin.

The sun came up and Ana-Maria hadn't slept a wink. She could hear various people starting to move around the house, and the subdued words of conversation as those who were awake tried not to disturb those who were asleep. In reality that was only Uncle Derek. He slept a little too much sometimes, and Ana-Maria's mother often chided him about it, along with his weight. Uncle Derek refused to have a medical examination though.

The Goblin still sat here on her desk, eating the candy that Ana-Maria had stockpiled after creeping down the stairs at around 4pm. That was when she had fully realised that she wasn't dreaming or hallucinating with some kind of fever, and that somehow, on this Christmas Day, her beloved new book had given birth to something. That something had looked at her expectantly when it had finished its first meal, and folded its arms like a pouting sulking child. Ana-Maria had just stared for a while and poked a little, feeling the Goblin's' frog-like skin and the Mohawk crest on its head that was like wire bush. His face was just two little black eyes and an underslung jaw that sprouted to fat tusks upwards, while his belly was bulbous and round. That, Ana-Maria decided, was due to all the candy.

Over time Ana-Maria had become an expert at creeping around, and the Goblin's hunger for candy seemed to be endless. They would probably run out before his appetite was sated, but she made the journey downstairs twice more anyway, more to give herself time to figure out what to do than anything else.

What would Uncle Francisco do? She didn't know. Uncle Francisco dealt with the monstrous things that roamed around the Wilderness. This Goblin was something else again. A thing out of a storybook that was just as real as anything. Was this, Ana-Maria wondered, what the woman at the cemetery had meant when she had given over that little piece of paper? Was this a gift from Ana Muerta? A wish made into reality.

Ana-Maria hoped so.

The Goblin finished its candy and reached out its arms like a needy baby. A little uncertainly, Ana-Maria reached and picked him up, placing him in the crook of her arm like she would one of her dolls. His skin was clammy and cool and soft, and he felt fat and pudgy in her embrace. He seemed to enjoy lying there too, and he smiled a lazy smile. This, Ana-Maria decided, was not an active Goblin.

There was knock at the door.

<Feliz Navidad Ana. We're having breakfast>, came her mother's voice, and before Ana-Maria had a chance to do anything Dr Sonja opened the door, planning to give her daughter a huge Christmas cuddle.

Instead all she could do was swear.

<Mama, you said a bad word.>

Dr Sonja blushed a little. <I'm so sorry *chica*, but…what…?> She pointed at the Goblin, who seemed to have drifted off into a contented doze.

Ana-Maria didn't quite know where to begin. She had told her mother about her encounter with the ghostly Ana Muerta, and that had been fine. But that had also been something that fit within expectations. Dia de Muertos was a time when people were supposed to speak to the ghosts of the passed-on. Even for the Wilderness, a place that spewed out brutes with skulls for heads and a hundred other grotesque things, this was new territory.

Moya appeared behind Dr Sonja. <Sonja, did you want the….> She tailed off as she saw the Goblin too. <Is that…a Goblin .>

Ana-Maria nodded, and Moya rushed over to look at him.

<Moya, what are you doing?> asked Dr Sonja.

<Oh look at him he's so cute,> said Moya. <Where did you find him.>

<He sort of came out of my book.> said Ana-Maria, a little awkwardly.

Moya picked up Uncle Derek's present, and she grinned widely. <Oh I had this book when I was a child. I loved it.> She showed it to Dr Sonja, who folded her arms decisively. <Did you ever read this.>

<No I did not. Did this thing…..>

<He's a Goblin mama.>

Dr Sonja sighed. <Did this *goblin* get into the house somehow. I didn't even know we *had* goblins.>

<We have something like them at home,> said Moya. <What's his name, Ana?>

<I don't really know. All I know is that he just eats candy.>

<Well, everyone loves candy,> offered Moya.

<Can I keep him Mama. At least for a while.>

Dr Sonja made an exasperated face, and decided it was futile to try and understand what had happened. Ana-Maria never really lied, and if she said this weird looking creature that was now sound asleep had sprouted out of a book, that was probably her understanding of the truth. Maybe it had, maybe it hadn't. No doubt Francisco would have a better explanation, but then again he had seen things nobody beyond the Wilderness would ever understand or believe.

<Ok, well. Another place for breakfast, Moya. Oh, and one more thing. Do we have any more candy?>

Deep down in the darkness, where only the ghosts lived like whispers, there was a sound.

It was faint at first. Little more than a pulse but regular as clockwork, that started to grow little by little until it became stronger. It became alive, a beat, echoing around the emptiness. Then a beat became a rhythm, breaking itself apart into individual little sounds and sections, forming patterns that wove in and out of each other.

Then came something else. Another rhythm, but different, more fluid. A heavy deep set of noises that followed the beats that themselves could have been some kind of mechanical heart. Together the two merged and became faster, more aggressive.

Suddenly there was music.

The guitars began. Hard and fast, a furious scale of four notes up and down, ramping up the intensity and the volume. As the hard drums and the thick bass and the thrashing guitars started to coalesce, the darkness quivered.

Almost as though it was afraid.

The music didn't let up. It raged against everything, powering louder and louder with every loop and every phrase. The darkness tried to pushed back, to smother this alien sound, but it had nothing to fight against. The noise, the music, was everywhere, surrounding everything.

The fight wasn't going to be so easily won though. Out of the dark came things, things with mouths and eyes that swam about in the gloom and shifted their shapes like jet-black mercury. Claws raked out and tongues lashed venomously, blindly hoping to rip away a chunk of the noise that was getting louder and louder, burning away at everything.

There was a voice now, somebody singing in a guttural growl words that sounded more like primal sounds. The drums shattered into complex pathways, the guitars raced, heavy and dark, pushing back whatever monster the darkness could give birth to. The embryonic creatures cried out in pain and faded back into their home while the music blasted away, washing away the sticky emptiness.

No respite, no mercy. Just the shape of rage in musical form, forcing back the demons. Like liquid, everything began to swirl into a vortex, and the endless void began to fracture. Light began to peek through, little seeds at first that soon bloomed into blazing sunlight.

The music raged, and for the first time in more months than he would ever be able to recall, Francisco opened his eyes to see a familiar face.

"Hey, welcome back. So you're not brain dead then?"

Francisco stared up, even the dim light bright to eyes that hadn't been used in so long. It took him a few seconds to realise that this someone was speaking English, and to remember that he spoke it himself. Then the person resolved themselves – a woman he knew, eyes covered by impenetrable sunglasses.

"Rae?" croaked Francisco.

Rae Tolly smiled. "Right first time. You know I kind of meant it when I said I hoped we didn't see each other for a while."

Francisco memory raced back to the past. He recalled the cenote, surrounded at its opening by the terrible thing that swarmed in the air and the madman with a gun who wanted to kill everyone. And then he remembered the reason he had been there in the first place.

"Is the…dinosaur…thing here?"

"Ol' Hooky?" Rae smiled. "Oh he's around here somewhere. He kind of does his own thing mostly."

Francisco tried to sit up but felt exhausted even by the effort of speaking, so he slumped back and just vaguely gestured to his eyes.

"Are you still….?"

Rae tipped down her sunglasses. Her eyes were yellow and reptilian, completely alien, just like they had been before. "Kind of used to it now. Had a few problems adjusting but me and Ol' Hooky have it all figured out." She slid the glasses back into place. "I just tell people I have an eye condition."

Francisco tried to move again. He wasn't used to feeling this weak and he tried to force the lethargy out of his body but everything felt heavy, as though his muscles were too dense for him to control. He realised that he was on a bed, in some kind of tent, and there was a drip-feeding fluid into his arm that made the muscle sore. He could feel the uncomfortable humidity in the air from outside as well, where the sun was fading to twilight. In the background, somewhere, a generator was running.

"Feel…not right…" mumbled Francisco.

"I'm not surprised. You've been out for…well, I kind of lost count after the first two weeks. You kind of stink but other than that nothing seems to be broken. Good job, as I'm kinda rusty on my basic coma care in the jungle, seeing as I'm not actually a medical doctor."

Francisco creased his forehead as he struggled to remember. "What…."

Then he realised that there were other people in the tent as well.

There were two people, a man and a woman that Francisco didn't know. She was the stronger looking of the two, and wore what looked like an elaborate embroidered mask across the top part of her face. Her companion was slim, tall, almost skeletal looking, and his body was swallowed by ragged clothes, a long coat and a hood that obscured his face. Even so, Francisco could see a green-yellow tint to flesh that looked dry, almost like an old mummy.

"He OK?" asked the woman, her English heavy with an accent and not comfortable on her tongue.

Rae nodded. "I can confirm that he is not dead." She looked over to the ragged figure. "No offence."

Francisco had no real idea what was going on. That last coherent thought he could summon up was of being in a hotel, searching for something. Or maybe someone. He remembered something so strong and dark and monstrous that it overpowered him as though he were a child, and after that……After that, nothing. Just the emptiness of oblivion, and now he was here.

"Perdita," whispered Francisco. "Is Perdita OK?"

Rae and the masked woman exchanged looks. They had never heard the name before.

<Girlfriend?> suggested the ragged man.

"There wasn't anyone with you when they found you. Sorry."

Francisco closed his eyes, making himself see Perdita's face in his mind's eye. Surely she couldn't be gone, could she? Surely he would know. He always knew if she was in danger, and she could always always deal with it. There was no-one he knew tougher than Perdita Castellanos. So she had to be OK. Didn't she?

He had to find out for sure, so he forced a little life into his body and swung his legs over the edge of the bed, an old gurney that had bowed a little under his weight. Every muscle in his body screamed out for him to stop, but Francisco tried not to listen. But he knew however much he fought it, he would have to take things in stages as his head swam and he felt sick. Strength was going to have to be earned back.

<He's..alot bigger sitting up,> observed the ragged man.

The masked woman smiled a little and walked over as Francisco tested his arms and legs, trying to find the right way to get them to work properly again. Up close, Francisco's chalk-white skin seemed even more eerie, and she could see why people called him Fantoma Palido – the Pale Ghost.

<We need your help, Francisco,> said the woman called Gloriana.

*

Sitting in a chair, beaten and bound, Estevez couldn't quite figure out how this had all happened so quickly. It had seemed like a normal day, just a couple of woman, touristas probably, passing through and looking to stop at a local bar. He'd switched on the charm, hoping to get some drink money out of them and keep his reputation for great tequila, all homemade. Then he'd seen the giant woman with the horns and everything had gone wrong.

Estevez winced as one of the women sat in front of him. She seemed the one least likely to kill him out of the three, but he still found her gaze hard to meet. His bar had been cleared out of locals and locked behind them, so he had nowhere to hide in his dimly lit establishment. Tequila and charm wasn't getting him out of this one.

<Now,> said Dr Sonja, fixing Estevez with her best hard stare. <I have a fairly simple set of questions for you.>

Estevez nodded, terrified. The dead-eyed woman with all the guns - her name was Perdita he had learned - sat at a nearby table, not even looking over as she stripped and cleaned a pistol. The horned amazon named Moya stood right next to him like some devil woman from the comic books. Dr Sonja frightened him fractionally less than those two but he wasn't going to take any risks.

<I have great answers,> babbled Estevez. <Just don't let her hit me again.>

Moya looked down almost apologetically. <Oh, you mean me? Sorry, but it's kind of why I'm here.> She shrugged a little, but Estevez didn't feel any better. For Moya it had been little more than a tap but it had sent him flying. Sometimes she forgot how fragile people were, and she had got so used to sparring with Francisco that reigning in her strength felt a little tricky.

Dr Sonja shook her head a little. She had been practicing her interrogator face, and was enjoying the role more than she should. <Now Estevez, you know everything that goes in and out of the Wilderness. What's gone out recently that could be carrying someone who's around seven feet tall and weighs over 115, aybe 120 kilos.>

Estevez laughed and regretted it instantly as Perdita shot him a look. Seven feet? Who was seven feet tall? Only things out in the middle of nowhere. He thought of just telling them anything to get them out of his bar but he guessed they would somehow know that he was lying to them.

<I…don't know. Nothing came out recently. Please don't kill me.>

Perdita stood up, looking for a moment like she would do exactly that. Then she holstered her gun and strode silently out of the bar.

Moya smiled widely. <Look like it's your lucky day.>

*

Perdita raged as she stalked back to the car. Two days! Two days of interrogating every Wilderness smuggler and information courier in the whole area and nothing to show for it. Estevez had been their last real chance of a lead, and again, nothing. She didn't understand how this was possible. How could a man vanish from the hospital without trace, with no one seeing him. Especially someone like Francisco.

She looked through the backseat window to where she kept all his things – his belt, his pouches, the poncho she hated so much. His sword was there too, the huge *Macuihuitl*, carefully wrapped up and sticking up out of where the roof would normally be if she didn't keep it down all the time, and the whipclaw was wound into a neat coil next to it. Sometimes it felt like that those that were all that remained of Francisco in the world now.

Dr Sonja and Moya watched from the bar entrance as Perdita sat in the driver's seat, and after a second or two of calm smashed the steering wheel as hard as she could. Once twice, five times in all.

<All that anger is so negative,> said Moya, sincerely.

<My sister is running on anger,> replied Dr Sonja. <This isn't going very well, and she's really worried.>

<So how long have they…..>

<Years. She likes to pretend she doesn't love him, but I think she forgets I'm her twin sister sometimes.>

<Why don't they get married, and all that kind of thing. Have little baby Franciscos?>

Dr Sonja raised her eyebrow. <I don't even know if that's possible anymore.> She turned to look up at Moya who dwarfed her. <Is there anything from your home that could help.>

Moya shook her head. <We always stay away from all this black magic stuff. There was this one guy Mama told me about, they say he got some potions and one night he mixed

it all up and ended up he turned himself into a pig. Then he got eaten.>

<Hey, you looking for strange?> asked a voice.

Dr Sonja and Moya looked down and saw a man not even four foot tall with one eye a different color from the other and most of his face covered in a huge beard. Neither had even seen him coming, but guessed he had been in the bar and stuck around.

<Oh he's so sweet,> said Moya.

The dwarf ignored her. < I know a guy who's real good at strange.>

*

Francisco landed on the ground hard. It didn't hurt his body as much as his pride, and that was good thing as it was easily the twentieth time it had happened in barely an hour. Standing over him, Gloriana offered her hand, mischief in her eyes behind the ornate luchadora half-mask.

<Want to stop for today?> she asked.

Francisco took her hand and got to his feet. It had been a day and a night since he'd woken up, and still had no idea how long it had been since the hotel. His strength was coming back but healing was a slow process. Even so he thought he'd be able to wrestle Gloriana, and he chose to hold back so that he didn't hurt her. Instead, she bent his body into shapes that would be agonising for a normal man, and threw him to the ground with casual ease. There was a skill in those compact muscles of hers. A power. Not for the first time, Francisco wondered if she was like him.

<No. Again.>

Gloriana nodded, smiling, and the two of them engaged again. To her, Francisco was like a block of stone. Impenetrable, strong, but with the right timing and the right positions, very easy to move. It took only a few seconds for her to misdirect him, then trip him up. He crashed down once more and she was on him, bending his shoulders back in a surfboard hold.

<You sure you want to keep at this?> said Gloriana. She let Francisco go and he himself down as he got to his feet once more.

<Where'd you learn to do that?>

Gloriana smiled. <Family tradition.> She gestured over to some tree growing nearby that bore a kind of makeshift gym. <Let's hit the weights.>

From the sidelines, Rae just watched. It all looked like torture to her, but she knew that there was a method if Gloriana's madness. This was her role. Just like it had been Rae's role to coax Francisco back from wherever his mind or soul had taken him, it was Gloriana's job to get his body working again. It was funny watching Francisco struggle so much. The first time she had met him he had seemed like a superman, walking through the ruins and forests where nature and the darker things sat side by side. Now, not so much.

Francisco began to work the makeshift weights that had been set up, hefting the rocks and twines draped over tree branches, trying to force his body to feel how strong it should be. He hated feeling so drained. He wanted to feel like himself again, not this weakened version.

Gloriana wanted that too.

Time was running out.

As Francisco worked out, he tried to picture the past. He tried to remember the face of the figure that had so easily beaten him, or what he had dreamed of while he had been unconscious, but there was nothing. Just a hole in his head where his memories should be. Instead, he had to make do with taking whatever his new friends told him. He wasn't good at asking questions or conversation, and he wished Dr Sonja was here. She would make sure that she got every last piece of information.

She wasn't here though. Rae seemed mainly preoccupied with keeping her hulking reptilian companion from eating everyone's food. She checked him regularly, while Hook himself ambled about. The creature was bigger and healthier now, curious like a dog that wanted to get its nose into everything. The ragged scar in his side was healed as well, and it seemed that whatever supernatural connection that Rae and formed with Hook suited them both. She fed him with raw meat regularly, and he had become a loyal guardian. Her own person sentinel.

As for the other two, Francisco had much less idea.

All he knew about Gloriana was that she was a hard taskmistress, or perhaps it was more that Francisco hadn't needed to work out for so long he'd forgotten what it was like. She was friendly though, and she had told him that they were in the Calakmul Reserve, in one of the old parts of the rainforest that was no so devoid of visitors that it had become almost entirely wild again. Francisco liked that, but the other man, the thin grey-green skinned man in the ragged clothes didn't share his enthusiasm. He said little, and seemed to have little interest in anything. Gloriana had said his name was Tempesta, but Francisco had opted to leave him along. He understood privacy, and he respected it.

Even so, he wanted to know who or what Tempesta was. There was definitely some of the unnatural taint of the Wilderness about him.

<Twenty more reps,> said Gloriana.

Francisco felt his arms and chest strain in a way they shouldn't have. He had lifted far heavier than this in his time, so he thought of other questions to distract himself. How had he got here? From Cancún to here was a long way, and there were no cars to be seen. Nobody knew the answer. Gloriana said they had simply found him in the forest, exactly where she had been told by somebody he would be. Tempesta hadn't said anything at all.

Everybody stopped dead as they heard a growling sound, one that anyone would recognise as a warning even if they had never heard it before. Francisco lowered his rock weights as quietly as he could.

Past the tents that formed the camp, out beyond the treeline and the campfire and the mound where Hook liked to sleep, something was moving.

Gloriana put her finger to her lips and motioned for everyone to take up their positions. It was a practiced routine, and Francisco had quickly realised that wherever it was that this makeshift little settlement of tents and equipment had been set up, it was by no means secure and safe. The inhabitants of the area didn't respect boundaries of any kind.

As Hook craned his dinosaur neck and moved over to the trees with unnatural agility, Francisco and Gloriana moved to pick up their weapons. Nothing fancy, and certainly not Francisco's sword or his belt of surprises. Just a couple of rifles, a few knives, a machete. The tools of hunting and survival, that could just as easily be used to defence.

Hook sniffed at the air, and after a second a few pigs broke cover and ran. They squealed as Hook gave chase, and for a moment everyone relaxed a little.

Only for a moment, however.

A dart whistled out from somewhere, and Francisco only just managed to dodge it. Something oily and green and corrosive oozed of the tip as it buried itself in the trunk of a tree. Gloriana dove neatly out of the way and rolled back to her feet, already peering down the barrel of her rifle. The treeline stayed still, and everyone's eyes fixed on the space, trying to see what was beyond it.

There were more sounds. There was rustling and a wet gurgle, then something heavy hit the ground. Something that wasn't Francisco for a change. The second were painfully slow as everything just hung, immobile, breaths held.

Tempesta emerged. Behind him he dragged a man, bloodied and barely conscious, who wore camouflaged clothes and a mask on his face into which an ornate cross had been carved. In Tempesta's other hand was a blowpipe, which he threw onto the ground in front of Gloriana.

<Another one,> said Tempesta.

Gloriana picked up the pipe and placed her rifle on the ground. She and Tempesta had seen all of this before, too many times now. Usually it happened when they were out foraging or hunting, but now it had happened right on their doorstep, and to have the plan to lure Hook away with the pigs was a smart one. But Tempesta was like a ghost, and the would–be assassin probably hadn't even heard him coming

<Looks like we're gonna have to move on,> said Gloriana.

Rae walked over from her cover and crouched down by the dart that still spilled its poison out onto the ground.

<Well this really isn't good.>

*

In an old rundown motel on a road that didn't have a name anymore, Erik Abrantes let himself out of his sweat-stinking room. He was distinctive as he headed down the stairs to reception, with his alligator-skin cowboy boots and his big ornately carved arcane belt buckle and his jet-black cowboy hat. He didn't look like he belonged out in the Wilderness, more like in an old Western movie.

Erik gave the young receptionist a big smile from behind his neatly trimmed goatee, then handed over his money. It wasn't an expensive motel, which was the reason Erik had originally come here. There were better places, even though the big chains had long since moved away, but Erik liked to save money. And then, as time had ticked on, he had grown to like the place. He was a creature of habit. He liked familiar things.

<You got visitors,> said the receptionist.

Erik looked outside into the carpark. It was usually mostly empty, and those cars that were there were old things that looked like they were about to fall apart. Today there was something new. Something that changed the routine. There was a car he'd never seen before, covered in road dust. It had what looked like a coffin strapped to the roof by heavy steel cabling, and next to it stood three women who looked very serious indeed.

Bounty hunters? wondered Erik. Or just hunters maybe. One was definitely a cop, and one that knew the Wilderness by the look of her. What made him stop and stare was the tallest of the three, a beauty with copper skin and horns that arced out from her skull. She looked to be very capable, and somehow he doubted the switchblade in his boot would be much help. Besides, Erik always preferred to talk his way out of trouble.

<Can I help you?> he called, standing fast at the motel entrance.

<Erik Abrantes.> said the cop. It wasn't a question. She clearly already knew the answer. Erik wasn't shocked. A lot of people had his description and he wasn't particularly hard to find.

<That's me.>

Perdita nodded. <I hear you're someone who can find people.>

This wasn't what Erik had expected. There was no confrontation, no violence and swearing and threats. There were no guns, and promises that he would be tortured or buried alive or left out in the hottest parts of the desert covered in honey and ants. He stayed cautious though, as he walked over until he was a safe and neutral distance from the three women, or at least as safe was he could be now he saw the gun tucked into Perdita's jeans.

<Ok, let's talk.>

As Erik stood there, waiting for the first words to be said, the horned Amazon looked at him.

<I like your hat.>

Erik nodded his appreciation. <You're from Ciudad Volcan, right?>

Moya smiled. <It's the horns, right?>

<Kind of a giveaway.>

<Do you like them?>

<Moya, can you stop flirting for just one second.> said Dr Sonja. She had only just managed to talk her sister out of beating this Abrantes character for information, and now it seemed Moya had a weakness for the cowboy type.

This was not the time, so she decided to take over. She extended her hand to Erik, who took it, a puzzled look on his face.

<Señor Abrantes, I'm Dr Sonja Castellanos, and I'm an associate of a man named Francisco Garza…>

Erik's eyes widened a little. <Garza? El Fantoma Palido?>

<You've heard of him?>

<In my line of work, everyone's heard of him. He's kind of a legend in the Wilderness.>

<Exactly what is your line of work Señor Abrantes,> said Perdita, who had no intention of introducing herself.

<I'm guessing you must know that already. How'd someone get Garza. Rumour says he's one of the strongest out there. He's taken down a lot of bad things out there.>

<He is very strong,> said Moya. <I'm pretty strong too.>

<Be quiet Moya. Señor Abrantes, we need some way of tracking Francisco down, and we hear you're the man to help out.>

Erik did his best to take everything in as coolly as possible. Out of nowhere, these three women had told him the Gravedigger himself was missing. Things like that didn't happen every day. There could be a hundred explanations, none of which would lead anywhere but the hidden world, the world Erik had made it his business to study, to understand. The same world that Francisco walked in – a world of the monstrous.

Finally, Erik said <Ok. I'll need to know everything.>

*

An RV, old but still strong, sped along a road that the rain was starting to turn into mud. The storm overhead was gathering strength, dark clouds forming and little sparks of lighting dancing down to the ground, and with every passing moment the rain got heavier and heavier.

Gloriana drove, peering out through the windshield and hoping that nothing would suddenly appear in the road. Next to her Tempesta just watched it all go by. He smelled a little of damp, and his ragged hood and coat seemed to hold onto the moisture for longer than they should. And like always, he was quiet.

Francisco sat back, regarding his new companions. They both had the touch of the Wilderness about them, the sense that something dark and unnatural had scattered a little of itself onto their bodies and changed them somehow. Made them different. Stronger. Clearly they had also known each other for a long while as well. They seemed to read each other's thoughts, knowing what actions to take and how to take them without the need to speak at all.

Strangest of all, they somehow knew Francisco. It was if they had been looking for him rather than discovering him accidentally. Francisco himself still had no idea how he had come to be this far West, deep in the Calakmul bioreserve rainforest, and more and more he got the sense that he was meant to be here. The dreams he had had were fading, the sense of time slowly returning, and when he slept he still saw spirits of shadow and blood flickering through the air in his dreams.

Next to Francisco, Rae was trying to sleep and he wondered if she dreamed with her own mind or that of Hook's, who happily ran outside in the forest, easily keeping pace with the RV just beyond the treeline. He was fast for his size, and Francisco wondered how much bigger he would get. Was he still just a baby? Would be become the size of an old extinct dinosaur, like a juggernaut of claws and teeth and horns?

<You OK back there?> asked Gloriana, as the RV hit a solid bump and rattled everyone's bones.

Annoyed, Rae looked up. "Where did you learn to drive?"

Gloriana smiled. She didn't speak a lot of English but the way Rae spoke was always funny. She was a woman who had received an incredible gift from the Wilderness, and yet she hated being here. To Gloriana the two of them were opposite ends of some kind of spectrum – at one end was the streets, without money and with only the ability to fight, at the other end education and privilege. It was strange that this place should bring them together.

Tempesta suddenly pointed, and Gloriana nodded acknowledgement.

<Hold on. We're going off road.>

The rain was torrential as the RV pulled up near to an old clearing surrounded by gnarled trees. There were boxes in the clearing, wrapped up tight and made weatherproof, waiting for their owners to arrive.

<Ok, we're here,> said Gloriana, and she looked back over her shoulder to Francisco. <You wanna help me set up. It's is no good in the rain.>

Tempesta shuffled in his seat but said nothing, and Rae nudged Francisco in the ribs, smiling a little.

"You look like you've got a new friend there. Maybe you could share a tent."

Francisco didn't answer. He had to admit there was something attractive about Gloriana, about the mask she never took off and the strength and skill, she possessed. But always in his mind was Perdita. For him, that could never change.

"Where's your dinosaur?"

Rae cocked her head. "Oh, he's just nearby. I think he's found something to amuse himself. He always does. Plus he's not a dinosaur. And don't strain yourself with those tents by the way."

"You helping?"

"Are you crazy? Take a look at the weather out there."

Francisco gave her a look and braced himself for the storm outside.

It was strange how the air could still be warm as the water fell. There wasn't the penetrating wind of cold that Francisco had heard of in other places. Here, the storms were different. Jagged bolts of lightning continually cut through the sky overhead, and thunder rumbled on and on without end. The clouds seemed to boil as well, moving like water slightly too fast than could really be normal or natural.

Gloriana was out of the driver's seat next to Francisco, and they waded through the rain to the first box. She had told him that they kept stocked bases like this all over, hidden away except for the map in Tempesta's head. She also told him they had to move around a lot, and that had got Francisco curious. The masked man with the blowpipe had been unexpected, but surely no reason to turn tail and run. Francisco didn't like running.,

There had to be more to this.

Francisco hefted the box, enjoying the feeling of his strength gradually coming back. Out of one ear he heard a whistling sound over the rain, and watched in disbelief as a heavy axe buried itself in the container.

Francisco dropped the box and he and Gloriana crouched behind it. It was only just big enough to cover them and offered nothing against the rain that continued to pummel.

<More of them?> asked Francisco.

Gloriana nodded, and carefully peeked out around the side of the container. <They're getting smart, figuring out how we do things. This isn't good, I can't see them. >

Francisco wished he had his belt or his sword, anything that might give them an advantage from their hiding place. But there was nothing. Instead, he took his own looked into the rainforest, peering as best he could through the curtain of rain and the dense woodland.

He didn't expect to be able to see anything at all, and yet, he could.

Not clearly, more like impressions of sight rather than sight itself, but there were there. Four of them, just outlines of different sizes and strengths, gathered together in a formation. Francisco narrowed his eyes to try and focus better, but the silhouettes remained stubbornly that.

He sat back behind the box, the wonder at this new skill he had not previously possessed quickly lost to the need to plan, to deal with the immediate danger. That was just how his brain always worked.

<You get anything?> asked Gloriana.

Francisco nodded, still a little confused about how. <Four of them.>

<Shit. Sounds like a raiding party. Probably the scout we got already tipped them off.>

<Raiding party? Who are these guys.>

Gloriana didn't answer. She was a quiet as Tempesta when it came to direct questions. Instead, she started running the options over in her head. Fight strategies, escape routes, numbers and weapons. Every possible outcome.

In the end, the decision was made for them.

An arrow whistled through the air and buried itself in a tree about ten feet off the ground just behind them. They both focussed on it, and saw that it wasn't just a normal arrow, there was something attached to it.

Something burning.

In the second it took to register the arrow it detonated, and a sheet of white-hot flame burst outwards.

The raiding party advanced, four men all dressed in the same fatigues and wearing the same featureless cross-bearing masks as the scout who still lay unconscious somewhere out in the forest. Each man bore their own weapons, with the leader at the front brandishing one of his collection of axes as he advanced. Behind him, the tallest man held a seven-foot serrated harpoon, and next to him a thicker set man wore his clawknuckles, burnished iron gauntlets smothered in heavy spikes. The fourth, the Archer, kept his distance at the rear, covering their movements - movements that seemed military in their precision and execution.

Magnesium fire raged across the boxes and containers, the wet air doing nothing to dampen it. Supply cans popped and melted, and tents burned to ashes draped in thick smoke. The Axeman moved closer, scanning for bodies, but he didn't see any. He'd hoped they might have got at least one of the targets, but it didn't matter. The plan had always been to isolate the stronger fighters from the weaker ones. With that done they could take the RV without too much of a challenge.

The Axeman signalled his companions and they centred on the vehicle. The Spearman advanced ahead. His job was always to deal with the first contact, which was why he was the strongest of them all, the one who could take the most punishment and pain. He walked towards the door, and then stopped. Something was off. Something that wasn't in the plan, something that hadn't been accounted for. At first it was just a feeling in the back of his head and then it grew into a whisper, and finally a voice that sang songs of fear to him. Harpoon tried to push them away so that he wouldn't embarrass himself in front of the others.

But the feeling wouldn't leave him, and as Harpoon looked to one side he saw something that surely could not have been there. A shape, an apparition. It was so pale and translucent it was almost like glass in the rain, and as he looked it seemed to resolve into the form of a woman. Not a normal woman though, instead an alien figure covered in feathers like a bird. The sight captivated Harpoon, mesmerising him so that he didn't even feel the hammering downpour anymore.

A few steps behind, the Axeman was suddenly concerned. His most trusted lieutenant usually didn't hesitate like this. He was always merciless, and yet now he was just staring into empty space, not moving, not stabbing, not wiping out the abominations, not doing any of the things that he was supposed to be doing. This wasn't right.

He looked behind him and things unravelled even more. Clawknuckle lay there, unconscious, and the Archer was nowhere to be seen. In the passing of a second the strength of the squad was completely gone, and its leader was left with nothing but his fear – his fear of the things that lived out in the forest, and what would happen if he failed to destroy them. His gut told him to run but The Axeman forced his body to action, ignoring the paralysed Harpoon and turning back to face the RV. His plan was simple, just like always – hack away at the filth inside that truck until it was all dead. Let the others face punishment for their weakness.

Instead, Francisco towered over him, waiting there in the pouring rain.

A single blow threw the Axeman twenty feet back, smashing him into a tree and cracking bone even through his body armour. Francisco advanced, leaving Harpoon as he still gazed at the beautiful ghost that transfixed him. Then she was suddenly gone, and in her place Gloriana was on him.

Harpoon stabbed out with the spear but she had already slipped out of the way, hitting him hard twice in the body where the plates of his body armour separated. She shin-kicked him in the back of the knee to drop him, and then wrapped the spear back around him, hauling it back to choke him unconscious.

The Axeman felt himself spit blood inside his mask, but he refused to let that stop him. Years of training, of conditioning told him that. His purpose, his reason to be fired him with strength and he stood, lashing out with his axe towards Francisco. There was no way on God's Earth, thought the Axeman, that this thing, this monstrosity, was going to beat him, however strong it thought it was.

Francisco dodged and The Axeman lashed out again and again, his actions half planned and half instinct. Part of the main blade caught Francisco's arm and he cursed as he bled. Still too weak and too slow, and the Axeman seized upon his opportunity. He leapt forward, and hammered down with the axe as hard as she could.

It buried itself in something, but not what he had expected.

Tempesta stood there. He had appeared seemingly out of nowhere, out of the shadows of the trees, out of the pounding rain and thunder and the axe was stuck into his chest. The Axeman and Francisco stared at him, expecting blood to gush forth, and the slight figure in the ragged clothes to pitch forward and die. Both were astounded when that didn't happen.

Instead, Tempesta just looked at the blade, and then at Francisco.

<All yours man.>

Francisco nodded, choosing not to wonder just what Tempesta truly was at this particular moment. Instead he turned his attention back to the incredulous Axeman, as Tempesta gave him the finger.

Rage brought out more violence, and the Axeman hammered out with his fists. Like so many before him, the blows were wasted on Francisco, and he just took them, feeling almost nothing as the Axeman pummelled uselessly.

<You fucking monster,> spat the Axeman, and Francisco just backhanded him away, leaving him agonised and broken on the half-liquid ground. Gloriana came up beside him, the Spear in her hand and it's owner unconscious and propped up next to the RV.

<Did you get the other one?>

Out in the forest The Archer ran, just like he had been told to. It wasn't cowardice, it was just orders. As he'd watched Clawknuckle be despatched so easily, one set of orders easily superceded the other. It was the Axeman and

Harpoon's job to engage. When things went wrong, as they had so very badly, The Archer's job was to get away and report back. Whatever the Axeman thought became irrelevant. Only the overall plan was important. Clearly they had underestimated this new variable, this hulking man with the chalk white skin. They had assumed he was just another creature that had staggered out of the Wilderness, primordial and thoughtless and easily subdued, but they had been wrong.

This Pale Ghost was something else entirely, and that new information had to be transmitted to base as quickly as possible so that plans could be reformulated, contingencies put in motion.

It wasn't far to the car, the one that had been reshaped and modified until it was more like a tank covered with blades. Once he was there, he was safe. If only signals worked in this place, he could radio ahead. But they didn't. Scouts reported it was the same all across the peninsula – the whole of the Yucatán had rejected electrical signals of any kind, so nothing worked. Like everyone else, the army to which The Archer belonged had adjusted, but it was annoying.

A hundred yards now, through the rain that fell so hard it was starting to hurt. Just a hundred yards, and then he could relax.

That thought had only just formed in his head when the jungle came to life. It wasn't explosion, violent and terrible, through the trees and water and mud, and before the Archer could even register it properly the savage power of Hook had him. He saw it, rearing up, clutching a bloodied iron hook in one claw and opening its jaws wide, and suddenly a hundred yards was forgotten.

He tried to loose an arrow but it was pointless. The beast called Hook lunged forward and hacked through one of his legs with his thick iron weapon. It was so sudden, so fast, that it felt numb as blood fountained form the wound. The Archer collapsed and Hook bit down hard, burying serrated teeth through armour and flesh alike. He raised up his prey, shaking The Archer and making him scream out, all his training and strength forgotten.

The scream carried through the trees, and Francisco and Gloriana heard it as if it was ten feet away. It was a terrible sound, followed by the primal roar of a predator.

<That sounded bad,> said Gloriana. <Glad he's on our side.>

Sitting in the RV, Rae shook bodily as she felt Hook tear his prey apart, and tasted warmth in her mouth. She could never admit to anyone, but as time went on there was tiny part of her that was starting to like those feelings.

Francisco surveyed what remained of the raiding party. Three left alive, two of them unconscious, one broken and barely functioning anymore. All of them bearing their own particular ways of dealing death, yet none of it enough. Armour, masks, tactics. It didn't matter. They were just men. Dangerous men, trained men certainly, but just men. Against the powers of the Wilderness, the powers that showed in Francisco's strength and in the axe that stuck absurdly out of Tempesta's chest, men just weren't enough.

<You need help with that?> asked Francisco.

Tempesta seemed to have forgotten the axe was even there, and he just nodded. <Its stuck good.>

As Francisco grabbed hold of the axe handle and Tempesta braced himself against the RV, Gloriana crouched down next to the Spearmen. She had jabbed his weapon point first into the mud now it had done its work, and was keen to try and get him at least partly awake again. Clawknuckle was out for the count, the Axeman was a mess, so the Spearman was the only real hope for information. She needed to know how they were tracking them, where they were, how many. She needed a plan now that their safety had been compromised.

Tempesta grunted as the axe came free, leaving a bloodless ragged hole in his body that would close up over time. It didn't even hurt that much as it came free – the continuous rain bothered him more.

Francisco tossed the axe aside. <So who are these guys?>

Tempesta looked around and caught Gloriana's eye. She nodded as she tried to slap some life back into Harpoon.

<Puritanos,> said Tempesta. <They been hunting us forever.>

<Why?>

Tempesta adjusted his clothes to cover the dry wound and made a cross sign across his dry scaley face. <God's work, man. So they say.>

<That isn't the God I know.>

<Hey, what can I tell you. They're all fucked up.>

Gloriana straightened up and left the Spearmen where he was. She had done far too good a job of putting him to sleep, and she didn't have the patience to wait for him to wake and start talking. If he did. Puritanos rarely spoke.

<They're killers who hide behind the cross. It's sick. And if they know about our safe places then we have to figure out where their base is.>

Francisco took a moment, and then said <I can help.>

*

Sun rose over the motel and Moya got dressed. In bed, Erik was still asleep, his cowboy hat perched on the back of the door and his slicked back thinning hair all out of place. Moya had enjoyed messing it up, just like she had enjoyed all of last night. Erik seemed much more like her home, back in Ciudad Volcan, where sex was never a big deal and nobody hid anything. It was a simple thing – if you liked someone, you enjoyed being with them. The rules were different out here though. Moya had never really understood why people made such a big deal out of it.

Especially men. They always seemed to get weird about sex.

Erik didn't stir. He just snored quietly, happy dreaming about something, so Moya put on her boots and left him there, blowing him a kiss as she opened the door. Maybe their paths would cross again and maybe not. Either way they had both had their fun.

As she clicked the door shut, Dr Sonja was waiting for her, leaning against the railing that ran along the second-floor walkway to the stairs.

<Enjoy yourself.>

Moya smiled. <Definitely. You should try it.>

<I'll pass, if that's OK.>

Moya peered at Dr Sonja, trying to read her expression. It was difficult because Dr Sonja prided herself on being impassive and emotionless.

<Are you angry with me?>

<Me, no. You can sleep with whoever you want. Just maybe a little quieter next time.>

Moya giggled. <Yeah, I think I might have broken him a bit.>

Dr Sonja rolled her eyes. <OK, we get it. You're an Amazon. Let's move on. We have a whole lot of driving to do.>

The two women headed down to the carpark where the familiar car waited. Moya still wasn't used to the coffin that was lashed to it. Off all the thing she had encountered since she had met Francisco, that was the one thing that made her uneasy. She wasn't really sure why.

182

As they approached, Perdita looked up from checking the engine. She had been up for hours, and lack of sleep was starting to take a toll in the dark lines around her eyes. She was living largely on coffee and adrenaline, and had no time for Moya and her one-night stands.

<If you're done being a whore, we need to get on the road.>

Two hours' drive put Perdita, Dr Sonja and Moya at the exact spot Erik had told them about. There was the crumbling pale mound of rocks he had said would be there, the old broken longhorn skull and the single tree that sprouted blood red flowers, even in the wilting heat.

The sun was fully up now, the sky primary blue, and although Moya relished the feeling of being outside in the warmth she had the sense she had worn out her welcome a little with the sisters. It was clear she had been brought along as muscle, and now they hadn't needed that she decided she would just wait and see what happened. She wanted to find Francisco too, but Perdita was far too tense and wound tight for her liking. She also had far too many guns than was healthy and Moya had no desire to get on her bad side.

How Francisco dealt with all of that Perdita stress Moya had no idea. Maybe it was a cop thing. Surely he would be much happier, Moya had thought more than once, with a good strong Los Cuernos girl.

Shrugging to herself, the horned woman lounged back against the car and watched the sisters get on with their task.

Perdita and Dr Sonja headed over to the mound. Perdita carried a bag over her shoulder, and she said nothing as she led her sister over, going about the instructions Erik had given them with methodically efficiency. First, unpack the mechanism. Three parts, made of brass and looking like the gears and springs of something old and clockwork. Then, click them together and insert the last element, the personal element. Perdita carried a lock of Francisco's hair in a locket that she hid underneath her top, and even Dr Sonja had been surprised to see it. She said nothing though – her sister liked her secrets, and to be so open about something so personal was unpleasant for her.

The locket slipped nearly into the mechanism, and Perdita placed the whole thing almost reverentially on top of the mound. There was no waiting. Instead the sun instantly triggered the function of whatever the brass mechanism was. Parts moved of their own accord clicking and grinding until they found their proper configuration. The sun lit the whole thing up until little rays flooded out in all directions like a tiny metal star.

Time for the final piece of this particular puzzle.

Perdita reached out to touch the mechanism, which heated up as it blazed, brass becoming infused with a hot white glow.

<You sure about this? We don't...>

<I have to,> said Perdita quietly, and she held her breath as she grabbed the stones with both hands, one each side of the device, just like Erik had said.

The glow of it consumed her.

*

Francisco clambered onto the roof of the RV as Gloriana finished tying up the three Puritanos. None of them had any real sense about them yet, and the Axemen looked like he might never quite be the man he was again. Had Francisco meant to hit him that hard, she wondered? Was it an accident, or was there something else there. Something inside the man that was not as gentle as the man himself.

The rain had eased off even though the thunder and lightning show continued, rolling off into the distance. The song of the animals was everywhere again, dominated by monkeys that seemed to have developed a curiosity about these newcomers into their part of the forest. They hung from trees all around, calling and howling to each other. In another life Rae would have observed them, taken notes, recorded everything. But now she saw through different eyes, and she could feel that Hook, who was happy laying down behind the RV with his jaws still stained with the Archer's blood, wanted to eat a few of them. It made her hungry too. Disturbingly so.

Tempesta had returned to the dryness of his seat inside the RV, and as he watched through the water-smeared windshield he prodded at the wound in his chest, that even after this short time was starting to close up. His new nature had taken time to adjust to, like anything radical, but now he preferred it to how he had been before, all soft and fleshy and easily damaged.

What was it that writer had said? Sometimes dead is better.

Gloriana looked up as Francisco settled down cross legged on the roof, adjusting his body until he just in the right position.

<So how does this work?> she asked.

<I kind of talk to them. In my head. Sometimes they tell me the way to things.>

<I got to say, sounds kind of weird to me. Sure you're not still just a little out of it? I mean, you were lying out there for a long time.>

Francisco nodded. <I've done this before. Just depends if they're listening.>

<Sure OK. I mean, we don't have anything to lose right? And if they have any great ideas about what we're supposed to do, please be sure to let me know.>

<I will,> assured Francisco.

Spirits. Gloriana thought, shaking her head. *Now we're talking to spirits.*

Above her, on the roof, Francisco started to breath in and out, slowly and steadily, and something ghostly and untouchable inside him began to reach out.

Everything was different this time.

There were no gentle whispers or dancers in the sky. Instead, Francisco felt like he was stepping outside of himself. It was a wrenching feeling that made him feel disorientated and drunk, as though he was falling and rolling inside his own body. The rain and the forest all around him began to shift and change, the water glittering as though it had been caught be some unseen light, and the trees and their leaves become brighter, lusher.

There was a sense of paranoia as well, of being watched by something.

It seemed to last forever as the rain suddenly began to reverse itself, falling upwards into the sky as the clouds opened to accept it back. Francisco tried to look around but his body felt like lead, and as he tried to shift his head his mind seemed to hang behind. If he had been standing he would have collapsed, and it was all he could do anyway to stop from falling off the RV. Nothing was solid or real, and he felt that queasy sense of being apart from himself, of being disassociated from life as though he was watching someone else through a lens or a window.

The sensations held him fast. There was no simple getting up and walking way this time. Something had changed, a commitment had been made, and now Francisco was drawn into it, unsure what was happening and uncertain where it was taking.

As he watched with sight that was half his own and half his imagination, he watched the raindrops clump together into larger and larger spheres, hanging in the air like balloons. Around them the storm continued to reverse itself but not in time, just in movement. Overhead, lightning sparked and flashed in every direction but it was silent now, mute and blinding flashes that lit up everything. Francisco saw bizarre shadows creeping in between the trees, shapes and forms that he didn't recognise - an army of something shadowy that was slowly emerging from the rainforest, released by the storm and given life by the flashes of natural electricity.

What door had he opened, Francisco wondered. *Why was everything so different? What was happening?*

In front of his eyes, a water globe hung there, and within it Francisco saw something very familiar indeed. The Dead Face, eerie and impassive, just like he had seen before. At the beach. At the mansion where he had found Moya. The same visage that always seemed to want to warn him of something, but he never knew what.

Slowly, straining against his own muscles, Francisco reached out for the globe and the face, and the second he touched its surface it began to transform into something else.

The water burst apart into a flower, and then into a thousand fragments of liquid diamond. It moved so slowly, unconcerned with the realities of the world around it which to Francisco almost didn't seem to exist anymore. There was just this dizzying vision now, this timeless weightless place that held him fast. As he watched, the fragment dissolved into smoke, and began to swirl, each one spawning a little army of air dancers that darted and whirled through the air. They were like the minuscule offspring of ones he had seen before, and rather than vague shapes in the air these were almost solid. They swam in the atmosphere around his body and Francisco could almost feel them on his skin, the smallest of impressions, like the rain itself that still gleamed so brightly.

The dancers became a whirlwind, and they started to draw together, losing their individuality until they were all one single whirling spiral. Then that too began to transform, reshaping itself like clay into limbs, a body, even hair. In front of Francisco, in the magnificence of his vision, a woman took shape, a woman who bore the head of an eagle that obscured most of her face and a body of feathers that spread out like huge phantom wings.

Francisco recognised her. Not just how she looked but how she felt. He knew this woman somehow, this spectre that was the most beautiful thing he had ever seen in his life. She was radiant in the glimmering raindrops, and a gentle smile grew across her mouth as she reached out.

<Diosa,> he whispered, in awe, and he held his breath as her hand, cool like stone, touched his face.

Instantly his mind was flying through the rainforest, faster than could ever be possible. He hurtled past trees and through thickets, passing every obstacle as something pulled him to what he was looking for. He saw animals and plants unknown to everyone, and felt the elements course through his spirit. It was exhilarating, as though he was a part of every part of nature, guided by it, powered by it.

Up ahead, he saw something. A compound of sorts, not big but heavily fortified. There were guards and dogs and barbed wire, and inside it he could see something glowing, a small twisted luminous shape alone in one of the small buildings. And there was something else as well. Something larger, more dangerous. Something that wanted nothing else but to kill.

Francisco gasped out loud and it was all over.

He sat there in the rain, soaked through on top of the RV, as though the whole vision had never even happened at all. It was only when Gloriana called up to him that he finally, fully, snapped back into reality and the last remnants of unreality faded away.

<I think I know where they are,> he said, quietly.

*

Dr Sonja drove as fast as she could, ignoring what road signs there were. Unlike Perdita who always followed the law, Dr Sonja had no issue with bending it, especially now when the police that remained had so many dangerous things to contend with, both human and otherwise.

Perdita herself was asleep on the back seat, half covered by Francisco's poncho. Dr Sonja was concerned. After the mechanism had drenched them all with its light, Perdita had seemed almost in a trance as she recited things to her sister, directions mostly. Then she gone to sleep, and that had been that. She needed rest, Dr Sonja realised, but it had been hours now and Perdita never slept for hours.

Moya sat comfortably in the passenger seat, glad to be able to stretch out her legs. There was no radio anymore, and so the two women had started to talk as Moya had worked out the route from Perdita's half-garbled, hypnotized instructions, and without Perdita's razor-sharp intention cutting through everything, they had started to learn about each other. As the time passed, Dr Sonja had become gradually more fascinated by the horned woman.

<So your home is half human beings and half Los Cuernos?>

Moya nodded. <Its all pretty relaxed and balanced out.>

<So you don't have issues getting on or anything.>

<Not really. We're all just part of the Volcano. We always find it weird that all you guys don't get on. >

<Believe me, so do I. Ciudad Volcan sounds like a paradise.>

189

<Well, I guess so. I got kind of bored so I went exploring. Some of us do that. My brother likes to stay home though.>

<You have a brother >>

<Yeah, a baby brother. He's like a tank now, and he has kind of big ram horns. He horned when he was just a baby which was kind of funny.>

<Is that unusual?>

<Yeah, it really is. Usually the horns come last, after the Marks.>

<Huh, I thought they were tattoos.>

On the back seat, Perdita suddenly stirred. She sat up and opened her eyes, still with that dreamlike blank quality to them that made her look as though she was under some kind of supernatural influence. That made Dr Sonja worry even more.

<We have to hurry,> Perdita said quietly. <Something's happening.>

*

In the harsh daylight, with the sky cleared and the storm passed, the compound Francisco had seen in his vision was an ominous sight. Not big - just a bare bones outpost of sorts, one of many perhaps, but what it threatened was much more. The guards, the dogs, the wire was all still there, but in seeing it for real the place was like castle, brutal and menacing as it sat there in a part of the forest that had been razed to the ground, leaving nothing surviving near its perimeter.

Gloriana had parked the RV a mile or so back, leaving Rae and Hook to act as a rearguard and a backup, while Tempesta had found a place to look out and keep watch. Once again, it was Francisco and Gloriana who moved together on the mission, slipping through the undergrowth as they did their best to get the measure of the place. They worked together better now they were more familiar with each other. It was a good team, and even Tempesta approved.

The two of them crouched down behind a barrier of fallen trees.

<T. says he sees about 12 or 15 of them.> whispered Gloriana.

<Any guns?>

<They never use guns. Only old-style weapons. They think its makes them closer to God, or whatever twisted version of God they have. So are you going to tell me how you found this place?>

<Not sure. It was different this time. Intense.>

<Spirits were talkative, huh?>

Francisco shifted uncomfortably. <Don't know what it was. It was….just…>

<Well, I'm not arguing. You found it.> She shifted a little. <You up for a fight, because those muscles of yours are going to be useful?>

<I feel stronger,> said Francisco. <Stronger than before.>

<And that's good, yes?>

<Guess so. So what's the plan.>

Gloriana sat on the wet ground with her back to the dead trunk. <I'll be straight with you Francisco. This is a rescue mission now. I really didn't think we'd ever get this chance, but we used to have someone else with us, and we think she's in there. Can't leave her.>

Francisco wasn't surprised. He had had a feeling something else was going on. Two people as unusual as Gloriana and Tempesta weren't just waiting around waiting for something to happen. There was always a reason, a purpose to things. And now he knew what that purpose was, it was time to act.

The two guards at the main gate focussed everything out in the jungle beyond the compound perimeter. It was their only task, and to fail in it would mean punishments of the worst kind. So there was no talking, no joking. There was just the two men in body armour and fatigues, their faces rendered anonymous by identical masks that bore the same cross as every other member of Los Puritanos, one carrying a heavy spiked mace and the other what looked like a vicious curved scimitar. Scimitar Man had made his weapon himself, and he loved it more than he had loved any woman. He dreamed of using it on the monstrous things that crawled in amongst the Wilderness, and sometimes those dreams went too far, although he didn't admit it even to himself. Those sorts of feelings were utterly forbidden.

Obsessed as he was, Scimitar Man missed something that his companion Mace caught straight away. Movement on the treeline. Once it might have been an animal but they had killed and skinned to many there probably weren't that many left and those that were, were too sensibly frightened to approach anymore. Mace pointed and Scimitar Man nodded. No words were required. Only the seniors got to speak. Guard's jobs were simply about action and violence, and it suddenly seemed like their weapons could taste blood today.

That excited Scimitar Man as the two of them moved forward, and both of them looked forward to teaching any interlopers a lesson. None of the Seniors cared if trespassers were alive or dead if it wasn't a capture mission.

A crunching creaking noise froze them both in their tracks, and they looked in shared disbelief as a tree came crashed down towards them, its trunk broken like snapped bones. Mace tried to leap aside but he was sluggish. He tripped, and even as he tried to roll out of danger the tree smashed down into his legs, destroying them. The agony was absolute, washing through his blood even as his blood washed out, but he would not scream, he would never scream, even as he saw the white skinned giant of a man emerge out of the rainforest in the moment before he passed out

Scimitar Man was paralyzed, unable to decide what to do. He couldn't rescue Mace and he couldn't fight this giant alone, and so his mind screamed at him to run, to raise the alarm. But something held him to the spot, freezing him in place, incapable of acting.

It wouldn't have made any real difference. Gloriana was on him, grabbing and twisting his arm and taking his beloved weapon from him before she expertly flipped him over her shoulder, driving him hard into the ground. He tried to fight back but he really didn't know how, and so Gloriana just turned him over and rabbit punched him in the back of his skull. He joined his comrade in unconsciousness.

The real fight had begun.

More of the Puritanos began to swarm, grabbing their preferred weapons and assembling as they had been taught. The treefall they had all heard couldn't have been natural, and so the One Law Above All was all anyone could think about.

Stop the intruders, at any cost.

Francisco and Gloriana were waiting. The gate was small so they could bottleneck the rush of bodies, and there was space to work even with the fallen tree and the two men already beaten.

<Why didn't we take their uniforms?> asked Francisco.

<Are you joking? Do you know how big you are? Nobody is that big. Plus, they don't have women here.>

The first three Puritanos came roaring out, all wielding their blend of blades and wood. A disc flew out, one that was ringed with razor blades, and Francisco dodged it and let it embed itself in the tree. Then he stampeded forward and smashed two of the attackers aside, feeling bones break against his body. They flew back and one cannoned into the fence, screaming out as the electricity neither Francisco or Gloriana knew had been there ripped through his body.

A machete hacked down and Gloriana redirected it back, cutting open armour and then kneeing hard before she rolled down, taking the man with her. She had the time for finesse and for finishing moves. Francisco was a juggernaut, a human barrier who the Puritanos seemed to just bounce off of, and so he attracted the majority of the attackers. They prioritised him just as their tactics told them they should, and for Gloriana that was a gift.

She picked another one off, buckling his knee down and smashing her elbow into the side of his head. Then another, this time kicking him in the gut hard and then spinning to sweep out his legs. The second man wasn't finished, and so Gloriana kneed though his face as he struggled to get up. His jawbone broke sideways half the width of his face and he was down as well.

Francisco lifted a man of his feet and threw him down, while another tried to tackle him but failed, feeling like he had thrown himself into the legs of an elephant. He looked up, almost pitifully, regretting his arrogance at refusing a weapon, as Francisco reached down for him.

One Puritan had somehow got behind the two of them and wrestled to release the razor disc form where it was stuck in the tree. He tried to ignore the ruin of his colleague, and when the disc wouldn't budge he hefted the too-heavy mace and turned to face the enemy.

The giant man and this masked woman had to die.

The Puritan swung his new weapon, but he wasn't used to it and the weight unbalanced him. He collapsed sideways, while Francisco and Gloriana just watched, bemused.

<Fucking demon scum,> spat the man, as he struggled to wield the mace. <Fucking ungoldly filth.>

<Are you new?> asked Gloriana, before she punched him out.

He joined the other broken and unconscious Puritans that lay by the compound entrance. Nine in all, all different shapes, yet all the same, their identities stripped away behind the clothes and their masks. Their weapons hadn't helped them, but perhaps they had simply been the cannon fodder. The pawns sent out to test the attack. Dispensable.

<How do you keep that mask on?> asked Francisco.

Gloriana gave him a smile. <Magic.>

Already the sounds of more men were audible, and Francisco and Gloriana braced themselves. This would be tougher now. The element of surprise was gone, and so these new attackers would be more prepared. More dangerous.

New Puritans rushed out, in a formation that allowed to them manoeuvre out of the gate and surround the intruders. Spite and vicious anger bled off these men into the air itself, and it was clear these were more experienced combatants. The way they held themselves and their various weapons, the way the seemed to move together as a unit. They had on single shared goal.

Three rushed Francisco and got a purchase on his, two of them trying to subdue his arms while the other stabbed at him with a forked blade. Francisco twisted but it caught him and he bled. Gloriana moved to help, but another Puritan blocked her way. He lashed out at her with hooks that replaced his hands, forcing her to bend her body out of the way almost to the point of losing her balance. As her hand touched the ground another man made to hack it with his blade but she was just that little bit quicker. A kick lashed out and hit the first man hard in the throat, and she managed to spring and scissor the second man around the neck as the first staggered and choked, desperate for air.

Francisco kicked out far too hard and the man with the fork hurtled backwards, his body smashed and his organs half-pulped. Gloriana saw another man moving to take his place, and she sprinted forward even as Francisco lifted the two man who had been trying to pin him clear off their feet. He smashed their together as she tackled the replacement, rolling for second to get a position where she could knock him out.

But they had missed one.

<Ungodly> hissed the Puritan. He had the razor disc in one hand and the dropped scimitar in the other, and he was clearly half mad with rage. He had watched his friends beaten down one by one and left as nothing more than human flotsam. Alive, but they might as well not be. There would be no coming back from this kind of defeated disgrace.

Her hurled the disc and it whirled past Francisco, and then brandished the scimitar. Too late Gloriana realised their mistake, and she called out to Francisco. He turned, and the disc cut into his arm. It had been designed to curve back in the air like a boomerang, and it was a stupid thing to miss. The cut was deep and Francisco felt it, the wound stinging as blood seeped out to stain his clothes.

Gloriana moved forward to intercept the Puritan, but he was much faster and much more agile than she had expected. She was getting tired too, with the exertion of the fight taking its tool. He cut forward expertly and caught her clothes, then again spiking at her leg and barely missing. She kicked out, missing as the man dodged her, and then went to try and take him down. The two of them collapsed and rolled onto the ground, and Gloriana managed to take away the scimitar just as Francisco's hand grabbed the Puritan by the neck and lifted him off the ground.

That was when Gloriana saw something had changed.

On Francisco's arms there were marks. Not smears or blood or dirt, but angular designs like ancient glyphs, forming in raised bruised black out of his chalk flesh. He saw them too, and he threw the Puritan aside as these new marks confused him.

Another change?> What was happening? What had happened to him since the hotel?

<Francisco, are you OK?> she called.

Francisco didn't answer. The pain of his wound was forgotten as he just stared at his arm in disbelief, unable to quite comprehend these new manifestations on his skin. He wiped at them but they were part of him.

The Puritan he had cast aside took advantage, and lunge forward once more, intend on using a dagger in his boot and plunging it deep into Francisco's heart. He would have succeeded as well, if the razor disc hadn't buried itself in the side of his skull and killed him stone dead. The body dropped sideways, and Gloriana felt a wash of relief as Tempesta stood in the clearing with them.

She felt like congratulating and chiding him all at once. She hated killing, but knew that it was a necessary evil of the world they had not truly chosen to inhabit. Instead, she saw a look on Tempesta's face that could almost have been wide eyed shock, and she looked back to the gate.

A true monster stood there.

It was bigger than Francisco, much bigger, a bulked mass of twisted flesh wrapped in gauze and bandages and armour. Its hands and feet were more like talons, raw down to the bone, but far worse than all of that was its head. There was no face, no eyes, no features of any kind. Instead there was just a skull buried under a metal structure like some burnished mantrap that made the monstrosity look though its entire face was nothing but one huge set of iron jaws.

Its name was Jawhead and it was the true weapon of the Puritan way. A thing, designed to fight fire with fire, and in its shape was realised all the lies and hypocrisy of the warped version of scripture that Los Puritanos had chosen to create for themselves. No God had made this thing, and it was their dirtiest most terrible secret, their own monster from the Wilderness redirected to their will.

One by one, Tempesta, Gloriana and Francisco looked at the monster. None of them could tell if it was looking back as it stood there, a Hellborn juggernaut, its chest expanding harshly in and out, in and out, each breath a grating wheeze dragged out through its metal trapjaw face.

It took a step forward, and Francisco realised what he had to do. It was bigger and stronger no doubt but he had no choice. Tempesta might survive its attack and knit himself back together in time, but Gloriana surely would not, however powerful and skilled she was. This abomination was the author of a thousand deaths already, bodies nothing but the softest tissue under its crushing hands.

<Run away,> shouted Tempesta, looking at Gloriana. <Why isn't he running away.>

Gloriana didn't know, but she couldn't look away as Francisco straightened up, facing Jawhead as it bore down on him. Faster than could ever be possible for something that size it was on him, and its claws smashed down.

Somehow, Francisco stopped them.

He met their force with his own, feeling the strain as Jawhead pushed down harder and harder. Francisco forced back, and he felt strength in his body, raging in his blood and in his bones. As he held back the assault, the black marks on his body spread everywhere, transforming his skin into an intricate tribal pattern. And then his face changed too. The marks formed around his eyes and his mouth and his jaw, forming a new face on top of his own. In a second,

Francisco's face bore the image of a skull as though it has been painted onto him by the brush of a demonic artist.

Raw power flooded through him, and Francisco roared out his defiance.

*

Perdita's head snapped up as the roar echoed through the jungle. Even through the jungle,

she would have recognised Francisco's voice anywhere, and she was off and running, loading her gun as she went.

<PERDI>. shouted Dr Sonja, but Perdita wasn't listening. There was so close now, the car not a hundred meters away from the compound, and now the power that Erik Abrantes had given her to find Francisco had led them all here nothing was going to stop her reaching him. Instead, she looked to Moya.

<Can you make sure….?>

Moya nodded. <Just let me get something out of the car.>

Perdita ran like a woman possessed. The mechanism that Erik had exposed her to had planted pictures in her mind - images and words and directions that had completely taken over her consciousness, forcing everything else out until she was a slave to them. Now, their work done, her thoughts were her own again, and she was free to do what she was meant to do.

To stop the bad guys, and protect Francisco.

Up ahead the compound loomed. She could see the tree that had crashed down towards the gates, and the first of the unconscious Puritans who lay there. Desperately she scanned them, looking for tell tales signs but they were all the same, all in the same fatigues. She ran faster, and hurtled out of treeline into the perimeter. Her weapon was ready, but there was nobody to aim it at. There were no howling attackers and madmen wielding machetes. No deformed psychopaths or distorted man-monsters who ate the flesh of children. Just men, beaten men, their faith gone.

Then she saw much bigger shapes, and ran over. She saw a huge hulking thing that lay on the ground next. A giant monster with a mantrap for a head. It was Jawhead, lifeless - its neck broken at a grotesque angle. And next to it lay Francisco, slumped and unconscious on the ground in amongst the Puritans to whom he had laid waste, covered in mud and blood.

She skidded to a haul a knelt down beside him, turning his head to face her as she looked to comfort him and bring him back to her.

Instead, all she could do was stare in wonder.

Francisco's face had changed again. The skull was gone, but more than that the white chalkiness of his skin that she had become so used to had gone to, faded away and leaving behind Francisco's natural dark color all over, everywhere.

The Pale Ghost was gone.

It took a moment before Francisco's eyes opened, and another before he fully focussed on Perdita. Then he smiled a warm loving smile.

<Hey.>

<Hey yourself. Got yourself in another mess?>

Francisco strained to look around, but it was clear he was in pain. His strength was used up, and he felt weak like he had when he had first woken up in the rainforest. The sun felt warm on his skin as well. He hadn't felt that in so long, and it felt good.

<What happened?>

Perdita just smiled down at him, just happy to see him alive. <Well, kind of looks like there have been some changes.>

Francisco held up his hand, his brow creasing as he saw his hand. His hand that wasn't chalk white anymore. <Woah.>

<Guess I should ask you what's happened?>

Francisco relaxed a little onto Perdita's lap. <Bad guys.>

<Yeah, always bad guys.>

Moya exploded out of the trees into the compound, and in her hand was Francisco's claw whip, the one he had almost forgotten he owned, the one he had never quite mastered since he had found it all that time ago in a cave in the wilderness.

<Wow, you went all human.> she said, realising that there was nothing to fight. <I…um, got your whip.>

Francisco raised a hand. <Keep it. I never really got that thing.>

<Really? Cool. Thankyou so much.> Moya grinned widely, and started to unwind it experimentally, as though she were a child with a new toy. The claw fascinated her, and she poked at it, laughing when it clutched at her slightly. <Magic whip. This is the best.>

<You're not going to give her the sword are you?> asked Perdita.

<No way.>

Perdita looked up as two figures emerged out of the compound.

Gloriana led Tempesta out into the perimeter, holding a small bundle in her hands as tears filled up her eyes.

<I think we were too late,> she said, quietly.

In her arms Gloriana held something that looked for all the world like a baby, wrapped delicately on dirty cloth and silent except for quiet hoarse breathing, in and out, painful and forced. From where he lay, Francisco wondered if this tiny bundle had been what this was all about – from the broken and beaten and bloody men that Moya was gradually hauling into a kind of pile of human beings, to the dead hulking Jawhead that he himself had somehow overpowered.

Francisco still didn't quite understand how he had done that. Jawhead had been a monstrosity, a juggernaut whose strength should have overwhelmed him. And yet he had prevailed. Then again a lot of things had happened that he didn't understand. Perhaps it was better to simply take things as they came, and lie there under Perdita's protection with his now-normal skin as energy slowly came back to worn out muscles.

For her part, Perdita eyed Gloriana and her masked face with suspicion.

<Who are you?> she growled.

<Its OK. They're friends.> said Francisco, and Perdita narrowed her eyes in a way that screamed that she wasn't convinced.

<Friends. Sure.>

Gloriana ignored her, and brought the bundle over, crouching down next to Francisco as though she were carrying the most precious thing in the world. And to her, perhaps she was.

<She hasn't got long,> said Gloriana, her voice filled with a deep sadness. <She wants to say something to you.>

Francisco hauled himself onto his elbows, and with Perdita's help managed to get himself up to something like a seated position. He still had no strength, as though the marks that had formed upon him had used everything up and left nothing to spare, so all he could do was look down onto the little being that lay in the rags.

It was a child, and yet not a child. Its body was shrivelled, almost embryonic, while its face held age and wisdom in eyes that could have belonged to some ancient shaman. Those eyes latched onto Francisco's gaze, and slowly the little being smiled like a newborn. Francisco couldn't help but smile back, and as a tiny hand reached out, he extended his own, letting a baby's fingers grasp at his palm.

<This is Zerafina,> said Gloriana. <The Puritanos took everything from her. But she still has the sight.>

Francisco was confused. What did she mean, the sight?

<I don't understand,> said Francisco.

Zerafina nodded almost imperceptibly, and offered out her free hand for everyone to see. In her tiny palm was a little caterpillar, fat and lurid green, that sat there, quiet and tranquil. Francisco and even Perdita started to feel that same sense of complete calm, as though nothing in the world was important – it washed out of Zerafina in waves, like a dam bursting. Los Puritanos had been denied this, this thing they had been searching for, something in amongst the devils and the spirits of the Wilderness. This precious gift that they had taken for themselves, and which they had been unable to open

As they all watched, captivated, Zerafina closed her hand, just for a second, and then opened it again.

Sitting there now, resplendent in jewelled reds and blues, was a butterfly. It was beautiful, perfect in a very way, as it opened its huge wings that bore patterns in gold and purple that looked like eyes. For a moment it seemed to regard Francisco, its faceted eyes meeting his gaze, and then it flew off into the sky and was gone.

Francisco followed it for a moment, feeling something deep inside him that connected him to it, yet completely unable to see it, to grasp hold of it. Something was changed – had changed. What would happen next? Surely there had to be more answers. Something that would help him understand. As the butterfly disappeared from view, Francisco's brain was full of questions, and he turned back to Zerafina.

But she was gone.

Her breath was gone, her eyes were closed, her face was serene. Whatever message she had had had been communicated, and now she was at peace - a strange little changeling that Francisco knew would live on in his mind and his dreams forever. Sitting next to him, Perdita wondered what had happened as well. Somehow, she had the sense that whatever life they were living, they were headed down a new road. One that wasn't expected or mapped. One that might change everything.

Gloriana wept a single tear, and placed Zerafina's little body tenderly on the ground. Tempesta had appeared, silently, out of the compound, and for the first time since Francisco had met him he seemed to connect. He placed a hand on Gloriana's shoulder and she placed hers there too. The dead man perhaps wasn't so dead after all, at least not inside. Whatever it was that Zerafina had been to them had been something unique, and now that was gone. But as she went, she had left something behind, a key of sorts perhaps, to fully unlock whatever it was the Francisco had experienced in this clearing, as his own body had transformed.

Now, it was time to send Zerafina on her way.

*

A makeshift funeral fire took no time at all to build. Francisco's natural urge had been to bury Zerafina, to give her the last rite she had been taught, but Gloriana had insisted on a pyre. That was the only way for the enigmatic little girl to depart the world.

It was Tempesta who lit the flames, and he stepped back respectfully, joining a strange group of people who watched in silence. Francisco stood now, a little unsteady and so Perdita helped him, not leaving his side. Moya had finished her work, and all the Puritanos were firmly subdued, bound and gagged and stripped of their masks so that their real faces were exposed for everyone to see. Dr Sonja was there too, solemn and respectful in the face of death as she always was, while Gloriana faced the pyre, looking away from everyone else, as she took off her mask.

She spoke something, a quiet prayer perhaps, or a poem of sadness. Nobody else could hear, because it was just for Zerafina. Gloriana had lost something vital today, and she hoped after all of this it had been worth it. After all, everything had been planned, everything had been seen in advance. Zerafina's sight had defined every single event down to the second, all for that tiny fleeting moment of connection with a man she had never met. But now she was gone. Now there was no guidance, no map of life. Now there was just this man, Francisco, and whatever came next.

The fire burned and burned, and eventually settled down to ashes, and then nothing at all. Only then did Gloriana replace her mask and turn back to look at everyone, none of them seeing her face.

Francisco nodded to her. <What do you do now.>

<I don't know,> said Gloriana quietly. She glanced over to Tempesta, who simply shrugged. Zerafina was the reason he existed, and he was just surprised that without her, he still walked and thought.

<You should come back with us,> said Moya, brightly. Everyone looked at her. <What? You should.>

<I hate the beach,> said Tempesta.

<I'm sure we can find a cave for you to mope about in. Can't we?>

<No problem here,> said Dr Sonja. <Ana always likes meeting new people.>

Gloriana looked to Francisco. In him she saw the authority of Zerafina, and regardless of what anyone else said, it would only be OK if he said yes.

Slowly, he broke into a smile. <I think I could do with some more of that training.>

*

From the treeline to the clearing, something watched. Something both human and inhuman, that picked up every scent and every sight with preternatural senses. Some people called It El Vivisector, and it had watched for a long time now, since it had come to the jungle from the wrecked city of Cancún months ago. It had watched Los Puritanos build their compound, and steal their prize, and celebrate with their oddly masochistic rituals. It had watched them crushed beneath the strength of a white skinned giant painted like a skeletal spirit, and a woman in a mask who fought like a demon. And now it watched their little group leave, not the same as when they had arrived. One by one they headed off into the forest, and after a while the sound of engines roared and then faded away into the distance.

Behind them, It wondered did any of those people, especially the giant man, truly understand what had happened here today.

El Vivisector clacked together long inhuman talons as its scaled flesh blended into the forest, making it like a chameleon or sorts. It was feeling the urge again, the need, and the horned woman had obligingly wrapped together the broken soldiers of this lost pointless deluded crusade. There had been others of course. But over time, It had taken them, little by little, forcing them into desperate plans of attack. When they had abducted the child, that had been the turning point. It knew then that something was coming for them, and all It had to do was bide its time. It was not built for combat but stealth with It's slim form and long spindly limbs. Let others do that hard work. Much easier to pick off the weak and carve spent bodies open before hanging them up.

Red eyes gazed and a mouth full of needle-sharp teeth salivated at the thought.

But before it did there was something else to consider.

It emerged out into the clearing, silent and unseen, and crept over to examine the corpse of Jawhead. This, It decided, was not something that should be so easily discarded. It had something of humanity about it, but most of that taint had been lost when it had been reshaped into something else. A tank of sorts, a hulking weapon that had true potential for the dealing of death. It had failed its first real test, but for It failures didn't matter. Only the future mattered.

And in It's future, beyond making sculptures of worthless dead men, was a quest. A journey. It knew that It was destined to meet the giant again, one day, in whatever form he took, with or without his friends. For so long the giant – the pale Ghost whose name was El Sepulturero - had seen It's work, in caves, in cities, and now it was time to reveal Itself properly. It had to be prepared though. Jawhead could be its instrument, but not yet. There was work to be done before it would be capable, and even though a little thing like death was simple to overcome It would need a different order of power, of strength, at It's disposal.

It thought a but this as it left behind its monstrous self and became a man, an average man with thinning hair and rimmed glasses, a little thick around the middle. A man named Charles Caleb Melville III whom nobody would suspect of anything as he walked away into the rainforest.

DIA DE MUERTOS
LUCHA DIABLO

Music and noise filled the air as the parade filled the streets. There were people everywhere, from the stilt men with their masks to the tourists who did their best to get photos. Every street and avenue was full and the atmosphere was electric as the floats and performers whirled and marched and danced. Best of all it was a break from home in Playa Del Mantarraya. Ana-Maria had got so worried about Francisco being missing and then her mother and aunt going off to find him.

Mexico City was a rare trip for Ana-Maria, and it was a special treat. But her Uncle Derek had had an ace up his sleeve to make her feel better and this was it. He had pulled out all the stops as well, and Ana-Maria was thrilled, even though she had to leave Gorguz her beloved goblin in the hotel room.

People just wouldn't get it, advised Uncle Derek. He was happy though – they had bought a lot of candy to keep Gorguz going. And the TV was on. Gorguz had discovered he loved watching the TV. After all, he had never seen one before. Ana-Maria had, but only when she was a lot younger before everything had changed. Besides, she much preferred the parades.

Dia de Muertos was always her favorite time of the year, and in Mexico City it was a whole new experience. It was long drive but it was worth it. She was spoiled with ice-cream milkshakes and hats, an got to perch on Uncle Derek's huge shoulders and point excitedly at every new thing she saw as the orchestra of parade sounds filled the air.

<There,> she squealed. <Look over there. Show me show me.>

Uncle Derek did his best to get her the best views. He was worried about his sisters too, but knew that Perdita wouldn't rest until she had Francisco back. She had always been the driven one in the family, and he felt sorry for anyone who got in her way. In the meanwhile he was happy to spend time with Ana-Maria and spoil her a little. He saw her infrequently. The Yucatán didn't agree with him, and he much preferred the hustle and bustle of Mexico City, even though it had its own share of strangeness. Not so long ago he'd heard stories about snake people, and had made a note to investigate when he got around to it.

A huge float came into view, bearing a huge head covered in colored feathers and sprouting huge red devil horns. It was surrounded by men in top hats and women in bridal dresses, all with their faces intricately painted into a legion of a hundred sugar-skull people. They beckoned the crowd around them, bringing forth the cheers.

<Oooh oooh, Uncle look at that. Did you ever fight a big monster like that?>

Father Derek Castellanos was a big man, even now he was too far on the wrong side of fifty. Barrel chested and covered in hair, and nowadays with a too-big gut that hung over his belt buckle, he often thought about his younger days when he had fought, before the church had become his calling. He could still smell the old places when the Lucha Libre matches had been held, and the thrill of fighting without rules. There were no fancy masks there, no heroic Luchadors unless a person got really lucky, or unlucky depending on a person's point of view, and landed a contract. Instead, it was blood, sweat and spit on the old ring canvas, and a contest of raw skill and passion.

El Oso Grande, they had called Derek. He was big and tough like a bear, and when he got a hold of someone they couldn't get away. Once somebody had counted his matched, and even when they discounted all the friendly bouts and practices, he still had over 500 fights under his belt.

No losses either, not that anybody could remember.

Those had been heady days where nothing else really mattered. He had been just seventeen, his sisters were young girls and *papa* didn't allow them to come and watch.

<Far too violent,> *papa* said. Then he would sneak out after they were safely in bed and cheer on his son, always winning a handful of notes and celebrating afterwards. Every now and then he would treat Derek to a beer as well, as long as he didn't tell *mama*.

Derek smiled as he remembered one night. Dia de Muertos like today, but a long time ago. He had been maybe nineteen years old, and he and his sparring partner Gabriel practiced as they always did in their old gym where old murals rumbled off the walls and age hung heavy on everything. The old stone walls made it even hotter than outside, but that didn't matter. It was all part of it. That's what made them tough. Sometimes Americans would come down to fight but they couldn't cope with the heat. One guy had even worn a mask and pretended to be a Luchador. He had got the beating of his life, but nothing got broken. Instead when they carried him away he was out cold from heat exhaustion.

Derek and Gabriel had laughed about and drank cold ice water from the huge pitcher Mariella had brought in. Mariella loved the fighters, and always wore her tightest tee-shirt and shortest shorts when she got to help out. Gabriel always charmed her but never any more than that, and Derek just sat back thinking of how badly it had gone for the last fighter, a new prospect with barely a month and two practice bouts under his belt, who had tried to court her and her boyfriend found out.

He was still thinking of that when a new figure was suddenly inside the makeshift gym, when nobody had seen or heard the door open.

<You lost friend?> called Gabriel, more as a challenge than a question.

The stranger didn't answer. It walked forward, its body hidden in a ragged cape dotted with flies that sat there contentedly as if it was home. The stranger's face had a mask, but nothing like Derek or Gabriel or even Mariella had seen before. His features were moulded into something grotesque, like charred half melted skin reformed into a burned horror mask with eyeholes and nothing else.

Mariella screamed and ran as the stranger pointed a long cadaverous finger at Derek.

<You,> it whispered.

<You want to fight?> asked Derek, a little bemused.

The figure said nothing. Instead it stripped off its cloak and revealed its body, a mockery of humanity. Raw exposed bone ribs surrounded the outside of its chest, and darkened tissue was taut across viciously honed muscles. Its hands were veined and tipped with fingernails like claws as they cracked into fists, and all that Derek and Gabriel could really see were two black eyes, staring out with nothing but malice behind them.

<What's the problem *pendejo*,> growled Gabriel. He didn't like the showy types. They should stay on the TV where they belonged. He took a few steps forward and as he did, the stranger was on him. Impossibly fast, like he had covered twenty feet in no time at all, and he had Gabriel by the throat.

<Brother,> shouted Derek, and he hurled himself forward to tackle the stranger. He rammed him hard and the stranger released Gabriel, but to Derek it had felt like hitting a mass of metal that felt no pain. Now he faced up to the stranger with its hideous face and satanic eyes, wondering what it was they were facing.

There was whisper in the air. A hint of voice barely more than breathing. A women's voice perhaps, that seemed to say two simple words.

<Not them.>

In that instant, the stranger was gone, as though he had just been a figment of a wrestler's imagination. No mask, no ragged cape, no flies. Just…nothing.

<Holy shit, brother. What was that?>

Derek just shook his head back then, and all these decades later remembered it all so vividly. It had been the first night he had seen the other face of Mexico City. The face of the dark. And it wouldn't be the last.

Ana-Maria snapped him back to the present day, and the sights and sounds of the parade swallowed him up again.

<So did you? demanded Ana-Maria. <Did you ever fight a monster.>

Derek just smiled.

<Maybe.>

EL VIVISECTOR

For so long, a lifetime it felt like, a man who sometimes called himself Charles had followed Francisco. He wasn't sure why – it was like a compulsion. The same kind of compulsion that had led Charles to slice open his victims in that very particular way and hang them up like sculptures. He had done it for so many years now, regular as clockwork. California had called him the worst serial killer in history, and they had never caught him. He was too smart, and that left Charles free to perfect his art.

The art of The Vivisector.

Charles had followed the Pale Ghost across the wilderness to the cave he himself had once kept as a base. One of his old victims was in there dying slowly, while another was strung up in the rotting heat. In his old life Charles would have been enraged to see Francisco rescue the girl, but things were different now. Instead, Charles simply watched, fascinated.

He wanted to claim Francisco's flesh as his own. To own that strength and power. Then he had seen the huge man-beast with the skull head that Francisco had used his strange magic on and that cut down. That was when Charles had realised that the cave held much more than just old weapons he had collected from a hundred Wilderness bodies and the stink of death that hung over them.

Francisco had opened a gate, and Charles knew that his destiny was to walk through it. That was the day of his transfiguration, when Charles Caleb Melville II truly became The Vivisector.

As he walked past the huge serpentine carcass Francisco
had left behind, and set foot across the threshold, visions
assaulted him - visions of things that would drive anyone
sane mad. But Charles was beyond their ability to touch. His
mind looked past the rotting faces and the claws that reached
from the walls. Part real, part imagined, they meant nothing
to him.

Charles wasn't afraid of anything.

He just felt a new hunger. He had spent time with the
body of the skull-headed beast, trying to understand what it
was. Now he wanted to see more. Killing could wait for a
little while as he explored this new path that fate had opened
up for him.

All because of Francisco.

Charles knew that he was meant to be like that. Strong
and tough, immune to the power of the elements and a step
outside normal human beings. In his head Charles was
already there, now it just a question of getting his body to
catch up.

Past the howling phantoms there was a dusty rocky
staircase that wound down into the Earth. That was where
Charles knew he had to go, and as he began to descend it felt
the Infernal Pit itself was waiting for him.

And he liked it.

Charles daydreamed of his first kill.

He was just 18 years old, and the girl he chose was a
pretty blonde girl who worked in an LA coffee shop. She
probably wanted to be an actress, and in his own way Charles
was about to cast her in his personal play.

The lead role.

"Hi, what can I get for you today."

"Just a normal coffee, that OK?"

"Sure thing. Anything else?"

"I don't go for the fancy stuff. Just coffee."

It had been too easy really. Charles had worn a suit and combed his hair, like he did every day for his highly paid salesman job with the new office and company car. He drank politely, made arrangements to meet after her shift was over and then let it all happen

When he slit her throat he didn't know her name or care. He just watched as her pretty smile died on her face and the life in her eyes faded away. He liked that part the most. After that it was work. Cutting, slicing, opening, then the system he had perfected to hang his trophies where everyone could see them, hidden away in the pit of night.

It amused Charles to hang her over the entrance to the coffee shop she had worked in, and he smiled for days after he read the headlines the next day. He hired some hookers to tie up and celebrate, but he didn't hurt them. He was smart enough to ration himself, even when the hunger screamed at him in the middle of the night.

One a month. Every month without fail, different places, everything meticulously worked out in advance. Routines memorised, people followed, research done. Man, woman, it didn't matter. They were all his meat, and he worked them all in the same way. He read books too, and learned how to hide, how to obscure the clues, even how to misdirect towards other people – the kinds of people who fit the profile of a killer.

On his fifth kill, the police called him The Vivisector, and Charles real life began in earnest.

When Charles first heard of the Wilderness they were just a story. Cable news said some sort of explosion had half destroyed Cancún, killing the holidaymakers and tourists and leaving the place uninhabitable. Terrorist were blamed, and the world moved on. Holidaymakers and tourists went elsewhere, and Cancún became a place nobody talked about anymore.

Except that they did, just in a different way.

They were like whispers at first, little urban legends that sprung up out of trashy newspapers or idle gossip on-line. There would be half glimpsed pictures of things that supposedly roamed the forests, and claims that nothing electronic worked there anymore. As Charles continue his monthly obsession, these tiny fragments of stories became to form into something else inside his head. He met friends he didn't care about at work and laughed about it all over drinks, but soon – unstoppably – they became a new obsession.

Sometimes he let the bodies watch over his research and his reading, sewing them up so they didn't leak all over the floor before his hunger drove him to cut them open and perform his own little ritual like he always had to.

As he looked deeper and deeper, way beyond the Dark Web, he found stories of a giant man who walked the Wilderness. It seemed ridiculous, like a comic book, but there were pictures. The giant, The Pale Ghost they called him, didn't seem to want to hide. Instead he carried a huge sword with him as he hacked down creatures that everyone wanted to pretend didn't exist.

Except it seemed down there, on the Yucatán, they did exist.

The stories said that whenever something prowled out of the Wilderness, The Pale Ghost was there to stop it. They said he was stronger than ten men, and could conjure fire out of nothingness. And that sword of his. The name they called it was one Charles that couldn't pronounce, but the stories said it was a magic sword from Mayan times, a weapon that could not be resisted by any demon or devil.

Charles studied the stories again and again, more excited each time. He had to go there. To him, the Wilderness sounded like home. Where the darkest things lived, where he could exist and hunt in the purest way without having to pretend he was a human being anymore. After all, he had known all along that something else hid under his skin.

The real him.

The floor of the second cave was cold when Charles woke up. The potion he had taken still burned inside his guts like acid but he had survived, just like the book said he would.

Yes, the book.

It had taken him a while to find it when he had reached the second cave, and instantly seen it was like a kind of laboratory. Everywhere there was equipment both mechanical and arcane, from chemistry sets to grotesque specimens that Charles couldn't recognise. Embedded in the walls were alcoves like crude metal coffins, some empty and open, others sealed tightly shut. It was a place of beauty for Charles, like a dark Wonderland that he was always meant to discover, and it would become his own place of power.

Then he had found the book. A grimoire of sorts, filled with words and pictures that it took time for Charles to decipher with his basic high school Spanish. Soon he began to gain his first understanding. And a name.

Baron Muzon.

Long dead, his body nothing but dust probably, that name spoke to Charles across time. Charles spoke back, and soon they began to converse. The voice of Baron Muzon told Charles where there was food and water, and told him of his Army. The Army Of The Skull Faced Men, created from hulking bodies and ancient powers of death that didn't even have a name.

<I made them to rule. They are true strength. My strength. My Army.>

The book said they had strength and power, but no mind. They were like primordial juggernauts, and those few that Baron Muzon had managed to let loose could do nothing but mindlessly attack whatever they saw. Like the one that lay dead outside at Francisco's hands.

<It frustrates me I cannot conjour even a single individual thought into the minds of my beasts. They cannot think, only destroy. I just look deeper, to try and understand why I cannot imbue my soldiers with even the tiniest fragment of a soul.>

Charles wondered how many more there were, roaming the Wilderness.

It was something else that really caught his attention. A kind of formula that was completely alien, and at the same time so familiar it was almost calling out his name. It only needed the chemistry that flowed through the apparatus of Baron Muzon's laboratory, and Charles wasted no time in drinking it as he read the words that changed him forever.

<You will realise yourself as the fear of all men.>

Charles felt different when he walked out into the sun for the first time. The burning inside his body slowly began to fade and his eyes began giving him sharper sight. He could hear animals burrowing under the ground, and a new instinct magnified his hunger to a new level.

That was the first time he let out his true self, and became The Vivisector.

With a thought, his human shape fell away and left something else in itself place, an emaciated thing of claws and fangs whose flesh could meld and transform with its surroundings. He was fast too, faster than anyone as he moved across the land, homing in on a heartbeat that spoke of a victim.

The Vivisector laughed. He was the new child of the dead Baron Muzon, walking the Earth as something much more than a man. He would be a success. Not like the Skull Men. No, this time things were as just they should be.

The days were rush of excitement as The Vivisector revelled in its power. More and more it felt this was Its natural state, the human identity of Charles Melville just a chrysalis that It had no use for anymore. Even becoming that form again was unpleasant, but sometimes It had no choice.

Charles' art still needed to be expressed, and he still needed to feel his human eyes watch the life drain out of victim after victim. That was the thrill, the desire he had. Then he could leave that and exist as The Vivisector for another 30 days, until the hunger called again.

Sometimes It wished It didn't have that need, but nothing was perfect, and in Its head the form of Charles was just an illusion leaving It free to roam the Wilderness amongst its brethren. It saw so many things out there, things no one, not even Francisco, had ever seen.

It took its world as though born to it. California, parents, sales jobs and flashy cars. That was all fading away into a past that didn't matter anymore.

Time led The Vivisector to Cancún, to see where it had all started. It founded the hotel that was smashed and burned out of shape, and sensed the powers that were still in there. Charles came out to kill again, and he hung the body he found high before hiding away to watch nameless people bring a young child in.

The Vivisector knew a sacrifice when it saw one, and Francisco wasn't far behind. Except this time Francisco didn't crush his enemy. This time he was beaten down, injured by something so powerful it tasted bad in the air, and It watched as they carried him out like he was almost dead. It saw the horned girl Moya and the police officer Perdita, and wondered what had happened.

Inside where just broken people and the dead, and It was left with only questions.

The Vivisector's senses drove It onward as It tracked down Francisco. It kept to the shadows, not wanting to tip Its hand, because this was its chance. With the Pale Ghost weakened, this was the time to find out what the real source of his strength was, and then take it for Itself.

That was why Charles had come here as a mere human, and that was why The Vivisector had been born. Created by the powers of Baron Muzon for one thing and one thing only.

It wanted Power.

The Power of El Sepulturero.

It was hard to keep on the trail sometimes. Paths became confusing, and the hospital at Playa Del Mantarraya was like a fortress. Outside the Wilderness, everybody seemed to protect the sick and injured so much more. Understandable. The Vivisector knew the Wilderness well now, and it knew the kinds of things that could swallow even the strongest people whole and not even notice. Weakness only ever meant death. Even the mighty Francisco had finally been beaten down.

So The Vivisector waited.

It was weeks away from any need to create its dead body art in the form of Charles, so there was plenty time to observe, and It learned patience. There were lots of people with guns, gang members led by a man with one eye who seemed to act as security, and The Vivisector had no desire to see if it was bulletproof.

On the third or forth night, It couldn't remember exactly, things changed.

There was a light, a red aura that fell out of the air and flowed through the walls and the corridors of the hospital. Nobody human seemed to see it, but the Vivisector saw it. Curious, It ventured closer to try and understand. It knew that there were spirits out in the forests, but this looked different. It didn't seem to fit even the twisted rules of the Wilderness, and the Vivisector wanted to understand. Baron Muzon's book had taught it many things, and it wanted to know more. So much more.

It wanted to be the God of the Wilderness.

Then the alarm was raised.

The Vivisector climbed up the walls on its spindly limbs like a spider and listened through the concrete, zeroing in on one voice. A doctor, It surmised, a woman who was close to Francisco.

Somehow, Francisco himself was gone.

It took weeks for The Vivisector to find Its way again. It returned to Baron Muzon's book and his laboratory, trying to understand. But there was nothing. That left It confused, distracted. When Charles returned to make his art of dead bodies again, it didn't have the same thrill, and his victim was barely cold before The Vivisector took Its true form once more.

It burned the cave and everything in it. The book had no more to teach It, so the pyre could claim the last remnants of the failed Skull Army. Instead, It tried to listen to the stories that flowed about the Wilderness. Everyone knew what Francisco was, but nobody seemed to know what had happened. They were all too shocked about him being beaten.

Everyone had thought he was indestructible.

As Charles, and hating every second of it, he found a library with books and magazines that he pored over. He killed the librarian when he was done and hadn't found the information he wanted, and strung her up in the entrance of her own building, letting her bleed down onto a pile of Bibles.

It hadn't even been a month, and The Vivisector realised that the petty killing obsessions and hungers of Charles Melville had no real meaning to It any more. There was just the primal need, the sheer desire, for that power, the ancient force that Francisco clearly held with his body.

The library wasn't a complete waste of time. The Vivisector had got a name. Erik. A man who knew things, and who travelled in and out of the Wilderness dealing in things that other people didn't. He wore black, and with his cowboy boots and a cowboy hat always rammed onto his head he was simple to find.

The Vivisector contemplated torturing Erik, but it had learned the value of listening, and instead It took all the information it needed as the sisters and the horned woman talked to him. It watched Erik and the horned woman Moya have sex, and watched as Erik gave them a strange contraption made of lenses.

None of it made a lot of sense. It had forgotten what human beings did, and It felt nothing as all these events happened in front of its eyes and in its ears.

It simply followed.

Things were coming together now. When they used the device Erik had given them to direct them, The Vivisector headed off, getting in front of them. It didn't know the rainforests the way it knew the Wilderness, and it needed time to become familiar so it could move freely. That would take time but it would be worth it. Not long now.

*

Francisco and Gloriana were a force to behold as they smashed their way through the Puritans. The Vivisector could only admire the strength and the skill from Its hiding place in the trees, and when the Skull Giant butcher emerged,

It almost cheered as Francisco became the Pale Ghost once again. Only even stronger, even more powerful, but somehow reduced to human again afterwards.

That was ideal for the Vivisector. It meant that his obsession was ripe for picking now, and It had a weapon of its own this time. From what it had gleaned from Baron Muzon's writings it had some chemistry to give the ruined Skull Giant life for a short while again. Not much, but enough to enact a plan that had formed in Its head.

It could almost taste the power as It slipped effortlessly between its human face and its true self.

Now was the time.

Up on the road ahead, Francisco's car and Gloriana's RV moved slowly. They were not in a rush, and the journey home was a long one. The first order of business was to find some water and found, and get some medical supplies of some kind. The Vivisector became Charles the hitchhiker, and acted his best human role so that they would squeeze him into the back seat of the RV. He had to listen to them all chattering about pointless things as they drove, especially the horned woman Moya. She especially irritated The Vivisector, so when the Skull Giant unleashed its fury on them, It had her attacked first.

The hulking monster smashed its way out of the trees.

<Didn't Francisco kill that thing already?>

The vehicles ground to halt and the fight began as Charles pretended to cower in the back with Rae, who didn't speak as much as the others. There was something about her eyes as well, behind her glasses. Perhaps she would become a new piece of art when this was all done.

Moya was thrown aside and the Skull Giant smashed its fist down onto the roof of the RV, buckling it in and forcing Rae and then Charles from the truck in the pretence of fear. They watched as Gloriana hammered down something heavy and metal onto one of the creature's knees while Moya got to her feet and unfurled her precious new whipclaw that spun in the air. The chain sang its song and lashed out, curling itself around the Skull Giant's next as the claw gouged its way into already failing flesh.

Charles slipped away towards Francisco's car, ignoring the coffin lying on its roof and seeing only Perdita in the back seat.

Alone.

What the f...?

Charles' senses told him nothing in the second before a hand grasped him and pinned him forward onto the car. The Vivisector asserted itself, slipping away from its human form as It lashed out with Its claws. But somehow, they didn't seem to work anymore. It felt weaker, not stronger.

As the Skull Giant succumbed to Moya and she climbed onto its back to break its neck, Dr Sonja emerged out of the trees. She had something in her hand – a piece of stone onto which had been carved some sort of symbol.

Hoy.

Instinctively, It knew what the Mayan glyph was. A grey face, and embedded within it a blessing to make right what was unnatural.

<Glad I got the right one.> said Dr Sonja.

Francisco nodded and smiled. <Me too.>

With every step Dr Sonja took, a little more of the Vivisector died away to nothing. The senses, the speed, the sharpness of tooth and claw, all of them faded until Charles Caleb Melville III the human being was all that was left, pissing out the powerful chemistry he had taken from the burned laboratory as his body rejected it.

Her own enemy broken and fully dead, Moya strode over to take over from Francisco as he felt weak and dizzy again, and lifted Charles bodily off his feet.

<What a little asshole,> she said, and she threw him hard against a heavy tree trunk.

"Ouch," winced Rae.

Charles the human being, drained of all that was monstrous and inhuman, realised his legs were broken as he looked up at what - who - faced him.

Francisco and Perdita, Dr Sonja and Moya, Gloriana and Tempesta, Rae and even Hook, who towered over them all and growled. The whole group of them looked down, and Charles tried to grasp how he had been so easily outmanoeuvred.

How could this have happened?

He was the Vivisector. His power came from the ancient alchemies of Baron Muzon. Except not anymore.

As Perdita pulled out her gun, Dr Sonja dropped something in front of Charles. A page that he recognised as coming from Baron Muzon's book, one he had never seen before.

"I think you missed something," said Dr Sonja.

A last fragment of understanding translated the page for Charles, the page that Erik had given to Dr Sonja and told her to keep safe until the time came to use it.

<Even with my greatest works, I cannot begin to comprehend the ancient power of the forgotten world itself, of the glorious past of Mayan times, that dwarf even my most profound methodologies. I dread the day the Pale Ghost comes for me, for nothing I have created will have power against him.>

All Charles could do was stare at it, and slump back, defeated in the final moment of a life spent devoted to killing.

"Well, shit."

NAVIDAD LOS CUERNOS

Moya lay back in her favorite pool and let the cool water wash over her. It was little way out of town, into the green of the trees where the surface rock had worn away and left a kind of ragged round depression in the ground, filled with crystal clear water that naturally fizzed a little. It was always the perfect temperature.

Nobody bothered Moya here, so she could feel relaxed in herself. It wasn't that anyone in town bothered her. Playa Del Mantarraya wasn't a place where people balked at the unusual. After all, when the sight a giant of a man with chalk white skin and a Mayan sword was an everyday occurrence, a tall woman with flawless copper-colored skin, intricate markings on her arms and those perfectly formed beautiful horns wasn't anything of a surprise. If anything she had admirers.

Overhead the sun shone, and Moya closed her eyes.

She thought of the people who had taken her in and showed her so much kindness. The sisters and the especially the young girl Ana-Maria who she was teaching how to cook. They were helping Moya adjust to the ways of the Yucatán peninsula, more so than they needed to, and so in turn she did everything she could to help.

Even with all of that, it could be difficult on certain days. Here, in Playa Del Mantarraya, something terrible had happened. The same thing, Ana-Maria had, said had happened all over the peninsula back when she had been a little girl. Maybe 2, 3 years ago. Moya found that hard to adjust to - all the modernity and technology she was used to didn't seem to work anymore. Cellphones, computers. Even simple TVs. None of the electronic signals got through anymore in the Wilderness.

Moya ducked her head under the water, soaking the thick mane of black hair that stretched down to her thighs and letting the water flow over the bone of her horns. Overhead, a scarlet bird flew over and Moya let its song clear her mind. This pool, her pool, could almost work wonders.

As she sat up again, she opened her eyes and looked to find a place where she could bask and dry off. Then she caught sight of something else, and it made her stop. She squinted through the bright sun. Somebody was there. A huge figure, bulky, just within the cover of the trees.

<Francisco?> she called. <Is that you playing games?>

The figure didn't respond. Instead it simply strode out into the clearing of Moya's pool and stood there, looking at her as the details resolved into a face, a body, clothes.

Moya looked back, not quite comprehending who she was looking at.

<Baby Brother>?

A hulking man, built like a bulldozer under board shorts and a bright orange tee-shirt, grinned widely through a heavy browed face. It was a darkened, copper face that was broad and a little worse for wear, topped with a thick pair of bullhead horns that looked as though they could pulverise whatever they were aimed at by the sheer brute force of their owner.

It was Buey's face, the face of Moya's baby brother, the man who everyone called Ox, and she hadn't seen it in far too long.

<Ola big sister.>

Moya hurled herself out of the water and wrapped her arms around him in a squeeze that would have crushed a human being. To Buey it was just a gentle family hug.

<Brother brother brother,> squealed Moya. <It's soooo good to see you.>

She finally let him go, and giggled as she let him stand there with his clothes half soaked.

<This where you been hiding?>

Moya nodded as she started to dry herself and put her clothes on. <A few months now. Oh, oh tell me, how is Mamacita. And little Gaciella. Is she still horning? Tell me tell me tell me.>

<Gaciella has half horns now. Like yours. Mamacita is old and grouchy. They all miss you.>

<I'm so so sorry I haven't contacted. This place.> Moya gestured around. <You can't get any signals here. I was going to write letters but there isn't even a postal service.>

Buey shrugged. <Hey, it's good. It's not like you never took off before. Rojas is still in mourning I think. He has pictures of you, and he cries like a child.>

<Rojas,> snorted Moya. <Isn't he over his silly crush yet.>

<Guess not. He's no good for you. Too weak.>

<You know, I keep saying this to everyone.> Moya rubbed her hair vigorously, trying to avoid the kinks and curls that the sun's drying power would create. <But they all keep saying 'Oh he's sensitive. Sensitive is good when you are from a Horned family.' I hate sensitive.>

Buey nodded his agreement. <Sensitive is for poets. So, you gonna tell me how you ended up here?>

Moya stopped. She looked her brother directly in the eye as she remembered the darkest time that she desperately wanted to forget. <Bad things happened....>

*

Long months ago, far back in time before she had ever even heard of Francisco Garza or Playa Del Mantarraya, was the first day Moya reached the Yucatán peninsula. A truck driver deposited her by the shallow waterway near the fences of barbed wire that didn't used to be there, a place he said was easy to get through. Never any guards or dogs, and nothing at all like the Mexican border had become.

<Not sure why anyone would want to go in there,> the truck driver said.

<Why? Its looks exciting to me.>

<I never would'a believed in demons, *chica*. Believe me, they exist. And they're all in there.>

Like everyone else Moya had watched the news broadcasts and read the endless chatter on the 'Net. But unlike most who had shied away from the place, Moya wanted to see it for herself. Even when Mamacita had begged her to go somewhere else on her new adventure, Moya was determined.

<Do I look like a girl who is frightened of a few demons.>

The truck driver stared at her for a moment. He had somehow got used to this young woman's appearance over the hours on the road, and had tuned out the unusual color and marks on her skin. He guessed there was something underneath her huge floppy hat as well, but he didn't press the matter

<I guess not. You just take care.>

<I will. Thanks for the lift, I really enjoyed meeting you.> Moya leaned over and gave the truck driver a peck on the cheek.

<Making an old man blush,> he said, and Moya hopped out of the air- conditioned cab with her backpack and slipped down into the burning heat. She slammed the door shut and the truck lurched back into motion, hurling up a storm of dry dust as its turned away down the empty road. Soon it was

shimmering in the haze of the road, and then it was gone completely.

Moya threw off her hat, letting her horns feel the sun, and got her bearings. She was used to the sounds of the scrubland behind her, the ever-present hums and the buzzes of the bugs, and now she wanted to see what the trees along the skyline held for her. The truck driver had picked well, and Moya quickly spotted a point in the fence where the wire had been part cut and part squashed down, just enough to climb over without getting torn on the vicious barbs. No doubt, she thought, she wasn't the first explorer here. It didn't immediately occur to her that it could just as easily have been people hasty to get out.

She made her away barefoot across the water and navigated the wire. As she did she felt a little cold shiver down her back, and on her very first step past the fence, everything felt different.

Moya had been in the rainforest many times before but this was different. The animals called like they always did, but the atmosphere here changed them somehow, making them sound discordant and wrong. Birds sang a little off key every few notes, some of the insects chirruped more like tiny buzzsaws than crickets, monkeys seemed to scream and the noises of other animals she didn't recognised crept out from between the trees.

The whole place made her uneasy. But that was why she was here. Back home, in the City, everyone had heard of the event that had consumed the Yucatán Peninsula, even though nobody really knew what it was or how it had happened. There were so many stories of strange things, spirits and devils that walked free in amongst a place that now seemed to live half in the present and half in the past. Enough to fill books. Moya had become fascinated with the new-formed legends this new place, this Wilderness, and had decided it was time for a new adventure.

She walked, taking everything in, listening to the heartbeat of the place. She found a path that she could follow and decided on a direction. That was always the best way as far as she was concerned. Explore and discover, because nobody ever knew what mysteries the wild places of the world still held. Especially places like this - unique and disconnected from the world.

A flock of brightly colored birds flapped in the trees high overhead, and Moya watched them. A monkey whooped and called further away. A huge blue and green butterfly danced in front of her, and beside the rocky path fresh water rushed by. Each thing she saw or heard filled Moya with a kind of joy that beat down the unease, and she felt like she could almost be alone in the entire world as she felt the ground incline a little under her feet and the going get heavier. There were no mountains here, but the earth still had its grooves and folds, and was never truly smooth.

It didn't matter too much. Moya had strength and endurance to spare, but she wanted to find one of the famous temples before nightfall so she could set up camp and relax underneath the canopy of the night sky and watch the stars peak through.

Something attracted her attention, on the ground up ahead. She headed for it and found something she hadn't expected, so she crouched down to pick it up. From a distance it had looked like a small rock, but now she had it in her hands Moya could see it was an old water canteen, cracked wide open like an egg and smeared in dark, sticky stains.

As she turned the canteen over in her hands she felt a chill across her skin, a feeling she wasn't used to, and a whisper inside her head said that something was nearby. Something she had never seen before.

Up above, she heard the flapping of leathery wings.

There was something moving up in the trees. It was large but it hid itself, moving from branch to branch, trunk to trunk, pushing everything else aside. Flocks of birds and troops of monkeys burst out of their roosts and hiding places. Everywhere life made away for whatever it was that crashed its way across the canopy, carried by that sound of flapping leather.

Moya braced herself. There was no sense running. She didn't know the landscape, not like she did back home, and whatever it was likely already had her scent.

When it came, it came like an explosion.

A figure hurled itself from the trees and down towards Moya. She had barely a second to register what it was –a face that was filled with predatory fury, a body that was toned and tensed for the kill. She dove aside and the attacker cannoned into the ground, and as she got to her feet she could see what it was she was facing.

As it shook off the daze of its crash, the attacker reared up. Tall, slim, its flesh almost jet black and almost armoured like a rhino. Its head was pitted and heavy, bearing vicious eyes and a mouthful of razor teeth, and its arms bore huge translucent membranes just like a bat.

There was no name for this thing.

All Moya knew was that she was going to have to fight, just like she did back home when she and her brother took a trip to the Mountains. There were nameless things there as well, but not like this. This place, this Wilderness, was so unique that nobody seemed to really understand it. All the rules had broken down, and now she was eye to eye with the bastard offspring of a human being and what could only be a demon.

It took a step forward, grinding its teeth in anticipation of ripping, but got no further. An object made of glass flew through the air and smashed into the creature's body. As Moya watched a slick fluid spilled out and the second it hit the air it burst into white hot fire. She covered her eyes against the dazzle of the flare. The phosphorus spread quickly across the creature's body and wings, clinging to it, and it screamed as it fled back into the rainforest

<Thankyou so much,> said Moya, looking to her saviour. She stopped dead when she saw them - three women, all tall and beautiful, dressed in colorful old fashioned dresses with faces painted like the most beautiful sugar skulls. But it was their eyes that scared her – dull, white, empty. Zombielike.

The one in front, the one with a black rose buried in cascades of red hair, held up a tranquiliser gun and pointed it at Moya.

"We love Doctor Horta," she said, and fired.

*

Moya shivered and dismissed the memory.
<That it?> asked Buey.
<That's it. I don't remember anything else until Francisco found me. Just weird dreams. Gross weird dreams.>
<You love Dr Horta too?>
<That's not funny. But I think his weird mind spell didn't really work on me properly so he locked me up.>
Buey clenched his fists. <Maybe we should finds this gringo, kick the shiii….> He tailed off suddenly, and Moya looked around. Ana-Maria was standing near the pool, watching silently with her beloved pot-bellied goblin in her arms as he stuffed a churro into his mouth.
<Auntie Moya.> Ana-Maria's eyes widened when she saw Buey. <Who's that?>

Moya grinned. <This is my baby brother. His name is Buey. Buey, this is Ana-Maria.>

Buey shifted awkwardly on the spot, and spied what Ana-Maria had in her arms. < They got those here?>

Ana-Maria nodded, still nervous. <He's my best friend and his name is Gorguz. Do you want to say hello?>

Buey clearly didn't.

<Buey is scared of goblins,> said Moya with a smirk.

<Not scared. They just eat everything. Like rats.>

Ana-Maria nodded. <He does eat a lot of candy. And churros. He loves churros.>

<Buey loves churros too, don't you baby brother?>

Buey just grunted, and recalled fond memories of churro-eating contests where he always won. Always. This goblin had no chance.

<Mama says that we're nearly ready to do the Piñatas. Can you help me with mine please Auntie Moya. Pleeeease.>

Buey looked puzzled. <Piñatas.>

<Las Posadas.> said Moya as if that explained everything, but it just added to Buey's puzzlement. Christmas was not something that he usually thought about. It was far too commercialised for his liking. <Oh baby brother, you are in for such a treat. And I can't wait to introduce you to Francisco.>

Ana-Maria grinned widely.

<Feliz Navidad>.

HORTA

The sun set over a little sandy bay with no name, overlooked by palm trees and spiky clumps of succulents that lined the top of craggy grey rocks. The sea had carved little arches and caves into the coastline and the waves crashed against them little, making white surf even on the calmest days. It was another little treasure of nature, hidden away from the *touristos* who used to swarm around the Yucatán, but it wasn't the beauty of this place that was important.

A makeshift gangway made of wooden slats sat little above the ocean and its waves, connecting out to something that shouldn't have been there. Lashed together from floating structures, old shacks and even what looked like the remains of an old seaplane was a kind of base, a platform bobbing gently in the sea away from the shore, lit up by a string on lamps powered by a noisy generator. There was no sense of how long it had been there or why it had first been built, but it was clearly a place to hide.

Sitting in Francisco's car, Dr Sonja took it all in. She sat in the passenger seat while Moya stood outside and leaned against a tree. Her brother, Buey was with her. Dr Sonja still wasn't used to him. He was a huge slab of a man, shorter but broader than Francisco, and the horns that curved out of his head reminded Dr Sonja of the Greek myth of the minotaur.

He said very little but he was clearly very focussed on the job at hand.

<How long is he going to be?> growled Buey.

<He's different now,> said Moya. <Maybe it'll take a bit longer.>

Different was right, thought Dr Sonja. She had got so used to Francisco's ghostly white skin that now it was gone and he looked Mexican again it still took her by surprise. He looked smaller now as well, still ridiculously tall like a giant but somehow not as strong, not as tough. Things tired him out here they didn't before. He seemed to prefer it though. Dr Sonja knew he had hated being called the Pale Ghost. Even so, he was taking a long time to return.

As the last of the light faded and the lights of the makeshift hideaway started to take over, Dr Sonja leaned out of the window. <Are you sure this is the right place?>

Moya nodded. <Erik said so. He did a lot of research for me.>

Dr Sonja snorted disdainfully. <So how many times did you have noisy sex with him this time?>

<You are just jealous I think.>

The image of Erik dressed head to foot in black from his dusty cowboy boots to his too-right jeans to his vacquero hat that hid his thinning hair popped into Dr Sonja's head and she winced. Definitely not her type. Then again, her ex-husband with his movie star looks had seemed perfect. Right up until he slept with every nurse in the hospital they worked at who would have him. Which had turned about to be a lot.

Dr Sonja sat back in the passenger seat, idly poking at the collection of thrash metal CDs that sat in the glove compartment.

<Come on Francisco, where are you?>

Francisco was chest deep in sea water, half-regretting agreeing to Moya's plan. It had all seemed pretty simple, and with Buey happy to handle anything physical all that was needed was a little sneaky sabotage. The trouble was that everything was harder than it used to be. Swimming tired Francisco out more, the sea felt colder, and he kept getting hungry. His emergency stash of churro's was in the car to stop them getting wet and disintegrating, which didn't help is growling stomach.

His part of the plan had taken a lot longer than he had intended it to when he volunteered, but at least he was nearly done now. The fourth and last piece of stone he had carved was ready, and he just needed to place it next to the generator that chugged away at one end of the floating platform.

Was it a platform? wondered Francisco. Or maybe it was more like a secret base? he had always wanted to raid a secret base, although he would had preferred it to be inside a volcano or something. With ninjas. Ninjas were cool.

Francisco eased himself through the water until he was just underneath the generator that sat on heavy wooden slats with little gas in them. Then he checked his stone, just to make sure everything was correct before he placed it.

Chaac.

The glyph almost glowed with power. Stronger than it ever would have before, as though a strange kind of rebalance had happened, where loss of strength had fed the magic and made it more potent. Francisco still wondered what other change had occurred since the rainforest and Zerafina. He still didn't really understand who she had been. Or maybe not who, but what she had been.

A little goddess perhaps, waiting to work her mystical gifts.

None of it made any sense. Even Dr Sonja was puzzled, and she could figure anything out.

Francisco pushed the stone up into one of the cracks in the wood, wedging it in place, and then he swam away as quietly as he could. He had seen at least eight security guard, all professional looking and all with guns that looked foreign and expensive. Any one of them would probably make short work of his vulnerable skin if they saw him.

Definitely a secret base.

Moya had said that it was a kind of safehouse, a hideaway for people who liked to do bad things and didn't want to be found. That sounded like exactly what this Doctor Horta person needed. As he swam Francisco remembered what he had done to Moya, the near-mindless zombie he had made her into. He remembered how strong she had been, probably stronger than he was now.

It made him smile that she was finally going to get her payback.

As he headed for the shore, far away from the lights that created luminous circles everywhere, he still felt the crackle of energy from the glyphs he had placed as carefully as he could.

Everything was ready. Time for Operation Get Horta to begin!

Soaked to the skin and his muscles aching, Francisco trudged up the slope that led back to his car. The last remnants of the day were nearly gone now, and the palm trees were nothing more than vague silhouettes. Behind him the lights on the floating platform blazed. He glanced back at them as he heard the generator make its heavy chug chug sound that bounced of the rock-faces lining the shore.

He hoped he'd timed everything right.

Dr Sonja was already out of the car with a towel as Francisco finally made his last few steps. She could tell he was weary and she had a couple of candy bars and a fruit juice on standby. He resented it, but she always got her way. Where the Pale Ghost had enjoyed some kind of preternatural immunity to being tired, the very human Francisco Garza didn't. He needed rest, food, looking after. All that time roaming the Wilderness, sword in hand with his chalk skin and his impossible strength had spoiled him.

Francisco's back hurt as he slumped down, and Dr Sonja handed him the juice.

<Guava,?> he said, pulling a face.

<Its good for you.> Dr Sonja folded her arms. <Drink it down.>

It was never a good idea to argue, Francisco knew. In a lot of ways Dr Sonja was tougher that her sister, and she had never lost that edge she had developed when she had lived her old life in the ER department, half her time smothered in blood and puke, the rest buried in paperwork. For a while she had even worked across the border in the US. She never talked about it, but Perdita had said over a few too many beers that it had somehow been even worse than the endless parade of gang members, junkies and tourists she had dealt with in Mexico City. When her three months was done, Perdita said, her sister couldn't wait to get home. Just without a husband.

Francisco decided it was better not to find out any more.

He drained his guava juice. It was so sweet it made him wince, but he forced it down. Dr Sonja knew best, after all. She had tested his blood so many times since they had come back from the rainforest trying to figure out the science of it all. What had changed? Why? Simple questions with answers that were determined to stay just out of reach. All she had found out for certain was that Francisco's blood sugar tended to drop when he insisted on still trying to be what he had been.

Hence the juice and the bars. Francisco had to admit he felt a little better after a minute of two. He didn't really want to admit it, but part of him missed being the Pale Ghost. He had hated the chalk white skin every second, but the strength, and toughness, they had been gifts.

Why had Zerafina taken them away from him?

He looked to see Moya. She had walked over without him even noticing and she put a hand on his shoulder. <You OK?> she asked, a concerned look on her face.

Francisco gave her a smile. <Yeah, I'm good. Just different.> He looked back down to the platform with its bright web of lights. <So, you ready?>

There was a pang of excitement in Moya's stomach as she answered. <I am soooo ready.>

The half-moon overhead made the sky glow a little as Francisco climbed into the driver's seat and handed Moya a piece of stone with little tiny carvings on it. It was thin and light, run through with hair-thin threads of blue crystal, and Moya was extra careful as she took it.

<So I just break this and it all happens?>

Francisco nodded. <Yeah. Then watch the fireworks.>

<And you're sure this is going to work,> asked Dr Sonja. <I mean, this isn't exactly precise. It's the M word.>

<Hey, I may be weak now but this still works.> Francisco tapped the side of his head. <Clearer than ever.>

On a sudden impulse Moya leaned down and kissed Francisco on the lips. He didn't have time to realise if he had kissed her back before she stood up and gave him her widest smile. <Wish us good luck.>

Francisco nodded, awkward. <You don't need luck, *chica*. Kick his ass.>

Dr Sonja snorted from the passenger seat. <How much are you going to pay me not to tell my sister about that. Oh you're blushing, how sweet.>

<Not blushing,> growled Francisco. He hauled the driver's door shut and fired up the ignition. Moya waved as he backed out along the dirt track that had brought them here the first place, and the last thing she saw of Francisco before he and his car with coffin lashed to the top and his bitchy doctor friend were gone into the gloom was his hand waving back at her.

Then they were gone, and there was just the darkness and the endless song of the insects.

Moya watched the empty pathway for a moment. She never liked goodbyes. The crunch of gritty sand got her attention and she turned as Buey walked up to her. He seemed bigger than ever in the dark, like he was part battering ram.

<You in love again, little sister,> he said, chuckling to himself.

<No. Shut up. I hate you.> Moya gave one final look along the path, seeing the car headlights witch on in the distance before they vanished as well. Then she turned away, and she and Buey walked back to the edge of the cliff where they had spent the last hour watching, studying, planning.

In reality it wasn't much of a plan. Mostly it would be hitting people. But now they had a better idea of how the security worked in this platform, this hideout that nobody should have been able to find. The men had guns of course. They always had guns. Some were probably private security, others were Cartel heavies drafted in through handshake deals and lots of money.

Moya turned her fragile feeling piece of stone over and over in her hands, and she lost herself in a little daydream until Buey nudged her and pointed.

<Look.>

Moya looked. A boat was coming in from the ocean.

Two people in suits walked along a wooden, bolted-together gangway lit up in the dark by a blazing white spotlight. They had been waiting for the latest shipment for what felt like days, and now it had finally arrived they would actually get to do something. It wouldn't be much, but it was a lot better than polishing brand new guns and staring out at the scenery being bored.

Working on The Barge always had two sides to it.

The money was good. A person could retire to somewhere tropical with the money that could be earned from a few months' work, living away from anywhere and doing little more than babysitting. Stories about former security staff who owned their own islands and had a harem at their beck and call were constantly told and retold. Whether they were true or not didn't really matter, because the stories passed the time and gave everyone something to daydream about.

The boredom got to everyone in the end, and nobody stayed more than a year. But that wasn't the worst thing about The Barge. The worst thing was always the people that paid to hide away here. They all had different reasons, and all of them were bad. Even with the kinds of things some of the staff said they had seen in the Wilderness, things that were only supposed to live in the depths of drug-induced hallucinations, the Barge tenants were monsters.

Valentina hated them all.

She led the way up towards the boat and the sight slim man she usually worked with another Colombian named Matias, followed quietly like he always did. They both wore the same brand of sunglasses and kept their suits and shirts pressed and clean with the oddly expensive facilities that hid behind the apparently shabby exterior of The Barge. That was its secret. To outsiders it was just a delipidated old mass of wood shackled together and dumped out to float by nameless rocks ignored by everyone. Inside it was a different matter. Inside it was luxury for the damned.

Valentina climbed into the moored boat while Matias stood as a sentry, his silver-plated handgun out in the open and obvious for everyone to see. That was part of their shared act and it always worked. Nobody ever caused any trouble, but Valentina still kept a watch over the two men in the boat as she checked the packages they had brought. If anyone tried anything she would simply break an arm or two. She had done it a great many times, and she had found it always sent a better message than just shooting people. In reality Matias's gun was just extra intimidation. He hadn't shot anyone since he'd come to the Barge nearly three months previously.

<What is this crap,> asked Valentina. The labels on the boxes were in a language she didn't know. <Supplies?>

The scared looking man at the helm of the boat shrugged. He didn't want to engage. The Barge security had a reputation and he had no intention of testing it out. <Not my problem.>

It was such a familiar answer that Valentina barely even registered it. <Fine. Get it unloaded. No surprises.>

Matias smiled a little, and he turned away to hide it. Then he froze. Somehow, a huge mass of a man who looked like he was half animal faced him. <Holy SHIT.>

Buey smiled back at him. *<Ola, puto.>*

There was no fight. Matias just flew through the air with one swipe, out cold as he splashed down into the water, his beloved gun sinking out of sight. Valentina drew her own gun and fixed the man at the helm with icy eyes behind her sunglasses.

<Ambush?> she hissed. *<Hijueputa!>*

The boatman held up his hands, his nervous disinterest transformed into panic in the space of a single second. Valentina took out her own gun – jet black and perfectly maintained - shot him in the head, right between the eyes. She let his limp body flop down with the destroyed brain matter hanging from the back of skull and slipping onto his expensive linen shirt. She aimed her weapon at the second man as he scrambled for cover, begging her not to fire. Valentina ignored him. She hated people who begged.

Then a hand grabbed onto her arm.

A woman's hand, impossibly strong, that locked Valentina in place and crushed her muscles. The pain was so ferocious, so instant, that she dropped her gun and gasped out loud in a way she had though she had taught herself not to over her years killing people in dangerous places. Suddenly she wasn't as stone-like as she thought she was.

Moya wrenched Valentina's arm back on itself, ripping the shoulder joint.

In the last moment before she was knocked out, Valentina saw the Amazon woman with the horns and the markings along her arms staring down at her, eyes blazing with anger, and realised she was hopelessly out of her league

<Its true,> she thought. <It's all true.>

From behind the crates on the back of the boat, the second man peaked out and tried to understand what was happening. He had already wet himself, and now the two people in the black suits had been replaced by a different man and woman. Guns had been bad enough, but this pair looked like demons standing there, looming out of the night time.

<*Madre de dios.*> he whispered, making a cross over his chest even though he hadn't been to church since he was a young boy.

The woman over up at him as she let Valentina collapse onto the decking with her nose broken and bleeding.

<Get out of here,> said Moya, and the boatman needed no second chance to comply. Suddenly he didn't care about getting paid for a delivery. All he cared about was getting way from The Barge as quickly as he could and coming up with a good lie when he dumped the cargo overboard. He ran the engine and cut the mooring rope with a knife, then accelerated back away from the gangway as fast as the throttle would let him.

Moya and Buey watched him go, as Moya kicked Valentina's body out of the way. Buey looked for something to fish Matias out of the sea. There was no reason to let him drown because he was just a man paid to do a job. The real enemy was somewhere else on The Barge, hiding.

"What the fuck is this?" snapped an American voice. "Turn the fuck around."

Moya and Buey raised their hands and turned, the spotlight half blinding them. All they could see was a hulking figure, wearing a suit like all the rest, who looked like he spent far too much of his time taking steroids and lifting weights.

"Don't you fucking move."

The new guard was named Caleb, and he liked to think he was big. But seeing these two, he felt a little insecure and he didn't like it. Moya was nearly a head taller than him, and Buey simply dwarfed him in body mass. It was time to assert himself. After all, he was always the Boss. Always.

<I don't speak any English,?> lied Moya, and Caleb felt the rage vein in his forehead begin to pulse. He knew two words of Spanish, because he expected everyone to speak to him with the appropriate respect in his language. The American language.

"Are you shitting me?" Caleb strode forward into the light hopping it would make him look bigger and more menacing. He had freshly shaved his head so he could show off his tattoos, and hefted his very large and very obvious high calibre gun. It was the biggest he had found back in the US, so he had bought ten with the expensive nickel plating. He loved the way they felt in his hand.

He saw Moya's horns and then Buey's ram-like head, and saw a chance to attack.

"What are you, a couple of freaks? Jesus."

<Now?> asked Buey.

Moya felt the slim piece of stone Francisco had given her in the palm of her hand. <Not yet.>

Caleb took a step closer, his weapon vaguely pointed at Buey but his eyes fixated on Moya. He looked her up and down in that invasive way that unpleasant dirty-minded men did, face to chest and then down to her waist, where his flinty eyes picked up her belt.

"What's that?" he demanded.

Moya knew what he was looking at. She had kept the whipclaw that Francisco had gifted to her coiled on her hip ever since they had left the rainforest. She had practiced with it, got used to how it worked, how it straddled a line between natural and supernatural. She had even got to the level where the large eagle-like claw on the end of the cord would almost respond to her thoughts, as though the thing had some kind of impossible life about it.

As Caleb moved forward it twitched, almost like it sensed what its mistress wanted to do. Moya felt the claw flex a little as Caleb called back over his shoulder. "Need some back up here."

It was just the right distraction.

Moya grabbed and lashed out the whipclaw in one smooth motion, letting the claw latch onto Caleb's gun and rip it from his hand. Caleb stared, dumbfounded, until Buey's foot connected with him and sent him flying twenty feet into crumpled, senseless, broken-boned heap.

<We may have lost the element of surprise here.>

It took only a few seconds for the clatter of footsteps to start, and then get louder and louder. Black suited figures seemed to pour out of every doorway and opening until a crowd of them had formed, blending into each other in the half light as they brandished their weapons. Guns mostly, but a few seemed to prefer knives, and one woman carried a katana that glimmered with wicked sharpness. There was one figure without anything at all, a brute of a man who looked eight feet tell with a misshapen face that looked like it was made entirely of scar tissue.

<Now?> asked Buey.

Moya nodded. <Now.>

She crushed the stone in her hand and felt it snap and crumble. As guns were cocked and the crowd began to form its identity of a mob, a sudden crack of thunder filled the air. Arcs of lightning spewed out of the Barge generator high into the sky, and electricity jumped from light to light like a sparking chain. The energy of it buzzed and burned in the air with the smell of ozone, and then it began its work.

The katana became a lightning rod and the woman holding it screamed as she burned. Current smashed its way through body after body, hurling them aside with the ease of a hand crushing a tiny insect. As the generator started to burst with released elemental power, the other sigils that Francisco had planted came to life as well. The arcs of power they produced formed a kind of net that died and reformed itself with each passing second. Sparks cut into the air and the lights caught fire as one Black Suit after the next cried out in agony. Some froze to the spot, others gave in to unstoppable body spasms, and other simply dropped. Everywhere, the power of the lighting was unmerciful, flowing from body to body, fitting to fitting, charring wood and scorching metal as it went in a blaze as hot and bright as the sun.

Moya and Buey shield their eyes as the elemental display danced its violent dance in front of them. Everything was lit up with the power of the storm as bolts of pure force burst up out of the floor and down out of the air. A few of the guards hurled themselves towards the water in a desperate bid to escape, but tendrils of energy lifted them up and cast them away. Caleb had managed to crawl to the edge of one of the walkways and drop in to the sea but the electricity fried him in the water until he floated unconscious, skin blistering with burns that wouldn't kill him but would scar his skin forever.

For Caleb, disfigurement was even worse than being dead.

The lightning started to coalesce, and Moya tried to look at it despite its eye-burning light. For a second, the briefest of instants, she thought she saw a figure form out of the arcs. There were just hints of it, glimpses of something both fish and reptile, standing over everything clutching the merest outlines of a gigantic axe that cast bolts of fury everywhere. It was the storm made incarnate like a God, and Moya could have sworn that it looked at her.

Then it was gone.

The light, the rage, the power. All of it vanished in a second, leaving the pier silent and quiet as the unconscious battered bodies of the Black Suits lay everywhere like beached fish.

Except one.

The Brute slowly began to get up. His body and clothing smoked and stank of burning, but he still forced his limbs to move. It took a moment as Moya and Buey watched before this one last Black Suited man had regained some measure of strength and stood in front of them again. His face was still the same mass of ruined flesh, and even in the gloom of the moonlight Moya and Buey had better sight that could see that there were other things about The Brute that set him apart. Not just his size and his bulk. His eyes for one – they reflected the light as an eerie orange glow. His hands too – they looked like they were fashioned out of flexible bone, ridges and skinless, fingers pointed into claws and knuckles heavy and raised like ballbearings.

<I think this one is a little different,> said Moya.

Buey nodded. Ever since he had come here to find his sister all he had come across were people who were just weak. It wasn't like back home, where he was just another Los Cuernos wrestler, thick-skinned and durable but by no means the strongest. Out here even the tough-guys couldn't back up their tough-guy talk, and they always resorted to guns. For her part Moya had told her brother tales of the strange beings that inhabited the Yucatán. Of witches and spirits and other things that didn't belong. The stories had fired up Buey's imagination, and he had wanted to meet them.

Now, it seemed, he had his chance. Whoever the Brute was he had the touch of the Wilderness about him, there was no mistaking that. He radiated a kind of strength that Moya had felt before, one that charged the air with supernatural energy that made akin crawl and hairs stand up on end. Buey felt it too, but he ignored it. The chance of a fight, a real fight, was just too exciting for him to pass up.

Moya could tell exactly what was happening.

<Is this the time for a dick measuring contest little brother?>

Buey didn't answer straight away. He was trying to figure out his opponent – what he could do, how strong and skilled he was. There was already that unspoken sense of commitment between him and The Brute, so all Moya really could do was let it play out.

<I got this,> said Buey finally. <You have to find that Horta *pendejo*, right?>

Moya just rolled her eyes. <Fine. *Dios*, why do you have to be such a macho shithead.>

She kept her eye on the Brute as she slipped away. He watched her go, but somehow he didn't seem too bothered. Instead his attention was focussed on Buey, with his rhino-hide skin and his bull horns. The Brute had never seen anything like him before, and he was curious. When he had taken the job here on the Barge he had been told he would see some strange things, and he believed it. The Brute had known all about the Wilderness since the day he'd woken up years ago covered in dirt with his body bigger and stronger, his hands turned into weapons, his face a scarred mess that had driven away his wife in fear.

He always knew there would be others. It was just a matter of time,

<*Lucha libre*,> said Buey, his body flexing and tensing in readiness.

The Brute nodded slowly and raised his bone fists.

*

As Moya vanished through one of the doorways that led to the inside of the raft the scent of sweetness hit her, like fresh oranges. There was light here too, dim but coming out of the roof and the floors where little glowing cubes had been placed at regular intervals. The walls were smooth and new and the whole place felt like it existed in a different world than the ramshackle wood structures outside.

Maybe it was, thought Moya. It wouldn't be the first time.

Oddly she could hear nothing from outside. The had expected there to be the grunts and shouts of fighting, but instead there was just a serene kind of peace and quiet. There had to be some kind of magic at work here, and it made Moya edgy as she started to try and navigate the corridors. Each one was identical, connected by junctions that created a kind of a maze that always ended in a door. The first one was ornate metal, the second painted green, but it was the third one – a heavy wooden carved thing smothered in a huge lurid mural – she found after what seemed like an eternity of sneaking about that got her attention.

Where the others had been silent, this one vibrated with sound

Moya pressed her ear to the surface and heard what she had been searching for.

<We love you Doctor Horta.>

Those words made Moya's mind race back in time. She was strapped to a gurney in a darkened room that was made of stone. She felt numb and drugged, unable to struggle as two women dressed like whores and nurses mixed together stood guard, both of them with faces painted for Dia De Muerte and their eyes blank and white like chalk. A voice that sounded muffled directed them like zombies, and they obeyed silently.

Moya struggled as the first needle pushed its way into her neck. The sensation it brought was horrible, like death worming its way through her veins and into her brain. It felt even worse in memory that it had back then, and Moya felt herself nearly throw up as she stood outside the wooden door.

It felt like her mind was being switched off.

More injections, and the fog took over. She felt something happen to her eyes, a coldness as they became as blank and empty as those of the nurses. There was no fight anymore, no struggle. Just the unnatural chemistry of Doctor Horta filling her up and turning her into a puppet.

At least that had probably been the idea.

It hadn't worked that way. Moya knew that rather than being a slave she had been a raging beast, a monster that wanted to tear everything and everyone apart until a giant of a man with white skin had found her. The feral fury had forced her to attack him but there had been something else, something like a voice. There had been the face of a woman clad in a cloak of multicolored feathers in her dulled mind and she had called to Moya through the fog. It had made her aware for a moment, given her a chance to get away.

Moya still didn't know what had happened that day, but she knew she had come to the end of what it had started as she kicked in the door.

The room inside was draped in luxury and lit by larger cubes than the corridors that gave it the feeling of being illuminated by candles. The walls were lined with paintings and the carpets were hand woven and expensive. A huge bed dominated everything, a four-poster structure smothered in silk coverings, and next to it was an antique table laden with junk food and cheap drink.

On the bed, a fried chicken leg half in his mouth, was Doctor Horta.

He stared in mute frozen shock at Moya as walked into the chamber, and she finally got a look at who he was. There was nothing impressive about him. He looked no older than 18 with a huge fat flabby body covered in a black gown stained with grease, and around his thick neck was a golden chain with a silvery pendant. His hair was slicked back into a ponytail of sorts but it was so thinning he looked as though he was bald from certain angles.

Moya stared at him. Could this lump of a manchild really have brought her too her knees? It was almost embarrassing.

"Are you like a hooker or something? Cool. I was getting totally bored of these DVDs. Hey, what's with the horns. You horny, huh? I like that."

Horta's voice irritated Moya. It was high pitched and childlike, laden with an accent that sounded so American that it came out of the movies rather than real life. She remembered the voice that had spoken to her before in Spanish, and realised just how much of an illusion it had been, like every word had been read form a script. Now she really saw how fake Horta really was. Even the voice she had heard through the door was just something being played back on a large screen hanging on the wall opposite the bed.

Bar the two of them there was no one else in the room. No naked obliging slave girl painted up for the holidays. Nobody.

Moya's plans to enact violent retribution fizzled out as she just kept looking at Horta in complete disbelief. <You are Horta?>

Horta chomped on his chicken. "Sorry lady. I don't abla Spanish. But if you said Horta, that's me." He tried to pose with pride. "Dr Sir Thaddeus Horta. So, you take your clothes off and bend over. Just need a moment to get myself revved up, know what I mean."

"You don't even know who I am, do you?" Moya asked, not quite knowing what to do.

"Should I?>" Horta threw his chicken leg back onto the table and hauled himself to sitting position on the bed. "So listen, I like my women to do what I tell them, so I have some panties and garter belts and stuff in that drawer. Put them on."

Moya realised what a joke it suddenly all was. There was no terrifying nemesis behind the name Horta. There was no monstrous evil to be conquered. There was just a fat idiot teenager in a dirt gown.

"This is bullshit," growled Moya. She stomped over to the bed and grabbed Horta by the ankle, dragging him off the bed and onto the floor. His head bounced off the carpet and he cried a little bit with the pain which wasn't really any pain at all.

"Jesus you freak bitch, that hurt. Hey, what are you doing?"

*

Moya stood on the roof of one of the Raft buildings and held Horta over the edge by the ankle. On the decking below Buey and The Brute sat, drank beers and watched.

<I thought you were measuring dicks.>

<It was a good fight.> said Buey.

The Brute nodded. <It was, but this Horta guy is such an asshole we decided he wasn't worth it. So we decided to have a beer instead.>

<This is the guy who made you his bitch?> asked Buey. <How?>

<Shut up,> snapped Moya, but she was asking the very same question herself.

Horta just screeched. His gown flapped a little and everyone was thankful he was wearing a pair of shorts underneath, just as stained as everything else about him. "Please please please it isn't my fault. This voice made me do it. I was just on vacation with my bros and we found this place with all this weird shit in all these jars and this voice gave me that thing and said I could have any woman I wanted. I mean come on who wouldn't. They gave all the chemicals and stuff and it all turned me evil. Please I would never do anything bad l really really respect women. Please you have to believe me." He paused. "Can I have my thing back?"

The thing was the amulet Moya held in her other hand that she had pulled from Horta's neck. It felt unpleasantly greasy, but the symbols carved into it were definitely from The Wilderness – arcane and unknowable in their meaning. It was impossible to see what unnatural hand had created them, only what they could do. <You mean this? This is how you do it?>

Horta seemed to realise he had said too much. <Maybe…Give it back. Give it to me.>

<What an asshole.> said The Brute

Moya flexed her hand and crushed the amulet out of shape. She felt a sensation of something as she did, of something almost ghostly leaving or fading away. Horta obviously felt it too was he wailed and cried some more, knowing that all his power was gone in instant. Now he was just plain Thad Hortenski again. The kid who liked to abuse people. The coward. The nobody.

Moya wondered how many women out there would now be free of his pernicious control. She desperately hoped some would come out of their trance alive and unharmed, like she had.

<Maybe now try getting a date the normal way,> she said, and she threw the amulet back behind her far out to sea where it sank instantly, lost to the currents.

<No hope,> said Buey, and he and the Brute bumped their beer cans together, sharing a smile. Shaking her head, Moya let Horta drop as well, this time just to the deck where he rolled off the wooden planks and into the water. He splashed desperately until he realised the water was shallow enough for him to stand. Then he did his best to run and swim away as fast as he could towards the close-by shore, focussed only on escape and safety somewhere. Anywhere.

After a moment there was screech and another splash, out of sight in the dark.

<You hear something?> asked Buey.

Moya simply took her brother's beer out of his hand and drained the can. <No.>

TEMPLO

The drive from Mexico City to Playa Del Mantarraya was a long and boring one that Francisco had made more times than he could count. He didn't really mind. It was for Ana-Maria's benefit so she could see Uncle Derek and the rest of the family who refused to settle in the Yucatán. Francisco couldn't blame them for that. Once a person crossed that fenced border everything changed. The eyes of thousand unknown things peered out of the forests, and without the safety net of cellphones and signals it was easy to feel frighteningly alone.

That was the nature of the Wilderness. For Francisco it was a home of sorts, and he felt he belonged there. But he often wondered why Dr Sonja stayed there. Surely Ana-Maria would grow up happier somewhere else, but she seemed as connected to the place as Francisco himself did so he decided not to question it.

Besides, without Dr Sonja to help, thing would be alot worse. Francisco often thanked the various Gods old and new for her courage in the face of things that sent most people running for the cover of normality. It was weird to think that in some ways he was one of things himself. That was why he never stayed in Mexico City. He belonged in the Wilderness, even now he wasn't the Pale Ghost.

About an hour's drive into the peninsula was a small old temple ruin that Francisco liked to stop at. Few people knew it was there, and it was set in a little clearing filled with birdsong. Sometimes he would see monkeys wandering the treetops or huge brightly colored macaws watching the world go by from their high-up branches. Today it as quieter, with the sun lighting up the stones of the ruin and glittering off the surface of a still pool close by.

Francisco parked quietly. Ana-Maria was fast asleep on the back seat while Dr Sonja sat in the passenger side drifting in and out of daydreams. She opened her eyes when Francisco eased open his door.

<Are we home yet.>

<No, just wanna stretch my legs.>

Dr Sonja nodded, her head a little woozy. She had enjoyed some drinks with her brother the previous night and she was feeling the after effects. A week in Mexico City had done her alot of good. She felt refreshed and happy, but somehow she still felt a pull back to Playa Del Mantarraya. Sometimes she couldn't really explain why to Derek.

<Going to call this place Templo Francisco,> she said. <Maybe make it into a holiday home.>

Francisco smiled as Dr Sonja closed her eyes again and shifted in the seat to get more comfortable. A hand drifted to check to her daughter, who stayed asleep as Gorguz slumped next to her curled-up body. He snored a tiny goblin snore that was somehow comforting.

Outside the bright morning sunlight was tempered the cover of trees and the air felt wet, like a storm was coming. Francisco walked out into the clearing, never out of sight of the car, and looked at the temple, his temple, like he always did. Usually it relaxed him but today it wasn't working. The odd quiet of the clearing made the atmosphere a little eerie, and Francisco felt a little feeling of unease in the pit of his stomach.

Somehow it all seemed different.

<Franciscooooooooo......>

Francisco looked around, his heart beating a little faster that it should. He would have dismissed it as the wind, but there was no wind. The trees were still and the animals and birds stayed quiet, if they were even here at all. Instead, it was the like air itself was spoken his name out loud. Dr Sonja and Ana-Maria were both still in the car, asleep or half-asleep, so it hadn't been them. There was no one else in the clearing either. It was just him and the temple.

It was not a huge ruin and nobody really knew what it had been or what it was for in times past. Something about the shapes just appealed to Francisco, the way it sat there in the clearing, surrounded by the tangles of the trees as though it defied them to take it back. There were vines that tried to take hold but hey never seemed to be successful. The one that had been there last time was withered and broken now.

Francisco took a couple of steps forward, keeping his footsteps quiet. Was there someone or something hiding in the ruins, rucked away, watching him. *Macuihuitl* was in the car and he was in no mood for a fight. But there was no guessing what variety of spirt or devil could have found its way here whether accidentally or on purpose.

<Franciscooooooo……>

It was definitely a voice this time, no doubt about it.

Francisco was torn. Should he run and or should he investigate. Now he was a normal man, stripped of the chalk-white skin of the Pale Ghost, he wasn't so sure any more. What was he supposed to do, he wondered. Was he supposed to leave it behind and be a normal man, or was this still something inside him, something he had always felt. A kind of drive to be the saviour of The Wilderness, to fight the monstrous things that squatted in the darkness and maybe even try to broker a kind of peace between human and inhuman.

None of it was really clear anymore, if it ever had been.

Francisco shook his head to try and clear it, and then he saw it. Or rather he saw her.

He recognised her. A faint ghostly shape, a spectre who seemed to be dressed in feathers. Barely there at all in the sun, she shifted shape like she was made of smoke. Francisco tried to find her eyes but there was something in the way, a kind of cowl shaped like a bird's head, perhaps an eagle. The ghost seemed to have materialised out of the stones of the temple and slowly she drifted forward. Francisco watched, rooted to the spot yet unafraid.

It was almost like he knew this woman. This spirit.

An ephemeral hand reached out. Francisco paused, and then slowly reached out his own. Flesh and blood met something else and they blended together for second. As little tendrils of smoke danced around Francisco's and a voice spoke in his head, a voice of picture and images.

They formed into one singular thing, one picture, and Francisco's eyes widened.

<Mierda…. he whispered.

Dr Sonja jerked awake as Francisco slammed the door shut and fired up the engine. Ana-Maria stirred too, not quite away yet but still wondering what was going on.

<What's happened.>

Francisco's face looked almost afraid as he said:

<We need to get home.>

EL SEPULTURERO

V

LAS BRUJAS

This was the end.

This exact moment, surrounded by the frozen dead, just the two of them. Francisco and Dr Sonja. Exhausted, hurting, suffering inside and out from everything they had had to face, and had to do.

In some ways, this was a relief.

Everywhere around them dripped with the cold, sealing everything into an ice blasted cage. Chichen Itza used to be a haven for tourists, and even after the fallout from the Black Ritual, people had still come here. Not now though. Now there were just skeletons stripped of their flesh by raging frost. The whole place was obscenely silent, with not even birdsong to break through the pall that hung over it.

To Francisco it felt like being in the past. Like he and Dr Sonja had taken a step back in time to before there was even a Mexico. All there was now, was this. This old Mayan city, dominated by El Castillo, turned into an apocalyptic nightmare where even the grass was burned away by cold and turned to blackened solid death. The rest of the world might as well have not even existed anymore.

And maybe it didn't. Neither Francisco nor Dr Sonja knew for sure anymore.

They had been here for what felt like forever, in amongst the ruins of the Mayan temples and observatories. The car had protected them as they had driven around, but now they had had to leave the safety of that behind as they stared up at El Castillo and the thing that stood there, screaming like a banshee foghorn that sucked the souls out of the unwary.

This is where it was going to end. So many people had died to get to this time and place. Cíclope and all his men had fought so bravely, but even they had fallen in the end.

Tempesta who should have been the most immune to death of all of them was cold and lifeless for real now. Rae was gone too, leaving Hook bereft and lost, not knowing what to do without his unique telepathy.

Francisco knew he could never have stopped them from fighting. This place, the Yucatán with all its Badland terrors, was their home and they had died to defend it. Even Moya with all her strength had fallen, and although she held on to life even Dr Sonja didn't know for sure if her brother Buey would pull through.

Only the two of them, Francisco and Dr Sonja, remained standing now.

The only two who had been there in the beginning.

The start of it all felt so long ago.

Years ago, Francisco sat in his little office at the Flor Azul cemetery with his favorite shovel, satisfied after a hard day's work tending the graves, greeting the visitors, and making things right for people to talk to the ones who had passed on in amongst the bright colors and the angelic sculptures.

He took a lot of pride in his work. After all, Flor Azul was *the* place to be buried. Everything was perfect here, and he had even painted the huge symbol of the flower on the outside walls himself. It looked like a work of street art, and touristos came from everywhere to take photos of it. They never came inside the cemetery gates though. That was reserved for the dead and their relatives.

Colorful birds chirped in the huge tree that overhung the far north fence. As Francisco drank some bottled water, he waved at the two people who sat there. A little girl and her mother, the girl wearing a summer dress and huge hat with a floppy brim.

<Hi Francisco> called Dr Sonja.

Ola.

<Sorry about this. She wanted to see the butterflies again. Is that OK?>

Francisco nodded and gave her a thumbs up. He didn't mind. He liked the fact that little Ana-Maria saw the cemetery as a place of beauty. This whole American thing of fearing the dead? He didn't get that. Surely it was natural, even special. That made Flor Azul a place of celebration to him, especially when Dia de Muertos came round.

He always made a special effort then. Lots and lots of candy.

Francisco and Dr Sonja didn't know each other well, but they liked each other. Just as friends, more like a kind of brotherly sisterly relationship. He knew she was divorced and had come out a hospital in the big city to set up a practice here, in this little town. Other than that he chose not to pry. In his experience people wanted to talk about things, they would talk.

<Long day?> asked Francisco.

<Senor Olan and his feet again?> said Dr Sonja. <You know I like the quiet life but once in a while I'd like maybe a serious injury or something .> She looked around the gravestones. <No zombies yet?>

Francisco smiled. She always asked that, and he always answered the same way, like a little shared joke. <We don't have those here.>

<Shame. I think I'd be good in a zombie attack. I have expert medical knowledge.>

A rumble like thunder in a clear sky stopped their conversation.

<Uncle Francisco?>

Little Ana-Maria's eyes had widened. Her butterfly was forgotten, and instead she pointed past the cemetery gates and out onto the far horizon into the trees.

<Uncle Francisco, what's that?>

The wave of shimmering half-invisible darkness had no name. It simple blasted out like the detonation of a warhead, consuming every soul it touched. Hundreds of thousands of people screamed and ran as the wave expanded, washing everything in its baleful demonic touch. Somewhere at its centre, a building, a huge hotel, had been ruptured and twisted out of shape, yet around it the structure, the stone and metal, remained untouched. Only living things perished at the wave's touch.

Perished, or were transformed.

Inch by inch, mile by mile, The Wilderness began to form. The earth started to fracture and things begin to crawl out from their forgotten tombs deep underground. Human beings became the shape of their fears and lusts, animals found new forms that defied evolution. Everything changed. Places of lost time and hidden imagination started to find a foothold out in the forests, in the cenotes, while dark songs that hadn't been sung in a thousand years howled out loud.

The spark of technology failed. All the advancements of the digital age, every computer, every cellphone, every signal, died instantly. They were permanently smothered by the wave, all the infinite little scraps of data sucked up and destroyed. Even engines would struggle now, and each second progress wound back ten years in its own little apocalypse.

At Flor Azul, Francisco and Dr Sonja both thought exactly the same thing.

Finally, the Mad President had done it. His all-consuming hatred had led him to push that big red button, and all anyone could do was run for shelter.

Francisco only had time to get Dr Sonja and little Ana-Maria into his hut before the wave hit and carried him away.

<FRANCISCO!!!!>

It could have been just a second before he opened his eyes again. Instantly he knew everything was different that it had been. He felt different.

His vision swam around him and he realised he wasn't in the cemetery anymore. The cemetery was gone now. He was inside Dr Sonja's surgery, surrounded by people who groaned with pain and loss.

<Uncle Francisco> squealed little Ana-Maria. She still wore the same flowery dress she had before, but no hat now. <Mama mama Uncle Francisco is alive.>

Dr Sonja was at his side instantly.

Gracias a Dios.

She didn't have time to prepare him before he saw his hands. They were chalk white, not covered in ash but as though the color has been sucked out of them. They felt oddly numb too. Somehow the heat outside wasn't touching him anymore.

<What's going on >

He tried to sit up, and felt heavy. That same hand grasped hold of the makeshift gurney he was on and effortlessly crushed the metal. He and Dr Sonja stared at it, then at each other, and then at his hand.

<I...don't think that was a nuclear bomb,> observed Dr Sonja.

<Uncle Francisco, are you Santo now. Or maybe Superman?>

People were making a fuss that doorway out onto the street, and one pointed.

<OK, now what is going on?> demanded Dr Sonja.

Outside, parked opposite, was a car with a coffin strapped to it, and laying across its hood was what looked like a wooden sword with razor sharp rectangular fragments buried into its edges. Francisco saw it too, and instantly a word popped into his head, one he couldn't have known and yet knew intimately.

Macuahuitl.

*

Moya dropped a bank note onto a rough wooden bartop and leaned over. Men were so easy to distract, and she had the bartender right where she wanted him – although she wasn't quite sure which he preferred: her horns or her chest.

"So, can we get some food on a discount?"

Buey watched and stayed sitting at the back of the bar, alone at a table with his water. Mainly his approach was to smash things, with his hulking body and huge horns that people seemed to take for granted here, but his sister had demanded they take a more subtle approach. He didn't much like it when Moya did her flirtatious thing. It made him cringe. Punching was much easier, and much more reliable.

The barman was captivated though. He was a young guy, American, probably on some kind of break from life to find himself. How he'd ended up in this dingy Mexican bar that was the same as a hundred other bars, Buey had no idea. It didn't matter though. He was simply a means to amend, and Buey decided that while Moya mesmerised him he could take some pride in his drawing of the infamous Doctor Horta. He had a knack for faces, and his sister's description had been so detailed it hadn't been difficult to make a decent likeness.

He was glad that Horta couldn't cause any more damage or take any more lives and minds. Once they got home they could burn the picture in a little ritual mand it would all be over. No more bad dreams his sister. Ever.

At the bar, the American was doing his best to turn Moya's interrogation into a phone number and a date. He had heard of Ciudad Volcan. Everybody had. But to meet one of their famous Amazon women in person was something else.

Moya had done a little too good a job. She started to realise that the American's mind was not focussed on trying to remember anything. Maybe she should have let Buey do his threatening thing in the first place. A while ago she would have, but Dr Sonja had taught her that not everything had to start in a fight.

"Young guy," persisted Moya, in her best English. "Bad person. Likes to do bad things to women."

So do I, though the American. He was going to roll out his best line when something caught his eye over Moya's shoulder. Moya saw his expression change instantly, and she turned to look at the doorway to the bar. Buey had turned as well, and both saw the same thing.

The afternoon sun outside, the dusty road and the cars had all gone. In their place was a churning sparking darkness, as though a cloud of night had flooded across everything. It pulsed as though it was alive, lit up by stormcloud lighting in reds and blues, and little tendrils groped their way into the bar.

As Moya watched, one of the tendrils found its way to an old drunk patron, and it snaked around his throat. He gasped suddenly and went blue, all the air sucked away from him as he pitched forward onto the table.

Buey was on his feet, using his own table as a kind of shield as he moved to join his sister.

<What's that?>

Moya shook her head, not taking her eyes of the malignant darkness and its swirling flashing mass.

<I don't know.>

A guttural sound came out of the darkness. Everyone in the bar felt it deep down inside, a growl that shook the bowels and shivered the heart. The American was already gone before a shape started to emerge, a figure forming out of the madness.

A woman, but not a human one. Moya saw a knotted mass of muscle, and claws where hands and feet should have been. Jagged hair was like spikes that shifted like snakes, and the woman's face was fixed into a rictus of the unrelenting need to kill anything she saw.

As she stalked into the bar, there was a rhythm in the air, like heartbeat that spoke a name over and over, drumming the fear into everyone.

La Mudo, it said. *La Mudo, La Mudo, La Mudo.*

<Don't think flashing your boobs will work this time,> said Buey.

The she-devil, La Mudo, hissed, her black eyes fixed completely on Moya as an echoing and sinister laugh fluttered through the air.

<I found you,> said a voice out of the darkness.

Images flashed in Moya's mind. She saw the broken hotel in Cancún. She saw Francisco beaten down and hurt. And then she saw the dark shape that she herself had beaten down. Humiliated, angry, full of vengeful bitterness. It was the same darkness that had infected the hotel. There was another name too.

Agathe.

The images battered Moya, and they hurt. Pictures of seven women, seven beings that crackled with violent power and purpose. La Mudo was there, hissing and snapping, and Agathe was there too, smiling as she cast her shadows and illusions. All round, a chorus of unseen babies howled out, their cries distorted and Hellish.

Moya opened her eyes and saw herself. La Mudo was a reflection of her now, the murderous mindless thrall of Doctor Horta in filthy clothes, its eyes blank white and its face drained of everything. Moya felt her mind slip back to that time, and how the man Horta had done his utmost to take out her mind, her very soul.

It terrified her.

Buey was afraid too. He saw his sister and the thing she had once been made into, and in that second of hesitation the reflection was on him. It howled and screamed as it smashed through the table. It tore into him, ripping open his tough skin down through every layer to dense muscle and hardened bone.

<BUEY!!!>

As her brother bled and fought desperately against the apparition, Moya forced herself to move. She forced the images Agathe put into her head away, and as the darkness at the door seethed in protest, she fought back.

It felt like walking in mud. Ghost after ghost assaulted her mind. Terror after terror, throwing her thoughts back in time to Doctor Horta. The pain of what he injected into her. And his laugh. That stupid high-pitched childish laugh.

<You love Doctor Horta, don't you Moya,> said Agathe, inside her head. <Admit it. You love him.>

La Mudo raised her talons to open Buey's throat, and Moya was suddenly there as she took hold of her arm, stopping the killing stroke dead in its tracks.

<No. I really don't>

The she-devil, still wearing Moya's deadened face and eyes, lashed out and Moya felt something break in her arm. But there was no time to feel the pain, or give into it. Instead Moya used the stabs of agony as her saviour, and she hurled La Mudo bodily against the wall.

Agathe's whispers stopped suddenly.

<You think you are scary?,> growled Moya, and she smashed her fists onto La Mudo's head. <I am *Los Cuernos* and you don't scare me, *perra*!>

The she-devil slid back into her own natural form – scaley, dried and mummified - and tried to defend herself. She touched her own peeling face, almost unable to grasp she was hurt and bleeding. It had never happened before, and now she was scared.

They had told La Mudo she could not fail but they had lied. She wasn't strong enough.

Then Moya hit La Mudo so hard her neck snapped and her head twisted around to face the wall. The she-devil was dead instantly, the spent body slithering down to the floor.

There was a sudden flood of horror everywhere. Images from every nightmare ran rampant, washing over everyone. There were terrible warped screams out in a monstrous wilderness, and the eyes of unknown things glittered hungrily.

A shotgun blast rang out.

Moya jerked her head around, and saw an old man in a big hat. He nodded to her, and Maya saw that the darkness was gone from the doorway. Sunlight fell in, and life returned. Instead, a second body lay there, most of its head gone – a dead woman in a tight velvet black dress whose Night Terrors slipped away down the drains and into the walls, forgotten and harmless.

<I really hate witches,> said the man with the shotgun. <Gonna call an ambulance.>

Moya winced. The pain was everywhere and her arm hung mostly useless, but when she looked at her brother she pushed all of that away. There was so much blood, and he looked like an animal had ravaged his body. His breathing juddered, and he lay there, broken in a way she had never seen before.

There was a single picture that had lodged in Moya's mind too – the image of the seven witches, surrounded by the sounds of crying babies as the world fell apart in an apocalypse of fire and ice. Two lay dead in this ordinary bar on this ordinary street, but five others stood there – their faces blurred, indistinct, but bidden by the same mission that had commanded Agathe and La Mudo.

Finally, Moya said, <I think this is really bad.>

*

Francisco and Dr Sonja could only stare, mute and dumbfounded, at what had once been their home. Their drive had been easy, bringing Ana-Maria and her beloved goblin Gorguz back from visiting the Uncle Derek. There had been talk and laughter and candy, and now that was all over.

Playa Del Mantarraya burned in front of them.

<Mama,> said Ana-Maria. She was crying already. She couldn't understand what had happened, that this place where she had been raised and lived with all her friends, strange and otherwise.

They had to have taken a wrong turn.

Dr Sonja knew that they hadn't. She desperately wanted to comfort her daughter, make her feel that everything was going to be fine.

<Its OK,> she said, even though she knew it wasn't. Francisco caught her eye, and she could see that he was ready to fight. Somebody had come to his town and razed what looked like the powers of Hell itself.

There was going to have to be payback, and he slid *Macuahutil* from the sheath lying on the back seat of his car. Dr Sonja began to worry. Francisco wasn't the man he had been. Ever since they had come back from the rainforest he had enjoyed the life of a human being, as Francisco Garza,

275

normal guy. Gloriana had continued to train him, but it felt like whatever magic there had been inside him was less than it had been. He sweated like everybody else in the heat, and even his sword seemed more of an effort to wield.

For months now, there had just been normality. Francisco had been devoted to Perdita, and even she had become less tense, less ferociously focussed on everything about the Wilderness. There had been meals and family and the kind of time they had forgotten even existed.

That seemed over now, as flames flicked in the burned-out shells of house after house, building after building, and bodies lay discarded across the roads. Francisco tried to understand. He was still strong, just different than before, but maybe the Wilderness had heard that he was changed now wasn't what it had been anymore, and it had come calling.

Maybe this was a message. Or a warning. Or something dark laughing at him, telling him how weak he was now.

<Mama, where's Auntie Perdi?>

Dr Sonja felt that stab of real fear in her gut, and she hugged her daughter closer to her in some vain attempt to protect her from the hard reality in front of them.

<I'd better check the house,> said Dr Sonja, and Francisco nodded.

<I'll take a look around.>

<Be safe.>

Francisco nodded, and took his first steps into what felt for all the world like a warzone.

He trod carefully. He could smell the taint of the dead and dying, and with each step he felt the life of Playa Del Mantarraya draining away into nothingness. He recognised a few faces, and as he reached a small intersection where children used to cross to go to school he found a cluster of bodies he recognised. Straight away he saw Cíclope, his single eye open and gazing, and around him the ruined bodies of his men. There were blades in all of them – blades made from metal and bone that were merged together into an unholy union. Carved, hooked and serrated, each and every one had cut something vital.

It seemed like this had been less a battle, and more of a massacre.

Francisco made a cross across his body and vowed to give them all the burials they deserved. Another body caught his eye, and he took a few steps to get a closer look. It was twitching, and even though its face was a death mask the corpse, a young woman in a summer dress, was trying to move.

<*Dios,*> muttered Francisco.

He had seen dead things walk before, and knew that whatever they were now, the soul was gone. It was not a person, and he cleanly cut her head off with *Macuahuitl* and knelt, whispering a prayer after the deed was done. When he stood he looked for other signs of non-life, feeling in his bones the arcane power that somehow could make bodies move again.

Where there was one, there was surely another. And then another. The dead turning against the living. It was always the way that happened.

<Francissssscooo,> whispered a voice, a sweet sound that somehow rotted in the air.

Ahead of him, out of nowhere in the bright sun and the blue sky, was a woman, her skin grey and her eyes sunken beneath strands of white oily hair.

Francisco gripped his sword, and felt the power that radiated off her even thirty feet away. A second figure shambled into view, horribly butchered yet hauled back into a mockery of life. The figure was a second woman, a beauty this time yet marred with bloody wounds and cataract eyes whose body and hands bore the same blades that were buried in Cíclope and his men, the men who had died trying to protect this place.

The older woman cackled. <He does not understand. We shall teach him that nothing can stop us. We are Las Brujas, boy. La Siete. I am Nixila. The dead are mine. Even Salvatoria walks until I permit otherwise.>

The second woman Salvatoria simply stood, a deadalive puppet waiting for the order to attack, as Nixila gestured towards the body of one of Cíclope's men. It started to twitch as the invisible strings were attached, and a groan seeped out of collapsed lungs. Then a second one began to move. The disease of non-life began to spread from corpse to corpse, and even Cíclope began to move under its influence.

Salvatoria stumbled forward as her stabbing weapons formed and grew like living things hungering for a kill. They began to squirm like snakes, and Francisco saw the unnatural venom that dripped from their edges.

<I'm ready for you, witch.>

Nixila cackled again. <Take him sister.>

Salvatoria screeched a dead screech and hurled herself forward, preternaturally quick like a blur. She plunged her blades towards Francisco's heart faster than he could react, and he braced himself for the pain.

There was nothing. No pain, no blood. Nothing at all. Instead, Salvatoria's weapons evaporated to nothingness the second they touched him. If she had been alive, perhaps she would have been surprised, even shocked. For her long long cursed existence before this, her blades had carved a thousand men's flesh, and she had relished every moment.

Now, all her power was suddenly meaningless. Against this man, her power seemed to mean nothing. A thought almost formed in her empty cold brain the second before she collapsed, inanimate. Nixila felt that last sensation too, that last attempt to formulate something in an undead mind, as her power over Salvatoria's body failed her.

<What have you done?>: she screeched, staring at the corpse that had once walked.

A huge roar echoed about the streets, and Nixila was suddenly terrified. She called to the others in her mind, begging for help, but that had not been the plan. Her's and Salvatoria's mission had been to bring the town of Playa Del Mantarraya to its end, and draw an army of the dead to their side. They were absolute in their conviction. They could not fail. They never failed.

And now here he stood. El Sepulturero. The ghost of a man they had all been told about, the man whom they had cast away like an old rag. His power was gone, they said. He was no threat anymore.

But the truth was he had new power, granted by the touch of some other kind of magic, something from deep in the forests. It was corrosive to Nixila, like an antidote to her own dark powers that she felt start to dissolve, juts the way Salvatoria's had.

Nixila felt every ounce of her energy fading away, leeching out of her somehow. Cíclope and his men retuned to the peace of true death and Salvatoria lay there, as dead as when she had been first shot down after first killing fifty people. It was as though Francisco's presence simply defied the warped magic – Nixila's necromancy, Salvatoria's blades – that the witches wielded.

Las Siete Brujas.

<But you are nothing,> spat the old witch. <Nothing.> She simply couldn't believe what had happened. <You are just a man. You are nothing.>

Francisco said nothing in response. He just lowered his sword and waited as Nixila sank to her knees like she was weighed down by a fear she desperately tried to keep out of her voice by spitting anger and rage.

It made no difference.

The roar came again, and now there were heavy steps that came with it, thundering along the street, getting louder and louder.

<What is that.> whispered Nixila, her eyes widening. <What have you summoned?> She was truly afraid, down in her bones, yet her supreme arrogance wouldn't admit it as she screeched and howled her final words. <This is nothing. NOTHING. I will live on. I will succeed. You are a pathetic husk. You are worthless. Weak. A speck. WE WILL PREVAIL.>

Francisco turned his back and walked away. He didn't need to see Hook emerge from the junction, a dinosaur titan wielding his huge iron weapon. He knew what would happen.

There was a single scream from Nixila, and that was the end of it.

*

Dr Sonja reached the Castellanos family house. It was standing at least, but the violence that had stretched across the whole of Playa Del Mantarraya was here too. She tried to hide Ana-Maria's eyes from the worst of it as they moved past the bodies of dead friends and strangers alike. There were so many of them, their faces grey and their eyes blackened, ridden with bullet wounds and broken limbs.

Dr Sonja counted at least twenty before she reached the door and made her way inside. That was when she saw the worst of it.

Rae lay there, her throat cut wide open and choking her last moments. She saw Dr Sonja and Ana-Maria with her snake-like eyes for all to see. Her sunglasses were broken just a few feet away.

<Auntie Rae?????>

Rae tried to smile even as Ana-Maria ran over to her side, kneeling down and holding her hand like she knew her mother had done to the dying so many times before.

<ANA!>

<Its fine mama. I'll look after her. I'll make her better.>

Dr Sonja didn't know what to say. Ana-Maria had seen death before but not like this. There was no way to make Rae better, and she and Rae knew it. There was only the comfort of these last little second of awareness, and the terrible whirlpool of emotions that came with them.

Ana-Maria clutched onto Are as hard as she could, trying to will her own strength into the dying women's body.

<Please don't go, Auntie Rae. We can make it all better. Mama can make it all better.>

Rae raised a hand up to Ana-Maria's face and touched it, oh so gently. There was a spark of sorts, a little surge of energy from skin to skin, and then the hand dropped. As she died, Rae sensed one final thing in her fading mind's eye, and it gave her some comfort at least. She saw Hook tear Nixila apart, and heard him roar his victory. That made her happy.

Ana-Maria tried not to cry as she saw that last glimmer of life leave Rae's body, and she was gone. An awful stillness hung over the room, a quiet that soaked up any kind of sound, and then Ana-Maria ran to her mother. They held each other, neither of them really grasping what had happened here, the ferocious suddenness of it all. But then again, death rarely made any sense. Violent or natural, it just was its own irresistible thing with its own unknowable rules.

Dr Sonja felt her daughter's little body wrack with sobbing as she hugged her, and then she heard someone else weeping as well.

Dr Sonja slowly pushed open an upstairs bedroom door, and saw Gloriana, reduced to tears as she huddled herself on the bed, knees to chest, her body shaking uncontrollably.

Next to her was Tempesta, his neck cleanly broken.

It was almost impossible to take in. Two people that had been a part of their daily lives, touched by the powers of the Wilderness, gone. And Gloriana, her mask thrown aside, broken in a different way.

<Glory> said Dr Sonja. <Its Sonja.>

Slowly Gloriana looked up. Very few people had seen her face behind the mask, the scars and burns she hid behind it, but Dr Sonja had. Dr Sonja had seen everything, right down to the very particular curse that Gloriana had to bear now – that even with all the pain, she could never shed a single tear.

<A witch,> whispered Gloriana, her voice choked on sobs and catching on itself. <She made him…do…..things. I had to stop him. I didn't want to, but he…..I had to stop him. But it wasn't him. It……>

There was nothing that could be done to console her. Whatever it was that had happened she would have to carry with her, and while in time Dr Sonja could help with trauma, the scars inside would never leave.

<Do you know what happened downstairs?> asked Dr Sonja, as gently as she could.

Gloriana just shivered. <One of them killed them and the other….that whore…she made them walk again. They….they were everywhere. She said all dead things….they were hers. And she got hold of Tem……she made him dance…..and….>

Tears claimed her again, and Dr Sonja realised it was time to stop talking. When Gloriana was ready they would speak again, and all that Dr Sonja could do was instinctively check Tempesta before she left and rejoined Ana-Maria where she had left her in the hall. It was pointless really – Tempesta had never had a pulse, but it was clear that whatever gave him his own brand of life had been taken away from him.

Another precious gift, all gone.

Silent, Dr Sonja held Ana-Maria's hand and they went downstairs again. She put a towel over Rae's head, and wondered what she else she could possibly do. Next to her Ana-Maria just stared and touched her face where Rae's hand had met her skin.

Someone, something felt a little different now. Like she could almost hear a voice….

They both jumped, shocked, as the door flew open and Francisco stood there. He wasn't alone. He threw a man forward, a cowering man who was terrified as he fell to the ground and begged for his life.

<Tell them what you told me,> growled Francisco. <And maybe you live.>

Clearing everything away seemed strange, but making the house neat again somehow made Dr Sonja feel better. Francisco finished burying Rae in the nicest place he could find, and he made a pyre for the other bodies. There were just too many to deal with any other way.

Hook had his fill with the meal the corpses of the two witches Nixila and Salvatoria had provided him, and now he seemed forlorn, lost without Rae's guiding voice. He roared in rage and sadness, refusing to settle as he hunted the streets of Playa Del Mantarraya for any last vestiges of the walking dead.

Ana-Maria sat quietly on the couch near the door as Gorguz the Goblin, somehow empathetic to what had happened, gently played with strands of her hair to try and

comfort her. Absently she fed him candy, but he didn't eat
it.

The sun was starting to set as they sat together for the first
time. Gloriana was asleep, sedated by something out of Dr
Sonja's medical supplies, and Francisco had gently taken
Tempesta away where he would never be found. He found it
sad that someone who had been so lucky as to live beyond
death, and even enjoy it, could have that twisted against him
so badly.

He cursed himself. He should have been here. He had
become so seduced by not carrying the burden of the pale
Ghost, of being Francisco again, that everything else – all
the evils and spirits out in the Wilderness - had become
almost a dream to him. Now it was real again – real and
blood, and nothing could be done to undo it. But at least they
knew what was happening now.

The man Francisco had found was a familiar, a bitch to a
witch named Miguel. Like a hundred men before him he had
succumbed to some sex and a need to be told what to do, and
Salvatoria had made the most of that. It had clearly been a
good deal for Miguel, better than his junkie past, and when
the time had come to betray his home town, it had meant
nothing compared to the pleasures Salvatoria granted.

His body had been cut so many times he was always
hurting, and the brand on his back was down to the bone.
Perhaps he had found some strength in that once, but Miguel
was a coward at heart, and they couldn't stop him talking
now his mistress was dead. Dr Sonja had persuaded
Francisco to let him go, and he had run. Maybe he would
never stop.

What he had told them hung in the room.

<There are seven of them, seven witches. Las Brujas.
They made it all happen in the first place, man. They called
it the Thousand Year Ritual. They made everything the way

it is, man. They are the *Wilderness.* And they got a plan. They knew all about you, and they knew you got weak. So they took care of that horned bitch of yours…>

Francisco had wanted to choke him for that, and Dr Sonja had to stop him. They needed information.

<They got a weapon man. *Apocalypsis.* They got it all figured out. They only didn't do it before because of you, man. You're El Sepulturero. Protecting people. Killing the things in the Wilderness. They've been waiting. And now that you're just a guy? That's it man. They got it all. They're gonna finish what they started man. Nothing stopping them.>

Miguel babbled on and on, terrified yet desperately trying to bask in the lost power of his dead mistress. He threatened and begged all at once, trying to be tough yet knowing he was completely impotent, and in the end Dr Sonja lost patience. Witches and doomsday weapons and rituals? She didn't care about any of that, not right this second.

She just had one simple question for Miguel.

<Where's my sister Perdita?>

Francisco shone his flashlight along a tunnel that burrowed deep under the wreckage of Cancún. Few people even knew about these places, but Francisco did. They were conduits to and from the Wilderness where things that weren't human could come and go as they pleased. A few he had managed to seal but plenty remained. They went everywhere, and held a thousand secrets nobody would ever know.

It was the only place they could be hiding.

Las Brujas.

Next to him, Dr Sonja held her own flashlight, and in another situation would have marvelled at this unknown place, with crystal spars that jutted from the earth and strange symbols carved out into the limestone. There were mushrooms that glowed, and pale bugs with no eyes that skittered everywhere like alien termites.

<I don't mean to sound like a *pendejo*, but are you sure this it?>

Francisco nodded. Even now he could feel the trails of unnatural things, and the path that Nixila the Necromancer and Salvatoria The Witch Of Blades had trodden blazed out to him as though it were actually footprints.

<There.>

Up ahead they could see faint light that shouldn't have been there. As they reached a branch in the tunnels they found a cache of things – talismans made of silver and gold, melted candles like wax sculptures, heated copper pots over flickering fires that simmered the fat of human and animal alike. It was a place of power where things were made.

Francisco slipped a slab of flat stone from his belt, the Mayan blessing sigil carved into it, and threw it into the biggest pot. Immediately it began to churn and sour, bubbling out its contents and evaporating them until only clear pure water was left. The candles and the fire went out, and the site was dead.

<How many of those do you have left?> asked Dr Sonja.

<It's all up here,> said Francisco, tapping the side of his head. <As long as I have the stone....>

<So how did I not know you were a wizard?>

Francisco shrugged. <It's not really magic. It's like chemistry. I don't know, like elemental or something. I woke up with this knowledge my head after it all happened.>

<I wish that had happened to me during my medical exams.>

Francisco smiled, and then raised a finger to his lips as they both heard something.

Something was coming, something that rustled and flapped like a bat in the darkness.

Francisco and Dr Sonja did their best to find a place to hide so they could watch. Their plan had been simple now that the witches familiar, Miguel, had babbled endlessly about sites connected by lines of force. It was like a network, he said, and all they had to do was interrupt the network until something paid attention.

Now, after what seemed like hours of walking, something was.

Out of the tunnel came a figure that crawled along the cavern sides, a deep blue cloak obscured everything about it was it formed almost like the same bat's wings it sounded like. It reached the dead site and stopped, almost confused. A wizened finger with a hook yellowed ingrown claw reached out and touched one of the candles but it wouldn't light. It tried again on another, but there was nothing.

Frustrated, the witch named Capa Azul hissed to itself, and reached for the pot Francisco had thrown his symbol into

<AAAAAIAIAIAIAIAIAIAAAAAEEEEE.>

It screeched and pulled back its hand, burned and in pain. It suddenly seemed to realise it wasn't alone, and as it looked around Francisco and Dr Sonja saw its face. It was hideous, a malformed mass of tumours that parted only for a slit of a mouth and two bulbous black eyes that looked like those of an insect.

Dr Sonja wanted to throw up. Anyone who looked upon the face of Capa Azul wanted to throw up, and as the witch started to investigate Dr Sonja did her utmost to stifle it.

She lasted longer than most.

Finally she wretched, and Capa Azul moved towards them. Next to Dr Sonja, Francisco hadn't felt the sickening influence. He didn't question it, he simply knew that in his body now was a new gift, one that replaced the raw muscle power he had lost. Now he had a different kind of strength, a kind of immunity that rendered Las Brujas magic ineffective against him. He'd felt it when Salvatoria's daggers had touched him, and when Nixila had died at the ravenous jaws of Hook.

That was his weapon now. How long it would last he didn't know, and so he acted.

He lunged out and tackled the witch more to protect Dr Sonja than anything else. Her cloak wrapped around him and dug into his body, thousands of vicious hooked thorns growing out of its substance. Then it lifted him and hurled him aside as she flew up into the air and attached herself to the ceiling.

<Why do you not cower, male filth,> growled Capa Azul, her voice impossibly guttural and deep. She couldn't immediately understand why Francisco wasn't vomiting everywhere, but it didn't matter. She had other weapons at her disposal. Her cloak was a part of her, and she willed stinging tendrils to spew out from his edges like a jellyfish.

Francisco rolled aside but some of stingers caught him. They hurt, but then pain seemed to die away and the stingers shrivelled when the touched him. The wounds from the thorns had closed up as well, but he didn't want to push his luck. There was nothing in his head to tell him how far this immunity of his stretched.

He slipped something out of his belt and threw it forward.

It was a spur of obsidian black that split into fragments in the air. Capa Azul was fraction to late in moving as each fragment cast a line to another and the whole structure formed into kind of web that captured the witch. She struggled but the fragments and the lines stuck to her, hurting as they cut into her unnatural skin, slick with something acidic. In the end she had no choice but to fall hard the ground, her back cracking on a spur of rock, close to the dead shrine she had so desperately tried to reignite

Francisco stood and moved over to her. She writhed in the web, hissing and cursing at him in a language he didn't recognise. The cape flipped and twisted, trying to form shape after shape that might let her loose, but the filaments held fast.

<Tell me where Perdita Castellanos is,> said Francisco

Capa Azul just spat and clawed, and he realised she would say nothing. All she was, was venom and threats as she tried to free herself.

Then Dr Sonja buried Francisco's carved piece of stone into her face, and all the struggling ceased. Her eyes stayed closed tight, refusing to succumb to nausea again as the witch's own buglike eyes popped and seeped down across her cancerous face. Then the cloak died as well, flattening out to nothing but cloth.

<Is she dead,> asked Dr Sonja.

<She's dead.>

Dr Sonja opened one eye to peak, and the other when she didn't collapse into wracking spasm of sickness. <*Muerde,* how many of these hags are there.>

<Miguel said seven.>

<Like I believe anything that lunatic said.>

<Too scared to lie.>

<Well, on the plus side that means there's only two to go. Maybe>

The two of them moved on, and left the corpse of Capa Azul to dissolve away behind them. Surely, Dr Sonja thought, after knives and zombies and the creeping madness a beaten Moya had told her about as she had tended to Buey's wounds, what else could Las Brujas throw at them?

The tunnel up ahead split again, and as Francisco moved forward he felt a tingle in his body. He stopped, without quite knowing why, and forced himself to look over at Dr Sonja. She was slowing too, as though the air was solidifying around them both. As they struggled, the solidity of the cave morphed away into something else and they felt the feeling of suddenly dropping in their stomachs.

<What NOW?>

In that instant they were elsewhere.

They faced a huge cavern filled with cries, and their paralysis sealed them in place. Eyes, six of them, ghostly and half–transparent and the size of soccer balls, glided into view, peering at every part of them inside and out.

<Did you really think I wouldn't see you,> whispered another voice, almost trembling with the pleasure of victory.

The voice came from a spectral woman, her dead-eyed face beautiful and terrible all at once. She was the mistress of the eyes, the eerie form of Señorita Oja clad in a dress of white lace and cobwebs that drifted on the air, half solid and half ghost, immune to everything. She observed Francisco and Dr Sonja and smiled a thin black-lipped smile of power and victory that showed teeth pointed like a vampire.

The two of them gazed at the witch and what lay beyond her. Neither could move at all now, strength leeched out of their muscles, and all they could do was stare at what was inside the chamber they had somehow been brought to.

They saw five cribs made out of burnished metal, surrounded by heat and steam that rose out of the cavern walls and cracked ground. In each crib there was a baby, a newborn, and each baby's head was marked with a different symbol. They cried and howled like babies did, their sounds bouncing off the ragged stone, and around them a circlet of flames flickered, transforming from yellow to white to blue and back again.

Señorita Oja regarded the cribs with tender glee.

<Do you see their perfection,> she whispered as the phantom eyes floated around her in the air, gazing at everything. <Do you see how this is the way it should be?>

Francisco fought to move, and Señorita Oja gently touched his shoulder in a way that made him shudder deep inside his bones.

<You are weak now, Francisco. Just a man. Your saviour mocks you. She steals away your strength and leaves you helpless. We are supreme.> The witch gestured towards the cribs with one hand. <Do you feel their power.>

Dr Sonja felt her life being sucked away, inch by inch. <They're just…babies.>

Señorita Oja drifted into her gaze and smiled a bitter smile. <They are so much more.>

Images began to play on the walls and in the air. There were blurred and vague at first, hints of shapes and colors that began to form into something more. It was as though a film was fighting to take shape in the emptiness, desperate to reveal its sights to its audience.

<*Fuego.*>

Nuclear fire swept across everything, charring and burning flesh and bone alike. The flames danced into the shapes of demons, all at the beck and call of the first baby that waved its hands in joy.

<*Plaga.*>

Men and women, young and old, all succumbed as disease took a hold of them, stripping away their vitality, and they shrivelled like the living dead, hearts, lungs, mind, all failing as the second baby watched, uncaring.

<*Mutante.*>

Beasts roamed free out of the Wilderness. Terrible things, twisted monstrosities driven by hunger and instinct. In a thousand different shapes they ravaged across everything, immune to guns and bombs, called by the third baby.

<*Fobia.*>

People became mad as they screamed and ran in terror, but there was no escaping the fear that sat in all their minds, haunting the new world. Every primal nightmare came to life from the mind of the fourth baby.

<Locura.>

Nothing made sense anymore as minds cracked and insanity flooded out. Thoughts snapped and people turned on each other in broken crazed fits – the real world lost to a spiral of psychosis as the final baby giggled.

Five babies in all, five anchors of power that would tear everything down.

<You see it now,> hissed Señorita Oja, savouring it all. <Don't you.>

Apocalypsis.

The witch cackled and the babies cried as something began to emerge from the flames. Like Señorita Oja it was a ghost at first, and then it became solid, taking on bones, flesh, skin, until it was a titan that stood before them. A skull faced brute, horned and tusked, a juggernaut of demonic muscle. It reared up seven, eight, nine feet, and it roared thunder and blood.

<Behold Baron Muzon's finest work,> crowed the witch, resolute in her victory. <Know that you your flesh feeds our mighty engine, and that you become a part of the great scheme.>

Francisco watched. He felt his heart race and his souls fight for freedom, and as he struggled inside him something clicked. A kind of mental switch flipped as he saw the horned beast, and he began to change. His flesh faded, becoming pale, his body grew, and power flowed in his blood. In his mind he saw the ancient pyramids of the Mayans and their gods who danced in feather and fur in the air and in the water. He felt all of it inside him, and finally, El Sepulturero burst free, his face stark black and white like a painted skull.

The true El Sepulturero

Francisco towered there, the chalk white titan of pure strength, no longer diluted by being half way between man and demigod. Now he was released, and as Dr Sonja saw him she realised how magnificent he truly was.

Señorita Oja stared, unable to quite comprehend what she was seeing.

<No,> she howled. <No NO NOOOOOOOO. Kill him. KILL HIM.>

The horned beast obeyed, and moved forward, and El Sepulturero met it, brushing aside the power that tried to hold him in place. When they clashed, the air itself shivered with the force of it all, and Dr Sonja was blown off her feet, her paralysis gone. Señorita Oja's eyes saw it all but did nothing. Instead, they watched impotently as the brutal fight took place.

Hammering blows that would crush even the toughest metal rained down. El Sepulturero smashed into the beasts armoured body and drove it back into the walls, and it fought back, bestial and ferocious. It stabbed and clawed, trying to gouge eyes and body, while El Sepulturero kicked it back. He leapt forward and tackled it down as it bit down into his body. It tasted blood, but the blood was biter, acrid. It was like poison, and the horned beast felt the liquid hurt it inside.

Señorita Oja felt it too, and as she did her own ghostly power stated to dissolve away, making her weak, cutting her connection to her beloved spectral eyeballs. They danced mindlessly, unable to focus on anything, and their mistress felt a fear she had never known.

The horned beast tried to stand but El Sepulturero beat it down with his fists. His blood streaked his chalk skin, but there was no pain. Just ancient Mayan power rushing through him as his heart beat faster and faster.

Then he took hold of its head, and as desperate eyes gazed up from behind the hideous skull, he snapped its neck and let the body drop to the ground.

Señorita Oja screamed as she watched her guardian creature die. The sound echoed and echoed. Then another sound began. The sound of singing perhaps, or a huge chord torn from an alien musical instrument. It grew and grew, and as Francisco slumped to the ground, spent and weakened next to the corpse of the horned beast, impossible light began to form.

The sound reached its crescendo, like a choir of music, as the light began to coalesce into the shimmering form of a woman, clad in a dress of feathers that made her look like a beautiful eagle in scarlet and blue ready to take flight. Around her, the faces of forgotten tribes watched and gave the spectre strength as they chanted her name.

IXTAL, they chorused. *IXTAL MEN, IXTAL MEN. IXTAL MENAAAAAAAAAA......*

Señorita Oja tried to get away. If she could get back into the tunnels she was safe, but already the eyes that had been severed from her control were starting to die away under the light that flowed from Ixtal's radiant body beneath her magnificent Mayan headdress and burning eyes. They collapsed like rotting fruit as Ixtal stood, a goddess in her splendour.

<How....> began Señorita Oja, but the voices of an army cut her off.

<*It has always been,*> they chanted. <*You can never succeed.*>

Visions swam in the witch's head as she saw terrible things, things so far beyond her understanding they instantly drove her mad. In that final second of awareness she realised that all she and her sisters had ever truly done was sip from a tiny cup, believing they were goddess. Now they faced the real thing. Now the entire ocean had come for them, and it was irresistible.

Ixtal drew a sword, a huge *Macuahuitl* of her own that smouldered with white-gold embers of force, and she raised it.

<Please,> begged Señorita Oja. <It would have been so much better....>

<No.>

Señorita Oja screamed as the sword hacked down, cutting through the witch's body and cleaving away her power.

In an instant it was over.

The light and the chorus were suddenly gone. Ixtal was gone. The circlet of fire was extinguished and all there was, was cool quiet in the cavern. Even the babies slept soundly now, and as Dr Sonja knelt to check on the wounds on Francisco's once again human body, she was already planning how she would get the five safely to a hospital and maybe try to find their undoubtedly panic-stricken parents.

How long the babies had been here this cave she couldn't possibly know. The image of Ixtal made it hard to focus, as though the goddess' light from the past dazed every thought.

Dr Sonja looked around. She saw where the horned beast lay dead, a felled titan, and on the ground next to it was slumped another body, its breaths gasping in chokes, barely coherent as it babbled to itself in the stink of its own piss. This was no longer Señorita Oja of Las Brujas. Her power was removed forever. Now she just a broken woman, insane and incontinent.

Beaten.

Dr Sonja stood over the nameless woman, hoping against hope there was some fragment of sense left in her mind that could answer the question she needed answering.

<Where is my sister. Where is Perdita Castellanos?>

The woman just laughed and started up with empty bloodshoot eyes that cleared for moment, just long enough to speak.

<La Perdida? She is with us. She has always been with us.   Fire   and   ice.   Ice   and   fire. AHAHAHHAHAHAHAHHAHAHAHAHAHAHAHAHA HA.>

The woman drooled, and Dr Sonja knew she was fit only for the madhouse now. There was never any coming back from where her mind had gone. But those last words resonated again and again in Dr Sonja's head.

<She is with us>.

<She has always been with us.>

Francisco heard the words too, and as he did he saw Ixtal's aura still glittering in the air. Slowly, pained from the exertion that his mortal muscles felt, he nodded that he was OK.

Ixtal raised a ghostly hand, and in the moment before she vanished completely Francisco and Dr Sonja both felt a horrible shared nausea in their guts, the certainty of dread, as the cave around them began to fade. A last gift, perhaps, from the goddess, a power that was transporting them somewhere else, with the sense of falling outside of themselves that was so familiar now.

They both knew that this was the answer to their question.

<Where is my sister?>

Around them the open air was appearing, but it was plunged into bitter arctic cold. The blue skies were smothered in dead grey, and cutting ice whipped all around. The old broken city of Chichen Itza materialised, solid as stone all around them, out of time, and they saw her, standing up on the steps of El Castillo – a new priestess of the ancient Temple Of Kukulkan.

The weapon of *Apocalypsis* was stopped, and the fire was extinguished, but the rage remained. The rage of ice.

The rage of the seventh witch. The final witch.

Perdita.

Where's Perdita?

Those were terrifying words to remember saying, and now that Francisco and Dr Sonja were here, facing the demon witch who had claimed El Castillo as her palace, the answer was nothing less than horrifying.

The seventh witch of seven. All the rest were gone, dead and beaten, even their great and mighty plan of Armageddon torn from them leaving only five innocent powerless little babies behind, babies who would have proper names and proper families now – babies that would grow up, fall in love, live lives.

All there was left was Perdita, and what she had become. Or perhaps what she had been all along.

As he stood there, Francisco simply didn't know what to do. It felt like his heart was frozen and broken at once. Like some cruel joke Las Brujas had taken something so vital from him that he would never recover. Not even the gift he had been given, that complete connection to his Mayan strength granted to him by a dying little child in the rainforest, could protect him from this.

Francisco felts tears in his eyes. <Perdita.....?>

The creature just hissed, uncaring about who or what she had once felt for him and revelling in his pain. Perhaps he was almost impenetrable, but she could attack him inside.

<It's not her anymore,> said Dr Sonja.

Francisco wanted to believe she was right. Dr Sonja had long ago learned to detach her feelings from the truth of life and death, and that gave her a power he didn't have. A power to be able to see through emotion, and be wholly clinical. Where he saw a person raging on El Castillo, Dr Sonja saw only a thing. Her grieving would come later. All she was focussed on was the cure.

Francisco still saw only Perdita there, and prayed that there was something left, some scrap of a soul.

Yet the longer he looked the more he knew it was all in vain. There was only the seventh witch now, the witch that had to be stopped. Francisco knew with an awful certainty exactly what that meant.

Power lashed and whirled like daggers around the pale witch's body, and she looked down with empty eyes, breathing her killing frost out into the still and eerie air.

Where's Perdita?

Here she was, but only her face. The essence of her, if there had ever truly been one, was gone. This was a hollow demon of a thing, a vessel of hatred that just raged against failed plans and the death of her sisters. All it wanted to do was hurt and kill and rip out the souls of innocent people.

Francisco stared up, wondering if there had ever really been a Perdita at all. Had she been stolen away and corrupted, or had she been this creature all along, concealed within the family, just waiting for the right time.

There would never really be an answer for that.

Dr Sonja stared up to. She looked into the mask of her sister and knew that she was dead. She had been dead a long time. Maybe longer than anyone of them really realised. Her shock had given away to understanding, the same as it did with her parent's deaths, or her divorce. What was left was purpose. She had watched so many people die that she couldn't save, and now all she had in her was grim determination.

Nobody else was going to die today. Nobody human.

<You've got to do it now, Francisco.>

Francisco gripped *Macuahuitl*'s hilt but all his strength seemed meaningless now. He felt weak inside himself, deep down in his soul, as though something vital as leaking away and leaving him hollow.

<I can't,> he said finally, and he let his sword drop to the earth.

Above, Perdita raged and screamed as her command of the deepest cold lifted her into the air on a vortex and hailed down spikes of sharpened bitter ice. Deep in her primal mind, she saw only this tiny human thing before her. She couldn't grasp how it had killed her sisters, how it had been able to resist their strongest attacks. She looked into him but all there was, was something ancient like her, the old civilisations coursing through his veins. She heard Mayan chants and saw Mayan warriors dressed as jaguars. That was where this power she and her sisters had been so unable to resist came from.

The power of El Sepulturero, a dead culture given life in the body of this tiny little human. The weapon of a forgotten civilisation that after so many centuries had come for them.

The power of the Maya.

If Perdita the Witch understood humour anymore, this was truly the greatest joke of all. The Ritual itself, the Witches years-long plans, the Wilderness they had spawned and their final weapon, *Apocalypsis*, that they had sent so long assembling.

It was all meaningless.

All the Witches had done was release that power of the Maya out of the dormant ground and given birth to their nemesis. In reality, they could never have succeeded. The land itself was against them. They were beaten before they even started.

Dr Sonja knew none of this. She just saw Francisco, standing there, seemingly accepting the end, as Perdita formed a whirlwind around her that would tear everything to shreds. The witches' plans were dead, just like they themselves were, and this their one final attack. If Perdita was to die, she would take everything she could with her. It was as mindless and primal as a savage beast.

Then Dr Sonja looked back to Francisco's car, and saw the coffin lashed to its roof.

There, through the cracks in the wood, she could see light. It was light she had never seen before, but she felt it inside her. Little slivers of a hidden sun that melted the frost and the air as they touched it, and returned life to lifelessness. It was struggling to be free.

In that instant Dr Sonja knew exactly what she had to do.

Without a single look back to the apparition she had once called her sister, Dr Sonja ran for the car.

Perdita The Witch saw her, and roared. She saw the light to, felt it, and knew what it was. She had to stop it. She had to kill these people and end it now.

Daggers of pure ice formed in the air and hurled themselves towards Dr Sonja as she reached the car. They penetrated her back, her legs, and Dr Sonja stifled her cries of pain as she felt the cold grow inside her. She had a few seconds before it took her completely, but a few seconds was all she needed. She grasped hold of the coffin, and tried to pry off the lid, to let the light out.

Everywhere the air raged and attacked them. It flayed and burned skin, tearing and ripping, unceasing in its barrage.

Just a couple of seconds more. Just a couple of seconds. If only she could shift it. Break the seal.

A hand landed on the coffin beside hers. A huge hand, chalk white, then another. Dr Sonja looked up, and El Sepulturero looked down on her one last time. He smiled that old Francisco smile, and Dr Sonja gazed at him sadly as she bled and the cold froze her.

<I'm sorry,> she said.

El Sepulturero nodded.

Then he tore open the coffin and let all the light flood out until it consumed everything.

*

Birds sang in the big old tree at Flor Azul where a new gravestone had been placed. Special people came to see it. Moya's arm was still bandaged, and next to her Buey's wounds were still vivid across his body. Gloriana came, slowly starting to find her way back again but still damaged by those last moments with Tempesta. The police were there, believing the lie that Perdita had simply died like so many others under the onslaught against Playa Del Mantarraya. It seemed too cruel to tell them anything else.

None of them spoke as Dr Sonja placed purple lilies on her sister's grave. Her face was like wet-streaked stone, and next to her Ana-Maria held her hand as she wore dark glasses and did her best not to cry. Ana-Maria herself just wept, wondering how it could be that her beloved aunt had left them.

The little girl searched for some sort of light to hold on to, and it came as a question she kept asking.

<Where's Uncle Francisco, mama? What happened? Is he dead?>

Hopefully if she asked enough there would be an answer. But nobody knew right now.

In her arms Gorguz was quiet, as though he understood somewhere in his little Goblin brain that something truly awful had happened.

Ana-Maria had a new friend now as well. She could hear him in the farthest corners of her mind like a whispering dream, ever since she had done when she had held Rae's hand one last time. Hook The Ceratocarnus was out in the Yucatán wilderness somewhere, living as wild and as happy as he could be. Ana-Maria thought of him often, especially when she looked in the mirror and saw the little hints of green and yellow in her eyes. She liked them in a way, but still hid them behind big pink rimmed sunglasses her mother had bought her a year ago.

They hid her tears as well. They came constantly. She missed Uncle Francisco and Auntie Perdida as much as she could anybody miss anything, and wondered if the hole in her soul would ever heal up.

Dr Sonja felt that too, and wished she could maker Ana-Maria feel better. They stared at the gravestone, a simple elegant thing bearing the flowers that became a little monument all their own. Purple lilies had been Perdita's favorites, and Francisco had always bought them for her on her birthday.

When the light had come, that vast cleansing all-consuming light, Dr Sonja couldn't really remember too much and perhaps that was for the best. There had just been a sense of raw power, as if lighting from Heaven had poured out from that coffin upon El Castillo and melted away every last scrap of ice and cold. It scoured away the darkness and cleansed the evil. The wounds that had bled openly as Dr Sonja lay on the ground healed up. A feeling of overwhelming primal emotions, all of them all at once, filled her up inside.

It was impossible, and yet it wasn't. It washed over her, and then faded to nothing.

When Dr Sonja's memory had started to work again there was the simple real solid feeling of the hard grassy ground, the sun on her face. That, and the knowledge she was alone.

Francisco was gone, the witch that had been Perdita was gone. Even the car. All gone now. All that was left was her sister's lifeless body, nothing more than an empty shell. Whether it had always been that way, or if Perdita had once been in there somewhere, Dr Sonja just didn't want to know anymore.

That had been almost a week ago,

Dr Sonja wept at her sister's grave, and she tried to push all those thoughts of everything else aside. All she wanted to remember was Perdita and her smile.

One of the policeman, the most senior one there, respectfully walked forward and placed a little gift on the side of the grave. He made a cross across his chest and bowed his head.

<I'm sorry for your loss,> he said. He had liked Perdita. She had been a good officer.

Gracias Senor Hernandez.

The funeral came to an end, and the crowd dispersed after a while. Things were going to be different, and Dr Sonja knew that it was time to leave Playa Del Mantarraya behind. It had become a place of the dead and soon all those who had lived would depart for a hundred different places. Francisco's old home town a hundred miles South-West was just fine, so Dr Sonja and Ana-Maria would stay there a while, help out a little. Towns always needed a doctor, after all. But it would only be for a short while.

After that, who knew?

Moya stood out by the gate to the cemetery with her brother and gave a wave goodbye. Dr Sonja waved back. She wondered if they would ever see each other again. She hoped so and so did Ana-Maria, but there was a shared pang of unspoken sadness as the horned woman walked away.

Dr Sonja couldn't help but wonder if things could had been different. Maybe if Francisco had seen the way Moya sometimes looked at him, there would have been less pain, less death.

Maybe if there had never been a Perdita at all…

She caught herself and forced that thought away. She was determined only to remember good things despite herself. But she knew deep down nothing would have been any different.

This whole life they had lived for years, event after event, from the first second of the twisted witches' Ritual to the Light that had erased the horrors of El Castillo, had been inevitable. Dr Sonja knew that now. An unstoppable avalanche of cause and effect that would always have played out in the same way regardless of the players.

What it all meant, she couldn't possibly guess. Her mind was trained for science, and what she had seen was far far beyond any such explanations.

Ana-Maria hugged close to her mother and they stood there. All around the sun shone and the birds sang, and the Wilderness themselves felt like they were fading away back into the background shadows. Maybe they were, maybe not, but right this second it didn't really matter.

All that mattered was this simple ceremony. This single moment to be remembered forever.

Dr Sonja looked down at the gravestone, shed her last tear, and said simply: <Goodbye Perdi.>

*

Uncle Derek walked towards the Castellanos family's new house. It was a lucky find, in a good area with a good school for Ana-Maria, and space for everyone, even Gorguz. There was even a spare room for Moya. Dr Sonja had insisted on that. Even though her brother Buey had left and gone home to recover from the injuries he had taken than in turn had nearly taken his life.

Moya wasn't ever going home to Ciudad Volcan by the sound of it. She had headed out to look for new adventures, far away from witches and out into the deserts and the wilderness. But just in case, there would always been a place for her to come if she needed it.

Derek smiled. He liked Moya, but not the way a lot of other people did. Even Francisco, Derek suspected. When he had been a much younger man he would have enjoyed fighting her, even though she was easily five times stronger than the strongest people he had ever trained. Maybe she would spar with them sometime, but in the meanwhile she was off on her travels. Dr Sonja had said something about going North, but nobody knew for sure.

Derek was glad Moya had finally got rid of Doctor Horta asshole. He was equally glad that his sister and niece had opted out of going on any new adventures and decided to settle back near family. He'd never really liked Playa Del Mantarraya, and with Francisco gone there was nobody to protect his sister and niece anymore. Persuading them to move to Mexico City hadn't been hard. The hospitals were begging for good doctors, and Dr Sonja would have a cellphone and a laptop again. Life would be a lot calmer, and there would be a lot less demonic forces to watch out for.

Hopefully, anyway.

Besides, if any of those little dark corners of the city spewed out anything they shouldn't one especially dark and smoggy night, Derek had a squad of Lucha Libre fighters who were learning the moves and all the tricks. His new gym boss, Gloriana, was teaching them everything she knew, and she knew a lot.

She always wore a mask though. Not the embroider dine but a plain black one that spoke of mourning and loss. That made Derek nervous, but Dr Sonja told him it was for a very good reason so that was that. He wasn't going to argue, not with Gloriana's way of fighting. SO far not one of the fighters had got the upper hand with her, and Derek guessed it would take someone very, very skilled to even get close.

He turned a corner at an intersection, the sounds of shouting and honking horns suddenly growing louder in his ears. He'd tuned them out like he normally did, but now he realised that something had happened here. A few cars had pulled up, their drivers had got out, and the street had slowed down, the traffic clogging up as person after person craned their necks to see what was going on.

The reason was something that Derek almost couldn't believe.

Smoking, half broken, but still intact, a car had been dumped on the side of the road and left for dead. Recently as well, perhaps just a few moments ago. People were already thinking it was an abandoned getaway car or a stolen vehicle cat aside by joyriders.

But Derek knew better. The color, the ageing, the things that hung from the mirror and the roof itself, scarred from what had once been tightly bound to it. All of it was unique and Derek recognised it straight away, even without the coffin.

Impossibly, it was Francisco's car. He took another look just to be certain, but there was no question.

The hairs on Derek's neck raised up, liked he was being watched. He reached to the cross on his heavy metal pendant as the sounds of the city faded away to a muted buzz, and he suddenly felt dizzy like he was drunk. For a moment, it was as though he had stepped outside of himself, and he looked up so see a faded crimson sky where clouds that once boiled ruby-red and angry were now golden, still and serene. There was the feeling of hot wind on his face, that felt like the last remnants of a dying storm that was finally giving way to calm after a very long time. All around the blurred ghosts of some other place shimmered in front of his eyes. They were peculiar mirages that didn't fit in middle of the urban maze of Mexico City – a road through peaceful empty countryside, an old shack that needed rebuilding, a garage that could be a waypoint for travellers.

Then he saw two people, faint and incomplete like ghosts of ghosts, but definitely there. A big man, so tall he was like a giant, and a smaller pretty woman with a vivid streak of blonde in her hair. They were holding hands, talking and smiling like any couple who loved each other might. They looked as though they didn't have a care in the world.

They looked free.

Derek stared as he suddenly recognised them, and opened his mouth to speak but no words came out.

Then the instant passed, and he was back in the city surrounded by people and the endless noise as drivers tried to figure out what to do with the car. Soon there would be arguments, and the *federales* would have to become involved.

But to Derek it just didn't matter for then and there. There was weird feeling of almost-joy in him, a sense that somehow, things were as they should be.

That everything was OK.

Maybe, thought Derek, there were happy endings after all.

ANA-MARIA
PARTE UNO

In her short sixteen years Ana-Maria Castellanos had seen so many things. She had seen past the veil of everyday life into other places. She had seen monsters come out of the sea and the dead rise. She had seen witches and ghosts, and she had watched her beloved Uncle Francisco fight them all. He had been her hero. Everyone's hero – the man they called El Sepulturero.

But now he was gone. Just like her Aunt Perdita. So many were gone, and Ana-Maria hadn't been sad after they had paid their respects at Francisco's memorial to leave the Wilderness of the Yucatán behind. She had enough sadness for a lifetime to carry and didn't want to be reminded of it every day. Her home town of Playa Del Mantarraya was wreck and ruin, Auntie Moya had gone off on her travels, and all that remained was one thing.

The Gift. The one she had been given by the touch of a dying woman.

At first Ana-Maria hadn't really understood it. She had been younger then, and it had been like strange dreams. But as she got older, as she learned more from friends of her mothers' – people like the half-masked luchadora Gloriana, usually just Glory, who had fought monsters herself, or the travelling man in the black vaquero hat called Erik Abrantes – she had started to believe there was more to it. Much more. They seemed to know so much about so many strange and impossible things. Ana-Maria could only guess at what they had seen compared to her. Sometimes he wrote little stories about them, in between schoolwork and Judo training, and wondered if she could ever imagine anything as bizarre than the things that really did exist.

But the Gift was something unique to her. Something she kept secret except to those few close people. It had made her eyes turn emerald green and her body stronger that it should have been for her size. She was small like her mother Dr Sonja, but she could wrestle bigger men surprisingly easily. Glory ran her own fight school and taught her a few things too on visits to the house for dinner. Dr Sonja didn't like Ana-Maria going to Glory's school. Far too dangerous. Maybe when she was older. That didn't bother Ana-Maria to much, because she had her friend to watch over.

Not her companion Gorguz. He never changed. He was still the little goblin who ate all the candy and liked to be carried around, and he had become like a kind of squashy teddy bear that Ana-Maria loved and gained comfort form. No, this was the other friend.

Perhaps 6 metres tall, he was a strange, unique beast. Part prehistoric and part something far more mythical, he was covered in armored scales that reached along a thick tail, with a head armed with crocodile teeth and heavy horns that had got bigger as he had had got older. He had had many names. Erik called him the Ceratocarnus, but Ana-Maria just called him El Rey Dragón after one of her Uncle Derek's favorite vintage comic books. He seemed to like just Dragón. He growled happily when he heard the name so she knew he understood. Dragón understood a lot of things. He made things too, and his latest project was a dead tree trunk that he was carving into a totem of some sort.

Every week, Ana-Maria travelled out of the city to the cave where Dragón liked to sleep. He didn't really need her to. He just liked to see her and they could talk. Not in words but in their heads, in streams of images and feelings. It was reassuring for both of them – for him, he seemed to need the connection, and for her it was reassurance that he wasn't going to eat anybody. Not that he would – that had been their agreement when he had finally finished his long long walk out of the Wilderness to find her.

Cows fine. People not fine.

Today was visit day, and Ana-Maria had other things on her mind than food as she finished the steep walk up to the entrance to Dragón's cave.

Behind her, view from a little way up the mountains, the vast and seemingly endless sprawl of Mexico City just lay there. It looked alien sometimes. It was a place that never really changed, and although it was her mother's home Ana-Maria herself had struggled to adjust. She had been born in rural Yucatán and she liked the feel of nature much better than the sense of concrete walls closing in on everything. The huge exciting parades of Dia de Muertos were still wonderful though. She always went to them with her Uncle Derek and he still told her stories of his past. She could never decide whether they were always true or not, but they were always good stories. Dr Sonja was working like she always did, but that didn't bother Ana-Maria so much. There would still be time to get home, and get ready to take bread and tequila to the cemetery. That was the really special part.

Except they could never celebrate Uncle Francisco. There was a little gravestone at the family plot near the hospital where Dr Sonja worked but it wasn't the real thing. They all knew wherever he was, wherever his spirit walked on Dia de Muertos, it was somewhere back in the Yucatán. That was his home, not like the Castellanos. Ana-Maria wanted to go back there, to the Wilderness, but no amount of screaming or arguing or begging would ever persuade Ana-Maria's family to let her. Not ever.

<Without anything to hold back the tide>, Glory had said to her. <All the ghosts and the devils roam free.>

The news streams on Ana-Maria's phone agreed. Cancun was abandoned, and all the tourists and holiday went to the big new developments in Vera Cruz. Only the locals lived on the Yucatán now – the locals, and other things. The news didn't call those things ghosts and devils of course, even though Ana-Maria had seen them. People just didn't want to believe in that kind of thing.

This year, Ana-Maria had decided that if she couldn't go to the Wilderness, it was going to have to come to her. Her mother didn't need to know – the usual excuse was Rico, who so wanted to be Ana-Maria's boyfriend she could get him to do whatever she wanted. She had saved up her money from her part time job and talked Erik into giving her the sigil she wanted. Nothing dangerous. Just something to let her know that Uncle Francisco was happy where he was, happy with her Auntie Perdita.

That's what Dia de Muertos was supposed to be, after all.

She had stolen one of Francisco's old tee-shirts before they had left Yucatán, one of the hundreds he owned that bore the names and images of endless different metal bands that most people had never heard of. Ana-Maria didn't like metal. It gave her a headache. But it was a special memory for her. Uncle Francisco had told her that music gave him strength, so she knew when Erik told her something personal was needed it had to be the tee-shirt. It even smelled a little bit of him.

That was everything. Now she was at Dragón's cave. It was the safest place she could imagine which was exactly where Erik had told her to go. Dragón would protect her from anything as well as bite off Erik's legs if he ever told her mother what she was doing.

At least that was what Ana-Maria had told him.

Rico was waiting a kilometre or so down the road looking after Gorguz. Ana-Maria had introduced them and brought the young man int her confidence. It wasn't that she didn't like hi in that way. She did – he was handsome and smart and liked animals. It was just other things were important to her. Today had obsessed her for months now.

Dragón looked up from his totem and the fire he had somehow made as Ana-Maria walked in and growled his greetings.

Dragón stood up on his huge, clawed back feet and gestured to his work. He looked pleased with himself, and Ana-Maria nodded as she walked into his cave.

<That looks so cool,>she said.

Dragón nodded appreciatively. The gentle glow of the fire flickered off the walls, and everywhere was the dinosaur's collection of treasure. It was junk of every description, from broken down cars and old abandoned machinery to colorful plastic shapes and abandoned toys. Dragón just liked finding things and Ana-Maria had no idea what he would eventually do with them. Maybe nothing. Or maybe he would create something amazing. Somewhere in amongst it all was the old iron hook Dragón had used to carry when Rae had been in his head so many years ago, when she and Francisco had rescued him from a cenote. He had outgrown it, but he liked his memories as much as any person. It was a keepsake now.

As she walked into the cave Ana-Maria rubbed the little pendant around her neck. It was a piece of carved old wood, varnished to preserve it, but it was very special. Back in the days when El Sepulturero had fought monsters, he had driven a car with an old coffin strapped to the top. The coffin was gone now too, but Ana-Maria wore a piece of it around her neck, always. Once a girl at school had tried to take it from her. That had ended badly.

In their connected minds Dragón had the general idea of what was going on. He liked protecting Ana-Maria so it wasn't going to be difficult. He had made himself a club for the occasion as well – a fat heavy bit of wood that he had pushed spikes of metal into. He didn't really grasp these images of people with painted skull faces, or these words Dia and Muertos. It was more human gibberish. He simply knew they were important to Ana-Maria and that was good enough for him.

She felt that too as she found herself a space and sat down, checking her cellphone as she constantly did. She spread out Francisco's tee-shirt in front of her and placed an old flat piece of slate on top of it. Like Erik had told her to, she made the sign of the cross across her body and spoke a short prayer to the Trinity. She was about to dabble in old things, and one had to be certain that the Devil wouldn't pay too much attention.

<I'm really nervous,> said Ana-Maria, looking up at Dragón. He looked back, baffled at what was going on. He growled and made a hammering gesture with his club, a bit too enthusiastically. Ana-Maria laughed. <No, this part is fine. You only have to do that if some sort of monster appears or something.>

The image of some skeletal horned thing in ragged colored robes spewing oily smoke from its eye sockets appeared in both their heads. Dragón immediately wanted to smash it to a pulp. He began to pace around the cave like a sentry as Ana-Maria concentrated. She took out the chalk that Erik had given here, and carefully drew the Mayan sigil she had committed to memory.

WAY.

For a moment, nothing happened. <Did you give me a fake, Erik?> hissed Ana-Maria.

Then, without any warning, something hit her from the inside out. She gasped once as her body went rigid and her eyes rolled back into her head. Her hands became stiffened like claws as a single word rebounded in her suddenly paralysed mind within a body that had become a living breathing statue.

All she could hear was a name spoken by whispers over and over again.

<Ixtal.>

*

The morning sun was bright as howler monkeys called out from their perches up in the trees. It was a familiar sound to Ixtal as she ran through the forest, always barefoot and so fast that only the strongest and speediest of the warriors who protected the nearby temple could attempt to keep up. Even with their body paint that they told everyone who would listen granted them the strength of the jaguar they would never catch her. Ixtal would smile and laugh as they gave up, screaming curses at her as she danced away into the lush green Mayan wilderness.

Ixtal loved to tease the warriors, but she still had purpose to her running. She had a mission, and as she moved through the forest – slipping over rocks and vaulting dead tree trunks – she prepared herself for the confrontation that was so close now she could smell it on the wet air.

The hunt had taken so long it seemed like it would never end, but Ixtal had persevered where others had given up. She had examined the smallest traces, the tiniest clues. She had listened to the voices of the rainforest where others could hear nothing – the songs of birds always told her things, and this morning the chorus of the monkeys guided her towards what she knew would be her quarry. They just couldn't tell her what it would be.

She ran faster, feeling her heart pound in her chest with that mixture of fear and joy that she loved so much as her jade amulet hung at her neck. She wore her usual skins – a simple skirt and chest covering – distressed and faded, and on her left bicep was an armband made of vine cord stitched with pointed teeth. She wore the face paint that made her tough and the bone piercings in her ears and nose that made her strong. Her long beaded black hair was cut away at the sides and braided with golden feathers. On her back was her beloved bow, and at her hips were her other weapons – her bone-handled obsidian dagger, her axe and her sling with its vicious multi-pointed projectiles. But no headdress or her father's old spear that was adorned with carve bones, the one nearly as big as she was. Not today.

Ixtal didn't need them. She was already prepared for the final moment. The confrontation.

Up ahead she heard something and she slowed down, barely out of breath as she crouched down behind a clump of thick foliage. She listened to everything. There was water up ahead, a small lake off a river where animals drank frequently. She knew the place well – playful black-haired tapirs liked to rest here when it was too hot and agouti swam in the cooling waters all the time. The howlers were there too, watching silently It was that silence that told Ixtal that she was where she was supposed to be, and it was time.

With practiced perfect motions, she jumped up onto a moss-covered rock and anchored herself in the posture she had been taught by her beloved Uncle, taking and drawing her bow in one fluid action with a single arrow pointing straight down into the grassy clearing around the lake surrounded by the trees. The animals froze and everything fell into silence as Ixtal saw her target.

A man, his dark skin dirty and dressed in nothing but a filthy loincloth stained in something that smelled to Ixtal like blood, squatted at the edge of the water. She could only see his back as he scooped handful after handful of water up, drinking loudly. For a moment it was like he hadn't even realised she was there, and then the moment passed. He stood up and turned and Ixtal saw his face.

It was not a man's face. It was a mass of melted flesh with empty eye sockets and a mouth that hung like it had no jawbone. Ixtal could see things crawling out the empty holes too, things that looked like worms, and as she watched the skull began to crack and split like rotten fruit. Two bigger worms forced their way out of the sides of the man's head, dripping wet as they stretched out into the air

Ixtal had no fear in her mind as her arrowhead burst into a dazzling white flame, and she fired.

*

Ana-Maria sucked in a breath as though she had fallen asleep for a brief second and jerked awake. Around her the cave was the same – the fire still flickered, Dragón still marched around being a bodyguard and no time at all seemed to have passed. She checked her phone again. Not thirty seconds had passed since she had sat down to do the ritual. And she had no memory at all of anything happening. Suddenly Ana-Maria felt stupid sitting there.

<Erik, I hate you. This is….aaagh, *pendejo pendejo PENDEJO*>.

She was about to allow her anger to come it full flow when she looked down and saw that the tile of slate she had marked had disintegrated gone, turned to dust on the top of Uncle Francisco's old faded tee-shirt. Dragón stomped over and looked down from his far greater height. Images of confusion flashed between their joined minds, and neither of them could quite decide what had happened. The slate had been there, solid and new, and now it was like it had aged a thousand years in no time at all.

317

Ana-Maria wondered if she had accidentally broken time. Hopefully there wouldn't be some kind of universe ending disaster like she had read about in some of her mother's less scientific books. She sat there for a minute then two, and nothing happened, so she started to feel a little more relaxed. Maybe it had worked after all?

<Uncle Francisco?> called Ana-Maria. Her voice echoed a little of the cave walls, but there wasn't a response. She wasn't sure what it was she had expected. She knew that the dead didn't really come back from Heaven – people simple sent their love out to them on *Dia de Muertos* and saw them in their memories and talked about in their stories. The dead Ana-Maria had seen come back were soulless empty things, not really living at all. She was relieved that hadn't happened either. No end of the world and no zombies. But the crumbled grains of slate bothered her. She didn't like things that couldn't be explained – that was why she spent so much time paying attention in science class, and that was why she was going to get her science degree. She was going to explain things and try and help her other, who preferred weird websites about unexplained phenomena and drinking too much. After all, Dragón could be explained. He was real and living and poking at the tee-shirt experimentally with his makeshift weapon, annoyed he hadn't had a chance to use it. So maybe all those other things could be explained too. Maybe.......

Then Ana-Maria touched her necklace and her heart skipped a beat in shock. She took it off and saw that it was changed too. The carved wood was gone, and in its place was an amulet carved in something green and translucent. Puzzled, she looked it up on her cellphone, and after a few seconds something came up on the screen that told her it was made of jade, and it was very very old indeed. It was a museum piece – an antique. A relic.

"*Mierda,*" she whispered, and Erik's face popped in her and Dragón's head. Dragón growled a little – he didn't like Erik. Perhaps it was the hat. He would have liked to eat at least one of Erik's legs, but it looked like that wasn't going to happen now.

Ana-Maria brushed off the dust and folded up Uncle Franciso's tee-shirt. It felt like it was more important than even now, and she knew that once she had spent time with her mother at the cemetery she would be calling Erik. She didn't care how late it was or who he was with, he was going to have to come up with some answers that made sense.

As she said goodbye to Dragón and headed out down towards Rico and his waiting car, Ana-Maria felt more and more with every step in that something had visited this cave on this Dia de Muertos.

Something…..forgotten.

BOOK #2
LA SEPULTURERA
500AD

CUEVA DE IXTAL

From her hiding place up in the trees Ixtal could feel the pulse of the rainforest in her blood and in her bones. It wasn't quite a sound, more like a vibration that flowed through everything. At first when she had started to sense it, it has been almost overwhelming, but now it was so much a part of her she couldn't imagine being without it. It had moods and rhythms she could read, and when she concentrated hard enough it could even tell her things.

All around the howler monkeys called and the colorful birds sang, and with the pulse in her mind Ixtal could understand a lot of them. Even the insects sometimes. Not like words - more like dream-like images that slipped in and out of her thoughts as her subconscious needed them. Sometimes Ixtal would see places she needed to go, or things she needed to find. Sometimes she would see the best way to kill, and sometimes she would know the perfect way to keep safe.

The wet morning heat rose of everything like steam as Ixtal watched Her deep brown eyes could focus on even the smallest details, and she let all the sounds of the rainforest filter through her hearing, trusting the environment itself to tell her what she needed to know. It rarely failed.

Today it told her of three people, men, smothered in dark mud and wearing vicious bones. They crashed through the forest undergrowth, not knowing enough to keep quiet as they pursued their prey. Whatever kind of instinct drove them, it overwhelmed everything else. Even the lowliest animal knew the rainforest better than these men.

Their clumsiness made Ixtal smile as she stretched out her athletic body and dropped silently down from her hideout, where she had arranged branches and leaves to conceal herself. Dressed in a long loincloth that coved front and back to her knees and a simple band across her chest, she crouched, scanning for the men of mud and bones. The monkeys hadn't raised the alarm yet so they were far enough away that Ixtal could easily keep the advantage. Where they were loud and aggressive, she would be silent and stealthy, slipping through the endless labyrinth of Mayan forest in the shadow of the mountains that had become her home and that she knew so well.

The feel of dried blood felt good on Ixtal's skin as she prepared herself. She had made her sacrifice to the Monkey Gods to grant her safe passage and the agility of the howlers, and they had listened. Along her arms and her belly and along the shaven sides of her head she had painted stripes of with her fingers, and she had tied her long black hair back with vine. All her weapons – her dagger, her sling, her axe and her bow – were checked and ready. All her muscles tightened with anticipation, and she felt strong.

She touched the armlet on her bicep, the one made of leather and bones – carved and smooth like the ones in her ears and though her nose - and whispered the scared name of her father - the one who had taught her all these things. Not the man who had made her mother pregnant – he was useless. All he did was eat and try and be important. Instead Ixtal spoke the name of her real father. The father of the forest.

Finally, in between the squawks and chirrups, she heard the footsteps she wanted to hear. They weren't the mem of mud and bone – even a child would be able to hear them. What Ixtal could hear was another set of footsteps, light and fast, belonging to some who was so frightened that their fear made the air taste bitter.

Someone who was being chased.

A young man ran for his life. He didn't know where he was or where he was going, just that he had to escape from the men of mud and bones who relentlessly pursued him. His chest burned as he sprinted as fast as he could, trying his best to keep under the cover of the trees as the world of the rainforest sang around him.

Only a single sunrise ago, Pech had been with his brothers and sisters. He was the eldest and he enjoyed the responsibility that gave him in teaching them. There had been laughter and play all the time. Sometimes they would leave their little village to see the huge green coated rock that looked like a strange monster, are head down to the waterhole and watch the animals. If they were lucky they would see a jaguar stalking through the undergrowth.

Jaguars had always been Pech's favorite. He often wished he had the magical power to turn into one. Maybe, he had hoped, if he made enough animal sacrifices, a god would listen to him and grant his wish. That had all changed today. When the men of mud and bones had arrived, everyone had betrayed him. His siblings had run and hidden, and his parents had gladly handed him over. They told him is was an honour, but Pech knew what honours like that meant. He had too many stories for the older men in the tribe who had spent time in the city of

Pech was to be sacrificed.

And so the men had bound him even as he screamed out for his village to help him. None of them did. To them, the loss of beloved Pech was a small price to pay for peace and prosperity in their tiny little section of the rainforest. The men of mud and bones gave them special tones and carvings to ward off the monstrous spirits of the night and told them that the maize harvest from nearby would be bountiful. Even the terrible plague of the worms would leave them untouched.

Some of the villagers even envied Pech. But none of them offered to take his place.

As he ran, Pech couldn't remember how he had managed to escape. Somehow the bindings on his wrists had been loose and he had wrenched free, stripping the skin off his arms. That didn't matter to him. He knew he was faster than the lumbering men of mud and bones so he had blindly run, vanishing off the cleared pathways into the rainforest. How long ago that had been he couldn't really tell. The sun was all but invisible through the tree canopy, and all he really knew that his legs and chest and heart all cried out for rest.

In the end he had to stop, sucking in breath as he tried to bury himself in thick plants growing all around the fat ridged exposed roots of a clump of buttressed trees. Ants crawled everywhere and Pech ate some, letting the others clamber all over his skin. He tried to make himself blend in so he was invisible, willing the insects to hide him.

Then Pech heard a sound, so quiet it was almost not there at all. He froze. Had one of the men of mud and bones somehow got ahead of him? Or were there others, quite like ghosts, waiting to trap him? He looked up, petrified, bracing himself for the inevitable blow from a club that would cave in his skull and leave him broken, stupid and nearly dead as he was dragged away to be sacrificed.

Instead Ixtal looked back down at him, her dark eyes searching.

<Who are you > she asked.

Pech stared up out of his hiding place, struck dumb. Everything in his life had been ripped away from him and now some kind of vengeful female spirit painted in blood looked down at him. What had he done to deserve this – what God had he so angered that they wanted him dead?

<Who are you?> Ixtal repeated, less patiently this time. The cowering man in the undergrowth looked so puny and frail it was almost pathetic, but Ixtal had no time for pleasantries. She could already hear the thundering footsteps of the men of mud and bone off in the distance, and it wouldn't be long before they found their way here.

Pech had picked a natural clearing and a poor hiding place.

Ixtal reached down to grab an arm and Pech cowered in terror, forcing himself back against the tree. He was crying now, and it looked like his mind had simply collapsed under the strain. Ixtal had hoped to someone lead him to safety – perhaps get him to a better concealed area that she could defend while she figured out exactly what the men of mud and bones wanted. That looked impossible now. Pech was degenerating into a blubbering mess and was useless.

Up above in the branches, a few howler monkeys had gathered. They often followed Ixtal, following the same quiet whisper of the rainforest, and they often acted as lookout. Sometimes it felt like theirs and Ixtal's eyes were connected somehow – that she could almost see what they could see. Not clearly but like looking through the early morning mist on the ground.

Ixtal looked around, following the howlers, and saw the hints of shapes to go with the crashing noises. There were still just three, all bulky and carrying heavy clubs that had been created from heavy wood and viciously sharpened bone. She had seen discarded weapons like that before – made to look like the arm of some wild animal that didn't exist. But this was the first time she had found the people who carried them – the men smeared in that stinking mud and trying to turn themselves into something other than human.

The disguise was enough for most, but Ixtal saw through it.

At her feet Pech just cowered. Now he had his hands over his head as he tried to pretend that all of this wasn't happening. He wished and wished that he had eaten something he shouldn't have, a rotten fermenting fruit maybe, that had made him see things. If he wished hard enough, maybe he would wake up from this nightmare and he would be home with his siblings again.

The howlers up above were becoming agitated now. Their calls were a warning and also a siren, alerting Pech's pursuers. Ixtal tried to will them to silence but there was no point. She had no control – she could only hear their calls, and act on what she heard.

Looking around, Ixtal tried to formulate a plan. She knew the men in mud and bones wouldn't speak. The stories of their mute cruelty were told time and again from parents to children and had been for endless sunrises and sunsets. They were the nightmare men who grew out of the wet earth and came for people. Anyone who resisted was brutalised with their bone clubs. They were demons, people said. Inhuman things who could not be fought.

Ixtal knew better than that. She needed to know more, and so she realised her only option was to fight and keep Pech alive. The howlers felt it too and they screeched as footsteps became like thunder, and finally the first of the men of mud and bone burst into the clearing.

He was a hulking brute of a man, misshapen and deformed. All the hair was stripped from his body, eyes stared wide and bulging from behind the mask of wet mud and a gaping mouth hung open, blackened teeth carved into points. As she looked more closely from the shadows she had concealed herself in, Ixtal could see a huge ragged scar on the man's scalp that stretched from temple to chin. It crawled with something alive.

She watched the man move. He looked like was broken somehow, like his legs didn't really work properly anymore, and he dragged his body forward. He held his heavy club, wood and bone that would need both hands for any normal man – ready to hammer down as he turned from side to side, sniffing at the air like an animal.

Pech's eyes were so wide with fear Ixtal thought they might burst out of his head. She kept her hand firmly over his mouth, making sure he didn't make any kind of sound that might give them away. With the man of mud and bone's size she knew a head-on attack would be pointless. She had to be cautious, calculated. And she had to be quiet.

Always quiet. That was how she survived.

She could hear the other two men in the distance, thrashing at the plants and vines, and guessed they had spread out to try and cover more ground. Perhaps it was sheer luck this first brute had stumbled across them, or perhaps he had some special insight. Perhaps the tactic was to make as much noise as possible to flush Pech out into the open where they could cut him down. Or perhaps this beast of a human was just that – a barely human shape that had only violence in its head.

Ixtal had seen all of these before, and she knew that what she had to do.

The howlers started their chorus again and the man of mud and bone looked up. It gave Ixtal the seconds she needed, and with her spare hand she slipped her slingshot from her waist, it's spiked projectile already loaded and ready. She let the man turn his back, just for a moment, and then she started to spin the weapon.

It whipped around, whispering in the air. Once, twice, and one final time to get all the power she needed. Once it had taken longer, even five or six spins, but now she had mastered the technique. She let her body twist and unwind, and the projectile flew out into the air.

The man heard nothing as the spikes buried themselves in the side of his head. He stood there, paralysed, a low gurgle coming out his mouth. Then his legs collapsed from under him and he dropped silently to the ground. The club rolled out of his grip, and Ixtal thought about retrieving it. If she had been alone, she probably would have. It would have gone well with the rest of her collection of strange treasures that she kept hidden away in a secret place nobody could ever find.

But she wasn't alone, so she turned her attentions back to Pech as the young man quivered in panic, his body saturated with sweat.

<We must run,> said Ixtal. <Come with me. NOW.>

Pech refused to move, Ixtal pulled at him but he just shook his head and pointed behind her. Frustrated, Ixtal looked, and she froze.

The man of mud and bone was getting back to his feet.

Ixtal stared at the body that should have been a corpse struggle to his feet. He staggered, thick dark blood staining the mud on his head and dripping down onto the ground.

<Why is he not dead?> she said, mainly to herself.

Pech didn't reply. The men of mud and bone were monsters of the rainforest as far as he was concerned. They weren't human, so they could do anything. Why should death affect them. All he really knew for certain was that if this frightening huntress and her lethal weapons couldn't stop his pursuers, nothing would.

Suddenly any hope of survival felt like it had disappeared.

The man of mud and bone lurched as though he was broken. He tried to grab his club but the effort was too much for him so he tipped over, crashing down face-first into the undergrowth. A hundred different insects scattered in every direction as the hulking form quivered for a few seconds, and then was still. Ixtal watched for a moment but the body didn't move again. When she was sure she walked over, each of her footsteps almost silent, and crouched down.

This time the man of mud and bone was clearly dead. One of his eyes was gone and the spikes from Ixtal's slingshot projectile had gone through bone. It had penetrated the side of his jaw, and poked out through the man's jagged sharpened teeth. This was always a killing strike, and yet somehow this figure had managed a few seconds of life when it should have been taken from him instantly.

How was this possible?

<What sort of magic do you have?> Ixtal asked herself.

The man's dead face sagged visibly as the one open eye stared back up at her. There was no answer – just the sticky mass of blood that stained everything. It took two or three attempts for Ixtal to tug the projectile free from the man's head, and as she did more wetness seeped out. Ignoring it, she looked at the mud coating on the man's skin. Now she was close up she could see that it wasn't mud at all, but rather something that had buried itself deeper, changing the surface flesh into something dark and rough and wet. Ixtal ran a finger over the man's shoulder. There was a coating on the skin that was sticky, like the sap of a tree, and when she smelled it was like nothing she had known before.

She began to wonder if this was a man at all. She had seen people cover their skin in all kinds of things, but this? This was different.

Pech stayed hidden deep in the bushes. Now the brute that had chased him was definitely dead his heartbeat began to slow down a little, but he still cowered and shook, sweat pouring off his body. Perhaps this young woman was more powerful than he had thought. Perhaps she could protect him, but that was no reason to sacrifice his hiding place. Not yet. He knew the other two other men of mud and bone were still out in the forest, out of sight and unheard for now.

But not for long.

A sound snapped Ixtal's attention behind her, and she rolled back to her feet as the howlers in the trees overhead hooted and howled at something new.

Ixtal notched an arrow to her bow and drew it back in one sleek motion, aiming straight at a natural archway in the trees that led to deeper darker parts of the wilderness. She knew she had seen something – the same something that howlers had detected. It was like a flicker, a ghost in the forest that was gone in a second. Her eyes did their best to peer past the leaves and branches but even with the sight she called on the howler monkey god to give her she could see nothing.

Yet she still knew something was there.

<Come out,> Ixtal barked. <I am a very good shot and I will not miss if you attack me.>

There was no response, no movement, no sign that anything had been there at all. For a moment Ixtal wondered if she had imagined the whole thing. There were lots of plants in the forest that gave out strange perfumes that made people see all kinds of things that weren't there. There were even stories of some huge bulbous things that ate people by mesmerising them with the exotic scent. Ixtal had always wanted to see one of those for herself.

Another moment passed and then something was thrown out of the jungle. Something round and hard that bounced and rolled along the ground leaving a trail of liquid behind it on the undergrowth. Ixtal saw straight away that it was a head, torn clean off the body of another of the men of mud and bone.

Pech squealed liked a child when he saw it, and Ixtal was quietly cautious as she took out her dagger and decided to take a closer look. For all she knew it would suddenly come back to life and fly into the air, chasing her as it bit and bit with its raggedy pointed teeth. She approached step by cautious step, and the head remained where it was. No flying, no biting. It was surely as dead as the man she had killed herself. She crouched and turned it over with her dagger, seeing the same deformed and stained flesh. Bulging bloodshot eyes gazed sightlessly out, and the expression on it was one that Ixtal had seen so many times before.

Shock. Pure and simple.

Ixtal wondered what it was that could bring that kind of fear to people like the men of mud and bones. They were the ones who made other afraid. That was the way of things. It wasn't supposed to the be other way around.

As Pech rustled in his hiding place, trying to decide whether it was safe to come out or not, Ixtal looked back to the archway of trees. A few of the howlers were creeping around, down out of the trees, investigating for themselves and clearly just as puzzled at what was happening. They had seen the head as well, and they were relieved, just like Ixtal was, that something hadn't driven them all mad with hallucinations.

No, there was definitely something there, something moving so quickly it didn't register. Not a human being or an animal. The glimmer of a shape with the power to take a man's head without a single sound. Or at least there had been. The howlers could see nothing now as they poked and prodded, while Ixtal listened out for bird calls in case there was anything in the voice of the forest she had missed.

There wasn't.

Ixtal sheathed her dagger and walked towards the archway of trees, wondering where the rest of the body was. Her bare foot stepped on something wet, and she looked down. There she saw the beginnings of a trail of fresh blood, and it screamed at her to follow it.

Beyond the archway of trees, the rainforest felt different somehow. Alien in some way. Ixtal had seen so many parts of this jungle in her life, but this was more like she was stepping over a boundary to somewhere else. It made her shiver and her skin came out in gooseflesh despite the humid warmth. Even the telepathic heartbeat that murmured at the back of her head felt it, its rhythms changing a little with what could almost be fear.

Everything felt wrong. The howlers felt it too. Their cries and whoops had subsided to almost nothing, and that unnerved Ixtal most of all

She checked that Pech was still firmly crouched in his hiding place, trying not to let the ants bother him too much. If he stayed there long enough the plants might grow on him, she thought. At least he was safe for the time being - he was invisible even from only a few footsteps away, and the jaguars rarely came through this part of the rainforest. The howlers would watch over him as well.

Ixtal refocused on the blood trail, dark and sticky and winding off into the deep gloom. She couldn't see much as she began to follow it except the sense of a thousand eyes watching her. Anything could be hiding here, any kind of animal or spirit or even something else. Everywhere was a mystery and so few people told stories of this place. Most stayed back in the city and worked the maize fields. It was only the little outlying settlements, places like Pech's home, that heard a few of the tales around their fires as they ate.

There were odd sounds around her as Ixtal walked, keeping her footsteps quiet and light. Overhead tree branches were festooned with vines and huge roots punched their way up out of the earth. The sun barely penetrated, just little spotlights here and there that gave tiny clues about what lay everywhere. There were flowers with no names and sounds there were no words for, and with each step Ixtal felt further and further from the familiarity of the Mayan jungle she lived in.

The blood track was easy to follow. Ixtal's eyes were well-used to dark places and she could see it glitter lightly like frozen jewels. Sometimes it was even like a tiny river, reflecting those little hints of sunlight. It wound around a gigantic mass of wood that was like no tree Ixtal had ever seen, and then snaked off towards a place where the plants had been hacked away. The branches and leaves were cleanly severed, and it puzzled Ixtal. She didn't know of a tool that could do that.

There was water on some of the nearby flowers, and insects buzzed and hummed around violet and purple petals. Their little air dance made Ixtal smile as she started to feel a little more about this hidden jungle with its unique life. She listened harder and picked up new sounds. Some were familiar, some were not. It made it hard to orient – there were no familiar landmarks to anchor her sense of direction, and no friendly voices that could point the way.

All she had was the bloody track.

It curved off a little further ahead, and as Ixtal followed it she found herself in a small clearing where a tall arrow-straight tree, stripped of any leaves it might once have had, stood all by itself, its bark shimmering a little in blues and greens. It would have fascinated Ixtal if that was all there was to see, but it wasn't.

Hanging down from a heavy branch, suspended upside down from some heavy vines, was the headless body of one of the man of mud and bones. Thick blood dripped out of the wound down to the base of the tree and onto the head of his companion – the last survivor of the hunting party that had searched for Pech. He was quivering and terrified, and missing both of his hands.

Ixtal stared down at the broken man of mud and bone, unsure what to do. In turn he looked back up at her and she saw the same malformed face and sharpened teeth as his companions, and the same changed darkened stained skin. But all the strength of his tribe had been taken away from him, and whatever it was that had cut his hands off in cleans strokes and also broken his mind completely. The man drooled and babbled incoherently, saying half words that made no sense and making croaking sounds that dissolved into tears and then hysterical laughing.

It was pure insanity, the same kind Ixtal had heard of before – the story was one of an old stone temple far away where people whose minds had been tainted by dark spirits were imprisoned to live out their lives screaming and eating their own waste. Now she could believe it. In comparisons to the babbling lunatic, the headless corpse hanging from the tree seemed to have been lucky in receiving a clean death.

The man of mud and bone held up his stumps towards Ixtal as though he was begging. He looked at her but she knew from those bulging eyes that he couldn't really see her. Madness was making him see other, terrible things. Whatever was happening inside the man's had was beyond any hope she had of understanding it

Ixtal cursed. She had hoped there might be some way to get information from at least one of the men. Her plan had been to kill two and then terrify the final one into telling her everything they knew. It had worked before, many times.

Now she had nothing except the eerie odd noises of this dark part of the rainforest.

She stook a step back, and as she tried to figure out a new plan, a weird high pitched scream came out from the trees behind and someone run full speed straight at her. Or at least she thought they did. Her hand went to her dagger on instinct, but when she turned she turned see saw Pech.

His face was contorted into his best impression of rage and he did his best not to trip over himself as he somehow lifted one of the men of mud and bones' clubs over his head. Ixtal was bemused, so she simply stepped out of the way as Pech stumbled towards the handless man, who just looked up and drooled as he saw whatever deranged vision it was he saw.

Pech barely made it to him before the weight of the club got too much, and it fell down onto the man of mud and bone's head. Pech tried to pretend he had wielded it like a warrior, but Ixtal knew that the weight of the weapon had done all the work. Its bulk and carved blade-like edge cracked the skull open and the handless man's eyes rolled up a little, as though he was not certain what was happening to him. The club felt odd in his head, and somehow in his last breaths he had a moment of sanity.

It was almost funny that he was dying at the hand of some sacrificial weakling.

The man died and pitched sideways. Pech stamped on the body ineffectually, trying to do his best war cry. Ixtal watched him for a moment or two, and then put an arm out to stop it. He wanted to think she was trying to hold back the strength he thought he had summoned, but for her the display was simply too embarrassing to put up with any longer.

<He is dead now.>

Pech held onto to his angry face for a second longer, and then he threw up everywhere.

*

The smell of cooking pig filled the air and Ixtal cut a slice off from the little peccary she had slaughtered for food. Once again the rainforest provided for her, but she only took what was needed. There was always a balance to be respected, a natural cycle to be maintained, and anyone who took too much would see the true face of the jungle – its rage and its immeasurable power. That idea scared even Ixtal.

Sometimes when she made blood offerings to the howler monkey gods she had visions that showed her shadows and outlines of terrifying things that protected the forest. She had no desire to face any of them. If the men of mud and bone had been destroyed by such a being, something so fast she couldn't see it or hear it, then even someone with Ixtal's skills would be like an ant under the foot of a godlike warrior.

Pech shivered nearby and Ixtal threw the meat she had carved over to him. He still looked pale and weak but his sickness had passed, so he hungrily bit into his meal. There was plenty of flesh on the peccary carcass but the smell would attract predators soon enough, especially when the sun started to go down. Ixtal always left what she didn't eat so a jaguar could have its own feast. That way the balance was maintained.

The body of the handless man lay slumped not far away, and occasionally he twitched. Like the one that Ixtal herself had killed, it seemed that it was hard to fully extinguish the life of the man of mud and bone. Even with his head bashed in the body still wanted to move, and she was sure that if there was enough strength left in those muscles it would do its best to get up again.

If it did, she was ready. Ixtal was always ready.

<Thankyou for feeding me,> gurgled Pech in between mouthfuls.

Ixtal nodded. <You are very weak. You need strength before I take you back to your village.>

Pech froze, the fear in his eyes flashing again. <I don't want to go back.>

<Why.>

<They hate me. They gave me to the Chac-Uayab-Xoc with smiles on their faces.>

Chac-Uayab-Xoc. So that was the men of mud and bones' real name. <Your family?>

<Yes all of them. Just so the maize harvest would be strong and the babies would grow up without sickness or worms. If my father was alive he would never have allowed this. But it was Bitol who made the agreement with the underworld and he always hated me. He made the others hate me too. With Chac-Uayab-Xoc magic.>

Ixtal listened to all of this and thought. Perhaps she and Pech could come to their own agreement. Her mission to track the Chac-Uayab-Xoc had largely given her nothing. Pech had information she could use, and as long as he didn't collapse from being so weak maybe he could help her.

<Do you know where they come from?>

Pech shook his head as he finished his meat and Ixtal carved him some more. Then he paused. <But I know where one of their meeting places is. They go there to make fires and talk to spirits and drink blood.>

Ixtal smiled. Perhaps Pech wasn't going to be useless after all. <Good. Then when we have eaten we will go there.>

Something like enthusiasm was starting to show in Pech has he ate more. Not much, but a little spark. <Can I have the club? The one I used to kill my enemy with great bravery.>

Ixtal nearly laughed as she replayed the scene of Pech nearly collapsing under the weight of the massive bone weapon. <I will make you one of your own.>

Pech felt stronger with his own weapon. Ixtal carved it to fit him better and he could lift it comfortably. She had made it spikier and sharper as well, and he wondered where a young woman, even as savage a huntress as Ixtal, could have learned these skills. The weapons she carried were all perfectly crafted, and though Pech had seen people carry and use them before they were usually soldiers, and men. Ixtal was on a higher level, her tools honed to perfection, her skills almost supernatural.

It made Pech feel safe as he moved through the forest that she was with him.

Ixtal didn't feel the same way at all. She was used to the familiarity of her usual terrain, and ever since she had followed the path of sticky blood she had felt an uneasy feeling in the pit of her stomach. All around her everything was different in a way she couldn't quite understand. She heard animal calls but they weren't the ones she usually recognised. She saw birds with blood plumage that she had never seen before, and worst of all the familiar call of the howler monkeys was far away and muted now. They hadn't followed her, and that bothered Ixtal most of all.

The howlers usually followed her everywhere. They were her little troop of soldiers who acted as sentinels and scouts, their chatter a constant comfort. She knew them all by their individual patterns and personalities. Without them she felt almost lonely. The sooner she was away from here the better. But for now, she had to focus.

<Tell me more about the Chac-Uayab-Xoc and their magic.>

Pech shivered at the name, even in the tropical humidity. His new bone club gave him confidence but it didn't protect him from his memories. <They commune with the underworld and it makes their skin darkened and tough and their teeth like the animals. You saw how they cannot die properly? If you kill them they always come back. Their magic keeps them alive as half-living things, and they take sacrifices so that they can become stronger. My father told me that they can summon the plague worms and raise the spirits of the dead to fight their battles.>

Ixtal didn't like the sound of any of that. <But they can be fought and made to fall. And perhaps we have a friend as well.>

She thought back to the flicker of movement she had seen back in the clearing where Pech had cowered, and the decapitated head that had been thrown to the ground in front of her. She guessed whatever had done that had destroyed the two other Chac-Uayab-Xoc, and with such an ease that it was frightening. She still didn't know yet if it had all been a warning, or a gift.

Next to her Pech was getting a little braver. He had taken a couple for steps out in front as he used his bladed club to clear through the vegetation. As he did, Ixtal started to pick up the scent of something. It wasn't an animal or the perfume of a plant, but something else. Something that smelt sickly and burned. It took only a second or two for her to recognise it, and she pulled Pech to a halt, forcing him to crouch down into cover with her.

In the branches above, a shape moved and when Ixtal looked up it was gone.

<What is it,> whispered Pech, determined to play his role as courageous scout. He had seen nothing up in the trees.

<That is the smell of cooking blood,> said Ixtal.

Just ahead, where the rainforest sucked in the darkness so much that it was almost night, the ground fell away into a kind of pit. It wasn't deep, perhaps half the height of a person, but it stretched around its raggedy edges to a size that could easily fit fifty. All the plants and trees had been stripped away and the ground inside the pit looked liked it had been scorched to charcoal. It looked like a hole had been punched through the forest right down into the ground by some kind of burning fist, leaving an imprint that made everything around it dead and silent.

Everywhere around it was that stink of burned blood, bitter and hot in the back of her throat as Ixtal got a little closer, the smell hanging everywhere in the air. She kept low and quiet, slipping from bush to bush, trunk to trunk, as Pech kept way back, gripping onto his club with all the strength his hands could muster. In his mind he planned to leap to Ixtal's defence if something happened, but deep down he knew that he would probably just run away.

Ixtal just hoped he would stay still and quiet as she lifted herself effortlessly up into the branches of a tree that overlooked the pit. From this angle she could see more a pattern – where the edges looked ragged before, now they looked almost regular, and the burned surface of the pit itself bore shapes, intricate ones that she didn't recognise. They weren't Mayan language and they certainly did not resemble animals of any kind she knew. They could only be things from somewhere else, Ixtal decided. Somewhere dark and unknown.

As she watched, a hunched little figure shambled into view out of the trees. It was a tiny thing, nothing like the bulk of the Chac-Uayab-Xoc, and there was no way to tell if it was a man of a woman. Its whole body was covered in a ragged black cloth, wrapped around as a cloak and a hood and a kind of dress all at once. It headed towards the pit, and the second it set foot on the blackened earth a kind of rumble rolled through the air. Not a sound but more like a feeling, one that Ixtal felt go right through her and make her stomach turn over.

It was so much like music of her own territory but twisted somehow. Diseased. It made her feel as though her eyes and ears were dulled, as though she was alone and cut off, and she felt her hand clutch at the hilt of her knife for comfort. She gripped it hard, knuckles whitening, and listened. There was nothing she could pick up, nothing to guide her either in her head or her ears. Even the loudest of the howlers were inaudible to her, and she felt lost.

Did this place, these people, have their own voices? Ones that spoke louder in the darkness and made Ixtal's own senses silent and useless?

There was nothing to do but watch.

The hunched figure shuffled to the centre of the pit where it was deepest and took out something from under its robes. A container of some kind made out of a gourd that looked rotted with age. It dropped to the ground and split apart, letting some dark liquid spread out. The carvings in the earth sucked it up hungrily and slowly, so slowly, the ground itself began to pulse. At first Ixtal wondered if the alien feeling in the air was making her see things, but when she cleared her head and focussed she could knew it was real. Solid had become like liquid as waves began to form in the pit. Dirt splashed around the hunched figure's feet and it started to dance a jerky, broken dance that was impossible to follow, as though time was jumping and going too fast all around.

Ixtal stared at the display, trying to understand, as something began to grow out of the pit.

Whatever was forming had no human shape, and nothing recognisable about it all. All Ixtal could see was something grotesque fighting its way out of the ground, perhaps even made out of the ground itself, dripping with sticky dried liquid that could only be the sacrificial blood of uncounted victims.

Suddenly the fate of all the people before Pech became horribly real to her.

Ixtal made her decision instantly. She could not allow this abomination, whatever it was, to walk. She notched an arrow to her bow and as she drew it back the vicious stone head burned with white phosphorus fire, sparking and spitting everywhere. She took aim and fired.

The movement alerted the hunchback creature, but it could do nothing as the arrow pierced straight into the growing creature's body mass. For a second the arrow just burned there and Ixtal thought whatever forces were at work might be immune somehow, that the fire might actually go out. But it didn't. Instead it burst outwards into liquid force, blinding and scorching at once, blasting open the creature and spreading its burning substance all over the pit. Wherever there were symbols new flames formed, pure and white and incandescent. They rolled and flowed, incinerating the blood that saturated the ground, and the hunchback screeched as it did its best to run away.

Ixtal watched, satisfied, as her fire consumed the pit. The shape melted away and the ground it had grown form started to crumbled as well, parts of it collapsing in on itself even as it burned. The pit gradually became a gaping hole, a gash in the land, and the cloud of smoke smelled so bad and acrid it made Ixtal sick.

She slipped down from her tree and retreated back into the undergrowth a little. She knew that the fire burned hot but very quickly, and in a moment it would be safe to approach. Overhead she heard the wings of unseen birds, huge and leathery, flap away, and the frightened calls of strange animals bark and screech as they ran too.

The thing that really surprised her was that Pech hadn't fled.

<What is that magic?> he asked, captivated by the sight of the fire.

<It is a special stone that was shown to me by……> Ixtal paused. <By my father.>

<It is amazing. You must have Xiuhtecuhtli's blessing."

Ixtal didn't reply. Her face was like mask, and her eyes peered forward, searching for any new threat that might hurl itself at them. Even without the lifeblood of the rainforest talking to her in her head her senses were still those of a huntress, and they told her to be cautious. This was unknown territory, and even though she had prevented some kind of monstrous birth ceremony she had no idea what else might dwell out here, where the sunlight barely penetrated the trees.

The phosphorus fire burned itself away to nothing and the heat faded. The bloody stink of the smoke still made Ixtal and Pech's eyes water as they moved forward, him hiding behind her, and she with her bow and arrow braced and ready. As she reached the edge of what had been the pit she saw that it was almost entirely gone. In its place was a vast chasm where the surface had fallen away completely to reveal a deep black hollow emptiness that smoked around its rim.

<That is the underworld,> whispered Pech. <It is Xibalba.>

Xibalba.

That word made everyone afraid. The idea of that underworld, that place of fear, waiting after life to claim the soul, ruled by the Lords Of Death and their monstrous subjects as they planned their endless tests and traps, was something that chilled the bones of the hardiest warriors. People dreamt of the vast city, its monstrous twisted landscapes and its boiling rivers of pus and blood in their nightmares. Then they woke up and wished for some kind of salvation. Soldiers hurled themselves into battle in the hope that their violent death would allow them to escape the torment of Xibalba, and everyone begged for some kind of mercy.

Ixtal knew that mercy was not the way of things. Nature was cruel, and the ways of life and death did not change for anybody.

Her mentor, the man she called her father, had told her the story of a gateway into the underworld city when she had been recovering from training wounds one night around a comforting fire. He said it was deep in the jungle, and that the unwary could find their way into the nightmarish realm even before they had died. Now, looking down into this hole in the ground that yawned wide like a demon's mouth, Ixtal could easily believe she had found such a gateway.

<Xibalba,> moaned Pech. He dropped to his knees and threw aside his club, giving up any pretence of bravery. <Xibalba Xibalba. May the Bloody Claws spare me from torment.>

Ixtal was scared too. The idea that has stood on the precipice of the realm of the dead made her want to freeze slid without the comfort of the rainforest heartbeat and the power of the sunlight. She had to force herself to move as she crouched and tried to see down into the gloom of the hole. It was pitch black, and even as she did her best to penetrate it she could see nothing.

A laugh made her look up. The hoarse rasping cackling noise that sounded like a person's dying breath hung in the air little and then faded, and Ixtal saw that the hunchbacked wretch had returned. Under its cowl was a wizened face so old it was nearly skeletal, with bulbous yellow and red eyes gazing unblinking outwards, and a mouth filled with rancid pointed teeth. In one hand it held a twisted dagger of bone as it shambled forward, wheezing as it came.

Once again Ixtal drew her bow. She was taking no chances. Who knew what this broken figure would be able to conjor up out of the ground.

The hunchback stopped in its tracks but kept laughing, waiving its dagger around. Nothing happened, and Ixtal felt herself relax, just a little. Perhaps, she thought, the wretch's power was gone now the pit and its blood and symbols had been burned away. Despite that, her arrowhead remained pointed unwaveringly at its target.

<Your bow is a child's weapon,> hissed the hunchback. <Do you think that fire matters to us. The Supreme Judges consume your fire as a delicacy. Your blood will nourish the ground, and Xiquiripat will consume every last drop to feed our army. Look, little child. Look down into the tiny little hole you have made in the world and see you small you are.>

Ixtal wanted to shoot the hunchback through its skull face, but she couldn't help casting her eyes back down into abyss once again. This time, somehow, she saw something down in the dark.

She saw jagged pointed rocks wet with blood, and they whispered like they were alive.

The sound of the rocks pushed its way into Ixtal's head and she clapped her hands to her ears to try and block it out. She made her mind hard like she had been taught, to force out the intruders, but it was so difficult. The whispers told her to do things, not in words but in sensations, and she found her body wanting to do as they commanded. One of her foot inched forward towards the edge of the hole against her will, and it felt as though some kind of strange force was doing its best to make her body into a puppet.

She wouldn't let it. She remembered the sounds of her home, the heartbeat in her bones, the call of the howlers and the voice of the rainforest itself and pushed back the tide. But even as she did she couldn't move, her body locked into place as she fought for control.

Next to her, Pech had no such strength.

The voices of the blackness flowed into his brain unhindered, and he all but ran towards the edge. He could see the jagged rocks, and they looked like teeth in some giant's mouth. He could see the blood that washed over everything, and he wanted to add his own to it. The urge to hurl himself down into the abyss was irresistible, and his mind was filled with that single terrifying word that he would do anything to escape from.

Xibalba.

XIBAAAAAAALBAAAAAAAAA…..

Ixtal saw him begin his leap, but her movement was slow and broken as she went to stop him. The effort of fighting the power of the whispering rocks was so much that her eyes were bloodshot and her ears were bleeding. Despite all of that she threw herself forward and caught Pech's arms. The momentum slammed her chest down into the ground and winded her, but she hung on to Pech's arms. She looked at him but her vision was blurred, and she felt the whispers like shards of obsidian picking at her body inside and out. Pech looked up at her, and his expression was caught between joy and utter terror. He didn't know why he wanted to be in the pit. He just did.

As Ixtal hung on, muscles straining and head screaming in protest, Pech felt cuts open up on the flesh of his legs. Invisible blades sliced him, and his blood there started to drain out as though it were being sucked away, down onto the rocks.

Finally, Pech screamed out in pain as Ixtal tried to pull him out, but some unseen vampiric force had him in its grip, leeching away at him drop by drop, vein by vein.

<Help MEEEEEEEEE.>

Ixtal tried to stand but Pech was too heavy and her arms felt like they were being pulled apart at the elbow. Cuts were forming all over Pech's lower body, the precious red fluid drawn away into the darkness like flowing water. Soon the rocks would have taken it all and he would be dead. Ixtal's arms were failing too, and she felt so weak as the war in her own mind took its toll. She wept red tears now and felt the back of her head throb so hard it could have burst outwards in a shower of bone and brain at any moment.

Silently she called out to the forest.

Somehow, it answered.

There was a flash of movement, the same blur that Ixtal had seen when she had watched the decapitated head of one of the Chac roll towards her. The air around her whirled and spun, and in the space of a breath she was hurled up into the air and down into a clump of soft leaves.

There was silence now. The malignant whispers in her mind were gone, and whatever power the cave had tried to exert over her was suddenly, completely gone.

Ixtal took a moment to breath and find some strength tog et to her feet. She was drained, as though the very essence of her had been leeched away a little, just the way Pech's blood had been leched from him. Woozy, weak on her feet, she moved back a little closer to the cavernous hole, careful not to get too close in case the rocks took her.

She didn't have to worry.

The air was solid around the edge, forming a barrier that stopped Ixtal in her tracks. She pushed at it a couple of times, and felt it bend under her touch, but it would not give. Even looking through it was difficult, especially with her eyes clouded with blood and tears that did her best to wipe away with a leaf. When she could finally look more clearly, she stopped dead.

Pech was gone.

Ixtal panicked. Had she lost the battle? Had some force been conjored out of the darkness to destroy her strength and claim its victim? Had she failed?

The hunchback was puzzled too as it tried to penetrate the barrier. It stabbed and stabbed the empty air with its bone dagger, and it cursed and spat and threatened. Nothing happened. The power of blood that the hunchback had wielded had failed it, and in that second of realisation Ixtal knew that Pech was safe. She didn't know how, and she didn't know where he was, but she knew, deep in her, that somehow that impossible flash of movement had helped her once again.

Somehow, the forest had provided her with a guardian.

Ixtal started to feel her strength come back to her as she traced her way around the barrier, feeling her way step by step. She felt focussed again without that terrible whispering that attacked her thoughts, and she locked in on the hunchback as it raged at the invisible wall. It seemed so consumed but its own rage that it didn't see Ixtal as she got closer and closer, keeping her footsteps quiet and making herself a part of the forest. Not invisible, but perhaps unnoticeable. Every breath controlled, every heartbeat measured. She had practiced this so often, and it had been so difficult to perfect. Now though she felt it was a part of her – she was hiding in plain sight, and it made her feel powerful as all her strength came back into her muscles and her senses.

It was only when Ixtal drew her dagger and moved fully into the hunchback's vision that it finally span to face her. It's skeletal face was contorted into something hideous, its lopsided mouth dripping with yellow bile as it brandished its own twisted bone weapon.

<What have you done,> it hissed. <What magic is this? This sacrificial place is sacred. You cannot desecrate it. You

are an insect. AN INSECT. WE WILL HAVE YOUR BLOOD.>>

Ixtal didn't listened to a word. Instead she simply launched herself forward, agile like a feral cat, and drove her dagger towards the hunchback's wizened throat.

The two of them smashed into the muddy ground in a tangle of bodies, but Ixtal's knife didn't find flesh, only earth. The hunchback twisted its neck to an impossible angle, cracking bones sideways and out of position, all the while wearing a hideous grin on its face. Its breath was rancid and made Ixtal gag as much as the stink of burning blood from the pit had. The hunchback's muscles were strangely strong as well, tight and sinewy underneath its raggedy clothing when Ixtal had expected them to be loose and weak.

She realised she had made a miscalculation as she rolled back away, keeping all her senses razor-keen as the hunchback snapped back to an upright position, its body moving in jerky spastic motions as though little pieces of time were being skipped.

Then it cackled. <You believe you are a strong huntress. But you are not.> It brandished its twisted bone dagger once again. <You are weak and I will have your blood. ALL OF YOUR BLOOD.>

A screech filled the air, an ear-splitting sound that spewed out of the hunchback's mouth and attacked Ixtal like it was a physical thing. It hurt, but this time Ixtal was ready. She had gained strength from enduring the monstrous whispering of the pit, and though her ears bled again she would not let this wretched little creature beat her. She had underestimated it once, but not again.

Moving too fast than was possible, the hunchback darted towards Ixtal, intending to pierce her heart with its dagger. Ixtal let her mind become calm, and let all her senses and her trained body do the work for her. The hunchback had power, that much was certain. But it had no skill. It wielded its weapon like a child might do when it was playfighting with its brothers and sisters.

The twisted dagger punched forward and Ixtal let it pass her by, cutting the hunchback's forearm with her arm knife as it did. The creature squealed and withdrew its attack, letting dark blood – too dark to be human – ooze out of the wound. Then it lunged again. This time Ixtal twisted her body and caught the creature's hand, twisting hard to snap its wrist and cutting the tendons in its elbow. This time the dagger fell to the ground and Ixtal kicked it away.

That would be her trophy for this fight.

The hunchback glared, half shocked and half almost impressed. All the people it had seen in its long life, all the supplicants and sacrifices, were not like this woman. They had all been easy to cull and bleed. Ixtal was something different to them. It was though there was a power in her that made her too strong to fight single-handedly, even with the power of blood and darkness at its disposal.

Ixtal waited, seeing everything, as the hunchback turned and tried to flee back into the rainforest, one arm hanging limply at its side and still bleeding whatever it had that passed for blood. But the creature moved slowly, staggering with age, and it gave plenty of time for Ixtal to notch an arrow to her bow and fire it with perfect aim. The arrow pierced right through the back of the hunchback's head, punching out through its forehead. It froze in place, eyes rolling up to nothing but a bloody and yellow mass as a single sound came out of its mouth. A sound of pure surprise. Almost as though it couldn't quite believe it was dead.

But it was

It toppled forward face first into damp earth and immediately began to break apart.

The hunchback's flesh dried out in a just a few seconds, becoming mummified, as joints dissolved and limbs fell away. Its chest sank and its head collapsed in on itself, spewing dust out of a hundred cracks in the dead parched flesh. Its eye sockets became empty, and its mouth to almost nothing. Ixtal reached to pick up her arrow as it fell to the ground without a solid skull to hold it in place, watching in a kind of disgusted fascination as the body parts started to fragment themselves.

In the end there were just the ragged robes left, and the remains of the hunchback became like a million ants made out of ash. They moved on their own, streaming away from what had once been their body and burying themselves down into the earth. Some headed for the pit and when they couldn't penetrate the barrier they just floated away like dust, and then nothing at all.

Ixtal sheathed her dagger, satisfied. Whatever creature the hunchback had been, it was dead now. It wasn't like the Chac-Uayab-Xoc. This time there was no body - nothing that could come back and try to attack her again.

She turned her attention to the barrier.

There, behind it, the pit was starting to knit itself shut. The twisted whispering of the rocks was gone completely as the barrier slowly began to fall away, and Ixtal pushed against it to test it again. It gave away a lot more this more, so she continued to watch as the chasm continued to close. The earth reversed in time, falling upwards into place, but dry and untainted this time. There was no blood and there were no symbols carved into the ground.

When it was over all there was, was plain ordinary earth as the barrier finally faded away, and the only sound was the faint chirping of particularly brave birds. They would return to the trees here to nest now, and then other animals would follow. Soon it would be like the pit had never been there at all.

Ixtal looked around. She wondered if her invisible guardian who moved faster than she could see would return. She wondered where he had taken Pech, or if Pech was even still alive after the hole in the ground had taken so much of his blood. She hoped he was, but she also knew that the rainforest claimed so many people, especially the weak, and especially in a part like this. A dark part, unknown and unknowable.

Maybe one day she would find some clue to Pech's fate.

But not today.

The darkness was heavy all around her, and she turned back towards the path that had led her here. At first the trail was hard to follow and she relied on her memory, but soon the trees started to thin out and the sunlight started to stream through again. She felt the warmth on her skin and it made her feel the familiarity of the rainforest – her rainforest. Sounds she recognised filled the air and off in the distance the howlers called for her.

She had missed them.

Ixtal headed out along a cleared path that she expected to end with the bodies of the Chac-Uayab-Xoc. But something had changed. Instead of trees and space there was a cave, hidden behind a curtain of hanging blue vines and carved into the side of a sheer dark rock face.

Ixtal wondered how she could have got so lost. The trail had somehow betrayed her and led her somewhere else even as the howlers called for her. She looked around, but there was no sign of anything familiar. All there was, was the cave.

She took a step closer, and a crowd of tiny emerald-colored beetles scurried away from their hiding place, hundreds of them, make a rustling sound as they went. Some had even clung to the vines, and those split their bodies and flew up into the heights. Ixtal tried to see where they went but up above was just thick canopy and huge twisted limbs of wood. The trees they belonged to looked strange, not like the usual rainforest. Instead, she was in another unknown place.

Was someone playing some kind of game with her?

Ixtal tried to put the little pieces together, looking for some kind of connection between all the thing she had seen. But there wasn't any. It was all so random and unnatural, beginning with a decapitated head and ending in a dissolving body.

A path that began with one death and ended in another.

Ixtal crouched to look at the trail of dark blood. It looked recent, and it made her think that this was deliberately new – a branch from the original path she had followed that was laid down for just one reason. To bring her here, to this place. This cave.

Was it her invisible lightning-fast protector again? Whatever it was it was so fast a new trail would have been a simple matter. And if it was that unseen spirit, what reason did it have to lead her from place to place, sight to sight. Even death to death.

So little of it made sense. All Ixtal could do was take a closer look at the cave and pray that there was some sort of meaning to be found.

She pulled aside some of the vines. They were fat and fibrous and warm, and they twitched a little as she touched them. It was an unpleasant sensation, almost like touching flesh. For one horrible moment Ixtal wondered if she had been led to the maw of some carnivorous plant. She had heard of them before, on the slopes of the mountain, and caught her breath.

Was this all some huge trap? Now that she had served her purposes, was she to be thrown to another monster?

But nothing happened. The thick vines just hung there, lifeless, and Ixtal felt a gentle rush of cool air from inside the mouth of the cave. She could hear water as well, running water, so she moved forward and kept every movement light and careful. The place defied her fears with every step she took – it was just a cave after all, like a hundred others, with wet moss on the lumpen walls and heavy stalactites hanging from the ceiling.

<*Raaaaaaaaaaaawr.*> shouted Ixtal. It was her jaguar call and it sounded exactly like the real thing. She had only made the sound so she could listen to the echoes. She had always loved that reflection of her own voice, and she smiled as her call bounced away into the depths. It also told her the cave was long and deep, and maybe it was too vast to investigate, at least for now.

That changed when she saw someone crouching down by a pool of clear water. It was a woman, young and athletic, and Ixtal stopped dead when she saw the figure had her face.

Encased in the skull of some monstrous carnivore and covered in multi-colored plumage, the woman stood up and Ixtal found herself looking at herself. Her face and her body, but not completely identical. This new version of her wore more ornate clothes, colored luxuriant animal skin that had been made into almost a dress, and jade jewellery hung from her throat and her arms. In one hand was a spear made from beautiful worked obsidian, and in the other was a small stone bowl that was half full of water.

The two looked at each other. Ixtal was shocked into immobility, while the other her with the headdress appeared calm, almost as though she had been expecting this meeting.

<You are the beginning,> said the second Ixtal, her voice soft and without any harshness. Ixtal stared at her and saw a kind of light in her eyes that shimmered like the amber sun. The same black hair cascaded down to her hips, but where

Ixtal kept hers shorn at the sides and held back with vine, this version had a vast thick mane woven with gemstones. Except for the spear there were no other weapons either. There was no sign of Ixtal's arsenal, the one she had dedicated her life to mastering with the guidance of the man she called her father.

<Are you a spirit?> said Ixtal.

The second Ixtal shook her head and laughed like music. She held out the bowl. <Drink, and it will begin.>

A hundred different things flashed through Ixtal's mind, a hundred different reasons why she shouldn't take drink form this impossible stranger. And yet something deep inside her told her it was safe, that this was what she was here for. To take a simple drink.

Hesitant at first, fighting the urge to run or fight, Ixtal reached out to take the bowl. The water inside glittered like liquid crystal, and it captivated her. <It is beautiful,> she whispered, and looked back up to try and understand. <What….?>

There would be no replay. The other Ixtal was gone. There was just the cave and the bowl, and gentle sounds of air over rock.

<So you were a spirit,> said Ixtal, letting her voice echo again.

Nothing answered.

She stood for what seemed like long minutes, the bowl of water in her hands, wondering what to do with it. It would so easy to just throw it away and dismiss all of this has some kind of waking dream. Perhaps the vines had their own kind of magic and had been her see things. But at the same time the stone bowl was solid and real in her hands, and the water still flashed inside it, perfect and pure.

Ixtal wished her father was there, her real father, not the man who had put the seed in her mother's belly. He had known so much, and he would have known what to do. But he wasn't there. He was long dead. There was no blood trial to follow on the ground from her unseen protector either. The voice of the rainforest was still too faint to help her, and the howlers were still distant, unwilling to take a step into the hidden rainforest borderland. All she had was her own thoughts.

Finally she lifted the bowl to her lips, hesitated one final time, and then drank.

Ixtal suddenly stood in a familiar place. It was light and bright, filled with life and so much a part of her that she recognised it even without seeing it. The rainforest spoke to her clearly again, in her blood and in her bones, and the excited chattering of the howlers surrounded her. She heard birds sing and insects chirrup, and nearby the sound of a small waterfall was like soothing music.

Ixtal looked up to see her beloved little tree hut, the one she had spent days building out of wood and vine bindings when the rain had become so heavy she simply couldn't sleep outside anymore. She had eaten here, made love here, carved weapons and collected her trophies here.

She was home, or as close to a home as she chose to make for herself.

What she didn't understand is how she was here.

One second she had taken a sip of water that had tasted oddly sweet, and in the next she was in the mostly familiar place in the world to her. It was like she had been summoned home by some kind of magic, but there had been no sense of any time passing. Yet Ixtal knew that it had. The sun was lower in the sky, while the sky itself was slowly taking on the colors of evening. She felt hungry too and she guessed her last meal of fire-roasted peccary had been longer ago than she realised.

It felt good to be here, but nothing made sense. She checked her feet. They were dirty, like she had walked for miles more than she recalled, and the stone bowl in her hands was empty. At her feet were her new trophies – a heavy carved club and a twisted bone dagger – that she couldn't remember picking up.

Ixtal closed her eyes and tried to force her brain to think. She tried to find something, anything, that would explain how she had come home without knowing, but there were simply no thoughts there to recall. No memory, nothing. Just blankness.

More magic? This was all starting to make Ixtal's head hurt with impossibility.

She decided to ponder these things when she lay down to sleep. First there were practicalities to consider. She needed to wash herself in the waterfall, and she needed to get some food from one of the nearby villages. It would be maize. It was always maize. But that was fine. Ixtal was too weary to hunt this evening and even the walk seemed like it would be hard work.

She would trade the bowl as well. She had no use for it anymore. There was no water, no magic. To her mind it was only good for holding food for clumsy children.

Relishing the sun on her body, Ixtal hauled herself up a knotted set of vines with practiced ease and into her hut. It was watertight and open, protecting her and yet not making it so hot that it was uncomfortable. The bed of thick padded leaves was inviting her to sleep, but it was still too early, and she never went to bed without feeling cleansed of the day's work. All the earth and sweat needed to come off first, so she placed her new trophies to one side and stripped her cloth from her body. It was damp and needed replacing, but she had her favorite skins to wear instead – dyed indigo and deep red leathers made into a split skirt and a band around her chest. They would feel good on her freshly washed skin. She could feel the waterfall on her body already and was keen to get clean as she arranged her weapons in a particular way.

Something whistled off in the distance. It was a bird, one of a flock that Ixtal knew well. They were large and friendly with huge bony crests, and she only heard them when the promise of rain was in the air.

Ixtal smiled. She could feel it too. It was about time for the sky gods to clear the oppressive humidity for a while. It meant she would be able to rest properly, perhaps ponder the mystery of the how she had found her way home before she travelled to the world of her dreams for the night.

It was a nice way to end the day, and so she headed off towards the waterfall.

RIO DE IXTAL

The rainforest was a relentless place. The punishing heat and the vampiric humidity sucked the strength from everything while the rain battered every plant and animal into submission. Everything alive from the smallest insect to the largest predator was on the hunt for its next meal. Even the earth itself was treacherous and lethal, hiding black pits and deep pools of sticky inescapable mud that sucked in even the most experienced explorers.

Sometimes even Ixtal struggled to find her way.

The rainforest was her home. She had lived out here, far away from the city and the vast fields of maize, for so long she couldn't remember a time before it. Yet even with all the knowledge and the strength she had gained as she had grown into a young huntress, she knew that the jungle always kept secrets. Above all, she had learned to respect that it was a place that was unremittingly hostile to people and that it not a place to be questioned. One little mistake would be all it would take to succumb to some hideous parasite that ate the body from the inside out, or be dragged away into hidden pools by the coils of a huge serpent with rainbow scales.

Ixtal had seen the result of those kinds of mistakes first hand, so she knew when it was time to struggle onwards and time to stop. As the thick storm-laden charged air made her muscles cramp she rested in a small clearing she knew well. All the routes she took through the rainforest were burned into her memory. Some were trails tramped into the undergrowth by jaguars on their regular hunting routes, while others were trails she had marked herself, invisible to most but given safe passage through the dense and endless trees. On this day it was a more open path, one somebody had cleared with tools and one she always used when she was carrying a carcass.

She found her familiar rock and placed the gutted peccary carefully on one of its flatter surfaces, safe for a moment from egg-laying bugs while she sat down and listened to the chorus of the forest. Birds and monkeys competed for volume and there was never a second of silence. Underneath it was the voice that only Ixtal could hear, that ghostly whispering in the back of her head that she could sense even over the thump of her heart.

It was so hot today that sweat dripped from her body in waterfalls. She had worn as little as she could, her lightest loincloth and a thin little band round her chest, and travelled light with just a few arrows for her bow, and her dagger and a little water grourd at her hip. She had to. All her strength was needed to get food to the village which was not far up ahead. The hunt had been fairly simple but with the stifling air attacking her every second it had been more exhausting than she would have liked. But the villagers needed their food. They had no hunters of their own, and Ixtal had made a bargain with them.

Supplies for food. As simple as that. It served them both well, and it also gave Ixtal that little bit if human company that even she sometimes needed. A peccary would mean a huge feast, and all the children would be laughing and running and playing while the adults discussed the next day's survival, and then the next. That, or they would gossip about people in the next village.

Ixtal took a sip of the water that had nearly boiled in the heat, and then stood to heave the carcass over her shoulders. It felt heavier than before and she forced strength into her arms and her back, making herself ignore the exhaustion.

She could hear the river now, so it wasn't far to go. Just a few hundred more steps.

The call of a familiar howler stopped Ixtal again. She knew the sound very well – it was louder and harsher than many others, and the howler who made it was bigger than most others. Ixtal had named him Mulac and whenever she heard his screech she knew something was not right – not at all. The voice of the rainforest whispered a little as well, and Mulac seemed to respond to it, screeching and wrenching at branches out of sight to make as much noise as he could.

Ixtal scanned the area as she put the carcass back down again. It was a relief – it had felt heavier when she had picked it up a second time.

Up ahead was a pathway that Ixtal usually took. It had been cut away along time ago and the ground had been worn to bare earth with the number of people who had used it. Animals used it too, and it wasn't unusual for somebody foraging away from the village huts to encounter a tapir or a porcupine or an armadillo. It always went the same way – the animal would take a kind of hesitant sniff, decide all humans were disgusting and then they would vanish into the forest. The children made up all sorts of names for them, gave them personalities and stories, and even fashioned crude models of them. The favorite last time Ixtal had visited had been Nacon, a bright green porcupine who had learned how to fly.

It made no sense, but children's stories never did. That's why they were so much fun.

Ixtal's mind was not on fun at the moment. The path ahead worried her, and she took a step forward towards it. Mulac was becoming hysterical up in the trees and she was sure he would be screaming insults at her for being so reckless if he could speak.

Then she smelled a familiar smell, and everything became clear.

Up ahead, lying half in and half our of thick fibrous green foliage, was a dead body. But it wasn't the decay that Ixtal had detected. Instead, she peered closer, her eyes, becoming keener and more focussed, and she could see that the corpse was infested.

Fat wriggling maggots the color of dried blood sat in dead eyes, ears and mouth. A few lumps were growing on the body as well, like boils that oozed sickly wetness that stank.

Ixtal's heart sank. The Worm Sickness had finally come this far.

It was by no means the worse she had ever seen. This unfortunate person had died long before the worms had been able to animate them and spread themselves across animal and human being alike. Instead the sickness had just killed them, anchoring the worms into the body. That was a relief. The body was barely a hundred steps from the river, and if it had fallen into the water the contamination would have been…

Ixtal shivered at the thought.

It didn't really matter how advanced the sickness was – the cure was always the same. Ixtal snapped one of her special arrowheads off a shaft and threw it over to the body. It took a second or two, and then it burst into pure cleansing white fire, incinerating the carcass and the worms, and like always Ixtal hoped they screamed as they died. She hated them beyond reason.

Mulac was quiet now so she knew there were no others to worry about. Instead, Ixtal could think of nicer things as she headed for the river bank and into the village.

The sound of the water always relaxed Ixtal. As she walked alongside the river she got lost in it, letting the gentle music wash over her. The short walk to the village was always like a short road through paradise, away from the merciless nature of the rainforest and out in the open a little.

The river was perhaps ten people across, and both banks overhung with trees as far as anyone could see in both directions. Sometimes they formed majestic living arches over the water where the monkeys could easily cross without fear of being eaten by caiman, although braver ones would jump off just because they could. A few lived, others met their end in a hungry reptile's jaws. There weren't many of either animal here today.

Caiman fascinated Ixtal. They were so different to anything else, as though they came from another time and place. They seemed so have been made specifically for what they did, with their huge jaws and their thick scaley armour-like bodies. They were beautiful in their own way.

But they were still killers. Ixtal respected that.

Birds loved the river too, like the herons nesting on the sandbanks that peaked out of the vegetation and the far louder more vibrantly colored kingfishers that perched on safer branches as they watched for small enough prey in the river's crystal-clear stream. As Ixtal watched there was a sudden flurry of squealing activity and a cloud of wings. She looked closer. A serval had tried its luck for a quick meal but had mistimed it lunge and ended up hanging but its forepaws from a branch.

Ixtal smiled as it clambered back up and tried to pretend nothing had happened.

As she walked on she did her best to ignore the endless swarms of little bugs that bit at the skin of the unwary. She had learned long ago to cover her skin in the oils of a certain tree, sweet-smelling like fruit but repellent to the bugs. But before that, she had had to experience the bites. It had been another trial for her youth, alone of so any she had lost count, and it had not been one she had relished. Salves had taken the worst of the swelling and irritation away, but it had still been days before the hundreds of pinpricks healed.

Since then she had never, ever forgotten to wear her oil. It was a part of what allowed her to go places that would make other people run away.

Ixtal often wondered if those other people saw the river the same way she did. Locals often came here to fish or wash themselves or their clothes or their infants. But did they come here simply to watch? Could they see the beauty of this little micro-world of water or were they too shackled to their work in the maize fields or to their oversized families to notice.

Most days it felt like Ixtal had the kind of freedom few others could enjoy. The rainforest was her world and hers alone, except for a few of the city's braver Jaguar guards who would sometimes try to follow her. But not many, and not for long. She enjoyed the games of unwilling tag she sometimes played with them, and especially enjoyed watching the guards get angry under their ferocious masks as she outran and outmanoeuvred them

The path up ahead curved away from the riverbank through a thicket of ferns, and barely a hundred steps later Ixtal reached the familiar entry point to the village, across a patch of bare dirt near a fat yellow-leaved tree that acted as a kind of entry sign.

As she walked past it, a peal of thunder rolled in from not far away.

Ixtal looked up as it began to rain. Only a few seconds before the sky had been bright blue and the sun had flooded into the clearing where the village huts had been built. Now, thick grey cloud spread like blood in water, and heavy drops punched into the earth.

<Over here, young huntress> called a familiar voice, loud and strident from the open entrance of the nearest oval-shaped thatched hut.

Ixtal looked and saw her friend Akna, an older woman who always wore a simple dress to cover herself up, letting the younger woman bare everything. She had grey hair that hung long around a face that bore scars and wrinkles alike, but she still retained the fierce good looks she had been born with. Akna wasn't the head of the village, but she was respected nonetheless. Deep brown eyes burned with undimmed intelligence, an intelligence had taught Ixtal a lot over the time she and Akna had known each other, their relationship like aunt and niece. That was one of the reasons Ixtal always wanted to help this small village and its people where she could.

Akna rushed out into the rain as it started to pound everything and helped Ixtal with the pig carcass. They took it into the hut and lay it out on a thick wooden slab that Akna always used for carcasses. She had taken over the duty of butchery and didn't trust anyone else to do it properly or fairly. The older boys always wanted more than their fair share. Akna's way avoided the inevitable fights. Even the village leader had agreed to it, not that he had much choice with Akn'as forceful persuasion. He was old and weak now, and it wouldn't be long before his eldest son took over. If he could ever get off his fat behind, that was. To Akna's mind that boy had never hunted or fought a day in his life.

Useless, lazy and weak as far she was concerned.

Many times she had asked Ixtal to teach him something, to show him some of the skills of the rainforest. The younger woman had tried once, but the leader's son had showed so little interest in anything other than sleeping she had given it up as a lost cause. Another reason to bring food to the village.

<Drink some *xocolatl*,> said Akna. She always had the drink ready for visitors, and even though Ixtal had never really developed a taste for its bitter cocoa taste she drank it gratefully out of one of the huge collection of clay pots that stacked round the inside of the round walls. Akna joined her – she was addicted to both the *xocolatl* and making the pots as well. It was a good thing they traded well.

As the chilli heat filled their mouths with warmth, Ixtal and Akna sat together and looked back out of the hut entrance. The rain was torrential, like a curtain of water, and already parts of the ground were turning into little rivers of mud. Thunder rolled in the air, heavy and powerful.

<This rain is strange,> said Ixtal. Normally the subtle voice of the rainforest warned her of sudden storms and the dangers they brought. But not this time. This tempest had come out of nowhere and its power was becoming louder and louder. All the children had run indoors and everyone hid away or peered out of their homes in the hope it would all pass quickly.

Akna nodded. <It is. But I do not think that this is Chaac's voice.>

<How can the rains fall without Chaac?> Ixtal was confused. Surely nothing like this could happen without the God Of The Rain. His voice was the law of all storms. But Akna seemed to have other ideas and she leaned closer, her voice dropping to a conspiratorial whisper.

<I think there is a dark spirit near this village.>

<A spirit?> repeated Ixtal, and Akna nodded as she drank.

<Something lost, from a place of darkness. It is not a true spirit of nature, but it pretends to be. It hides, and it laughs at Chaac as it makes us suffer with its bad rain.>

Ixtal found her mind casting itself back in time, to that hidden dark place in the rainforest she had been led to not so long ago by some unseen prescence, and the shambling men of mud and bone that had hunted both her and the young man Pech.

Pech. Ixtal still didn't know what had happened to him. He had simply vanished.

<Do you know something?>

Ixtal realised that Akna was staring at her intently, reading every little movement of her face. The older woman was good at that. It was like her own special kind of magic, and some people said she could even see a person's thoughts and memories. This was why Akna lived along. She was valued by the village, but nobody wanted to spend too much time with her in case she peered into the privacy of their minds.

There was no point in lying, Ixtal knew. Akna would know.

<I…found something. In a part of the forest I have never seen before. It was…wrong.>

<But you know the forest. You have the knowledge of your father. You hear the voice.>

Ixtal felt awkward, as though she didn't quite know what to say. But she had to say something. Akna's eyes pierced into her, and despite her ferocious reputation as a huntress Ixtal felt as open and exposed as anybody else. Sometimes she wondered if Akna enjoyed making people feel that way. <I saw…men. Their skin was black like the earth, and they carried their own bones as weapons. They were not like any other men. And they would not die like other men.>

<Tell me,> ordered Akna.

<I cannot remember what they were called, but I found a place where they were born. It was a place where men were buried, and there was …somebody there. Something. Something whose back was bent and who called dead men out of the ground. And then….> Ixtal shivered a little. So many images were swamping her, from the blood being

leeched from Pech's body to the mirror of herself in the cave. And yet still there was that gap – that missing time between the cave and her tree home that Ixtal could not explain.

That would have to be a question for another day.

<And then…> urged Akna.

<And then I killed them, but the ground opened up. And I saw…I saw the Underworld. I saw Xibalba.> Ixtal shook the sudden fear out of herself. <But that cannot be. We cannot see the Underworld. We are living. The world of the Dead is invisible to us. Is it not?>

Akna was silent at first. Ixtal's words hung in the air as the rain continued to pound the earth outside to mud. When the older woman finally spoke, her voice has heavy with understanding.

<No. I have seen it too.>

Akna remembered what she had seen with perfect clarity. She had been a younger woman then, more willing to follow the life of a wife and mother. Men had wanted her because she had handsome and strong, and one man in particular had caught her eye. A tall man named Xomocan who wanted nothing more than to be a Jaguar Warrior. He trained constantly, and Akna enjoyed the benefits at night. They talked of children, but Xomocan's desire to become a warrior and wear the skin of a Jaguar was so much stronger than anything else, even his desire for Akna. So she had agreed to share his dream - to travel to the city where he could be noticed and perhaps chosen, and she could try to turn her talent for pottery into something to sell in the stalls to the nobility while they waited.

Besides, she had always wanted to see the city with its temples and pyramids. It was a tragedy that they had never made it.

Akna's eyes still filled with tears when she recalled what had happened to her beloved Xomocan. As she spoke, Ixtal sat with her and put a gentle hand on her shoulder.

<He did not cry out. He was brave. But when I found him, the rains fell from the sky without warning and the ground had opened up. I heard….I heard the voices of the Lord Of Xibalba. They called out for his soul and he threw himself onto their spikes. They took his blood and left only his shell behind, and his rotten bones. It spat them back out. And then….then it was gone. As though the mouth of a great Death God had opened and closed to breath in my Xomocan's soul. And I cursed it. I cursed all of it, with all my anger.>

For a moment there was only the sound of the rain. Ixtal had no idea what to say. She had always looked to Akna for her guidance and advice, and now the older woman was doing her best to control her sobbing Ixtal raised she had no idea how to return that gift. She was a huntress - those were the skills her father had taught her. Tears defeated her.

<I….> Ixtal began, and Akna put a reassuring hand on hers, knowing it was probably better for the younger woman not to say anything.

<You would have liked Xomocan very much.>

Ixtal smiled. <It is sad I never knew him.>

With one final deep shuddering breath Akna shook off the grief as best she could, pushing back into it little box in her mind, and fixed Ixtal's eyes once again with her piercing eyes. <But do you see now? Perhaps the thing afflicts us…>

<Do you think a spirit of the Underworld has followed you?>

<Or perhaps you,> Akna replied, a little ominously. <Has it found me after all this time through you, and now it punishes this village for my words then. Does everyone suffer for my curses?>

Ixtal didn't reply. She had no idea what to say. All she could do was think back to how she and her unseen guardian had rescued Pech, scrabbling inside her head for some kind of answer. There had been plenty of time for something to escape, and if Akna was being punished just for words, surely Ixtal would be torn apart for denying the Underworld a fresh soul. It was a thought that chilled her bones.

Both women looked up as a shuddering figure appeared at the entrance to the hut, a young mother named Nenetl to whom Akna taught pottery. She was soaking wet and clearly terrified.

<Please,> she cried. <Please, mother Akna, I need help. My daughter. She went down to the river with her brother but she has not come back.>

Ixtal got to her feet, all of her instincts switching on. Understanding Akna's pain had been hard, but finding people? That was just another kind of hunt. It was the kind of thing that she had been made to do.

<Which part of the river> asked Ixtal.

As Akna put her arms around the young mother to comfort her, Nenetl pointed a shaky finger in the direction back out of the village and away the path that had led in.

<By….by the tree with the blue flowers……I told her not to…….>

Nenetl's voice choked off, and Akna held her

Ixtal knew the place and its tree – it was much wilder than the areas that had been cleared away for living, and children weren't supposed to go there. It was a perfect place for a jaguar to watch, or a snake to wrap itself around a tree. With the rain, the whole place was likely a quagmire deathtrap by now. Clearly Nenetl's daughter was the adventurous type, but that kind of curiosity was more dangerous than anything for a young child.

Ixtal knew that too well. She also knew how lucky she had been that she had been rescued, all that time ago. That kind of luck rarely happened twice. But she kept silent. She had learned that these were not the kinds of thoughts to say out loud to people, so she did her best to adopt her understanding voice, the one Akna had tried to bring out of her.

<I will return her.>

Akna had already known what Ixtal was going to do, so she pointed to a piece of dark brown material on the ground neatly folded by a large pot, almost as though it had been preprepared. <You will need this to stop the rain.>

Ixtal remembered how thin the cloth she was wearing was, intended for the heat. The rain would ruin it in seconds and so she grabbed the material, slipped her quiver and bow off and wrapped it around her body. It fit comfortably like a cloak and its surface felt almost oily to the touch. It was an odd feeling on her fingers, and Ixtal wondered what strange potion Akna had applied to it.

She would ask when she got back.

The rain seemed to be getting even harder and the thunder sounded so close that it was almost inside the hut, deafening with every peal. Ixtal checked her dagger was at her hip, and she decided to leave her bow. It wasn't far to the tree with the blue flowers and her plan was to move quickly and quietly. There was no need to shoot anything today, and she didn't want to scare the child. Ixtal knew that even without her blood markings a child might be terrified at the sight of some unknown huntress and run deeper into the rainforest. Or worse, fall into the river itself.

Nenetl had disintegrated into hysterics and it was all Akna could do to stop the woman from having convulsions. Not even some fresh *xocolatl* was going to help at the moment. Soon other villagers would descend on the hut to help, drawn by the wailing that pierced the air between thunderclaps, so Akna nodded silently that everything was under control.

Ixtal nodded back, braced herself and headed outside.

She had never felt rain like this. It moved like it had a mind of its own, changing direction on a whim and spinning with impossible whirls and vortices. Each drop was almost attacking her, trying to push her the way it wanted her to go and force her back into the hut, just like all the other villagers. As she tried to walk she hauled Akna's cloak tightly around her as rainfall bounced off the oily surface and protected her from the worst of the onslaught.

Every step was a trial. Any hope of moving as quickly as Ixtal had hoped to was crushed. The mud all around was thick and sticky, and her feet sunk up to her ankles in some places. It squelched and sucked at her, trying to stop her. Anyone else would have turned back instantly and retraced the few steps back to the relative safety of the hut.

But Ixtal had promised. She would not be defeated by some raging spirit throwing a tantrum, however violent and punishing it was.

The route back to the river felt so much longer than it had been when the sky was clear. Liquid muck formed tiny streams like veins all across the ground and the sound of thunder was deafening. Somehow the heavy clouds were not moving on like storms normally did – instead they were fixed overhead, right on top of the village determined to wreak havoc with the elements.

Ixtal looked up but the sun was gone. She hoped it was still there behind all the clouds and that everything wouldn't be plunged into cold and dark. Up head she could see almost nothing as well, the curtain of rain filling the air around her up so much it was blinding. All the noise and all the water threw Ixtal's senses off, and she did her best to hear the voice of the rainforest.

It was there, but so faint. Just enough to give her a vague direction and nothing more. The monkeys that often accompanied her were quiet too, driven into their favorite hiding places. Even an offering to the Howler Monkey God wouldn't have dragged them out into this storm. No animal with any sense ventured out in this weather. Even the hungriest predator seemed to want to wait for it to pass. Jaguar, caiman and anaconda. All quiet and still.

That was all so wrong to Ixtal. Rain didn't usually bother hunters, and as everything added up in her mind, she couldn't shake off the sense that none of this was as it should be. It was more like the storm had brought with it a bad dream, a madness with an unknown method that frightened everything into submission. It was a feeling that unnerved her as she pressed onwards.

Ixtal nearly fell as the ground gave way to a bank down to the river's edge. Carefully she probed with one foot to make sure no treacherous roots were waiting to snap her ankle, and nothing sharp or angry that might cut her open. There wasn't. There was just water and mud, torrents of it, with no end sight as the rain beat down and did its best to drive Ixtal back.

Instead she persevered. She always did.

Finding the path at the edge of the bank, Ixtal shielded her eyes with her hands to try and see a little further. The sound of the river churning was just as loud as the storm now, so there was no point calling out. Besides, Ixtal didn't know the little girl's name. All she could do was trust her senses and try and pick through the power of the storm, just like she had been taught. To home in on one single thing - the sound of a cry perhaps, a lost child wanting her mother.

Ixtal swept aside a mass of broad spiny green leaves with stems taller than she was to clear the way, forcing a group of colorful beetles clinging to the underside to scuttle off, and there it was.

The tree with the blue flowers, looming large out of the storm.

The tree was a beautiful thing, its branches symmetrically curved and its flowers large and ripe. They shone in the rain as well. But as Ixtal moved towards it she smelled something – something bad that caught in her throat like smoke. She felt her senses flare and a shudder washed across her whole body. Every part of her crackled, screaming at her that something terrible had happened, and as Ixtal placed her hand on smooth bark of the tree she knew that she was too late.

The voice of the rainforest whispered through the wood and the flowers. Not in words or pictures but simple feelings – the joy of play, and then a sudden all-consuming terror. And then…nothing. The rush made Ixtal feel sick. She didn't want to know any of this. The voice was supposed to guide her and help her on her hunts, show her things, not torture her with guilt.

Anger rose up in Ixtal's gut. The rain still hammered down but she didn't feel it. Instead she looked and listened as the rainforest fell away, and knew that someone else was here with her, in this little clearing around the tree. Not an animal but a person but a racing heart and heavy breath. There was fear and excitement in equal measure, and Ixtal's hand went to her dagger as she turned to face the threat.

A shape charged out of the rain. It was one that Ixtal knew straight away, a body that desperately tried to be frightening and no doubt was to a little girl. But not to a huntress. All Ixtal saw was a flabby man, unfit and untrained, lunging forward in a desperate attack. He was slow and moved like an old man to Ixtal as her own senses lit up even more, slowing down time and locking her into his every movement.

It was the son of the village elder. Cuchum The Lazy. Cuchum The Unliked.

Cuchum The Killer Of Children.

He was bigger than Ixtal remembered and she felt more strength in him as tried to grab her but she still effortlessly slipped aside and cut him across the arm. Not deep, just a taster of what was to come. Ixtal was going to punish the elder's son. Then she would cut out his heart and feed it to a pig, because that's all it was worth.

Cuchum clutched his wound and wailed loudly. Ixtal cut him again, and then a third time. The wanted him to suffer. As she hoped he tried to lash blindly back at her and she was ready. She caught his arm and cut the tendons at the elbow as she wound the limb around her body and threw himonto the ground.

He lay there, terrified, his eyes so wide they looked like they might bulge right out of their sockets. The sight of the Huntress, the one who lived in so many village stories now standing over him with death in her eyes and a bloody knife in her hands, was like a nightmare come true. He remembered the young woman Ixtal from when he was younger. She had tried to teach him things, but that had distracted him from his obsessions. His desires. The thing that towered over him now looked like that young woman, but now it was something else. Something that had come to kill him.

As she put a knee hard into Cuchum's chest and raised her dagger, Ixtal caught sight of his fat neck. There was a pendant there, half buried in the flesh – an angular amulet made out of materials she didn't recognise, something dull and solid and grey embedded with crystalline purple. Carved into it were symbols she didn't know. They were alien, unnatural, and they seemed to move a little as she watched them.

For the briefest of seconds Ixtal was distracted, and in that tiny moment the rain came to life, swirling into a vortex all around her. It whipped around and held her fast like it was a solid thing. Cuchum scrabbled away, smothering himself in mud, desperate to save himself as his cuts bled and his arm burned with pain. Behind him the rain became like a raging monster, every drop glowing with a ferocious red light that came from nowhere. The water formed a vast mouth and vicious eyes, and then two huge limbs. It roared with thunder and lifted Ixtal into the air, holding her for a moment in the way a person might study a tiny bug.

Then it blasted her away into the river.

Ixtal hit the water so hard she thought she was going to burst. Every bit of air was pushed out of her and she gasped as she sank into the river, desperately trying not to choke. Her head rang with pain, and in her daze she couldn't make her arms and legs coordinate to swim properly. She went under, once, twice and then again, the rainproofed oiled cloak around her body tangling up with a life of its own.

For a brief moment, Ixtal panicked that she going to drown. The river seemed to have the same life as the rain, trying to pull her down and hold her. That terrible feeling that her lungs would split apart with strain grew and grew until it was overwhelming.

It felt like she could not escape.

In that second under the water she remembered her father's face, his glittering golden eyes and his dark furred skin. In her mind he held out his hand, and she reached for it.

The river churned all around with the rain and Ixtal found some strength to haul herself about the surface. She sucked air into her lungs, relishing each breath. It took a moment for her to calm down and for her heart to cease its frightened palpitations. Her body found its rhythm and she was able to hold herself properly and get a sense of where she was.

The bank where the blue flower tree had was gone, lost to the storm. Whatever demonic beast it was that had created itself out of the elements had thrown her a long way down river, and the current was far too strong to work against. It was easier to go with it and let it guide her to somewhere safer. Then she could try and rest, and ponder what had just happened.

How could Cuchum possess such power? How could he make the rains come to life? And the amulet buried in his neck - was that the source of the spirit that had frightened Akna?

The questions rolled around inside Ixtal's mind as the river swept her further and further, past banks where caimans bathed and birds roosted in overhanging trees. The screech of the howler monkeys was following her too, and she knew her troop of companions wanted to rescue her. How they planned to do that, Ixtal had no idea. The river had such power that it could not be fought against. All she could really do was wait for somewhere safe and try and guide herself towards it.

Jagged logs reached out but Ixtal knew that trying to grab them risked real injury. Once, long ago, she had seen someone impale themselves on sharp wood from a fallen tree in a river just like this one. That was not the way she wanted to die – slowly and in agony.

Further still down the river and the storm faded away to nothing. Sun streamed through the trees again and Ixtal felt a little of her strength return. As it did her senses cleared and she guided herself through the current better. There were all sorts of fish swarming in the water around her, some curious and some hungry. There were piranhas here but they rarely attacked people. Ixtal just hoped she hadn't been cut, otherwise her blood would create and irresistible trail. Another horrible way to die, and one that was the subject of far too many nighttime stories.

Finally, up ahead, a gap in the rainforest canopy shone light down onto a tiny inlet filled with thick roots that intertwined with each other. The water was still there, and the river's current was slowing enough for Ixtal to direct herself towards it. She could see it was more mud than sand, but she didn't care. She just wanted to be out of the river. Even the shadowy shapes of unknown animals lurking back in the dense forest did nothing to stop her. Instead she focussed on a loop of wood that was just close enough to catch hold of. It came up on her left side, and she reached out for it.

Still weak, her grab missed.

In the instant it took for Ixtal to realise what had happened, and as the current threatened to pull her under again, a hand reached out. Not a person's hand – instead colored blood red with jet black nails that were almost like talons. It was strong too, far stronger than anything Ixtal had felt before. It hauled her bodily out of the water and dumped her on the wet bank where she slumped for a moment, gasping in breath after breath as she tried to take in her surroundings. She was in a small grove, where the plants and flowers were greener than anywhere else. It was like they had a glow to them as the mud gave way to solid ground, and a slight sweet perfumed filled the air.

It was a relief for Ixtal to be back in control of herself again. She hated not being strong enough, but she knew that the river showed no deference or mercy to anyone. At least she was free of its grip, and she looked up to see who or what it was that had saved her.

Towering over her was a woman. All the skin on her body was as red as her hand, and her eyes and her lips were as jet black as her nails. Her hair was black too, but it shimmered in the light with faint rainbow colors as it cascaded down to her legs in a way that looked like vines or thick stems. Thick strips criss-crossed the woman's chest and a short ragged hunting skirt was wrapped around her waist, all made of something scaled and copper-colored.

The woman's face looked almost human, but not quite. Ixtal could see her ears were more pointed than they should be, and she had no hair on her brows. Instead the skin on her forehead arched downward into her face, and made her look as though she was angry all the time. The woman radiated strength, and Ixtal knew that she was looking at another kind of huntress.

She didn't know how. She just felt it.

The blood red woman seemed to feel it was well. She tossed something to Ixtal, a fruit of some kind with a thick yellow skin, and crouched down as Ixtal bit into it. It was sweet and bitter at once, and juice dripped down her chin. The insides were so slippery she didn't know whether to eat them or drink them. In the end she managed to do both, and felt it make her a little stronger.

She decided this was something she very much needed to get some supplies of.

<Thankyou,> said Ixtal.

The blood red woman just stared with those deep black eyes. It was as though she was scanning Ixtal, and she quickly locked in on a wound on her left arm, one that Ixtal herself only realised was there as it started to hurt. The red woman reached out her palm, and Ixtal flinched. The palm wasn't a threat though. Instead the gesture was more like asking permission, and there was no sense of an oncoming fight. Besides, it was clear that this woman could have crushed Ixtal any time she wanted going by how easily she had pulled her from that churning water.

This encounter was something else.

Ixtal offered her arm, and the blood red woman's hand clamped on, not hard, but enough that it made Ixtal gasp a little. The touch brought something that was felt like a sting except not unpleasant. Instead it was like a warm balm. There was a kind of pressure inside her head as well, one that made the whole grove spin a little. It all lasted only a few seconds, and then the hand hauled Ixtal to her feet.

<I speak with you now,> said the blood red woman.

Ixtal hauled the heavy oiled cloak off her to get the sun back on her body, and she stretched her arm. The blood around the wound was gone, and the gash itself had sealed up. In a day and a night, there would be hint it had ever been there at all.

<Thankyou,> said Ixtal again. She didn't really know what else she could say to this woman who stood at least a head taller than her.

<You are Huntress yes?>

Slowly, Ixtal nodded, not understanding how this woman could speak the same language and look so…different. Was she from the underworld, or some other place of spirits? There was no way to know, and she wished that Akna was here. She knew a lot more about this kind of thing.

<I am called Ixtal.>

The scarlet woman processed this for a moment, her forehead creasing even more. <This is your place?> She stopped, knowing that something was wrong. <Your tribe?>

<It is my name. Do you have a name?>

This seemed to confuse the blood red woman. <We are….Bolera. We are all Bolera.>

<I do not understand…>

<We, where I am from. We are Bolera. We are not Ixtal Huntress.>

The Bolera gestured towards an arch that was neatly carved into a kind of wall that had formed out of thick fibrous roots that stretched up overhead. The glow to the plants was stronger here, and Ixtal could feel a kind of energy all around her that made her skin buzz. The perfume was more intense as well. It drew her in, intoxicating and almost hypnotic in a way, and Ixtal walked over to the arch. It led to a den of sorts, made from criss-crossed stems and padded with leaves. On it was a second scarlet woman, a second Bolera, but this one had none of the strength of the first. She lay, almost still, her breathing shallow and painful. As Ixtal looked closer she could see that there a deep wound had been cut into the second Bolera's belly. The blood from it was dark and sticky, almost purple, and there was so much staining the leaves that Ixtal couldn't believe this woman was still alive.

Ixtal was horrified at the viciousness of the wound, and it only reenforced the sudden and inexplicable sense of kinship she felt for these women. She wanted to get angry, but the aura of the grove and its scent kept it suppressed. It felt like only peace was allowed here.

The First Bolera struggled with the words she had found in Ixtal's head. They were hard to make sense of, and so she decided it was better to show rather than try to explain.

<Look, Ixtal Huntress> she said, finally. <We know you are strong.>

On the other side of the grove there was an opening that gave way to the rainforest that Ixtal recognised. Birds chattered again, ones that the grove had muted, and her beloved howlers called in the distance, still searching. They would be reunited soon and there would be a lot of hooting and whooping, but first Ixtal had to see what had happened here. She was almost compelled to. She took a step, and even before she peered through the opening she could smell the blood of human beings and knew what she was going to find.

The horribly destroyed corpses of five men stood there, locked into their poses of death.

Every man looked as though he had been flayed - skin ripped from bones, muscles burst, flesh somehow blasted away and then frozen into bizarre new shapes that hung there as if time had stopped. To Ixtal, it was like something had some burning windstorm had melted and broken them, but surely no kind of fire could do this. Then again, she would never have thought the rain could come alive to attack her either. Ixtal's father had always told her the rainforest had so many secrets that only showed themselves when they had to. Now, it seemed, they were. There was no sense trying to understand them either – they just existed. People were not meant to be able to grasp these things.

Ixtal turned back to the First Bolera, who waited.

<They took from us. Bolera came to…..be peaceful. They wanted us.>

The First Bolera opened her hand and took a small sharp tool, one that was not stone or crystal, out of a pouch hanging at the waistband of her hunting skirt. Then she cut into her palm. Thick purple blood oozed out, moving in a way that spilled blood wasn't supposed to.

Ixtal instinctively took a step back. <What are you……>

<We share our blood. Ixtal will understand us.>

Ixtal wasn't sure about this. Yes, this powerful woman had snatched her out of the river, but now she had seen the Bolera companion who had almost cut in half, and the corpses of men that she couldn't explain. Not to mention that whole feel of this grove with its glow and its scent and its odd sense of calm. Like it wasn't really part of the rainforest at all.

In the end, like it always did with Ixtal, curiosity won out. She felt compelled to know before she judged anything. She had always been that way since she was a child, and her father had nurtured the instinct as she grew up. Every cave or clearing held new mysteries, and the two of them exploring together had always made her feel so much excitement. It was built into her as a huntress. And so she had to know.

As she nodded the First Bolero reached out towards Ixtal's breastbone and gently pressed her palm to it. The blood felt cool, and as it sank into the skin the whole grove, the whole clearing, transformed. A whole other reality was superimposed onto everything, and Ixtal could see both at once.

The dead men lived again alongside their bodies, wielding their weapons and spitting threats. Ixtal saw them for what they were now – marauders from some far village, brutal and merciless, not caring who they hurt or what they destroyed as long as they got what they wanted. The wounded Second Bolera was here, as well as lying in the grove. She crawled away from her attackers, clutching at her belly, screaming out for help with a voice that echoed over and over.

The First Bolera reappeared, in two places at once - running at the same time as she stood with Ixtal. All around the air was suddenly burning red hot. Another whirling vortex formed, just like the one that had made the rain come to life back near the village. But this one was made of the pure rage of fire, and its tendrils pierced like spears. It stripped the men of their lives – torturing them, paralysing them. They cried and begged but the ferocious power just destroyed them.

And then, lying on the ground between them all, Ixtal saw an object in middle of the vision, heavy and grey, its shape built of odd angles and curves, its surface burning with amber crystal light. It looked so alien, and yet Ixtal recognised what it was made of. It was the same material and bore the same carvings as the amulet that had been buried in Cuchum's neck.

Ixtal reached down. Her hands simply passed through the object as the illusion faded away. The First Bolera drew her own hand away, all the blood she had shared seeping back into the wound she had created. When every drop was recovered the cut sealed itself up.

<I know this.> Ixtals' voice was almost excited.

<This was taken from us. It gives us our….strength. Of the sky and the air.>

Ixtal understood. She had long known that people in nearby villages had deals with marauders, mostly out of fear than anything else. Usually the threat was for someone to be taken into slavery and sold at the city if people didn't cooperate. Sometimes people were taken anyway.

Akna's village wasn't like that. The marauders usually stayed clear. So something realise had happened. Somehow, Cuchum The Lazy had found his way into some kind of a deal. His father had influence, so perhaps he had traded that for a favor from the marauders. He wouldn't be the first person to do that. The village needed to be protected. And his son, Cuchum had always wanted to be strong so he could take over when his father died, but he never wanted to work for it.

Had they both found a shortcut in the Bolera? Ixtal was sure he had. It was the only possible explanation.

<We know you are strong,> said the First Bolera. She had said it before and this time it stuck with Ixtal.

<How do you know this.>

<We…see you. Before. When the ground opened up, Bolera came. Our…..soldier protected. But you could not see them. >

Ixtal remembered the thing that moved so fast she couldn't see it, the thing that had beheaded the Chac and stolen away Pech in front of the Xibalba Pit. It was a startling thought to realise that she had been watched the whole time. And not only watched, but defended. The whole episode replayed inside Ixtal's mind, and everything felt so different. Like she was a part of something much bigger.

<I want to know more,> she said. <I want to understand.>

The First Bolera nodded. <Help us. Then we shall all…understand.>

Ixtal felt that familiar determination rise up in her gut. That hunting instinct that defined her. It didn't matter what reasons Cuchum and his father had had, they had to be held account for what they had done. They had violated something far beyond their understanding. They had stolen some kind of power from the Bolera – a power that could shape the elements. And as Ixtal thought back to her fight with Cuchum at the blue flowered tree, she realised that he very much did not know how to control it.

<I know who has this power. He is Cuchum.> She paused. <What will happen?>

<The Cuchum will destroy….like them.> The First Bolera gestured at the corpses. <All.>

<But there was no fire. The rain came to life around him.>

<It is the same. All the same. Air and sky.>

Ixtal didn't quite grasp what she meant, but she knew what she had to do. <When shall we leave?>

<We cannot leave.> The First Bolera gestured around the grove. <We are weakened. Not strong. This….heals us. We cannot leave.> She took something else from the pouch at her waist – a small oddly angled totem that was shaped

almost like a figure and it fit right in the palm of Ixtal's hand. Like the object in the illusion and the amulet in Cuchum's neck it was dull grey and its surface was adorned with crystalline inlay, green in color this time rather than purple or burning amber.

The little symbols moved like liquid, and Ixtal stared at them, fascinated.

<What is it?> she murmured.

<It is Bolera gift to you, Ixtal huntress. When you find the Cuchum our…soldier will come.>

Ixtal knew what would happen then, but she realised that she didn't care. To her Cuchum was lower than the lowest bug in the dirtiest muck. She could only guess what he had done to the little girl he had followed to the blue flower tree. The very thought of it it made her sick. She didn't care what kind of strange power he tried to wield – for that crime alone he deserved to die. And if it avenged the attack on the Bolera as well, if she was able to return what was theirs to them, all the better.

The power of the hunt began to rise in Ixtal, the excitement filling her up.

She had no weapons so it would take time to prepare. From the amount of time she had been in the water she could estimate how far away she a was form the village. But she also knew that Cuchum would have panicked. He would be too scared for his secret to come out and his father to spit on him, so he would try to run away. And if he was carrying the Bolera's object with him he would be moving slowly, especially with his weight. It was likely he would leave at night under cover, and use the pathways that everyone used in the dark. The ones that were safer.

There was a small settlement down one of those paths. People lived there who would shelter anybody for money.

That was where Cuchum would go. And that was where Ixtal would take him to his punishment.

Empowered, her senses snapping into sharp focus, Ixtal slipped out of the grove as The First Bolera watched her go.

The river still churned at the little muddy inlet, but now Ixtal was confident again. Strength and agility flowed through her body as she darted up onto a fallen tree branch and ran along it, jumping the gap to an overhanging tree and riding the vines down to the other side. She picked up a trail quickly. The river had all kinds of paths that wound along it, and she took one that took her deeper into the forest where she could fashion a bow and some arrows.

The voice of the rainforest led her to where she wanted to go. A thicket with all the right materials to hand, so she got to work quickly. Stripping bark, tensioning vine, measuring shafts, sharpening arrowheads. The result wasn't perfect but it would do the job. Someone like Cuchum wasn't worth any more.

As she worked the howlers finally found her, chattering excitedly. She welcomed them as they clustered around her, like her own little private army - extra eyes and ears and useful hands. When the bow was finished she made her offering to the Howler Monkey God, and Mulac the biggest of the howlers sat on her shoulder as she did, puffing out his chest. She spoke the sacred words that had been ingrained into her, built the little makeshift shrine and drew the stripes of blood on her face and her arms, drawn from a dead body that her howlers had brought her. They often gave their own to her, ones who had just died from injury, but never illness. The blood had to be clean so that Ixtal could bathe in its strength.

As the sun began to set, the howlers danced in the trees. They shared in the deep and heavy sounds between the trees

that grew and grew as the voice of the rainforest called Ixtal
The Huntress to her mission.

*

Cuchum always knew he would have to run away from
the village one day, but he didn't care anymore. Now he had
his Great Power he could go anywhere, and now he had seen
the demon shape of the great Rain rise up to do his bidding
and watched it throw Ixtal away like she was nothing, he
could do anything be wanted. There would always be more
little girls to play with, and nobody would be able to stand
up to him. In his mind he turned all the terror he had
experienced at the blue flower tree and did his best to make
is strength. It was all just pretend but again Cuchum didn't
care. Despite everything else, in that moment he had felt the
power of Gods and he wasn't going to let that go. Not for
anything.

Cuchum decided he had been clever in the lies he had told
the village. He had told his weak and ageing father that Ixtal
had gone insane and attacked him, and the wounds on his
body were enough proof for him to be believed. If she ever
showed her face at the village again, she would be shunned.
Akna had disagreed, but then she always did. Cuchum's
father had dismissed her because Cuchum called her a mad
woman, and any other arguments were over.

That made Cuchum smile. He didn't like his father
particularly, but he had his uses. If he had wanted, Cuchum
could have just taken over the village as his personal
kingdom with just a few words. He had dreamed about it –
taking whatever woman he wanted, crushing anyone who
tried to fight him. Now, that just wasn't enough. Now
Cuchum's eyes had been opened. He wanted bigger, better
things. Even the City maybe. He was sure he could take on

390

the Kings themselves soon. Not yet though. First he needed to get away, to find somewhere that questions wouldn't be asked. The village would never find the little girl's body, but there would always be doubters – especially Akna – and in the end nobody would ever believed Ixtal had killed her. Cuchum hadn't even bothered trying to sell that lie.

Instead, when the moon came up and he had finally been able to stop the rain from falling, he had gathered up his idol and a few possessions and vanished into the darkness after wishing his father a pleasant sleep. He hoped he would never see the old man again.

There was a path that led into the forest a little way. Not the quickest route that went up the hill, because Cuchum was far too unfit for that. Instead he headed away from the river and towards some open land where nothing grew properly. Cuchum knew it well – he used to go there because the idea of things being dead made him feel good. He didn't worry about the hundreds of predatory eyes watching from behind the trees – his idol would protect him. Ever since it had planted a little piece from inside itself in his throat, silently and painlessly, Cuchum knew that for sure, once he had stopped wetting himself with fear.

The idol had given him its special mark, and that meant nothing could hurt him. Especially not Ixtal, and he had her dagger tucked into his loincloth to prove it, the one she had dropped when the power – HIS power – had beaten her. Maybe the knife gave him her strength as well, so now he would be the perfect hunter.

Every few steps Cuchum stopped, out of breath. He pretended that he was stopping to admire the idol instead. It was an odd-looking thing – the same object Ixtal had seen in her vision. When he had first heard of it, Cuchum had contacted people he shouldn't have, promised them things he never intended to deliver. He was glad when only one of them came back, one who had sneaked back to get the prize and who told a story of his fellow marauders being killed by something so horrible it had made him half mad with fear. That man hadn't been able to run away quickly enough when he handed over the idol. He didn't even ask for anything in return.

That was good, because there was nothing to give him. Except a stab in the back perhaps.

As Cuchum got his breath back, the idol began to glow a little, its crystals pulsing and shifting across the dull grey surface. Was this some new magic, he wondered, that was going to be revealed?

That was when he heard something whisper in the night air.

It wasn't the sound of jaguars, the ones that so often filled Cuchum's nightmares. The ones he imagined were coming for him to punish him for all the terrible things he had done that he buried deep down in his mind and pretended had never happened.

No, this was something else.

The idol glowed a little brighter, the patterns on its surface reforming into something new. It hummed as well, starting with a tone like a person's voice and then building, adding higher and lower sounds that merged together into an unsettling powerful wall of noise.

Cuchum decided it was time to leave, so he reached down in the hope he would last long enough to escape whatever was going on. But as his fingers touched the surface of the idol they arced with violent pink sparks, and he snatched his hand back. Stupidly he tried again and then again, not understanding what was going on. It didn't make sense – the idol and all of its strength was his supposed to be his now. He had taken it. Earned it. It had given him the amulet. Why did it reject him now?

What was HAPPENING?

Cuchum was suddenly very scared indeed. A hundred ways of him being killed appeared in his mind all at once, and only once idea to save his skin - head back to the village? He could easily come up with new lies, tell everyone how marauders had attacked and taken everything when he had been trying to help somebody. It didn't matter who. As long as people believed him. Maybe he could tell them the idol had made him do bad things, that it wasn't his fault about the little girl. Who cared what people said – his father would support him. The old fool always did.

Yes. That was the plan. He still has the amulet after all.

Cuchum hadn't got ten steps in a shambling run before an arrow came from out of the darkness and punched right through his leg.

<AAAAAAAAAAAAAAAAAAAAAAAAAAAAAAAAAAAAAAAA AAAA.>

He screamed as loudly as he could as he collapsed, hoping the village would hear and come to his rescue. The arrow stuck out of the front of his thigh, slick with blood, and it almost looked unreal. The pain was ferocious, like something inside him was opn fire.

<Why do you not SAVE ME,> he howled at the idol, while its light reflected off everything and its humming tone echoed between the trees. <Bring the RAIN. Make my enemies go away. KILL them all. > Tears flowed down his fat cheeks as he begged. <PLEASE. PLEASE make the rain spirit come. SAVE ME.>

The idol ignored him, and as Cuhcum looked pathetically upward form where he lay, Ixtal strode out of the trees like the specter of death. Around her, her howlers whooped in victory, scampering all around the overhead branches as though they were taunting Cuchum in his failure. And perhaps they were.

As Ixtal The Huntress approached, Cuchum realised just why people said she was so terrifying to so many people. It was like the forest itself had made her from nightmares and blood, and the look in her eyes penetrated into him like the arrow that had penetrated his body. She walked towards him, every step deliberate and purposeful.

<The girl. It wasn't my fault. The idol. It made me do it. It is evil. I tried to stop it from attacking you.> He realised his words meant nothing now and finally he just whimpered. <Are you going to….kill me>

Ixtal towered over him, and when she finally spoke Cuchum's blood froze.

<No.>

<What…..?>

Cuchum tried to understand as Ixtal lowered her bow, but his panic-addled brain couldn't make sense of anything. He watched as she took something from her waist and tossed it to him. He caught it awkwardly in both hands, feeling a little electrical charge run through his skin as he did. It was the figure the First Bolera had given her, and it glowed in time with the idol, pulsing with a heartbeat of light and resonating with the sound.

Was this a trick? wondered Cuchum. Had Ixtal come to save him after all?

Whatever he had expected Ixtal to do, this was not it. The pain in his leg subsided a little and he became fascinated with the new object with its strange figurine shape. He decided he liked it better than the idol. It was much easier to carry for one thing. And no doubt it had its own magic that he could control.

<Why do you not kill me?>

Ixtal moved away from him a little, out of the light a little, then turned back, her face just as merciless as before.

<Something else is coming for you. >

Cuchum's heart stopped dead.

<No,> he wailed. <No no no,> He threw the little figurine away and tried to crawl, but Ixtal just watched, without pity. <No no no no no no.>

<You cannot run,> said Ixtal. <And your stolen idol will not hide you anymore, killer of the young.>

<I did not mean it. It was her fault. She…..It…..>

Something flashed across Cuchum's line of sight and silenced him. It was like blur, an outline of something moving so quickly it was impossible to follow. Not an animal, not a man, but something else entirely.

<WHAT IS IT? WHAT HAVE YOU SUMMONED?>

Ixtal did not answer. All there was the synchronized humming of the idol and the figurine, and the light they threw out. If Cuchum had had some wits about him he might have recognized them for what they were. Ixtal doubted it. But she knew.

They were a beacon, calling out for something.

Crying more tears than he ever had, Cuchum hauled himself up to a kneel, opening his arms out as he blubbered like a child.

<I beg you. Take her and not me. She has killed so many people. She killed the little girl. I tried to protect her, but she attacked me. Looked at my wounds. She is a demon. A monster. TAKE HER….>

The blur came again, and it flashed so fast across in front of Cuchum that it took a second for Ixtal to realise what had happened. Then she saw that the amulet had been torn out of Cuchum's throat, along with most of the skin that had surrounded it. Blood spurted forwards as a disbelieving Cuchum put his hands to his neck, not knowing what else to do. His voice was gone, and his blood felt warm on his hands. Absurdly it was comforting, like dark mother's milk in the gentle embrace of death.

When the blur returned for one final time, it sliced Cuchum's head clean off his shoulders and let it roll away along with ground, eyes bulging widely in its last seconds of sight.

Ixtal felt nothing for the headless Cuchum. She just watched the body and the head bleed into the ground. In a few moments they would be fodder for animals, and then there would be nothing left at all except for a few bones. In time even his memory would fade away to nothing.

Cuchum, dead son of the Village Elder. Cuchum The Lazy, The Fat. The Uncaring. Cuchum The Killer of Little Girls. Cuchum The Coward. Now he was nothing more than meat for the animals of the rainforest, and his soul would plunge down into the endless roads of blood and pus that filled the Underworld. Maybe the scorpions would consume him as he screamed forever.

At least they had a use for him. Nobody else ever had.

Ixtal moved over to the body and reached down, taking back her dagger. She would like to have punished him for the sheer insult of carrying it, for offending her father's memory. But it had tasted his blood at least. That was enough.

As she tucked her knife away and slid her newly made bow over her shoulders, the light of the idol caught her gaze, and she saw something outlined there against the blackness of the rainforest.

A figure, built like a man but not a man. It was taller, thinner, its fingers long and sharp and its head wrapped in a kind of black cloth that hid everything – everything bar its mouth. That mouth seemed to smile at her, and it was filled with jagged pointed teeth that caught the glow as it picked up the idol and the figure. As the sounds and the light began to disappear, Ixtal saw that this apparition's skin was the same blood red as the Bolera, and the vicious claws on its hands and feet were the same jet black like obsidian.

It seemed to acknowledge Ixtal, and she swore she heard it say something. Not in any way she could understand, but more like the voice of the rainforest. The sound was a kind of rasping in her head, sounds that had no meaning and at the same time she knew that they did.

Maybe one day she would understand what it meant.

Then it was all gone. The apparition vanished in an instant, the light and the sound disappeared, and all that was left was Ixtal, her eyes seeing only Cuchum's corpse in the moonlight. There was just the beautiful chorus of the forest, all the insects and the frogs, the sounds of the air that only she could hear sometimes, and the gradually quieter calls of the howlers as they settled down to sleep, the excitement over for now.

A jaguar was prowling nearby. Ixtal could feel it. It was far enough away to be safe but it had obviously caught the scent of blood. It would no doubt take Cuchum's body as it was still warm enough and fresh enough to count as a kill. It would save the jaguar a lot of effort as well. Maybe it was a mother who wanted to feed her baby jaguars. Ixtal liked that idea. It was nice to remember life came from death. Her father had always taught her that.

The rainforest wasted nothing, and everything was a circle with no beginning and no end.

Ixtal felt tired. Her body was aching and she needed sleep to recharge herself. It had been a long day, and it was too far to go to get to her own home. She didn't want to return to the village, and so she dropped her bow and arrows, slipped effortlessly up one of the trees and made a bed of fat leaves with the howlers.

*

That night, Ixtal had a dream.

She saw herself back in the cave where she had seen that different version of herself. It started out like a memory and then turned into something else, warping and changing with bizarre little pieces of her imagination. The cave flowed into peculiar shapes and huge figures wandered. Things didn't match – everything seemed larger inside than out, and her body felt like it could float in the air and pass through rock.

But there was something else.

She saw herself sip the water from the bowl, and where she expected to be instantly back at her tree home like before, instead she saw…something. There was a sinking feeling, as though she had fallen through something and remembered in her dream what had been empty space when she was awake.

There were sounds and smells she couldn't believe. Dirty acrid stinks like smoke but a hundred times worse, and the howl of terrible things, screaming and screeching endlessly. Buried deep in a kind of thick bitter choking fog there were shapes that lurked just out of sight.

It was a horrible place, and Ixtal was relieved when she woke up.

The forest was still dark, but the first hints of sunrise were just about to peak over the tops of the trees. It wouldn't be long before the night gave way to day so Ixtal waited, laying on her comfortable leaves as Mulac snored on her belly. He often did that. Maybe her heartbeat comforted him, or maybe he was just being territorial. But he certainly liked being Ixtal's favorite, and anyone who tried to take his place usually got beaten down.

But not too much. Mulac didn't want to break up the harmony of the troop.

Ixtal gently stroked the top of Mulac's head and thought about her dream. The details were fading now like dreams always did, but enough remained that she knew she had seen something during the hole in her memory. Some…place? She didn't really understand it, but then again so many things were new to her now. She had seen things far beyond what her father had taught her about, and she began to wonder of she was charting unknown territories that even he hadn't visited.

Like always she wished more than anything she could share it all with him – her adventure of blood skinned woman and spirits of the rain and strange idols that called for…..what had the Bolera called it? Their soldier?

Ixtal was glad it had been on her side. She wondered if it was still watching. And had it really watched her before, when the Xibalba Pit had opened up and tried to steal Pech away?

Always questions.

Like her father said, those were always far more common than answers.

The first hints of warmth hit her skin and howlers started to stir as early birds started to sing, waking each other up in their funny early morning daze. Mulac shifted too, and Ixtal moved him off her while he kept on snoring. He was always the last up. Mulac The Sleepy.

Ixtal dropped back out of the tree, landing neatly on the ground. She picked up her bow and arrows from where she had left them and looked up into the sky where the sun finally rose.

A new day in the rainforest.

EL ORO DE IXTAL

Far away from the settlements that surrounded the city of Oxhuitza as it sat nestled in the mountain foothills, the vastness of the rainforest held a million secrets. Buried deep, unseen by all but the bravest, there were dark places where the sun couldn't penetrate the heavy canopy of trees overhead. The shadows beneath formed a kind of other world, a world of strange plants that grew inside the bodies of the dead, and of ferocious clawed animals that burrowed in the ground without eyes.

This was the home of the Chac-Uayab-Xoc.

Those few that had heard of them and lived – people like jaguar soldiers hunting escaped prisoners who tried desperately to find hiding places – called them The Men of Mud and Bones. Their flesh was thick and dark like the earth, and bones were their brutal weapons. The stories said they couldn't be killed, that they had the strength of five men, and that they wielded the forces of the Underworld to steal the souls of their victims.

Ixtal had seen them with her own eyes, and she knew that the stories were true

In the Chac-Uayab-Xoc's shadowy world there were pits, huge craters in the ground where flesh and blood were offered to Xibalba and its Lords of Terror. Ixtal had seen one of them too. It had tried to claim her and her young companion Pech, as its guardian – a hideous hunchback thing that could only have been a dead person corrupted by dark spirits – tried to kill her. The dark magics Ixtal had seen at work that day still made no sense. All she knew is that she had taken a look into the realm below the Earth, the realm of the Dead itself, and somehow she had survived.

Anyone else would be too scared to look again. Ixtal was different.

It had taken time and effort, violence, gifts and sex, to finally get the information she needed. The entrance to another hidden pathway that other people couldn't find, the same as before. Only this time there was no invisible guide to help her. Ixtal didn't know why. She had hoped her guardian, her soldier of the Bolera that she had glimpsed as it had taken Cuchum The Child Killer's life, would be here. But he wasn't. Ixtal didn't know why, but she couldn't wait. This new pit had to be destroyed.

Like before, her troop of howlers refused to follow her into the gloom. Whatever it was in the air that they sensed they wanted no part of it, even the bravest. So Ixtal had made her offerings and painted her skin in blood to give her the strength she needed. Her senses took everything in even as the voice of the rainforest left her, and she clutched her dagger for security.

The path she had found was damp underfoot, and as she walked it the trees and the flowers became more and more alien. Huge growths punched out of massive trunks distorted into monstrous shapes, and clumps of giant black blooms pumped out their bitter, choking perfume. Green became the blues and purples of bruises and the reds of wounds. The familiar sounds of birdcalls, monkey whoops and insect trills all faded away, and all that was left were curious whispers and the growls of things nobody would ever recognise.

Ixtal tried not to think about those things as the humid air closed in on her, hotter with each step.

She could almost feel the pit up ahead. She recognised how it made her skin tingle, and she notched an arrow to her bow as she took step by careful step towards a clearing made of sharp ragged tree stumps. When she finally reached it and peered through the barrier of carved wood, she expected to see what she had seen before. A ceremony of blood sacrifice as the Men of Mud and Bone lumbered about at the command of their hunchbacked master, waiting for the pit to give up its gifts.

Instead, Ixtal stared in disbelief.

The pit was gone, nothing but a shallow pool of useless black sludge, and all of the Chac-Uayab-Xoc were dead.

Ixtal counted easily fifteen bodies and she was certain there were more hidden away amongst the ruins of the trees or buried under the ground where what had once been a blood pit had reclaimed them. Slowly she began to circle the clearing, scanning the first corpse to see if she could see any kind of clue. But there was nothing. No signs of a death worm infestation, no wounds, no disease or poison. Like all the others, he had simply stopped living - eyes open, mouth drooping.

The hunchback was there too, its twisted body looking like a skeleton in rags. Ixtal casually put an arrow through its skull just to be sure, but she didn't need to. It was as though the life had simply been taken from all these bodies in an instant, leaving just husks and useless bones behind.

Insects were started to swarm, flies arriving to lay their eggs and strange beetles looking for food. That was always the way of the rainforest. Ixtal had been taught that since she was a baby – that the forest wasted nothing. Whenever something died, it would be consumed, and the spirit of the forest would go stronger from the essence. She had watched it happen, seen fungus grow over dead plants and maggots sprout out from slaughtered animals. It had fascinated her. Ixtal's father had explained it to her like a circle, that all things began, and then ended, and then began again but different.

<But how can people come back from the Underworld?>
Ixtal had asked, a wide eyed eight year old. *<Do the
scorpion demons not eat them.>*

Her father had just smiled in that enigmatic way he
always had and left his daughter to think about it for herself.
It was always infuriating, even now. But Ixtal had to admit
that the sense of curiosity her father had built in her had
served her well. It had led her to so many things – not least
her connection to the rainforest itself, and its voice that she
still couldn't hear in this dead place.

She checked a few more of the bodies, but there was
nothing new to see in any of them. She almost left it behind
until she caught sight of something else – a kind of rough
wooden structure that had been formed out of roots and
branches of blackened twisted wood just near another exit to
the clearing. The earth had been churned up all round, like it
had just been grown, but Ixtal didn't care about that. Instead,
she caught her breath at what he saw next.

A woman hung suspended by vines in the structure.

Ixtal ran over, snatching her knife from her waistband.
Closer up she could see the woman had been stripped except
for an ornate gold collar around her neck and bands around
her forearms that looked so tightly bonded to her skin they
would never come off. Her skin was covered in red cuts and
lesions, and as Ixtal cut into the vines she remembered the
vampiric powers of the Chac-Uayab-Xoc pit and how it had
sucked the blood from Pech before he had disappeared.

The vines spewed fluid that burned a little but Ixtal
ignored it. She cut and cut until she could free the woman,
catching her half-lifeless body as she collapsed forward and
carrying her away for the darkness of the Chac-Uayab-Xoc
clearing as fast as she could.

It felt like forever before Ixtal heard the voice of the
rainforest again. It led her to a small shady spot next to a pool

of fresh cool water and orange-leaved plants that healed and took away pain. She lay the woman down and began to try and clean up the wounds as she had been taught. There were so many of them, and the woman's skin was so pale that it would be a miracle if there was any blood left in her at all.

How long had she been hung up in that trap at the mercy of the pit?

Ixtal daubed water on the woman's face, hoping that the leaves natural painkillers would ease the torture she had suffered, and suddenly her eyes snapped open.

Blue and gold and glittering like precious stones, they were utterly inhuman.

Ixtal was frozen, transfixed by the unnatural colors until she realised that the woman's eyes weren't up looking at her at all. They weren't looking at anything anymore.

<Can you hear me?> asked Ixtal, even though she knew she was wasting her time. All the medicines in the forest wouldn't have made any difference to these wounds. It was as though they refused to heal, cursed somehow to remain until there was no more pain and in jury to inflict, no more life to take.

Whoever the woman had been, she was dead now.

Ixtal sat back on the ground and just looked at the body for a while. She had seen the dead many times before but there was something different about this woman. It wasn't just her eyes. Ixtal started to take in details, and she could pick out things that weren't right, that didn't fit a human body. Parts of the skin that weren't ruined by wounds looked almost too smooth, and when Ixtal pressed her fingers into one patch it felt nothing like skin at all dead or alive. It felt more like the thick velvet feel of a flower petal but without any hint of sweat or moisture. And when Ixtal looked at the woman's hair she could see it wasn't hair at all, more like thick vines that coiled around and back over itself. But it had been hair, just a few minutes ago.

Ixtal could have sworn to it.

She watched more and realised that the body was starting to change. It was beginning to glow a dull amber light that pushed its way out of a hundred little tiny holes in the unnatural skin, and in turn that same skin began to dissolve and flake away. Cracks began to form and the glow began to well out of first the woman's mouth and then through her eyes, consuming them with light.

There was a sudden ringing sound in the air that got louder and louder, and underneath it a crackling of static energy as the woman's body continued to transform. Filaments of energy sparked off into the air as finally the last pieces of what had been a human form burned away to reveal…

..what?

Ixtal had no idea what she was looking at. A skeleton but not a skeleton, encased in light and only there for a brief second before it was gone as well. In that second, Ixtal though she saw not bone but wood.

But that was impossible.

The ringing sound faded away into an echo that bled away into the background sounds of the rainforest, and the body was gone. The only evidence that the woman had ever existed at all was the gold collar and wrist bands that were left behind, immune to whatever process had consumed their owner.

Ixtal started at the metal, and then moved a little closer. All three pieces were perfectly matched, and so beautifully worked and carved she wondered where they had come from. Nowhere she knew of, certainly. Even the best craftsmen followed the trends, and the patterns on the collar alone were nothing like anything any Mayan city would produce.

Gently, Ixtal picked up the collar, feeling its weight. It was certainly solid gold, and as she turned it over in her hands its mysteries began to spark ideas in her mind. She had to know more.

The sun was starting to set as Ixtal sat cross-legged in her hut tucked up in the trees. The walk back had been consumed by thoughts of the dead woman and what she might have been in this or any other life. Even as Ixtal climbed the knotted vines up to her bed and her possessions, the vision of the body dissolving away into light and then nothing at all haunted her.

She knew this woman had come from somewhere else, somewhere maybe even Ixtal's father had never heard of. But where? What unseen world had the woman with the gemstone eyes come from, only to be captured and tortured by the Chac-Uayab-Xoc. Ixtal's father had loved to talk to her about all the things he had seen on his travels as he taught her about the hidden world of the rainforest Maybe this was something new. Something truly unknown.

Ixtal was starting to believe he had only scratched the surface of what was out there, and now she was started to dig a little deeper. Her plan had been simple - to hunt down as many of the Chac-Uayab-Xoc as she could and punish them for the things they had done to all those innocent people – to Pech especially. She hoped he was safe, despite the fact she had never been able to find a single clue as to where he had gone or who had taken him.

Sometimes she dreamed of him, smiling and happy in his oddly young way.

But not tonight. She wouldn't be able to sleep. Instead she stared at heavy gold that bore indecipherable symbols and wondered just how it was that one thing led to another, like an endless processions of things that defied any attempt to understand them. Was some cryptic god, or worse a bored Lord of the Underworld, somehow guiding her to something – putting mysteries in her way and stubbornly refusing to explain anything at all.

Ixtal was getting frustrated as the day came to its end. Her father had taught her to read different signs and symbols to understand language and how it worked. But this was meaningless to her. For all she knew it could simply be random carvings that meant nothing to anybody. Her instincts, the ones honed by her father, denied that.

She heard his voice, clear as day.

<People had closed heads, daughter. We must make sure ours are open. Not all the answer are in plain sight.>

It didn't help, and Ixtal looked up as Mulac, the largest of the howlers, clambered downed form the roof of her tree hut and made himself at home. He did that often, and Ixtal didn't mind. Most of the rest of the tribe were asleep up in the trees but Mulac seemed to share Ixtal's curiosity, and he picked up one of the gold cuffs, sniffing it.

<That is not food,> said Ixtal, smiling a little despite her annoyance.

Mulac frowned and started to turn the cuff over and over. He bit it once or twice, and then decided that Ixtal was wasting her time with this nonsense. Casually he tossed the cuff out of the hut entrance, and Ixtal lunged forward in a vain attempt to try and catch it. Mulac barked and hopped out of the way, startled.

<Why did you DO that?>

Mulac made a sound he often made that Ixtal assumed was him laughing, and she shook her head, frustrated by the mischief-making as she peered out into the encroaching night-time to try and find her treasure down in the gloom.

The shadows of the trees were deepening by the second, bringing with them another warm and humid night. Only the strongest of the rays fading sun could penetrate the overhead canopy. They were fading too as Ixtal strained to try and see the golden cuff down on the forest floor.

It was there, but not how she expected.

She had hoped for some brief glimmer of sunlight on the gold, just enough so she could slip down the vines and retrieve it before the jaguars started to begin their nocturnal hunts. They would never try and scale the trees where Ixtals' hut was built – they were too smart for that. But they would certainly stalk the areas around it, and as strong as Ixtal was with all her training she was still only human, and certainly no match for a hungry predator without her weapons.

It had never come to that kind of confrontation and Ixtal hoped it never would. Sometimes she wondered if there was some kind of unspoken truce in place. Even Mulac and the howlers felt safe. Perhaps the voice of the rainforest had brokered something only the animals could hear.

It whispered to her now, not in words but in ideas. From its telepathic flicker in her mind Ixtal could feel the sense of the cuff, that it was something special, and when she saw finally saw it she understood why. There was no golden glint, but instead a flow of amber light, just like the light that had consumed its owner. But it wasn't overwhelming this time. Not a flood, but focussed. It seemed to be drawing lines in the air like a spider weaving some kind of luminous web, and Ixtal was fascinated as she watched it take shape. She even forgot to light the special fire brazier she kept in her hut.

A minute passed, then another, and finally Ixtal slid down the vines to investigate. Mulac watched her go from the roof of the hut, still curious but not enough to follow.

Hanging in the air was a maze of gossamer energy. It pulsed a little, and tiny orbs moved along the lines and shapes like droplets of burning water. Up close Ixtal couldn't make sense of it so she took a few steps back, and when she did everything became suddenly clear. She was looking at a picture.

Woven from all those little threads of light, it was the image of a place. She could see the familiar rainforest, but in the centre of it all was somewhere she didn't recognise at all. It looked like huge vertical ripples of stone half a mile high, as though the side of a cliff had been fractured or melted into a new form. As Ixtal looked closer her senses could pick out more and more detail where others would have seen nothing. And she committed everything to her memory. She could see caves with gigantic entrances and carvings into the rock that looked something like animals, but no animal she recognised.

Were they gods? Spirits? Ixtal didn't know. She had seen so many statues on her travels depicting so many things, but nothing like these. Her father had always said that the Mayans lay at the crossroads of other civilisations, but she had never really believed him. Not before the Bolera anyway. She couldn't deny they were from somewhere else she didn't really understand. But that was surely beyond the rainforest. If a place like this image existed in Ixtal's domain she would know about it. There would be some story, some whisper.

Wouldn't there?

Ixtal stepped forward again and picked the bracelet up from the ground. The image vanished, letting the cloak of night drop onto everything even as a few sparks of amber still flickered over the surface of the gold. It tingled in her hand, and Ixtal clipped it to her wrist as she hauled herself back up to her hut. A hundred different thoughts filled her thoughts as she lay down, knowing she wouldn't sleep as one single-minded idea dominated everything else.

She had to find this place she had seen.

*

Sometimes the rainforest seemed endless and Ixtal had walked for nearly a whole day. It was a wet day, and the air was so thick it drained her. She stopped too often to eat and drink at places, but only at places that were familiar and safe, careful to avoid danger spots and then heading only for the little settlements she knew. Three of them had given her nothing, but the fourth, little more than a single hut made of branches and leaves occupied by an old man and his little family who lived so deep in the forest they were almost a part of it, gave her hope she was on the right track.

<Do you know this place?> Ixtal asked. She had made a scratched drawing of the cuff's vision on a piece of hide with her knife, and she was pleased with how accurate it looked. Things like that satisfied her, and she wondered if different parents raised her she would have been an artisan of some kind. But they hadn't, so those thoughts flashed across her mind and disappeared in brief seconds.

The old man peered at the sketch, then at Ixtal, and then back again. He had cloudy eyes that made her wonder if he could even see, and the chattering of one of two of his younger children was distracting to him.

<Perhaps....> the old man's voice creaked.

This sort of thing annoyed Ixtal. She much preferred people to be clear and direct and answer questions with simple yes's or no's. All this uncertainty wasted time. She wanted to be at her next camp before the sun went down.

<Can you be more certain,> said Ixtal, a harsh edge in her voice.

411

One of the children, not much older than Ixtal herself, presented herself a little too aggressively for Ixtal's liking. <Our father's wisdom takes time. You should do well to remember this.>

Ixtal felt like punching this woman but then, she knew, there would be no kind of information forthcoming at all. Her father had taught her about the value of diplomacy over fighting but if Ixtal was honest she had mostly ignored those lessons in favor of learning to use her bow, the same one which hung cross her back now to accompany her dagger and her sling and her dyed skins that covered her chest and reached down to her knees, split up both sides to her waist.

The woman seemed to notice all this for the first time and subsided as her father waved her to silence. His eyes blazed with a sudden spark of life and even his voice sounded stronger when he spoke again. <It is the cave where Kukulkan spawned a hundred children.>

Ixtal did not like the sound of that at all. Kukulkan always meant snakes. Ixtal didn't like snakes. <Is it near here.>

<It is near and far. Kukulkan rested at the caves, and as his children were born the rocks themselves became like water and waves before they became rock again.>

Near and far? Was this old man toying with her or simply feeble in the head with age?

Ixtal realised there was little more to be had here, and she hoped that one more questioned wouldn't send the old man into delirium and his family into a protective frenzy. The last thing she needed was a fight.

<In which direction must I walk?>

The old man pointed a shaky finger to the North of the sun. <There. A day and a half travel across the bad ground. You should rest here before the journey.>

The old man seemed to have no name, but as others of his daughters brought out stone jugs filled with some unidentifiable liquid he became more and more friendly. Ixtal sat with him, sipping a little and trying to pretend it didn't burn her mouth and throat.

<What is this?>

The old man chuckled into his beard. <It is my favorite thing in the world. My own special drink that is made from fruit that is left to rot, and then it becomes potent.>

Potent was the word. Even a few small mouthfuls made Ixtal feel woozy, so she made sure she didn't have any more. If this was some kind of elaborate trap to drug her, she wanted to have her reflexed working. But the more time she spent with the old man she more and more had the feeling he was simply harmless and was glad of some company.

Perhaps that was because his family endless fluttered around him. Having that every day would make anyone happy to see a new face.

The sun overhead was heading downward and it made sense to rest here. Ixtal had spotted a good tree nearby where she could make a bed for the night. The old man himself seemed not to have a bed at all. The hut was filled with his family and he clearly preferred the open air. Decades of sunlight had caked his skin almost to leather and his hair was silver, thin but still long down his back. He wore nothing, and Ixtal guessed that somebody like this simply wouldn't care where they slept.

<Have you always been here?> she asked.

The old man swigged some more of his drink. <The city disgusts me. > He cackled. <This is my world. I was born here, and the underworld will open for me here when it is my time.>

Ixtal believed him. <How do you know of the cave?>

<Ahaah. I know many things. Many secrets. Do you know as many secrets as me?>

<My father taught me of the rainforest.>

<Indeed. And did he come to tell you of the cave?>

<He walks in the afterlife now. I found something...> Ixtal shoved out her arm where she still kept the gold cuff in her wrist. The other two pieces hung for her belt, and the old man peered at them closely. <They showed me this place.>

<Yes, I see I see.> The old man cackled again. <Tell me huntress, did this prize come from a woman with eyes like jewels?>

Ixtal caught her breath. How could this man possibly know that? <She..how....>

<Secrets. Yes. Secrets. Hahahahaha. The cave is where you just go. You have been shown the path. Hahahahhahaa.> The old man took one final huge gulp of his drink and then pitched backward into the undergrowth, barely conscious as the contents of the jug spilled over his face. Two of his family were there instantly, and they set about trying to make him comfortable. From their speed and efficiency Ixtal guessed this was something that happened a great deal.

They ignored Ixtal, so she headed for her tree and the beginnings of making her bed.

The old man and his family were gone when Ixtal awoke. She took soe water for her leather bottle and slipped down to the ground, yawning and clearing her eyes to try and peer through the early morning mists. The sound of the birds was already loud and she guessed today was going to be hotter than the previous one. As she looked around the abandoned hut she was already planning her route, remembering waypoint to rest at, places to drink and get shelter.

A day and a half the old man had said. And what had he meant by bad ground?

The hut itself was empty. Every little hint that people had lived there was gone, and Ixtal pondered if anybody had ever been there in the first place. There were many ghosts of the rainforest, some friendly, some deluded, and utterly malignant.

Ixtal ran her hand over the gold cuff on her wrist. Sometimes she could feel a little vibration through it, but not this morning. Today it was just metal, heavy on her arm.

There was no sense delaying any further, so Ixtal orientated herself to the direction that the old man had pointed and headed out. There was a path of sorts to follow, a faint track worn into the rainforest ground where thickets and bushes looked to have been slashed away. As she walked she ate some of the preserved meat she kept in a pouch at her hip. It didn't help the curious dryness in her throat but at least it would give her strength, and she didn't want to waste more water until she could find somewhere safe to refill. This place was unknown territory, and she listened closely the whispered pictures of the voice of the rainforest in her head as she opened up her senses to everything.

She saw amazing flowers in rainbow colors, and heard every bird as they sang and swooped and nested. There were pigs and monkeys everywhere, and baby caiman swam in water close by. She smelled a hundred different scents both subtle and powerful, and tasted the humidity on the air as it rose with the growing heat. Once ore the sheer beauty of the rainforest made her marvel at this new place and she felt at home as she tracked her way down to a small winding river perhaps the height of a person across. The baby caiman were there, pretending to be adults, and Ixtal washed herself as they swam nearby, not quite bold enough to bite.

<Is this the right direction to the cave of Kukulkan?> she asked them

The sun dried Ixtal's skin quickly and soon she was moving again, following the river as it ran parallel to the path and headed exactly the way she wanted. The canopy overhead wasn't as thick as other places, and that told her that it might thin out soon. There were plants here that bathed in the sun, their flowers growing big and strong without the trees to smother them. A lizard with golden skin scuttled across one of the petals and caught Ixtal's eye, and a blue feathered bird with long thin legs waded in the water, poking at the surface for little bugs to eat.

Ixtal had ever seen neither of the before, so she added them to her memory so she would be able to dream about them alongside all the other animals she knew.

Finally the forest thinned out so much that Ixtal could see into the distance, and she felt the full strength of the sun on her skin. Even with the paste from a plant from near her home to protect her she felt herself burn a little as she came to a halt where the forest itself came to a kind of dead stop, forming a rocky border beyond which was a place that looked like it wasn't meant for people to even exist. The ground was harsh and ashen, and spike-like vicious looking plants grew from everywhere across blackened earth that split into yawning deep, dark cracks that silently spilled grey smoke into thick air.

With that sight, Ixtal realised exactly what the old man had meant by bad ground.

Doubt flashed across Ixtal's mind. She began to wonder what kind of a place the golden map of light had led her too, and what would happen now she was here. Her father had often cautioned her against being too impulsive. He had always been a man who had plan upon plan for ever eventuality, and it was like nothing ever surprised him.

But Ixtal's nature got the better of her too often. For her, everything was about the moment. There was no real past and nor real future. Just the rainforest and all its dangers , both known and unknown, that could snuff out a life in an instant. The things she had seen over the past weeks and months just reenforced that for her. She simply couldn't make plans when there was something impossible behind every tree and in every shadow.

She regretted at a little as she took in the vista of the bad ground.

Perhaps it had been the same rich green forest as everywhere else once, and something cataclysmic had transformed it forever. Or perhaps it had always been this way – a place of death in amongst all the teaming life. Whichever it was it looked like nowhere else she had ever seen. As she looked, it was if something out in this wasteland was looking back her – something unseen yet something so real it made her skin crawl.

Again, Ixtal wondered if this journey had been worth it. Following a trail from a dead woman with alien eyes and her gold could be called a kind of madness by others. She had been called a lot worse. But perhaps there was a kind of insanity to this as she looked up to the sky. It was smothered by unnatural dirty purples that made the sun look red like blood., screaming at her like a warning to turn back and leave. The voice of the rainforest, faint and almost gone, said the same thing.

But Ixtal felt compelled by some other instinct, maybe one that wasn't even her own, so she put first one bare foot and then another forward and walked out onto the bad ground.

It crunched under her, like a billion bones ground down into dust. The heat here was different, oily and dirty as she felt her eyes, her nose and her mouth all start to sting. It clung to her body as the huge spike plants moved a little. She drew closer to one and she could see it was turning as though it was trying to look at her through a little bulb on its very tip, one ridden with veins that pulsed arranged around core that was round just like a human eye. But it wasn't a human eye, and Ixtal had no idea how it could sense her. Other spikes followed, moving with her, always focussed on her. Some were five times the height of a man, other barely the size of a child.

She kept her distance from them all, keeping her footsteps as she skirted one chasm in the ground after another, avoiding the smoke columns that made her breath difficult. She guessed breathing any of it in would make that so much worse, and so she wrapped her hand across her face as she pushed forwards, keeping the discolored sun as her guide. She only had the old man's word that this was the way to go, but the path she was finding took her away from the worst of the bad ground. There had to be some meaning in that.

The gold cuff felt suddenly hot on Ixtal's wrist and she slid it off. The unexpectedness of it distracted her and as she checked for a burn it took her a moment to realise what had happened. The gold was warning her.

There was something up ahead, looming out of a smoke column.

At first Ixtal couldn't see clearly. There was an outline of something, but it wasn't solid. It was more like the steam that vented out of the crack in the earth was forming a shape inside itself, as though it was giving birth. At the seconds ticked past things began to become more clear – there were misshapen limbs and the sense of a large distorted head, and to Ixtal it looked like it could almost be the shape of a baby, a newborn growing out of the earth and the gas.

It struggled inside the column of smoke, its features constantly shifting from one thing to another, and Ixtal tried to find a way to get away from it before it finally decided on its final self. There was no cover anywhere, just the flat burned earth. The spike plants and their eye bulbs kept staring, and Ixtal realised that all she could do was run.

The bad ground gave nowhere to hide.

She looked back to retrace her steps back into the safety of the rainforest and stopped dead. The trees were gone, and the bad ground stretched everywhere in every direction now. Ixtal tried to understand but couldn't. Nothing made sense to her, and all the rules he had learned about how the world worked suddenly seemed meaningless.

This whole place, this bad ground, has its own rules, its own laws.

The Smoke Baby finally began to move, its heavy arms and legs ending in points and its head dominated by a single eye that began to peer around itself. Two sets of split curved horns grew where ears should be, and when it finally opened its mouth to cry out its first sound all Ixtal could see was a huge slit around its head filled with jagged masses that could be teeth or something else.

There was just no way to now, and Ixtal began to distrust her own senses. The very thing she relied on every day to survive felt like they had started lying to her. Even the voice of the rainforest was garbled, unable to penetrate through the bad ground.

Without the forest, Ixtal began to feel utterly lost. She had nothing familiar to latch onto.

The air stung her throat as she started to run, trying to follow the direction of the red-colored sun overhead and hoping that it wouldn't just disappear like the forest had. Her eyes watered and she fought down the constant urge to stop. The sky stayed its filthy purple color and all around the empty space felt like it was fighting her every move like endless unseen fingers - the bad ground almost had her, and she knew it would do anything to keep her from getting away.

Ixtal cursed the old man who had sent her here. Had he tricked her? She wasn't sure, and she still couldn't shake off the sense that something compelled her onwards and that there was some reason she was here. Maybe the gold itself was in her head. Or the woman who had worn it.

Maybe maybe maybe. So many uncertainties, and only one thing for sure.

She had to escape.

Behind Ixtal, the Smoke Baby took its first steps. It was still not quite solid - still part some kind of flesh and part the choking gas that had spawned it. Its body flickered in and out of focus and it made sounds like the world itself was being ripped open. Each footfall was thunder that shook the ground and split it even more, and that one single eye groped for focus so it could do what is had been born to do.

All around her, Ixtal could feel a power in the air that made it feel hotter and denser with every moment she ran. It sucked away her strength and made her gasp for breath until finally she had to stop running, The cracks in the earth around her spewed out more and of their choking gases, the same gases that the Smoke Baby was gaining strength from with each titanic footstep it took.

Ixtal turned to look at her pursuer.

It had grown bigger, nourished somehow by the hostility of the bad ground. Bigger and stronger and heavier, judging by the sound it made. But it still seemed unable to quite focus on anything, just like any newborn. Its thick arms reached to grab for some of the spike plants as though it was trying to gather them. They tried to withdraw and furl themselves up but the Smoke Baby managed to grasp one and tear it out of its roots. As it put the sharp stalk in its mouth Ixtal was sure she heard a little scream, so faint and yet filled with pain,

The Smoke Baby spat out the plant, the raggedy mouth that took up half its bulbous head shrinking in disgust. Ixtal watched, sucking in breaths as best she could into burning lungs and trying to will some strength back into her body. The creature seemed far away but with its stride it would make up the distance in seconds, and surely Ixtal would have no chance once it gained its focus. Already the single eye was starting to make more sense of things, so see more clearly.

She took her bow off her back and notched an arrow to it, waiting for its special tip to ignite. For one sickening second she though the special material might not work here, but finally it burst into a fizzing white fire. When it did she wasted no time and fired. The arrow flew straight and true until it got close to the Smoke Baby. Then it just dove into the ground and exploded, throwing up a sheet of fire and a shower of rocks. The creature shrieked out, trying to cover its face against the attack, and Ixtal felt a sudden pang of sorrow for it even as the cursed the bad ground for taking away her weapon.

Flames surrounded the Smoke Baby, and it stumbled forward, larger than ever. The fire didn't hurt it but it was afraid, and it tried to sweep it away. Its hands just passed right through, and the single eye tried to take it all in. Even from her distance, Ixtal could sense a kind of confusion in the Smoke Baby. She had assumed it would automatically know the bad ground it had born into, but it didn't. Instead like any child it was all instinct as every new sensation hit it.

<What are you?> whispered Ixtal, and the Smoke Baby bellowed out.

Finally it caught sight of her, and Ixtal raised her bow again for another shot. She knew she wasn't going to be able to hurt the creature but if she could scare it enough, maybe she could get away. There had to be hiding places somewhere in this burned ash wilderness, places she might be able to exploit the newborn's confusion to try and make herself invisible.

The Smoke Baby was more solid now, more like a real thing than a phantom, and it was easily five times Ixtal's size.

It seemed to see the arrow, to recognise what it was, and it stopped moving. Its eye looked, studied. And them, silently, it held up one of its huge clawed hands.

Ixtal didn't have any time at all to try and understand before the ground began to crumble away at her feet, the solid earth disintegrating without any vibration or warning, and she felt herself backwards into a gaping new chasm.

<NOOOOOO!>

Her balance gone, there was nothing for Ixtal to grab for. The gold weighed her down, and time slowed to an agonising crawl as she felt more choking hot gas billowing up from deep deep down. There was nothing but blackness, waiting to claim her body.

Was this the end?

She remembered her father's words.

<Daughter, it is the kingdom we cannot see, but it waits for us at every moment. When your moment comes, face it with courage.>

He had talked about death many times, about the long journey after life through fear and hardship that awaited every Mayan. She had seen the mouth to Xibalba herself, or at least she thought she had. And now it seemed it had come for her this time, and her alone.

Ixtal tried to steel herself, to have the courage her father had talked about, but she was terrified.

She didn't want to die.

At the instant she felt herself begin to fall into the hot dark maw, the air around her spun and whirled itself into new life. A wind blast like something from a storm hit her hard, knocking the wind out of her, and she felt something clasp around her, taking her body and lifting it out of harm's way. The steam made her eyes bleed a little so she couldn't see or understand, only make out the huge crack in the earth grow wider and wider as she flew across it, suddenly weightless.

It grew fast, desperate to claim its prey. The gas roared upwards like ghost fingers but Ixtal defied them. Even as the chasm became so wide it could almost consume everything around it its power couldn't catch her. Instead, heavy again, she crashed down on the other side where the ground was solid and unbroken.

For moment, then two, Ixtal lay there. She was hurt, bleeding, and things felt wrong where her ribs were. She tried to deal with the pain by concentrating on feeling things again, letting her senses do their work. The ground was softer, more like sand than ash, and the harsh vicious density of the air was gone too. Now it was more bitter, like rancid fruit, Unpleasant, but a lot better than the burning gas she had sucked into her lungs. When she finally opened her eyes the sky was clearer to, its poisoned mauve color giving way to a murky blue.

Ixtal wiped the blood from her face as best she could, and that was when she saw the Smoke Baby towering over her. It was huge yet still with the proportions of a malformed infant, its head too big for its massive distorted body. Almost wholly solid now, wisps of smoke leaked from its skin, while its single eye gazed down at her not with any kind of rage or hostility, but with an impossible sense of calm. Even its jagged mouth seemed at peace.

<Did you save me,> gasped Ixtal. Each word hurt as she tried to breath normally.

The Smoke Baby said nothing. It simply looked at her, the bone of its split horns catching the muted sunlight a little.

<You cannot speak, can you?>

Ixtal knew her question was meaningless. Even if this giant being had developed an ability to say anything since its unnatural birth she doubted it had even the smallest idea of what she was saying. The only reply was that serene stare from that one eye. It just watched her as she struggled to pull herself upright, wincing at the pain she felt.

There was a small leather pouch strapped to Ixtal's left thigh, and she reached for it. It held medicines she always took with her when she was away from familiar places – seeds, flowers, pods. She had memorised every single one over the years, and knew exactly what each was for, how it was to be prepared and mixed, and how long it would last. First was a blackened nut that she crunched and ate quickly, letting its ability to kill the pain ash over her in a matter of a couple of minutes. Then she squeezed a kind of yellow paste from some swollen leaves and rubbed it into the worst of the cuts, wishing that she had access to the strange healing blood of the Bolera.

Wherever they were, wherever their soldier who could move so fast he was invisible was, none of them were watching her now. She guessed the bad ground was beyond even their ability to see or patrol.

There was just the broken pain in her side to deal with now. Ixtal took out a green shiny fruit and peeled it into long strips that she wrapped across her side where dark bruises were already forming. It clung to her skin and she cut it into patches with her knife, breathing through the burning acidic sting that always came before the relief. It wouldn't fixed whatever was broken, but it would help, for a tie at least. She ate the fruit as well, just because it tasted good.

But that was all her medicines gone. Whatever came next she had no way to recover from, and the bad ground no doubt had a thousand other surprises in store for her. It had already revealed its ability to warp moments of time and distort space so that it made no sense, and even transform itself when it wanted to. But that still didn't explain the Smoke Baby. It had been born from something else, Ixtal realised, something that seemed to want to protect her.

She looked up at its monstrous face as she got to her feet. All the pain was still there but the bleeding had stopped, and everything was bearable now. She could move, run. Maybe even fight.

<I am sorry that I fired my arrow at you.>

The Smoke Baby's flesh showed no sign of injury so Ixtal guessed that the explosion she had caused hadn't been any more than a slight shock to the newborn.

<Do you know here I have to go. Can you point the direction? I must find the caves of Kukulkan's serpent children so I may return this.> Ixtal hauled one of the gold cuffs from her clearly overburdened waistband and held it up high to show it to The Smoke Baby.

This time it reacted, and it made a kind of low grumbling sound in his belly.

<Do you know what this is?>

For a moment Ixtal felt like some kind of communication might begin, but it was interrupted as suddenly as it began. The Smoke Baby stomped forward with sudden speed, shielding Ixtal behind its bulk as the bad ground began another metamorphosis.

Twisted shapes began to sprout out of clumps of pointed eye plants. Part earth and part something else, every one of them was different – there were sap-dripping bladed limbs and clusters of jet black eyeballs and bloated bodies that pulsed with veins like leaves. There were beaks and tendrils and flowers and claws. An army of something terrible was growing, each member pushing up out of the cracked ground and pushing its way out of the stalks.

Ixtal started at them in muted horror, while The Smoke Baby bellowed and attacked.

It smashed through four of the shapes with its first blow and then stamped down onto another two. Others took their place and tried swarm the Smoke Baby, ripping at it as best they could even as it peeled the away and crushed them. The aura of dark steam that still surrounded burned at the shapes too, and some fell away and dissolved before they could do anything.

But some were getting through. Some would always get through.

Finally, something in Ixtals' mind penetrated her fear and she drew her bow, firing into the largest mass of shapes she could see as they tore their way into existence from another clump. The arrow detonated like it had before and they all burned in silence.

As the Smoke Baby did its best to decimate each grotesque member of the bad ground's army as it could, Ixtal saw that one was focussed on her. It was a faceless thing made of half assembled parts and in the hollow nothingness that should have been its chest a nest of writhing tendrils lapped at the air. Ixtal drew and fired again and the explosion should have destroyed this creature completely.

Instead it walked through the cloud of smoke and fire unharmed.

Ixtal realised that this shape was different. Where the army that attacked the Smoke Baby were just automatons, mindless and replaceable, the faceless thing had a purpose. It walked towards her, shambling on its barely formed attempts at legs, and too many arms reached out.

But not for Ixtal. Suddenly she knew that whether she lived or died was irrelevant to the bad ground's army. She was just a carrier.

What they wanted was the gold.

The assault on the Smoke Baby raged on, wave after wave, shape after shape, and Ixtal drew her dagger as the faceless thing raked out at her. She slipped sideways and cut what passed for its flesh, and again there was nothing. The shape was as dry as the ground and there was nothing to hurt.

It lunged again and Ixtal rolled out of the way, trying to again as much distance as she possibly could. She looked around. The army of shapes was everywhere – relentless, remorseless. However many were destroyed more would grow, and the Smoke Baby could only old back the tide for so long.

Ixtal had no choice and nothing to fight with, and so she listened. Not the familiar voice of the rainforest that had guided her along so many hidden paths in her life, but the new voice. The one that had been there since she had started this journey, since she had seen the woman with the gemstone eyes.

It was the song of the gold itself, and it told Ixtal what to do.

The sky began to roll with a dark sound like thunder but different, more like the call of some monstrous voice straining to reach down. Ixtal clipped the first cuff into place and immediately the faceless thing stopped in its tracks, regarding everything with its empty nothingness head. It had wanted the gold, its only purpose was to retrieve the gold, and now something unexpected had happened. Something…wrong.

Ixtal clipped the second cuff onto her other wrist and felt a surge of something, a rush of power that flooded her from the ends of her hair to the toenails on her feet. The sky overhead roared and the army of shapes began to falter as the song of the gold sang louder in Ixtal's head. It danced alongside her own thoughts, her own senses, not trying to control but instead merging with them, trying to search out something that could link the two together. Now she could see the face of the woman with the gemstones eyes so clearly. Not the beaten dying boy she had found, but now vital, charged up with the same force that ran through Ixtal's bones, her muscles, her veins.

The faceless thing tried to attack again, slashing out as others of the army of shapes broke off their attack on the Smoke Baby. Or at least they tried to. They couldn't get away fast enough and were crushed down and burned away just like all the others. But there were so many the Smoke Baby couldn't pause for an instant to try and get to Ixtal.

Ixtal threw herself aside again as she pulled the last gold piece to her neck, but the faceless thing seemed to anticipate her movement this time. It lunged, its arm impossibly long, and just caught a little piece of clothing. Not much, but just enough to unbalance Ixtal.

She dropped the gold necklace, and fell to the bad ground between them both.

The faceless thing hurled itself forward, not caring about its own existence because in truth it had no existence. It was just a vessel, and only the gold mattered. Ixtal leapt forward too and plunged her dagger deep into the faceless thing's head, driving it down and twisting it hard. There was no resistance, nothing to fight against. Instead her blade sliced and crushed all at once and the faceless thing staggered backwards. Its head was nothing but wreckage now, deprived of whatever kind of sight it had possessed, and instead the tendrils in its chest cavity lashed out blindly. One cut across Ixtal's arm and burned her like acid as the sky roared again

The pain cut through the power of the medicines she had taken and she felt herself sink to her knees, the strength ebbing out of her, her cuts opening up again. Blood dripped onto the bad ground and the faceless thing tried its best to track Ixtal with it. Perhaps with the sound, perhaps with the taste on the air, or perhaps with some other kind of sense Ixtal couldn't fathom.

It didn't matter. The poison from the tendril was seeping in, making her eyes blurry again, paralysing her. The gold necklace was just out of reach, and she knew she only had a single chance to garb it, even as the faceless thing started to lock in on her. It shambled forward again, its walk sickeningly unnatural and its tendrils picking at the air, oozing in anticipation.

Ixtal thought of her father. She tried to make herself strong with the song of the gold, and managed to fall forward and clutch the necklace in one hand. She was barely able to lift it now, but she had no more time left. All she needed was a couple more seconds….just a couple….

As the faceless thing pounced for the killing blow, Ixtal clipped the last piece of gold around her neck, and everything was filled with light.

Golden power gushed from Ixtal's body as she knelt, arms wide, head gazing to the sky that called to her. Her mind was filled with the song of the gold. The force of it swamped everything, howling and ringing, the sound like water hammering off cliffs mixed with the music in Ixtal's mind that reverberated everywhere.

It built to a crescendo, filling up the bad ground, purifying it, erasing the army of shapes and the faceless thing, until there was nothing left except the light.

And then it was over.

Ixtal slumped back, and wondered for a moment if she had died. Gently, she moved her arms and then her legs. She breathed in and out, slowly and deliberately, until she was happy that somehow she was alive. She had not been plunged into the depths of the Earth so suffer in the pits of the Underworld City. Her eyes were clear again, her body moving, all of her cuts and wounds gone. And all around was so quiet it was impossible to accept. Not even a single insect chirruped.

She sat up and saw that she was in a field of amber grass where the sun beat down from a perfect blue sky. Everything smelt sweet like honey, and everywhere felt so serene and so safe.

<Thankyou Ixtal,> said a voice.

Ixtal looked up, and standing over her was the woman with the gemstone eyes. Floating a little off the ground and lit up with an aura of gold, she wore the gold cuffs and necklace, as well as a shimmering robe made of a material so beautiful it almost took Ixtal's breath away. The woman's skin shared that same ethereal beauty, and they could almost have been the same thing.

<Thankyou?> repeated Ixtal, puzzled. She reached for her dagger as it lay just nearby, just in case. <What is this place? Where is the bad ground.>

<You have brought me home,> said the woman. She smiled a smile that filled the air up with joy, and Ixtal started to think that she had always meant to come to this place, to finish this journey. <I give you thanks. The bad ground is healed.>

<I want to understand,> said Ixtal.

<Like your father understood.>

Ixtal felt herself begin to weep. <My….father…..Yes. Please.>

<The bad ground held me here. Your father could not help me, but he gave you to the rainforest so that I would be free.>

<All these things…I have seen. It was for you …?>

<The Bolera have watched over you, and now you have become more. You will walk in eternity, Ixtal, and you will never truly know death. The Underworld cannot claim you. It will try to unleash its horror, and there will be those who will try to control it. But you will protect others in this life and far beyond.>

Ixtal knelt there, tears falling freely. Her mind was filled with her father's kindly face, and in the aura of this beautiful woman, this goddess, she – just for a moment – truly grasped everything.

*

A man lay at the bottom of a pit, thrown there by the savage killers who had tracked him down without mercy. They had had slaughtered everybody else, but for this man there was a crueller punishment. Surrounded by the dismembered bodies of his friends, soaked in their blood, he would suffer and die alone and in fear.

Then Xibalba would take him, and the Lords Of Death would consume his spirit for eternity.

And that would have happened until a woman with red skin and black eyes found him in the darkness. She had power about her, he could feel that, and the world changed as she approached. Where there had been only the coldness of the pit there was the sense of somewhere else . As the woman with the red skin lifted him to his felt almost effortlessly, the man felt as if he could see something, but not with his eyes. It lay just out of reach, a doorway to another place beyond the pain and violence and blood of this life.

One thought filled up the man's head. One single word that change everything.

Bolera.

*

The savages were dead now, all of them.

A legion of barbarians who ate the flesh of men, woman and children, whose bodies were not human like the Maya but something else, had believed that they were strong enough to defeat any threat. They had always taken what they wanted, laughed at the so-called power of the

The man looked down at the bodies, utterly dispassionate.

Around him, Bolera stood. They had brought power like the man had never seen even in his most feverish nightmares. Just eight of them in total, and not a single weapon between them. Just strange objects and changed and warped their shape and glowed with light. But the and had still watched them rip bodies apart, turn them inside out, set them ablaze with liquid blue fire and turn them to dust, one by one, until there were none left.

The whole barbaric tribe, gone. All of them.

*

The man sat alone now in a cave. He felt different now he was back from that other place, and he looked different too, not like other men. And he had now knowledge too. Special knowledge. Knowledge the Bolera had given him.

In his arms he held a tiny baby, and he gently washed her in the clean pure waters of a pool he had found, a pool whose waters tasted so sweet that they made the senses swim and disconnected the mind from the body. The first time he had tasted them he had seen himself, but differently, like a reflection. Real or imagined, it had started him on his own journey, just like the little girl in his arms would start hers one day.

All he had to do was give her a name, and there was only one that would ever be right.

Ixtal.

*

Ixtal opened her eyes.

The amber fields were gone, the beauty was gone too, and everywhere around Ixtal was noise and stink. She could hear so many things, howls and voices and whirrs and bangs, and she realised that she knew this place. It had been in visions and dreams, vague at first but getting clearer every time.

Now she saw it all properly for the first time.

She stood on the side of a mountain and looked down onto an endless vista of lights. It was city, but not like the city she knew. This was so vast it consumed everything and its was filled up with life and movement, never ending. Some of the city builds reached up so high it looked like they touched the clouds, and in amongst everything were huge roads of stone that strange creatures moved along, with people inside them. The creatures shouted at each other with weird honking noises, and spewed smoke from their rear ends that turned the air dirty.

But there were no trees, no rainforest. This was not the world she knew, nothing like and she turned away from all the noise to try and see something else.

As she did the noises ceased, and she was in the forest again. But it was different. She walked a little way long a dirt track that soon became a road. The land became flatter and clearer and she clutched her dagger as she saw people dressed in strange clothes. They didn't see her though. They all looked wounded or hurt, and Ixtal saw that something had happened here, something terrible but something so agonisingly familiar. A catastrophe had occurred here, and something of The Underworld was everywhere.

A little further and Ixtal found more buildings, all painted bright colors and festooned with what looked like vines overhead. It felt like a place that should have been happy, filled with families and homes, but now there was just anger and pain and terror.

There was a building she was drawn to, and she approached it, unseen by anyone, a man emerged from it. He was a giant and his skin was chalk white, and even at first sight Ixtal felt connected to him. There was a strength in him, a knowledge, that had been granted from somewhere else. Again it was so familiar. Just like the memories of her father.

A woman followed the giant out into the street, chiding him in words that Ixtal couldn't understand. All she could make out was a name.

<Francisco!>

The name made Ixtal stop dead. It was like she had always known it, and she realised that one day she would be here again, just as she had been here before. She would be with the giant with the white skin not as Ixtal The Huntress but as something… different - a guardian perhaps. A spirit. She would help him and guide him, and when the cracks in the world had to be sealed up again, she would be the one to give him the strength to do it. They were forever connected now.

Francisco looked across the street, thinking that he saw something out of the corner of his eye. He was still dazed and not quite understanding what had happen to his skin. His mind whirled with strange new thoughts too, and even Dr Sonja wasn't making a great deal of sense to him. Then whatever he thought he had sensed was gone, and something else grabbed his attention.

Just nearby was an old car with a wooden coffin tied to its roof, and the man people would know as El Sepulturero was born.

*

The bad ground wasn't bad anymore.

Ixtal got to her feet and saw everything was as it should be. There were trees all around and the sounds of birds and monkeys was everywhere again. The sun shone down into the clearing where she found herself, warming her body, and she felt the comfort of the voice of the rainforest in her mind once more. Even the gold was gone from her wrists and neck.

There were no vast cities and creatures that howled and spewed smoke anymore. There was just home, in the jungle where her father had raised her and the Bolera had watched over her all her life. She wondered if they were watching now, hidden in their own places, just out of sight.

She hoped so. Maybe she would find a way to see them again one day.

Smiling, Ixtal turned to find a way home, and then she stopped.

Somehow, looming up ahead, vast and awe-inspiring, were the huge caves of Kukulkan. She didn't try and question how she had found herself here. She just accepted it. Their openings were so big Ixtal couldn't really grasp their size, and as she took a step or two closer she saw that the stone ripples all around had a life of their own. Closer still and she could see the children of Kukulkan themselves – serpents of stone ten times the size of a person, each swimming in the rock. They dove down and came up again, writhed and spiralled, never stopping.

Ixtal had sometimes doubted that this place was even real. But now here it as. An old place of gods, deep in the rainforest. The place where Kukulkan had touched the world of humanity, and wondered where those huge caves might lead.

<Ixtal, shouted a voice. <Ixtal. I am so happy to see you.>

A figure was running out of one of the smaller canes, though they still looked like an ant in the doorway of a house. She couldn't feel any kind of threat, so she let the person come closer and as they did she saw a young an with a cheerful face and scars all across his arms and his legs.

She couldn't believe who she was seeing.

<Pech?>

Pech ran up to her and threw his arms around her, ignoring any chance that Ixtal The Mighty Huntress might simple kill him with a flick of her wrist. <Yes, it is me. Pech. I have found my way back to you so that we can have more adventures. Do you think I am brave.>

Ixtal nodded, smiling. <I do. Where…where have you been. I searched for you….>

<I do not know. I think I was in another place, and I was surrounded by beautiful women with skin as red as blood. I remember the pit, but something saved me from the horrors.>

<I think I know what that was,> said Ixtal.

<Look, look, I bought you a present.> Pech opened his hand and Ixtal saw a leather necklace, and hanging from it was a beautiful green crystal carved into an amulet of Bolera shapes. It captivated her, and Pech was thrilled when she put it on. <It is beautiful. They said you would like it. It will protect you.>

Ixtal nodded appreciatively. She liked the idea of protection, especially now.

<What shall we do. Where shall we go,> asked Pech, excited liked a puppy.

Ixtal thought for a moment. The caves lay ahead, and behind her lay the familiarity of the rainforest. There were so many questions to ask and mysteries to solve. The caves could lead anywhere, and it was exciting, but she was so tired and there was another path that could be taken now. A life where people could be helped and things could be made right. Where a protector was more important than a huntress, and where a father's beloved daughter could be what she was always meant to be.

After all, the future was waiting for her. She had seen it.

Finally, Ixtal said. <Let us go home.>

EPILOGO [ANA-MARIA PARTE DOS]

Ana-Maria Castellanos woke up at just after 3am. Around her neck her necklace, the one with the jade amulet that she never removed, tingled like it sometimes did. It felt a little like the tattoo she had had just had done on her left arm, the ornate Catholic crucifix to replace the one she should have worn around her neck.

A tattoo was much more her. Her mother had even approved it, grudgingly.

Over on a cushion on the floor Gorguz the goblin was fast asleep, snoring his little snores and gorged on candy. He always slept through the night and the sound was a comfort in amongst the endless urban symphony of Mexico City. In the back of her mind El Rey **Dragón** was in his cave, keeping out of trouble and looking after his pile of treasures. Their connection was a strong as ever, and Ana-Maria had even come to like the green eyes she had received as a result.

The dream she had been having was fading fast. There were little fragments left but even they were disappearing like melting ice in the sun. It was always this way, and sometimes it bothered her, as though she was supposed to remember something important but never could.

Real life always got in the way.

Time had passed and she had come to accept that Uncle Francisco was gone. It had taken time and therapy, and a lot of scolding from her mother about trying to conduct strange ceremonies in the middle of the night. Instead they had made a little memorial to him in a room in the house to remember him buy, dominated by his huge smiling face. It still made Ana-Maria sad but whenever she felt that pang she thought of her dreams and touched the green crystal.

Somewhere deep down, in her subconscious, there was the sense that they were all connected. If she had the time she could probably try and work it all out, but there was never time. She and Rico were celebrating their first anniversary, shifts at the hospital as an orderly were coming thick and fast now, and she had university applications to prepare. Not medicine though – hospital work had put her off that for life, and she only carried on the work to save money. Sick and dying people were not her thing. Ana-Maria had decided marine biology was what she wanted to explore.

<At least,> said her mother. <It's still kind of science.>

Time always passed, and the strangeness of the Yucatán was distant from her now. She still had Gorguz and **Dragón**, but they had become more like pets in a way, weird pets that Rico was doing his very best to adjust to. One day she would have to let **Dragón** go and find his own territory, and she imagined that Gorguz would become old like everything did. So she had decided it was best to live a life that was as normal as she could possibly make it, and lock up all the dark unnatural things she had seen when she had been younger in parts of her mind not even her therapist could reach.

Like everyone and everything always did in the end, she had begun to move on.

Ana-Maria yawned and settled down to sleep again, letting Gorguz lull her into a pleasant relaxed half-doze. The alarm was set for 7am, and the world was waiting as she slowly drifted back to her dreams.

And in another place, deep in the heart of the Mayan rainforest of centuries past, Ixtal The Protector welcomed her.